SHADOW CHILD

Also by S.F. Taylor

THIS SQUALID LITTLE ROOM

Based upon Lawrence of Arabia's stays in Hornsea, East Yorkshire, at the end of his career in the RAF

CRUMBS ON THE CARPET

Covering Wilfred Owen's final year in Scarborough, before his death in France in 1918

PARIS, PICASSO AND ME

Novel. A single mother moves to find an elderly neighbour with a remarkable past living next door. (Publication due 2022)

S.F. Taylor

Shadow Child

Published by Southfield Writers/Coffeehouse Publications

Copyright @ S.F. Taylor 2022

ISBN: 978-1-8382517-3-4

Cover design by Thom Strid

Printed in Great Britain

Acknowledgments

Thanks primarily go to Mandi Allen at The Coffeehouse Writer for her support, encouragement and suggestions, and for getting the author to actually finish a work started many years ago.

To Thom Strid for another brilliant cover design

And to my beta-reader friends: Elaine, Tricia, Debbie, Jayne, Val, Pam and Fran. Thank you so much for taking the time to read and give your useful comments

Chapter 1

1669

Chateau Colombe, France

IN THE LAVISH surroundings of the Queen's bedchamber, candle flames flickered from a breeze snaking through a crack in the door. In the early hours of the morning, silhouettes on the wall shimmied a ghostly dance above the bed and an eerie silence fell over those in attendance. Sumptuous tapestries of red and gold, now tied back, revealed a frail body lost beneath heavy covers, and shadowy figures hovered over her. An attendant priest prayed for forgiveness and the salvation of the Queen's soul, and physicians ministered to her last bodily needs.

She had lived long beyond her husband Charles; fifty years had passed since his execution, fifty years without the man and the king she had always loved. Now, after years of illness and suffering, her time had finally come, following a too great administration of opiates by a well-meaning physician.

In the silence that followed, and the few minutes of remaining darkness, no one moved until a sign was given that she had gone. Queen Henrietta Maria, widow of Charles 1 of England, was at peace, although the agonies that dogged her final days at Colombes could still be seen in the deeply etched lines on her face, and in the haunted, sunken shadows of her eyes. Drugs that had once brought blessed release from pain, now gave oblivion and the final release.

On the tenth of September 1669, a cock crowed in the distance and light smeared the sky as though an artist had been in a rush to finish the final stroke on his canvas. Dawn arrived, and with it life went on as ever outside the castle walls, in the rough dwellings, and on the scattered farms around. The people of the town awoke from their slumbers.

The long summer days were shortening, and the stultifying heat of August would continue into September until the rains arrived, bringing relief to the parched earth and wilting crops. Dogs, too tired to even chase the rats, skulked in whatever shade they could find, and children, irritable and moody, hid from the burden of their chores.

At the back of the bedchamber, the servant, Jehanne, carried out her final duties for the Queen. She moved quietly and unnoticed; replenishing jugs of water and taking away soiled linen left by the door. Working quickly and without fuss, invisibility had been attained by virtue of a continued service since childhood, as well as a regime of fear and coercion.

Today, trembling hands and a fast beating heart impeded that efficiency. A leather pouch, retrieved from behind an old chest, lay tucked into a hidden pocket of her long brown dress and she held it close to her breast, the gold cross reassuringly protected through a sheaf of papers. The bruises on her body, sustained from years of abuse, had subsided as Fabrice had bent her will towards his in a final act of obedience.

It hadn't been easy for the orphaned Jehanne to make her way in the world, but she had little choice; it was work hard under servitude, or starve. Both parents had served in the Queen's household and she had been accepted too when she demonstrated how efficient she could be, slowly working her way up to the royal chamber. Fabrice, from the confines of the kitchen, and waiting at the Queen's table, instructed her in what was required and how she should conduct herself, but mostly it was in the form of keep your mouth shut and your eyes open. Ever conscious of a beating at his hands if she did otherwise, she obeyed in every respect. His advice had served her well, kept her in employment, and fed. Young, impressionable and bidda-ble, he'd groomed her long and well over the years into obeying his demands. Threats to her position and security had always been the right side of enough to ensure she would do exactly as he wanted despite her fear of being caught.

Plans had been made on just how useful she could be to him since learning of the Queen's last illness and petty thefts had provided rehearsals for the greater prize. He was stupid, but not so much that he didn't know the value of the girl in his charge and what her position of trust could mean. He needed to ensure that her actions were seam-lessly performed as though part of her duties, quickly and without fuss, and so far they had worked well.

The flurry of activity at the other end of the room focussed the attention of the mourners, the priest and the physicians around the Queen's bed. Plans were made and preparations for the body and extraction of the heart would soon begin. Jehanne knew that her services would now come to an end and after a quick glance at the backs of the small gathering, prepared to leave the bedchamber. The priest, with head bowed, closed his book and made the sign of the cross. Drops of sanctified oil were dripped on to the head of the Queen catching the morning light that began to filter into the room and two of the women began to cry. The long wait was over. Jehanne, trembling in fear of what she had done, quietly slipped away with the Papers, the cross in an old leather pouch, having performed her last duty at the Castle.

She left the chamber and went outside via a door hidden at the back of the kitchens, grateful for the absence of Fabrice who had not yet risen. Jehanne's breath was fast and shallow as the pouch rubbed against her skin beneath the rough brown dress. It was a stark reminder of what she had done and the stolen items needed to be hidden quickly before anything was discovered.

There was much activity to divert any attention she may have attracted; attending to the Queen took a great deal of preparation, enough to allow a serving girl to get on with her duties unnoticed. Placing a hand across her belly, stroking it gently, the life growing inside could not be hidden much longer and would soon be noticed. With no husband the child would have no father to support them. Fabrice, despite promises to the contrary, would not take care of her, let alone a baby. She would be thrown out of employment and the only hope of salvation lay in the contents of the pouch – a gold cross, wrapped in papers that she could not read, and optimism that they had great value.

Jehanne understood exactly how much his anger would turn on her when he found out how little she had taken, but there had not been enough time; her fumbling fingers refused to obey the task in hand and too soon she was no longer alone. She needed to act quickly before Fabrice came for the hoard of valuables he'd envisaged, and before he discovered the hastily formed plan she's made for herself. She would escape to Paris and sell the cross to give her and the baby a new start in the anonymity of a big city, away from Colombes, a place where no-one would know how much she had sinned in the eyes of God.

Consumed with greed, and working on the suspicion of a forthcoming baby, Fabrice already knew that his future life did not involve a needy wife and a screaming child; the opposite of what he had promised. He awoke to the news of the Queen and quickly dressed to seek out Jehanne.

Jehanne was already skirting the formal symmetrical gardens, weaving in and around carefully tended shrubs and beds to a far corner of the castle grounds. Beyond the immaculately tended lawns, stood a group of ancient cherry trees, hidden and forgotten when they were so far from the main gardens. Their branches merged like witches' fingers, interlaced and held aloft, providing a little protection from the worst of the winter weather to any lost soul. Many times they had hidden and sheltered Jehanne following beatings and abuse at the hands of Fabrice; it was the only place she was ever left alone in peace. The trees understood; they took her in, enfolding her, keeping her hidden and safe, in times of pain and suffering. The beauty of the delicate blossom in Spring, and the lush red fruits of summer gave her hope that there was a better life waiting somewhere other than this one of dread and fear.

Jehanne's exposed ankles chafed in the long grass as she carried her tired and aching legs behind the largest of the trees. Having never known her real mother, she referred to this particular tree as 'ma Mère' and liked to think that somewhere beyond her world a kindly woman was looking down, guiding her through the long, dark days.

The fruits from the trees, those not taken by a succession of hungry birds and small animals, lay on the ground, rotting, with just a few left clinging tenaciously to the branches.

Urgently, but with great difficulty, Jehanne scraped out a small hole beneath the tree with a sturdy piece of wood, digging as far as she could between the knotted roots, to bury the pouch. She planned to tell Fabrice that she'd had no chance to take anything and prepared herself to endure a final beating before making her escape. She could not afford for him to think that anything had been taken, and would not risk being followed. The hole was shallow but time was pressing; it was deep enough for its purpose and the pouch laid inside. With splintered nails and bleeding fingers from her endeavour, she was satisfied when loose earth, twigs and stones provided sufficient cover. The job was finished as best she could manage and Jehanne stood on shaking legs.

The trees swayed and rustled in a rising breeze, whispering their warning. She looked around in fear that she might not be alone but there was no one in sight. Satisfied, Jehanne kneeled once more by the covered hole and hung her head low in prayer, weeping silently, over the burial mound.

'Pour tu, bebe. We will leave very soon and start somewhere new. Just you and me. Protège moi, maman. Keep us safe.'

There was no time to waste; the job was done. She was confident that the cherry trees would protect her treasure. It was time to get back and finish her work before she was missed.

But Jehanne was not alone. The figure that had closely followed her every step since leaving the Chateau had succeeded in keeping his presence hidden. Jehanne barely registered the man behind the flash of glinting metal when it blinded her eyes. In shock, she hardly felt the point of the knife as it pierced through the brown woollen dress to her heart. The life inside would become a shadow of a memory in the last moments of the young serving girl as their blood flowed freely into the gaping hole beneath the ancient cherry tree.

Chapter 2

1969

Yorkshire

JULIA LAY in her small cramped bed crushed against the wall of her bedroom. She felt like Lewis Carroll's Alice, flung down a hole into a room she had long outgrown. She'd woken up unusually early this particular morning for three reasons: first was the vivid violence of the dream she'd had for two nights in a row; the second was her uncontained excitement for the day ahead; and lastly, the sultry heat of a room that had not cooled down from the day before.

One leg flicked aside the thin sheet covering her body. Her foot found its way to the floor where it came across a school tie, trailing from the rest of the uniform stuffed under the bed. None would be needed for the sixth form and would not be missed. She caught the tie between her toes and brought it up to her outstretched hand. The fraying blue and white fabric still held the badges of 'Prefect' and 'Constable House', both of which should have been handed in at the end of the summer term. She threw it back on the floor where it snaked across a well-read copy of Wuthering Heights flattened open at Mr Lockwood's grip of Cathy's arm when she demanded to be let in. What Julia lacked in life, she made up with a vivid imagination and the passage never failed to give a shiver of excitement. She became Cathy, wanting her own Heathcliff.

Julia yawned and stretched her legs, pushing aside the memory of the nightmare. The woman in the long brown, blood stained dress, was no more than a dress of her own hanging from the door. It wasn't the first time sleep had been disturbed by bad dreams. They usually came after reading torrid passages of books that gripped her. She looked at the dress and remembered that it was too tight. 'Nothing fits any more! Everything is too frumpy, too small: clothes, shoes, this awful house. I want to scream!'

The clock in the downstairs hall chimed eight. Julia curled up in the bed ready to feign sleep before her parents left for work for the day. She heard her mother downstairs in the kitchen; the aroma of toast making its way up through the thin walls and hollow staircase. Audrey Cavaner was at the sink; hands plunged deep into hot foaming water, washing up with regimental efficiency. Tightly permed hair framed a ruddy complexioned and her mouth was pursed and set firm. She wasn't happy, as she often was nowadays, when facing yet another battle of wills with her daughter. The loss of the compliant little girl grieved her with its intensity, and the lack of control brought a seismic shift in their relationship. Friday night's argument, still unresolved, made her tense. Tom was no use with his 'Let it go, Audrey, she's growing up, you'll only make yourself ill fretting so much.' He was never any use, preferring a quiet life, and let things go too easily, but it would come to no good, of that she was sure. Getting home so late, and where was she anyway until that time?

Audrey dried her hands on the tea towel and draped it over the oven handle to dry. The flush of the toilet upstairs signalled that they would soon be ready to leave. Audrey looked up to the ceiling as if she could see through to Julia's bedroom but remained seated at the kitchen table waiting with her bag and cardigan. Tom started early on the docks and Audrey was always first in for the early shift at the grocer shop in town.

Julia too read the signal of departure and turned on to her back, relieved that her mother had chosen not to come in. She looked around her room. Maybe it wasn't all bad and at least it was a space she could claim as her own. It was some consolation for having to live under the same roof as a mother who understood absolutely nothing.

The walls of the bedroom, or what could be seen of them beneath the posters, prints and photos were 'French Grey' according to the colour chart she had eventually been allowed to choose from. Audrey hated it of course. Julia had picked out the colour not because she liked it, but because it was French and sounded sophisticated. She had been reading Madame Bovary at the time and was introduced to Rimbaud at the beginning of last term by the new young English teacher, Miss Hamilton, who was evidently pleased that one of her pupils took such an interest outside the curriculum. And there were only so many times she could re-read Wuthering Heights. 'Julia', she would say, 'you are a star pupil' and would bring in works that Julia had never even heard of, including poetry. Rimbaud's 'Voyelles' caught her imagination and she loved the words long before discovering the translation. It was now written out in a neat sans serif script and pinned up on the French Grey wall above the single bed: "Je dirai quelque jour vos naissances latentes". The secret birth…it sounded so deliciously mysterious. Not something Maggie, or Billy and the others would take an interest in. Maggie would want every detail of the gory nightmare though; she would love that.

Rays of sunlight shone knife-like into the room revealing piles of clothes around the floor, all tried on and discarded the day before. The dressing table displayed a fabulous rainbow of colours spilling out from tubs and tubes of cheap makeup bought from the market in town. After hours of practise, the remains waited for today's effort. 'Why can't I look like the models? How do they do it? Easy to achieve the look of the season, yeah right.' Magazine photographs were taped to the mirror. Beautiful girls, beautifully made up, shone out from the covers of 'Jackie' and 'Teen', pictures of perfection and endlessly happy lives.

Julia's reverie was broken by footsteps sounding on the stairs. She held her breath in the hope she would be left in peace, but it was short lived when a tap on the bedroom door preceded her mother's face appearing in the room. 'Julia', she said, 'Julia…we're going now.' Audrey waited for an answer, hoping to end the feud between them, but Julia's response was to turn and face the wall and pull up the covers over her head. 'Don't be like that love…you know it was wrong. We were worried sick.'

After Friday's confrontation, Julia was still smarting from its repercussions and had no intention of giving way. Arriving home from the school dance two hours later than promised had not gone down well and she might have apologised but for the prolonged and relentless arguments that followed. The result was her mother demanding an apology that never came, and promises that would not be given. She strode into the room, opening the curtains with a flourish.

'Stop it, it's too bright!'

'It's gone eight Julia and I've left you a list downstairs of jobs to do for me; it's time you got up anyway. Think about what I said last night and we'll talk about it when your Dad and me get home.'

'No,' she groaned, 'not again…I've told you…we just…'

'I was worried sick'

Audrey looked down at her daughter, at a loss to what more she could say or do. With arms folded tight across her chest, she sighed, lingering in the hope of a response but none was given. 'We'll be back at six. Don't stay in bed all day, will you?'

Julia lay still until the sound of car tyres crunching over the gravel drive reached her ears. She stretched over to the little radio behind the clock, turned it on and Fleetwood Mac echoed through its tinny little speakers as she lay back down, remembering every minute of Friday night.

Chapter 3

The School Dance

SOUTH BRINSLEY SCHOOL hall resonated with the music brought in by the fifth and sixth forms. Mr Brice, bored and disinterested, acted as DJ, selecting records he could tolerate the most, and slipping in a few of his own as the evening wore on. He knew from derisory snorts and sniggering that they were not to the taste of his pupils, just as he knew that it wasn't lemonade they were drinking from the plastic cups. He chose to ignore both, but at the same time wished he'd thought to bring something for himself to get through the evening.

Julia danced with Maggie and a few other girls in their year. The boys just watched, trying to act cool as they finished the cheap Spanish wine Dennis Cowan had decanted into the lemonade bottle, taken from his Dad's collection. When it started to get too raucous, Mr Brice decided that the time was right for something to calm them down. Nothing wrong with a little Dion and the Belmonts he thought although it only managed to empty the dance floor amid catcalls of complaint.

On a bench lining the wall, Billy Sanderson made space next to him for Julia, newly arrived with a group of girls who were out of breath and pink from an energetic dance. As she caught her breath he put his arm around her neck, emboldened by another slug of the 'lemonade'. Horrified, Julia pushed him off. They'd been to the pictures once and she let him hold her hand, but had drawn the line at letting him kiss her. He was nice enough but it wasn't Billy's attention she was after tonight.

At the other side of the hall, Mr Weston leaned against the wall. He'd been watching the juvenile crowd on the dance floor with benign amusement, and an expression that clearly showed that he too, like Mr Brice, would rather be elsewhere. Julia looked over in his direction; she'd been waiting most of the night for the right opportunity. She knew he'd noticed her dancing with the girls, demonstrating the moves they'd been practising all week during lunch hours. Julia hung out with only a small group, including her best friend, Maggie; a studious nature meant that she often spent time alone, but she'd joined in the excitement over the end of term dance. In their first year, Maggie had been placed next to her in class by virtue of surname but they got on well enough to form a close friendship too. Maggie knew what Julia had planned; they talked and giggled one night during a sleepover about the merits of Mr David Weston and his flirting with the girls. It had all started as a joke and Maggie never thought for one minute she would carry it through, but when the time came she offered herself as a distraction to Billy when Julia went to the toilets to check her hair and makeup. Maggie had no problem with that and had secretly envied the interest Billy took in Julia. On her return from the toilets,

Julia was surprised to see how closely they were both dancing in the dimmed light of the hall, but relieved at the same time that the pressure was off.

It was getting close to the end of the evening and for once Mr Brice's choice of music went down well. 'Hey Jude' floated across the hall as those who were still left on the floor paired up, swaying to Paul McCartney telling them it would get 'better, better, better.' The other half sat bored in small groups, waiting for the dance to finish and the resumption of something faster. David Weston took the opportunity to sneak outside, gesturing to one of his colleagues with two closed fingers moving to and from his mouth, the need for a cigarette. Julia saw her opportunity too. It was the first she'd had all evening and she followed closely behind.

Outside, a thin light shimmered down from the toilet window in an otherwise darkening sky and it took some time to adjust. The cool refreshing air was welcome after the stifling heat of the hall and she took a large intake of breath before finding David. He pulled out a pack of cigarettes, frisking himself for a match. Its spark briefly illuminated his face and he inhaled deeply. He looked as relaxed and happy as Julia felt nervous and unsure.

This had been David Weston's first post from teacher training college at St John's in York. He had not taken greatly to teaching but had been in the school long enough to make his mark. He was young and fresh and funny, but no pushover, and Julia was smitten from the first day he arrived in class. At well over six feet tall, lean and good-looking, he couldn't present any greater contrast to the rest of the staff as they sat up on the stage for daily assembly. In truth, he wasn't much older than some of the pupils he taught. The boys liked him; he went to watch Hull City on a regular basis with Mr Brice and spoke with authority on the merits of Wagstaff and Chilton. The girls loved him for the attention he paid to what they said and what they did; even commenting on a new hairstyle when one appeared. To him it was a bit of fun that alleviated the tedium of school life, but all too soon, he was desperate to leave, and when the opportunity arose, was grateful.

David Weston was musing on his last day, and half way through the cigarette, before he saw Julia emerge from the shadows. 'Are you following me?' he asked, bemusement replacing the automatic irritation he felt at being disturbed when he saw who it was. Julia moved a little closer now that she'd been seen. At five foot two with a slight frame, he towered over her and Julia wished she'd worn heels. He took another drag of the cigarette as he weighed up the quiet girl in front of him. Julia was one of the prettiest he taught, clever too, promising. The small figure shyly hugging her arms about her body looked down at the grass.

'It's hot in there,' she mumbled. All the witty and clever remarks she practised earlier had taken flight in a fit of nerves. 'Looks like both of us needed to cool down then,' he replied.

She looked up and locating a little of the courage it had taken to follow him, and went on as casually as her racing heart would allow, 'Can I have a cigarette?' She had never smoked in her life and regretted asking as soon as the words came out, but it was too late now. Their eyes briefly met in the dim light, dark enough that he couldn't see her burning face, but light enough to detect a glimmer of expectation. David raised an eyebrow, brushing back a fallen lock of hair through his open fingers.

This should be interesting, he thought and took a cigarette from the packet. 'I wouldn't have thought that you smoked,' he said smiling and offered a light; then watching in amusement as Julia tried not to cough. 'Perhaps Gauloise are not such a good choice for a beginner.' He laughed openly, but not unkindly, at her childish attempt.

Julia fought a rising mortification but determined to go on. The cigarette became squashed between her fingers and was held down at a safe enough distance from her face. It was disgusting of course. The experience and sophistication of smoking that some of the sixth form girls had acquired had not reached her and Maggie yet. Neither had they found the opportunity or confidence to buy any cigarettes to practise with.

'So…what are your plans for the summer then, Julia? Spain? Butlin's?' he asked between enjoying the cigarette and wondering why exactly she'd followed him. Was it a bet? Schoolgirl crush? She wouldn't be the first if it was the latter and his memory of Caroline on the history trip to Lincoln crossed his mind. Julia pulled a face at the question; she knew from classroom talk that these seemed to be the two most popular holiday locations that year. 'No' was all she managed in reply when the reality of her home life did not include a holiday destination remotely interesting or exotic. Family day trips to Scarborough and Filey in Dad's Bedford van were not places she cared to share with anyone, nor was the thought that her Dad had already suggested Butlin's. Even her mother had rebuffed the idea by saying it was too common. As for Spain, none of them even owned a passport.

David looked at his watch; 'Time to go I think.'

Julia, struggling to find the words that would keep his attention longer, was acutely aware that the dance would soon be over. He would go back inside and her opportunity lost for good. As if in confirmation, a loud noise carried across the night air when the hall door crashed open. The brightness of the light inside suggested that indeed the dance was close to over. Three girls ran out squealing, chased by two boys, two of whom she could make out as Maggie and Billy. The music had stopped and a low rumble of chairs and equipment was scraping across the floor, confirming that it was time to go.

Darkness resumed when the hall door slammed shut. They were still alone; there was still time, but it had to be now; there would be no other chance. She reached up to kiss him but at that very moment he'd turned his head to exhale smoke from the last of his cigarette. Julia's searching lips missed their mark, brushing his cheek instead. For several seconds that seemed like an eternity, they both remained perfectly still, caught in a moment of surprise. David stepped back, ground out his cigarette on the wall and flicked it away. He smiled at her shocked expression. 'If I'd known you were going to do that Julia, we'd have come out earlier...now how about we go back inside and help clear up?'

'But you're leaving! Don't go yet...please. Won't you kiss me first?' The words were blurted out and spoke more of the desperation of the moment than any fear of rejection. She had nothing more to lose. David looked around, unsure and surprised, but not entirely annoyed by what had just happened. He paused for no longer than it took to make a swift decision that perhaps one kiss couldn't do any harm. She was a sweet girl with a crush on her teacher, it happens, but from tonight he was no longer that person, not her teacher at least. He cupped the imploring face in his hands and gave the longed for kiss: short and hard and full on the lips. Her heart pumped ferociously, pleading inside for him not to stop, the words hammering in her head.

'We should go back in,' he said as he pulled her hands away ready to guide her back in.

'No...you can't...not yet...'

'Julia, you know...this isn't....' For once he was the one struggling for the right words. He wanted to let her down gently, but in the determination for more, she reached her arms up around his neck, and offered him once again her soft pleading mouth. In a fraction of a second, in the security of darkness, he responded to those parted lips with more than either expected. Reasoning that he would be leaving soon, what was the harm? With that second kiss, the gentle touch of his hands stroked and slowly felt their way down her back, exciting Julia with feelings she had never experienced before. This was beyond expectation and once again the words don't stop played over and over in her head. He didn't this time, and exploring hands reached down to the bottom of the short skirt that rode up as he pressed her body against the cold hard wall behind.

Chapter 4

Friday night stayed with Julia, playing over and over on a loop of longing and hope of where it would go next. She treasured the scrap of paper on which he had written down his address, given along with the promise that she could visit his house on Monday, today, before he left England for good.

She snapped off the music, no longer caring for its distraction from the morning's preparations. The bedroom was too hot and, dressed only in a short nightie; she went out into the garden to think about the day ahead.

A velvety scent rose from the damp grass crushing beneath her bare feet. Fine spider webs hung between the posts of the fence, dancing in the sun like slender jewelled chains. The warmth of the sun on her face and the certainty that it was going to be a beautiful day, came with such intensity, she could not remember ever being so happy. It was going to be a perfect day.

Julia took a long bath, after which she stood in front of the full-length mirror in the hall and let the towel drop to the floor. Damp hair dripped and hung in tendrils around her cheeks and she looked at herself with a newly critical eye. The once straight and narrow hips now curved in to a slim waist and a recently flat chest showed breasts that were growing at an alarming rate. Thoughts vacillated from fear to pleasure at the changes. She did not want to be a child any more but the alternative scared her too.

Lost in thought, she gave an involuntary gasp as a flash of light behind reflected a figure in the mirror. She froze, afraid to move, eyes shut tight. A chill fear shuddered through her body and she turned to face whoever was there. But it had gone. Facing the wall, she saw nothing but an old painting, a Madonna and Child bought by her mother from a jumble sale, and the morning sun gleaming, mocking, from the glass in the front door. She grabbed the towel from the floor and ran back into her bedroom, slamming the door behind and leaning against it. When her breathing had slowed down enough for her to function and think more clearly, she walked past the bed, her foot catching the paperback of Wuthering Heights still on the floor. She picked it up and put it back on the bookshelf where it sat amongst the Poe, Radcliffe and Shelley, other volumes that stirred a fertile imagination.

AS PREDICTED FROM FIRST LIGHT, it was a hot day. The temperature rose throughout the morning and a baking sun blazed through dirt-smeared windows on the top deck of the bus. The air was suffocating and Julia's white shirt, picked out as particularly flattering and not yet too tight, began to show two dark patches underneath the arms. She felt them in horror and held her arms out as far as she could to cool. The bus was full for most of the journey but still swayed like a drunk around the curves and bends of the winding road to the coast. The rail link had closed five years ago and buses took the strain, especially during the summer months. The heat and noise were overpowering on the long and unfamiliar route, not one her father used when he took Julia and her mother out for a Sunday drive. Villages appeared and disappeared in clouds of fine dust and the yellowing grass at the verges flattened in their wake.

It was with great relief when the bus eventually pulled into the terminus; the smell of diesel had made her feel sick and the windows hadn't opened far enough to make much of a difference. The bus rolled lazily into a concrete yard, where a another idled in front of them, already waiting to take the return journey. She watched, uncertain, as the driver jumped up into his seat and wondered, for a moment only, if she should go back. The rest of the passengers, mostly families with children shrieking in delight at their escape from the confines of the bus, scrabbled around for bags and cases. Julia stood alone. For the hundredth time that day, she stared at the crumpled piece of paper on which David Weston had written his address. When he'd finally agreed to let her visit, it was on the understanding that it would have to be brief; they were packing and leaving within days. Julia had no idea where the house was and looked around for someone who might help with directions, but the last of the passengers had already gone and there was no one else in sight. The driver had long since disappeared with his newspaper tucked under his arm, and the vanishing second bus left only a ghost of smoke and dust in its place.

A sea breeze played around the frill of Julia's skirt as she tried to hold it down with one hand and tightly gripped the piece of paper with the other. Her hair flew up and floating strands stuck to the pale pink lipstick carefully reapplied on the bus. It was just as hot outside. The breeze was welcome apart from fine particles of sand that caught her eye. Seagulls screamed and whirled high above before settling down on distant rooftops.

A sign pinned to the door of a squat building in the corner of the yard read: 'Enquiries 9am to 5pm Mon-Fri'. It was Monday, and the station clock showed eleven. Julia tentatively went inside to find that the only person around was a cleaner, tunelessly humming whilst making a half-hearted attempt at mopping the floor. Years of grime stubbornly clung in the crevices where wall and floor met and cobwebs were left to freely sway down from the ceiling. The sole desk in the room held a pile of newly arrived timetables and an empty, brown-stained cup, but the seat was not occupied.

A nylon overall flapped loose over a thin flowered dress worn by the cleaner and coarse bleached hair fought to escape from a turban tied at the front. An inch of cigarette drooped from the side of her puckered lips with an equal length of ash defying gravity on the end. She stopped mopping when she heard the door open and quickly threw the tab into a bin, an act she regretted when she discovered that it was just a lost young girl looking for directions. Her eyes swept the length of Julia's body, swiftly appraising and registering disapproval of her outfit with a downturned mouth. 'You want to be careful going out in a skirt that short, love', she announced with authority. Julia thought of her mother saying the same thing and said nothing in reply. 'Can I help you, love?' the cleaner persisted as Julia looked around for anyone who might be in charge of the office. With no one else in sight, she showed the cleaner the address on the piece of paper.

'Do you know where this is, please?'

She considered the request and announced, 'Yes, dear,

I'm sure I do. There aren't many places around here that I don't know of.'

She took the slip of paper and studied it for a moment to ascertain whether or not she also knew who lived there, but was disappointed when she realised that she didn't and handed it back.

'Not from round here then, love?' she asked, but it was really more of a statement than question.

'No…I'm not.' Julia shook her head and followed the cleaner as she beckoned her back outside with a bent and bony forefinger. She reminded Julia of one of the witches in Macbeth.

'It's a long walk…and uphill, y'know', the cleaner said after giving directions and turning her gaze down to Julia's new platform sandals. They were already hurting her feet from sitting so long in the overheated bus. The cleaner questioned her with two raised, thin and pencil-drawn brows.

'I'll be all right'

'If you say so, dear…I can call a taxi if you want one?'

Julia could not fool her. The eyebrows shot up again as she leant towards her, breathing stale tobacco close to Julia's face.

'I'm sure the boss won't mind me phoning,' she croaked, tapping her crooked nose.

'No, it's fine, really,' Julia backed away as far as she could to escape the smell of her breath. The cleaner's eyes strained to follow her as she walked in the direction given.

'You'll regret that, dearie,' she said out of earshot.

Julia determined not to wince from the pain of the blisters until she'd walked out of sight.

The streets of the town were unfamiliar and the sound of the sea, close to the bus station, faded as she walked in the opposite direction. Every other house on the street displayed 'Vacancies' or 'No Vacancies' at netted windows; the kind of houses Julia and her parents stayed at on summer holidays; memorable mostly for creaking floorboards, lumpy beds, as well as awful fried breakfasts where the only edible part was toast. Each step brought fresh anxiety over how David might react to her visit; would he still want her there? It took twenty painful minutes to reach his house. Julia slowed as she got closer in an attempt to settle highly wrought nerves, as well as manage the pain in her feet. By the time she arrived her scalp prickled with the heat and small black flies were clinging to her damp white shirt.

Was this it? Julia stood at the front of a small semi-detached house half way down a long street. The front garden was badly neglected, overgrown and full of weeds; nothing like the garden at home with its neat striped lawn and tidy flowering beds. This garden was abandoned and unloved, unlike its neighbouring gardens on both sides. She checked the piece of paper one last time having clung to it like a talisman during the walk. There was no mistake; it was definitely the right address. A rusting metal gate to the path was held fast by an equally rusting sneck and took several attempts to free it.

Julia stood on the path, her body giving an involuntary shiver for the second time that day, despite the heat. Close to the gate stood an old tree, resolutely clinging to life. Several of its branches had snapped cleanly off, quite recently judging by the freshness of the yellow exposed wood. On one side a few black cherries tenaciously held on to a slender branch. She looked up to the top of the house where the curtains were still closed despite the lateness of the day. At ground level, white blinds at the windows were also tightly shut. She knocked on the door and waited, heart thumping remorselessly, hoping that he wouldn't notice how nervous she was. She took a deep breath but nothing would calm her as she stood at the door. An unnatural silence fell around the house broken only by the distant echo of a raging seagull. A fresh gust of wind rustled the leaves on the tree beside the gate and Julia looked behind her and down the street. She sensed being watched although there was no one in sight.

What if he's forgotten? What if his wife's there? What do I say? With no other choice but to dismiss such thoughts she knocked again, louder this time, until muffled footsteps could be heard, followed by the sound of a key turning in the lock.

The door opened and David stood before her, looking the opposite of how Julia felt. He was relaxed and smiling, pleased to see her, but appearing nothing like the teacher at school. Navy shorts that didn't quite reach his knees, and a pale blue tee shirt, were worn in place of the usual corduroy trousers, check shirt and tie. His feet were bare and his face, legs and arms had already started to tan. Julia, pale and nervous, was acutely aware of the contrast between them, hot and uncomfortable as she was in damp shirt and tight shoes.

Chapter 5

'Well, hello there, you made it' His smile was warm and welcoming, but Julia doubted that he really could be pleased to see a pasty-faced schoolgirl at his door.

'Hello'

'I thought you'd changed your mind...was the bus late?' he asked and she wondered again if he wished she hadn't come. He glanced, almost imperceptibly, down the street before ushering her in.

'No, no, I-I just got a bit lost,' It was a feeble response and she hoped that he wouldn't think she couldn't find her way around such a small town.

'Come on through.'

He led her to the room with the closed white blinds, his hand brushing her back as it had done on Friday night, but this time stopping at a more respectable height. She flushed at the memory as it flashed back in vivid detail. Her throat closed so tight she could barely speak. The confidence that came after drinking cheap red wine at the school dance was long gone. She was in a strange house with a man she barely knew beyond the confines of the school history room, and one night in a pub after the dance.

'You look rather hot,' he said and put his hand against her burning cheek. 'Wait in here where it's cool and I'll go and get you a cold drink.'

'Thank you…I'm really ok', she managed to whisper but he merely led her over to an old leather sofa under the window.

'I won't be a minute.'

She sat down on a worn, old sofa that sagged in the middle and creaked beneath her weight. In no time, her bare legs stuck uncomfortably to it.

'Make yourself at home,' David called out from the kitchen.

The living room was in disarray, looking just as neglected as the garden, but at least it was cool. Windows, shaded from the sun, provided welcome relief from the heat. Julia's face began to return to its usual colour and the agitation she'd felt on arrival eased just a little, at least enough to look around and take in the surroundings as David clattered in the kitchen.

Tightly packed bookshelves lined two of the walls. She had never seen so many books in one room before, apart from the library in the village at home, and the one at school, of course. Her parents were not great readers beyond Dad's daily paper and Mum's 'People's Friend'. Julia was the exception in the family, but even so felt woefully inadequate against the volumes on display in this room. Her eyes skimmed along a line of Orange Penguin paperbacks nestling alongside older leather-bound volumes of history. She stood up to relieve the discomfort of the sofa and walked towards a narrow shelf above the electric fire. A row of dusty framed photographs caught her attention and curiosity got the better of her. In one of them,

David was laughing, standing with his arm around a woman's waist. They were obviously happy, posing beneath a sky so clear and blue it could have come straight from a child's paint box. She picked it up to take a closer look. Of course it must be his wife but in the haste of replacing the photograph in exactly the same spot, a letter, tucked behind, was disturbed and fell to the floor. She picked it up and saw a postmark that read Paris, France, and the sender as M. G. Gaudet. Julia was about to tuck it back behind the photograph when a second rogue wind whipped down the flue behind the electric fire, and almost snatched it from her hand, but then, just as quickly as it began, died away. Julia shivered and looked around for David's return as she went back to the sofa. A paperback sat on a small table, a well-thumbed copy of 'L'Education Sentimentale'. Its cover was badly creased and spine bent from reading. The sofa creaked again as Julia's legs came unstuck and she leaned across to pick it up. A tasselled bookmark fell out at the moment David walked back in with a glass of orange, ice cubes clinking at its sides. He wiped the drips underneath and set it down where the book had been.

'Sorry it took so long, couldn't find the juice.'

Her cheeks flamed afresh when she replaced the bookmark in an approximation of where she thought it had been.

'Ah, that's Simone's, not mine. I could only manage the translation I'm afraid,' he joked. 'Have you read it?' He took the book from hands that had suddenly taken on a life of their own and trembled uncontrollably. 'Not yet,' she said in a low voice, before taking a sip from the glass that wobbled as she drank. She rested it on her knee to try to stop the shaking and watched as David carelessly threw the book on top of an already overflowing tea chest. The bookmark fell out again, this time dropping behind a pile of papers underneath. 'I think Simone finished reading it last night.'

For the second time in three days, Julia tried desperately to remember the conversations so carefully rehearsed in her room, and on the bus, but nothing came to mind apart from the fact that his wife might come in any minute. She didn't even know her name and up to this point hadn't considered the implications of her visit if Mrs Weston had been there, or what she would say to the inevitable question of why she had come. He must have read her mind. 'It's all right, Simone's not home until after six'. 'Oh' was all Julia could manage in reply, but the relief was palpable. Of course he knew what she was thinking. She was as much an open book as the Flaubert sitting in the chest. David slumped in a chair opposite. 'Anyway, I have a few history texts that you can take back with you…be good when you do 'A' Level. I presume you are still doing 'A' Level history?' Julia sat primly on the edge of the seat, bolt upright, knees clamped together, arms held into her side, and glass held tight.

'Yes…yes I am.'

'Good…good.'

What am I doing here? I can't speak, can't even drink from a glass without shaking.

'It is lovely to see you again,' he offered but she knew he was just being kind and bit her lip. David did most of the talking and Julia managed to smile once or twice, but it was painfully obvious she had little to say.

How could I ever be like you? So cool and calm, so relaxed? He glanced at his watch. This is it. He's going to tell me to leave.

'Right then…Julia…what shall we do now you're here?' He leaned forward in his chair, smiling. Julia was taken aback at the directness of the question. 'I-I don't know… anything really…I hadn't thought…'

The morning's confidence, so carefully built up on the journey, dismantled minute by minute and to top it all, her stomach gave an embarrassingly long growl. She'd eaten nothing since yesterday's tea and even then, it had been very little. The excitement of today's visit had taken away any thought of food. David laughed, and relieving the tension said, 'Let's start with some lunch, then.' He retrieved the half-drunk glass of orange glass with one hand and reached out for her hand with his other. 'Come on, I'll make some sandwiches…if that's all right with you?' He tried to make light of the visit and led her to the kitchen table, from which he retrieved a bus timetable collected the day before and tucked it back behind a teapot.

Lunch was a relief; doing something so mundane might ease the tension and the knots inside her stomach. The kitchen was equally full of boxes and debris. His going away had been pushed to the back of her mind, but the evidence lay all around the house; in the hall and in each room they passed.

Sandwiches were made from a lonely block of cheese retrieved from the fridge, coated with ketchup from the last remains of an almost empty bottle. Julia felt herself revert to the schoolgirl she still was as David once again asked about summer holidays. He had obviously forgotten their earlier conversation on Friday night. Nothing was said about Friday night.

Julia watched David prepare lunch, but all she could think about was his arms around her and that kiss in the dark outside school. Could he really have forgotten that? Or had he dismissed it altogether in the cold light of day? An almost-conversation at the kitchen table wove around sandwich preferences, ketchup or not, and another glass of orange juice. When it was set before her, she managed a few mouthfuls, enough to stave off the pangs of hunger, but no more than that. David apologised for the lack of ham or, anything more imaginative, but Julia had no interest in food. Unable to take another bite, she pushed aside the half eaten sandwich.

'I thought you were hungry. Are you sure you've had enough?'

'I can't manage any more, really.' David had eaten his with obvious relish and looked across at her plate.

'Sorry...but thank you...it was nice.'

She looked down, her eyes turning away from his gaze as he reached across to wipe a crumb from the side of her mouth. 'It's all right, Julia...it doesn't matter.'

It does matter she thought, it matters that I'm here and I don't know what to say or do and I feel stupid. Sensing that nothing had alleviated her discomfort, he felt sorry for the sad, young girl sitting opposite at the table.

'You look pretty today, you know. Any lucky boyfriend on the scene?' David tried to be upbeat.

'No, not now.'

'I thought you and Billy Sanderson were an item?'

'No'

How would he know that? Billy didn't really count and she wasn't about to go into detail of why she rejected him at the dance. She fidgeted in her chair, conscious that what remained of her pink lipstick was now smeared around the glass of orange, and the blue eye shadow so carefully applied this morning must have all but rubbed away in the heat. Underneath the table, she nervously picked at the cuticle around her thumb. It was red and sore, but the pain was nothing to her inability to think of what else to say.

'Well then, Julia; what shall we do next…stay in…or go out?'

He caught her attention. Was this the defining moment? Was this where he made it clear that it was time to leave?

On Friday night, after the dance, he'd taken her to the 'Royal Oak', an old pub, hidden down a side street where neither of them were likely to meet anyone they knew. It felt so grown up and special. He'd bought her a glass of wine after checking that it was all right for her to be out a little longer; and he agreed to drive her home afterwards. She could hardly remember what they had talked about then. The unaccustomed wine helped her relax into his company and the euphoria rose as the evening went on. But now, now was different. Despite the nerves and the shaking hands, she recognised that the opportunity she'd craved was here, but felt helpless in the undertaking. He had finished for good at school and within a week would leave for France. The whole class knew that; they'd collectively signed a card to wish him well and bought a framed photograph of the Hull City team he supported as a memento. Of course she knew that he was going but gave it little thought until now, just as she had never really considered that his wife might have been here either. He didn't ask her to leave and 'I want to stay', was her quiet response.

Chapter 6

David pulled Julia to her feet. Her head barely reached his shoulder so she rested her face against his chest where the woody scent of cologne and the warmth of his body seductively drew her in. Against the slow steady beating of his heart, and his arms wrapped around her, she at last felt loved and wanted. She believed that he loved her at that moment, as much as she did him.

'Are you sure?' he said.

She nodded, certain, and he led her upstairs. It took a while to adjust to the darkness of the bedroom until a bedside lamp was switched on. The curtains were thick and effective, but the lamp's dim glow was enough to see that the bed had only been roughly made. At the other side of the room, half-empty drawers gaped open and coats, with hangers still left inside, were draped across a chair. More boxes spread out along the floor, waiting expectantly to be filled by shoes, boots and clothing strewn around the room. It signified nothing against the passionate kiss that took her breath away, and strong firm hands gently stroking her face and hair and neck.

Prior to this moment, sex meant little beyond giggling conversations with Maggie; smutty suggestions of boys in the playground; and Billy's clumsy, and rejected, fumbling after the cinema and at the dance. This was different; this was real.

David momentarily let her go, undressed by the small light and stood before her in pale striped shorts. His chest, also starting to tan was toned and hairless, apart from a stripe down the centre, leading down into the shorts.

Julia tried to undo the buttons on her shirt, but her trembling fingers failed to respond, so David took over the task, releasing the shirt, the skirt and the bra that was already becoming too small. He pulled back the covers on the bed, kissing her lightly now on the lips, and lay her down before climbing in too, but stopped suddenly and raised his head, taking in Julia's expectant face and shining eyes. 'You can change your mind if you want to, you know. Just say'. 'I don't want to, no', came the reply at which he pulled her close. Small kisses were planted over her eyelids and mouth, slowly working their way down to her neck and shoulders that prickled with pleasure in response. Yes, this was what she wanted. She gave an involuntary shiver to David Weston's sure and experienced touch. The scream of the gulls and imperceptible creak of a decaying cherry tree were the only accompaniment to the lesson learned in the stillness of his bedroom.

THE MIXTURE of pleasure and pain that came from their lovemaking was not disappointing. It was her first time and if it wasn't exactly as she'd imagined, it was just as beautiful as she'd hoped. David had been caring and tender and Julia had relaxed enough to lose herself in him, but it was over too soon. When he kissed her cheek and got out of bed, she tried not to cry but couldn't help herself.

'You do love me, don't you? Don't leave me.'

'Of course I love you, but it can't go on, you know that. You're a sweet girl Julia, but I can't love you the way you want me to. I do love you but I'm in love with my wife. I thought you knew that; I told you on Friday.'

Did he? She couldn't or wouldn't remember that part of the evening. 'You have your whole life ahead of you... you're a pretty, bright girl...you'll have plenty of boyfriends and you'll soon forget about me.' She did not remember that part of the conversation.

'Will I see you again?'

'That won't be possible... not now...I'm so sorry... we leave in a few days time. Simone finishes work tonight and we're going back to France, to live...not for a holiday... and probably for good.'

Julia's tears fell freely on the sheets and all trace of the happiness she had felt just a few minutes earlier, vanished.

'You don't regret this, do you?' he asked, retrieving his shorts from the floor and kneeling beside the bed. 'This was what you wanted?' He pushed back her hair and wiped her tears with the sheet. 'Yes, I love you,' she told him, her voice, cracked with emotions she had no control over. He stroked her hair, as she lay still on the bed. 'You are very special, Julia,' he said and reached over for the tissues at Simone's side of the bed, once again wiping the tears that freely flowed down her face. After pulling on the shorts and tee shirt, he stood in thought for a few seconds at the bedroom door.

'Julia...' he began and her imploring eyes looked up, cutting him short; this wasn't what he was used to or even expecting, '...the bathroom's just across the hall if you want to…you know…freshen up a bit. I'll wait for you downstairs.'

Julia slowly made her way to the bathroom, feeling a warm stickiness between her legs, and locked the door behind her. The mirror above the sink reflected a mottled face and unflattering bloodshot eyes.

Downstairs, David whistled as he filled the kettle and sought out a couple of mugs, calculating that hot, sweet tea might be called for. After ten minutes, Julia appeared.

'Hello…I thought you might have sneaked off out… are you ok?'

Julia's face had been washed clean of the last vestiges of make up and with hair tucked behind her ears, looked more the fifteen-year old schoolgirl she was. Two mugs of tea were put on the table where they had sat together barely an hour earlier, 'Here we have the last mugs left in the cupboard… I'll take the one with the chip, of course' he gestured with a flourish, trying to lighten the mood, and pulled out a chair.

'I've got an idea,' he said, replacing a stray wisp of hair behind her ear,

'Why don't we go for a walk down to the beach before you go?'

'That would be nice,' she agreed, trying to smile and sipped the hot, sweet tea. She hated tea, but right now it was a welcome distraction.

With all emotion spent, what else was there to do? Hopes of yesterday flew away like smoke in the wind and she could do no more than agree to whatever he suggested. Maybe on a walk they could talk and he would tell her that he really did love her? As the minutes passed, it became increasingly obvious that the last hour might have never happened. David cleared the table, wiped away the crumbs and put plates, glasses and mugs into the sink. When he was done, he smiled across, 'Ready?'

It could have been her Dad standing there before a nice day out, hurrying to get her and Mum out of the door, anxious to be off before 'the traffic gets bad'. David picked up the house keys and tucked the bus timetable into his pocket. His manner reverted to how it had been when she first arrived. He told her what a promising student she was and how he was glad that she'd decided to stay on at school.

David walked Julia down the backstreets, towards a part of the beach where few people came, unless they were backpackers, or dog walkers, who liked out of the way places. Visitors filled the beach at the other end of town, they weren't inclined to walk far from the pub, the amusements or the fish and chip takeaways. When the houses had become a distant blur, and they were far enough from any sign of life, he took her hand. The gesture was kindly meant but was given with the understanding on his part, that by tomorrow this afternoon, and Julia, would be no more than a memory of a summer's day. Julia was grateful for the crumb of kindness and took from it rather more than had been intended by the giver.

At the cliff edge, the sea looked magnificent, bathed in a warm afternoon sun whose bright orange orb blazed on the horizon. The sky was clear enough to see for miles along the coastline. In the face of the beauty before them, Julia was ready to believe that perhaps everything would be right after all. She turned to him for any sign of confirmation but he was somewhere else, looking out to sea and deep in thought. She might not have been there at all.

'What are you thinking about?' she asked.

'What...oh, nothing much...how close...and how far we are from France,' he eventually replied.

David had already moved on from the hour after lunch. Julia was still in the darkened room, in his arms, and in his bed, and winced a little at the soreness between her legs.

'Come on, let's get down to the beach.'

His words spoke more to the breeze blowing across the North Sea than Julia. He let go of her hand and led the way along the edge of the cliff. The steps down to the beach were steep and narrow, rough-hewn out of crumbling rock. It was a precarious descent and the only form of support a line of rope attached at intervals to wooden stakes on both sides. Over the years the steps had worn smooth and it looked as though it wouldn't be long before they too disappeared, along with chunks of the eroding headland.

Julia lost her footing half way down when a gull screeched close by her head; it flew up like a beacon as the light caught its feathers underneath, and it was borne aloft by a shift in the wind. She screamed out, slipping on loosened earth, catching David's attention only when a hail of stones rained down on him. 'Are you all right? Do you want a hand?' he called up over the noise of seagulls and sea, more amused than worried at the predicament they found themselves in.

'I'm fine,' Julia called at his back.

On the beach, they took off their shoes and walked along the water's edge where the sand felt warm and soft between their toes. Their two sets of footprints were fleeting as the rolling waves smoothed over any sign that they had been there at all.

It wasn't too long before the tide started closing in and the sun drifted behind a bank of cloud in the distance. All too soon, the sea no longer looked as inviting as it had at first and the gentle breeze of earlier gave way to a chill

North wind making its presence felt. Shadows drifted in and out of crevices along the cliffs and for the third time that day, Julia felt a chill run down her body, along with a sense that they were not alone. She looked around, but there was no one else in sight.

'You ok?'

'Yes…fine,' but how could she explain the same fear she'd felt in the hallway at home, the same foreboding that something was wrong? The girl in a blood stained dress and a dream that wouldn't leave her alone. She wanted to tell David but thought better of it and didn't want to appear childish. After all, it was just a dream, a dress and a flash of sunlight, wasn't it?

She held on to David's hand a little more tightly when she saw his eyes going down to his wrist.

'We'd better get back up now or you'll miss your bus home.'

Shivering in her short skirt, she forced her swollen feet back into the tight strappy sandals, wincing as the leather rubbed against fresh raw blisters that had already formed on each heel. They walked along in silence; not that there had been much of a conversation while they had been down on the beach.

The return journey to the bus station held none of the optimism of her walk away from it. Julia struggled to keep up with David's quickening pace and the terminus came in sight too soon. There had been no time to collect the promised history books. 'I'll send them with Mr Brice for next term.' The visit had come to an end.

'Sorry, we had to rush', he offered by way of apology, 'but I didn't want you to miss your bus…there won't be another before seven tonight.'

A dust-coated bus was already waiting at the depot, its driver impatiently tapping the steering wheel. He revved the engine, keen to be off, and a cloud of noxious smoke blew out from an ancient vibrating exhaust. Julia was relieved the cleaner was nowhere in sight; the office stood in darkness, closed for the day.

Julia waited in vain for words of kindness, of consolation, before she left, but there was little time to say much beyond goodbye. Her face told more than she could ever put into words and David tried not to notice.

'I'm sorry I have to rush off...I did warn you I had a lot to do today and you've definitely kept me from it' He laughed, 'It's all your fault I've done no packing yet!' A light, chaste, kiss was planted on each cheek, between fast falling tears. Firmly taking her arms away from his neck, and holding her hands in his, he implored her, 'Don't say anything more, Julia. You have to understand we can't meet again. It's been a wonderful day; take from that what you can. I was pleased to see you but now make the most of the holidays...and keep up with your studies. I mean it when I say that you were always my best student.'

'But...'

'No...really...I have to go...you take care won't you?'

'Doors closing now...mind yourself please.' The drivers voice softened when he saw Julia's face, 'Time to go, love.'

The doors closed and she watched David as he stood and waited to see the bus leave. She opened the window as dark clouds overhead started to release a shower of rain. David was surprised to see a young woman sitting beside Julia and thought perhaps it was someone she knew. He needed to get back home before Simone arrived and look as though he had at least made some progress on the packing.

Julia put her bag on the empty seat beside her and made a brave attempt to stem the flow of tears. There considerably fewer people on the bus than when she came. Outside, and fading into the distance, David was already on the road home and did not turn round again. Julia watched rivulets of rain snaking their way down the streaking glass and immersed herself into the hours that had passed.

JULIA WOULD MAKE ONLY one other visit to the little house at the seaside. Two months later, it revealed a 'sold' sign pegged into the front lawn and grass reached almost half way up the wooden stake. The cherry tree had completely died and its remaining branches hung useless from its decaying trunk. The house was empty and David had gone, just as he'd said he would.

Julia's experience of first love decreed that it was nothing like the romantic novels she read and left nothing behind beyond the memory of that one afternoon, along with a permanent reminder.

Chapter 7

Simone came home tired after her last day at work, hoping against hope that David might have made a good start on the packing now that school was over. The elderly Citroen Dolly she had driven for the past couple of years had taken its last commute into the city and stood on the roadside awaiting collection. Tomorrow it would be hauled away by an enthusiast and both were pleased considering its one last breakdown the week before. Even though the mechanic had sounded the death knell when repairs would cost more than the car was worth, it sold remarkably easy. Simone affectionately patted its roof before going inside. That was the final nail in the coffin of their life on the east coast. David had always hated the car and was more than happy not to have to do yet another oil change or tinker around under the bonnet wondering if the clacking noise indicated something more sinister. Whatever they did was now followed by the thought of 'this will be the last time'.

Simone, gratefully prising off tight shoes and dropping her briefcase by the hall table, called out to David that she was home, unaware how close he was until a rustling noise behind a pile of boxes caught her attention. Peering around, she found him kneeling amongst a pile of junk that had never seen daylight since they had first moved in. She looked in dismay at boxes still only a quarter full and sighed deeply after kissing the top of his head. He looked up in obvious delight at seeing her back; ever thankful for an excuse to stop doing something he took no pleasure in.

'Ah good, you got off early then?'

'They wanted me to go out for one last drink, but I said no. I needed to get back to my husband who has been on his own all day…to help him with packing …which I see he has barely started, lazy man.'

She peered into the living room with equal dismay when she saw that it was still very much as it had been that morning.

'Really? David?'

Simone's accent was faint and her English almost perfect, spoken with a trace of French but she still pronounced his name 'Daveed'. David loved it, found it sexy and basked in the envy of his friends when he'd introduced her. It had also added to her appeal in attracting new clients to the firm she'd found employment with in the city. It was not something she would capitalise on, but there were those above her who made sure that she sat next to the most receptive of clients. Simone let it pass; being more than good at her job, she chose to accept the vagaries that went with the post in the hope that it would all pay off some day. She had not been treated the same as her predominantly male colleagues but her ability was quietly admired beneath the banter and the occasional slight of her position. She had confidence enough to ride it out and bide her time and that ability won out when clients often asked for her by name. Quite simply, she was a lovely person as well as talented and it paid off. Knowing for some time that her salary would always make up the bulk of their income, she saw no problem with that and was grateful to David for not making it an issue. Teaching was never going to be in the same league as financial management. It was not something they'd discussed in particular, each preferring to let the other find their own level, their own place in the working world. There was no envy or comparison, making life easy to navigate once they'd both eased their way out of student life in France. David had not been able to find employment there and Simone had been more than happy to give England a try. Over the past few years, the combination of monetary acuity and a pleasing, easy manner ensured her a great return for the company that employed her and now they were keen for her to head the Paris office when a vacancy came up.

'These things can't be rushed, you know. Packing takes a lot of careful planning.' He pulled her down and kissed her full on the lips.

'I'm a man of leisure now, ma cherie, I can take my time.'

'That may be so but we have three days David. Three, not twenty-three. And there'll be much for you to do when we move. I'll be under a lot of pressure to prove myself with this new job. It's not a walkover, you know.'

David draped his arms around her neck, stroking her cheek and hair, his voice as soothing as hers was building with anxiety.

'You worry too much…everything will be fine. You concentrate on your job, and just leave the rest to me.'

'Hmm, that's what worries me,' she said as she eased her way out of his arms and went upstairs to change, 'Give me a couple of minutes and I'll make a start on the kitchen,' she called down, 'Then we must sort out this bedroom, it's a tip,' she shouted from the other side of the door when she saw that little had progressed there either.

'I changed the sheets,' he called back.

'What? What for? We go in three days…'

Her response spoke more to herself than David when she wondered if this was a sign of things to come. He'd never done that before, even when it was badly needed. She changed into comfortable trousers and a baggy top, happy to be free from the stilettos that crippled her feet and the tight black suit that was designed more for effect than comfort. Simone sat on the bed, rubbing the throbbing pain at her temple, reflecting on life in the little house that sat in a quiet corner of a quaint seaside town.

The contrast with Paris could not have been more acute; it had been difficult to adjust at first but she embraced change with her usual good grace and realised now that she might actually miss it, if just a little. The move would happen with some measure of regret at least. They had been happy here but change was inevitable. In a few short days they would leave for Paris for good. There would be much to occupy them both and such reflections would be a luxury she could not afford. Simone, excited and worried in equal measure, walked to the window that overlooked the garden and pulled back the curtain. Looking down, she was sad that they never seemed to make time to do anything with it beyond harvesting a pathetic handful of cherries from the old gnarled tree at the gate. Even that had taken a battering in last week's high winds and would soon have to be taken down before it caused an accident. 'The next occupants can have that problem,' she mused.

Simone's new role was already demanding her attention; it was something new and exciting to focus on, not just for herself, but also for a future life with David. His boredom with teaching was a nightly complaint to which the answer was generally a large glass of red, or preferably more once a bottle was opened. Teaching was always going to be a stopgap, he said, but he gave little indication of what he really wanted to do next. She knew that for the foreseeable future they would both rely on her, not insubstantial, salary, but that wasn't what was foremost in her mind. There was always a need to prove herself to her father. Even in death he held great sway over his daughter; Bertrand Lefebre's love came at a price. Not an easy man to impress, she'd fallen far short of his expectations when they'd parted and following only two meetings with David, he did little to hide his disapproval. Bertrand had not considered him good enough for his daughter, that he would bring her down and take her away from the family business; on top of which he thought him too lazy to even care. No argument from Simone could persuade him otherwise, not even when her mother, whilst she was alive, had interceded on her behalf. In Bertrand's life, love came a firm second to a successful business.

For the first time in her life, Simone had stood up to him although it did not take away the compulsion to prove that she could make a successful career on her own *and* be with the man she loved. Their arguments had spilt over into a bitter feud but then a fatal heart attack had taken away the opportunity of showing him what she had achieved. Bertrand had died at home, alone, discovered by Mme Rubin when he had not appeared for three days. Now, standing at the window, holding on to the ledge and gazing out, she felt a stab of remorse that it was no longer possible to make him see how wrong he had been. Life was good and she was happy, with David and with her job.

Going to her father's funeral without David had been a difficult decision, but it felt right at the time. She was stronger on her own, like her father, and held back the oppression of grief when there was so much to organise and prepare. She'd even paved the way for their move. The apartment, her childhood home, was part of the legacy and it was soon decided that this was where they should live – to begin with anyway. Bertrand had been a very wealthy man; David had little idea of how wealthy, but Simone was an only child and the inheritance substantial.

Simone took a deep breath and slowly exhaled. Straightening the cover on the bed, she then made her way back downstairs. She smiled at the thought of the glass of wine that David would be pouring in the kitchen; always his answer to any problem at any time, and tonight it would be her answer too. She chose to ignore piles of clothes on the floor and hope for the future replaced small disappointments of the present. David was right; it would all get done in time.

Downstairs, as presumed, two large glasses of a dubious red sat on the mantelpiece in the living room; the bottle having been left over from their leaving party the week before. Looking at the bottle, it was most likely the one brought by Phil, one of David's university friends. Simone took a sip and grimaced, 'What on earth is this?'

'Phil's disgusting offering, but there's nothing else left 'til we get to France'

'Thought so…I can't drink that, you have it.'

David downed his glass in one and replaced his empty glass with Simone's full one. He picked up the letter sitting behind the clock as Simone set to work on packing already started. Ruthless efficiency was required over sentimentality and piles of discards soon outgrew the packed and wanted.

Happy to let Simone take charge, David momentarily focussed on the letter and name on the back of the envelope before slipping it into his pocket. Georges' proposal was tempting, it might even keep him occupied for a while but it could wait until they had moved before he got back in touch. There was no hurry. The letter itself was at least six months old anyway; a few more weeks wouldn't make much difference. He had always intended to reply, but the usual apathy and prevarication meant he had not. Poor Georges had sounded troubled; but when wasn't he? The unread part of the letter would have told David his wife Sybil was ill and he was struggling to find the time to do all he needed on his collection of historic papers dating back to the time of the Civil War. It was always going to be part of his retirement project but something invariably cropped up to make it impossible. The Papers, at Georges' home in Paris, now languished in a box at the back of a cupboard.

Years earlier, when David asked the questions of why, what and how he came to possess them, Georges insisted they were nothing to do with the Paris Archives where he worked; they had come into his hands from a trusted source; they needed careful handling. They were his. David wasn't entirely convinced they were genuine, however. The likelihood of something like that surviving unknown from the death of Charles 1's widow was remote, but Georges insisted they were the real thing. He said there were links that needed to be followed up in Yorkshire and asked David to make a start as he was so close, but that too never happened, one more promise he'd failed to fulfil.

Georges' health was poor, it had been for some time, and he'd retired early from his job, but, David reasoned, he still had time to finish writing. In truth, it was Sybil's illness that held him back, that and the grip of a Catholic faith he'd returned to in desperation when her cancer took a firm hold.

The letter was tucked deep into his pocket where the

offer remained like an unused gift he wasn't sure what to do with. He would get back in touch with Georges again soon and in a half-hearted attempt to assuage the guilt of not replying, it did not go in the pile of papers marked 'rubbish'.

David had no regrets about leaving; the house and job had always been a temporary phase in their life, and he looked forward to finding something new. He loved France and couldn't wait to get back. Life had been so good back then. Teaching was always a means to an end, not something he actually wanted to do, and he discarded the job as easily as the pile of work clothes on the bedroom floor; just as easily as he discarded thoughts of the young girl who had visited him that afternoon.

Chapter 8

Paris

In a warm afternoon sun, the taxi from Orly Airport pulled up outside the Belle Vue Apartments on the Ile Saint Louis. Two battered suitcases had been deposited on the street and now sat incongruous to the opulent building before them. David and Simone stood side by side as the taxi, with bent bumpers and grinding gears, quickly disappeared to his next fare. They looked up without speaking – Simone, in remembrance of her last trip home, and David in awe and disbelief at where they were about to live.

Below them, the Seine shone and glistened with broken reflections of the beautiful buildings along its banks. It was a moment of tranquillity amidst the frenetic activity of the journey as both were lost in the perfect moment of arrival.

David was first to break the silence and gave a low whistle, grateful that the rest of their belongings were not lined up with two cheap suitcases sitting at their feet. He tried to remember how it was that he had never actually been here before this day. Simone's father had disapproved of their relationship it was true, he'd only met Bertrand a couple of times in Paris and the meetings had not gone particularly well, but Simone had never attempted to persuade her father to invite him home after that, even after they'd married. It was only now, standing together outside the building that David began to fully understand the extent of the wealth he'd married into, and the reason why her father might not have wanted his daughter to be stuck with a penniless, left wing student with limited prospects.

'Well, what do you think?'

David couldn't find the words and laughed incredulously. He picked up Simone and swung her round, until she shrieked and begged to be put down.

'Do you think you could like living here?' she panted as the squeeze took her breath away.

'Like it! What do you think?'

'I think it's a bit different from the less than desirable holes we used to live in over here'

'You told me you would live penniless in a garret as long as you were with

me'

'Yes well…those days have long gone, mon cher'. I like a bathroom I don't have to queue for nowadays… and one with plenty of hot water. Come on, let's go in.'

They giggled like children, excited and happy at the prospect before them. Simone, despite initial misgivings, appreciated this big leap in their lives, albeit an unexpected one. The death of her father was sudden and had thrown everything into turmoil, not least because of the opportunities that had arisen since. David's reaction to her suggestion that she should take up the job in Paris and move back there was to write his letter of resignation and ask who they should invite to the leaving party.

'I love you Mme. Weston.'

He heartily kissed her on both cheeks as Simone struggled to break free, her anxiety rising in the midst of excitement.

'I want to savour this moment…just wait a minute longer,' he pleaded and held her closer. He recalled with clarity the first time he'd met the young, opinionated French girl with the short black bob and striking features, someone who instinctively drew people to her when she entered a room. The minute David saw her and heard her voice at L'Etoile Verte, he wanted her. She wasn't conventionally beautiful; her face was long and her nose pointed, but with sculpted cheekbones and exquisite mouth. The confidence in what she said, and the way in which she held court with friends, was captivating to the extent that he had to be with her. She attracted men and women with her gift of making them at ease and with her charm; quite simply, she was funny and fabulous to be with.

Since arriving at university in Paris, David had not met anyone else who came close. It had not stopped him flirting elsewhere when the occasion called for it, but he always went back to Simone. He had no idea of her background and assumed that she was just as penniless as the rest of them, studying economics and politics and having fun on very little income. She had always been reluctant to talk about her family and he'd never pushed the subject, but within a month they'd moved in together, and after completing their final year, married and left for England. The brief introduction to her father had not been a success and was never repeated despite David's attempt to persuade her to try again. Bertrand disapproved of the match and would not give his blessing to a marriage that was not to be held in a Catholic Church. He'd also wanted his daughter to join the family business and couldn't see the need to practise in England of all places.

Simone, in turn, overlooked David's occasional slip into indiscretion when he overwhelmed her with love and attention, physically and mentally, as no other man had before. It was always in full belief that he would never actually be unfaithful to her and so she loved him in return without reservation. He was nothing like a Frenchman; they were supposed to be the passionate ones, the lovers who knew how to make a woman feel wanted and special, but David exceeded all expectation in that respect. He asked her once why she loved him and she told him it was for his soft brown hair that curled at the back of his neck; she liked to run her fingers through it, and he laughed at that.

'And what about me?' she replied.

'When I heard you talking about jazz with such passion, I couldn't resist…and I saw you long before you even noticed me.'

'Rubbish,' she retorted, but there was probably a hint of truth in it.

She struggled successfully this time to get free of his clasp and grabbed David's hand, 'Come on!' She was impatient now to get inside until he reminded her that they should also take in the suitcases.

Chapter 9

The cavernous lobby was empty; church-like in its opulence where a marble and stone interior was equally as impressive as the outside. A delicate scent of jasmine hung in the air, coming from an abundant display of flowers beneath a large window. They were reflected to advantage in one of many large gilt mirrors that hung around the walls. David turned full circle, taking in as much as he could in one fell swoop. Again, he was speechless.

Simone stood to one side with hands at the back of her head, watching his reaction, but they were not alone for long. Silently, without warning, a dark skinned woman swathed in vibrantly coloured clothing appeared from a small office in the far corner. She scowled at the intrusion of unknown visitors disturbing her sleep – that is until she realised who had walked in. The scowl transformed into a look of delight and her face broke into a broad smile. She strode over to them, quickly now and remarkably agile for such a big woman. She enveloped Simone with a warm hug of familiarity. 'Simone, Simone! Bonjour…ma cherie je n'avais pas idée…' Madame Rubin's dark eyes lit up with pleasure, her face animated with delight. She had known Simone since childhood and had followed the family's rise and fall in fortune from a close but respectful distance, perhaps knowing more about the family than she would ever care to admit. Her head was encased in a bright red turban, and her unlined features gave little away with respect to age. It was difficult to guess her nationality too, her colour was dark but not deeply so, and her accent difficult to place. Her clothes clung to a voluminous body in several layers, equally brightly coloured in vivid contrast to the pale, subtle décor of the lobby.

'I know, I know, I'm sorry, I wasn't certain when we would get here...but we're here now and...' She wasn't allowed to finish before Mme. Rubin stopped her short with a raised hand, interrupting Simone after seeing David standing smiling behind. 'Qui est-ce?' she asked in clipped tones, but a raised eyebrow gave away the fact that she possibly already knew the answer. 'C'est mon mari, David. My husband.' Simone took David's arm and brought him forward to meet the colourful concierge, leaving the suit-cases standing in the centre of the lobby like unwanted guests at a party. Mme. Rubin slowly and solemnly looked him up and down, taking in the curling unkempt hair, faded jeans and crumpled denim shirt. A cold shiver ran through him despite the warmth of the lobby where the afternoon sun continued to stream in. Simone stepped back knowing how Mme. Rubin always liked to inspect any new friends, and a new husband would be no different.

For several moments, Mme Rubin stood firm before David, her face betraying nothing of what was going on behind her penetrating gaze. His discomfort did not bother her, but after several moments she broke into another broad smile and threw open her arms. She greeted David with a hug and firm kiss on both cheeks. She held him close, the scent of patchouli and spice overwhelming in the process. The hold was longer than he expected and she spoke in a voice that did not quite match the warmth of the greeting:

'I expect you, David. Look after my child. Be happy, mais prenez soin. Take great care.'

The smile dropped again when Simone walked over to call the lift and her eyes looked closely into his own as if she could read his mind and every thought held there.

The exchange was lost on Simone, as was the grip Mme. Rubin had on his hand before she let him follow. 'Come on David...bring the other suitcase. We'll see you later Mme. Rubin, I promise' Simone called over her shoulder.

David rubbed his hand and gave her a puzzled look, 'Don't worry...Simone is safe with me. I always look after her.' She nodded and returned back to her office, disturbed by the shock of electricity that had run through her body when she'd held David's hand. She gave a deep sigh as she watched them from the small window in her room, one that gave her a perfect view of the comings and goings in the building. 'So, it start,' she murmured to herself as she helped herself from the dish of cherries on the table.

'I think she likes you...what did she say when my back was turned?' The lift doors had closed, the inside proving just as fabulous as the lobby. Simone sat on one of the suit-cases and held on to David's leg. Exertions of the past week were finally catching up with her, and anxiety beginning afresh. She was curious to know what kind of impression he had made though, aware that Mme. Rubin took no pris-oners, and her views, one way or another, were liable to be extreme. David stroked the top of her head,

'Just that I had to take good care of you.'

'Hmm...is that all?'

'You could have warned me about her'

'Sorry…I completely forgot in the rush of packing and clearing, flight booking…'

'Ok, ok, I know I made a bit of a mess of that but we're here now…and just look at us'

Simone was still thinking about Mme. Rubin and would question her later. Now was not the time and the thought of being there with David, in her family home, was a big milestone in their lives.

'You have to take good care of me, eh?…Well then… that is quite right. Make sure you do.' Her hand reached up to stroke his thigh. The David of old would have taken her there and then in the lift, but he behaved with unaccustomed restraint in anticipation of what lay ahead.

The lift was old and slow and in the time it took them to arrive at the third floor, to their home, Simone grew quiet. Her whole body tensed as they reached the apartment door. Her smile fell and the happy, carefree, look was replaced by deep creases between her brows.

Bertrand, had bought the apartment in the early fifties when, as a well-established financier in the city, he could finally afford to invest in property. It was at the time when prices in the area had been reasonable, comparable even with other areas in Paris, but over the past twenty years, its value had increased out of all proportion. The Isle de la Cite was an oasis of serenity and beauty, not too far from the city centre, but far enough to disassociate itself from the hectic life there. It was cocooned in seventeenth century splendour, almost frozen in time, and for a moment had made David think of Georges and his project, set around that same era.

Simone unlocked the door and insisted that David walk in first. He stared in amazement at the extravagance of the main salon and wandered from room to room like a child in a sweet shop, almost forgetting that Simone was with him. The size and beauty of the place was so beyond his expectation that he was lost for words.

Simone hung back as familiar sights and smells overwhelmed her with their poignancy. Flowers on the table, once brought in weekly by their housekeeper, had been left over from the funeral. They were damask roses, Celsiana, and their strong musky fragrance haunted the air. Their perfume had always filled the room throughout summer months and a hint of it remained even though the blooms had long since died. Simone had bought them in remembrance of her mother, just before her father's funeral. They had been her favourites, but now dry, brown petals, lay scattered around vase and floor, blown about by a draught from the door when it had opened. Her eyes chased around the room. She saw her father's grim features as she told him for the second and last time that she would marry David with or without his approval. It was the first time he had refused her anything. Bertrand had always come round before and she had been so sure that he would again. But she was wrong.

Simone blew her nose before gathering faded blooms and dropping them into a bin beside her father's desk. She glanced at the black and gold Mont Blanc pen alongside a blotting pad of indecipherable ink marks, a present to him from her mother on his sixtieth birthday – the same year in which Simone had seen him out with a young woman who was obviously more than a friend.

'Well this is slightly better than the rooms we stayed in last time we lived in France.' Finding his voice, David crept up behind Simone and grabbed her round the waist. She stiffened in response.

'What's the matter?' he asked, when her reaction not what he'd expected. 'if it's too much living here, we don't have to stay you know…I know the memories weren't always good ones for you darling.'

She turned to him and put her hands up to his face, 'It's all right,' she replied, 'It's good that we can stay here until we get sorted…then we'll see'

'Are you sure?' he asked, but in his own mind they had already moved in. If she wasn't keen now he would do his best to persuade her it was the right decision. He could not give up an opportunity like this.

'And I promise you two things David…one, I will make this a happy home…in memory of my mother, and two, that any child of ours will always feel loved and wanted… and…and listened to no matter what they want to do.'

'Our child…you're not are you?' It was David's turn to stiffen, his immediate reaction a mix of excitement and horror at the thought of a baby so soon. It was something they had talked about but it was always an event set out on a far more distant horizon.

'No! No, not now, silly…but maybe soon,' she said tilting her head. Her slender arms draped across his shoulders and her soft brown eyes locked into his of piercing blue. 'Let me make myself indispensable in this new job first, and then perhaps.'

She smiled, bemused at his initial enthusiasm and happy that the thought of a baby had not been an entirely unwelcome one. She was fully aware that they'd never really talked about children as a reality before now, just as a vague idea. She always assumed that they would know when the time was right. What she did know for sure was that David did not feel any particular affinity with other people's children, and certainly not those he taught. He had become a teacher by default when no other options had been open to him, but a child of their own, that would be a very different matter; of that she was certain.

Despite misgivings, memories and the legacy of her father's belongings, some of which were soon boxed and stored out of sight, the apartment was transformed over the coming months. When their pathetically few items arrived from England, simple Stoke and Hornsea Pottery sat alongside French ormolu, and an early small Picasso kept company with their faded impressionist prints. Then slowly they too were replaced with something more in keeping and original. It was a happy, busy time for them both, possibly the happiest they had been since those first passionate, exciting months when they were getting to know each other in student digs. David had a chameleon-like gift of being all she wanted and lived up to expectation. If she did have a sense of his holding back at times, it was held at bay and soon forgotten when he overwhelmed her with his attention and praised her to his friends. She could never quite put her finger on what it was about him that made her feel so special, but she loved him all the more for it.

Over the months and years, friendships were renewed and new ones made. Everyone loved this gregarious, friendly man who waltzed into their lives, bringing with him excitement at dinner parties and impromptu get-togethers. He charmed women and men in equal measure, although perhaps with a little jealousy on the part of the husbands and boyfriends when they saw how their wives and girlfriends responded with 'why can't you be more like David?' But they all fell in with his exuberance and lust for life and were happy to be part of their circle.

Simone won over all who knew her in a different way. Her calm, gentle ways and concern for everyone's welfare above her own, not only brought her friends but also success in her work where, once again, she was frequently asked for by name.

In those early days, David cleared the messages from the answer phone and took on the job of calling back those who had not heard what had happened to Bertrand. But one message he couldn't respond to was the last on the tape. He was glad that Simone had not been around to hear it. It had been made a long time ago, but for some reason Bertrand had never erased it. Spoken in a faltering, quiet voice, he heard:

'Bonjour Papa...c'est moi,' followed by a short silence, then: 'Te me telephoner, Papa? '

Chapter 10

1980

Paris

'How many is it tonight?'

David languorously stretched out his long legs on top of the unmade bed, breathing in his expanding stomach. Having decided that it wasn't too bad, he relaxed, indolence displayed on every facet of his body and face. An unlit cigarette hung from his mouth as he rolled on to his side and felt across for a lighter. It flared briefly before the first longed for drag of the morning. Leaning back and reflecting on the day ahead, his eyes looked up at the ornate ceiling. Nothing too heavy today, he mused, nothing another hour in bed would inconvenience.

Simone was at the dressing table having showered half an hour earlier as David still slept. Her hair was dried and arranged away from her face, and she sat putting on make up, ready for work. The table held a vast array of expensive creams and lotions; Estee Lauder and Chanel No. 5 spread out amongst tissues and a collection of brushes.

Simone stared at herself in the mirror; soon she

would be thirty-six. Turning her face left and right and smoothing her neck with a perfectly manicured hand, she was happy with the desired effect. Simone was never vain but at the same time understood the requirements and expectations of the world in which she worked. Whilst denying that success and ability had anything to do with looks, she equally understood that grooming was an absolute necessity, especially in Paris. She looked across at David whose attention was now drawn towards his wife; it was with a mix of feelings that swung from concern that he had never really found his place in the working world, to relief that he showed no rancour or resentment of her elevated position. David, on his part, was merely enjoying the spectacle of his wife dressing for work in the belief that he played his part well enough. The lack of a child in their lives was unspoken nowa-days; both successfully hiding the pain of each miscar-riage that took them further and further from the reality of a baby.

Today was Friday. Friday was cleaning day, and also, as it was the last Friday in the month, they would be enter-taining.

'Just twelve of us tonight.'

'Does that include your boss?'

'Claude? Yes, of course. There's a senior partnership vacancy he wants me to go for and he knows how keen I am. I want to talk to him away from the office… more travel of course, but you won't mind will you? And you can keep his wife entertained tonight…you seemed to manage to keep Rene occupied well enough last time.' Simone spoke with neither irony nor rancour, having lived long enough with David's predilection for female guests who were not part of the corporate world. They had somehow slipped into a routine that worked well for them both, but as ever, since her inheritance, it was Simone who provided the financial security and picked up the bills.

She applied the latest shade of peach lipstick in a final flourish, rolling her lips together to achieve the desired coverage. She wasn't too sure if it was her colour, pouting for effect, but the girl at the Dior counter insisted it really was most flattering and it was definitely better than the earthy brown she'd first produced.

'Did I? Can't remember'

'Come on, she was all over you after the first course. She flattered you and you loved it.'

'Mmm.' David smiled. Of course he remembered. It was a thoroughly enjoyable night. He closed his eyes, enjoying the rest of his cigarette. The evening filtered through his mind with each slow drag of the Gauloise. They had sat next to each other, close, thighs gently rubbing together without any effort from either to move further apart. When his hand felt down to stroke the top of her leg with light fingertip pressure, she merely smiled and commented on the pleasure of the company that evening before raising a glass to Simone at the other side of the table.

The sounds of morning life reached up to the apartment, reminding Simone that she must get a move on. David stubbed out the cigarette and thought of bringing a coffee back to bed when Simone had gone. She had had her breakfast over an hour ago. David could not face food until closer to noon. Eleven years had slipped by with little to disturb the pleasures each enjoyed in their own way. Simone fulfilled the promise secretly made to her father after his death, content in the thought that he would not have been disappointed in her. Since his fatal heart attack, she had all but forgotten his infidelities to her mother, along with his bitterness over David's appearance in her life. She chose to remember the happy, indulged childhood in the apartment she now inhabited with the man she had chosen for herself, and whom she still loved despite everything.

By the end of her first year in the city, Simone had already proved her worth with a remarkable combination of enthusiasm, ability, long hours and sheer hard work. All went in her favour, as did the connections she brought from those who knew her father; they were not lost on the company's board of directors, as she was beginning to realise.

Thoughts of children had been pushed aside during that time, but in rare moments of introspection, she had liked to think that they would consider a family in the not too distant future, before she got too old. The apartment was big enough, and in the occasional time alone, she would sit in the second bedroom, plan a nursery and imagine how she would like it furnished. They could afford a family certainly and perhaps it would rein in David's excesses of drink and cigarettes, and lack of settled work. Tutoring had been intermittent, too much like teaching at school for his liking, and did not last long. Other efforts came to nothing when he was content to run their domestic life and be on hand when friends needed help. For several years he had been unwilling to consider they might have a child of their own, wanting to get as much out of life as he could squeeze from it first. The close call when they'd arrived pulled him up short and he had been thankful since then that there was still no child to disrupt the pleasures of life as it was now. He had even got used to the constant gaze of Mme. Rubin following his every move as he came and went in the building.

Simone stood up, giving herself a final inspection in the cheval mirror in the corner. 'I'm going now. I'll be back by six. The caterers are coming at five…please don't forget.' She went over to kiss David's proffered cheek, but when she leaned in he pulled her close, unable to resist the warm sensuous perfume that drifted over with her. Her attraction was still a powerful magnet that he couldn't resist.

'No! I must go, really…David…' She managed to escape his grip but was secretly pleased that he still wanted her as much as she did him.

'Caterers at five…remember….not like last time'

'Don't worry….don't worry… I know my job.'

He watched Simone leave but could still smell her reassuring presence in the room, it always lingered long after she'd gone. His cigarette was stubbed in an ashtray along with the two butts from the previous night. He'd cut down after a bad chest infection, but the pleasure of smoking far outweighed the warnings from his doctor. And Simone knew better than to start that argument up again. It was one she would never win.

Shortly before twelve, after a late breakfast of two pain au chocolat, he left the apartment on orders to pay the florist and the fishmonger. He was in no hurry and appreciated the as yet absence of midday commuters. Lost in thought and enjoying the warm sun at his back, he was pulled up short at the sound of his name being called out from across the street. He squinted in the sun to where it came from. An old man was shuffling over as fast as his legs would go, anxious not to lose sight of David.

David could not have been more surprised. Despite the changes due to old age, there was no mistaking him.

'Georges!'

The old man's breath came in short bursts by the time he reached David, but his eyes lit up. Ignoring David's proffered right hand, he tightly embraced his long lost friend.

Any feelings of guilt he might have felt at not contacting Georges were set aside and he greeted the old man as though they had never been apart. 'How are you my old friend?' Guilt was not an emotion David was inclined to indulge in at any time, preferring to gloss over any failings he may have been responsible for.

'David...I am so happy to have found you! My last letters were all returned and I didn't know where you had gone...you didn't tell me.' Georges hid the hurt beneath a broad smile that conveyed relief as much as happiness.

'I'm sorry Georges. In the move back here I lost your letter and wasn't sure where to find you either.' The lie tripped easily from his tongue but whether or not Georges believed him was irrelevant in light of the sudden and unexpected reunion.

David was shocked at the old man's appearance, from the deeply lined face to the stooping gait, but let it pass in seeing Georges' obvious pleasure.

'I can't believe I've found you after all this time...how are you...where have you been...are you working here now...is Simone...?'

'Whoa...slow down Georges'

'I thought I would never see you again...we must catch up...can we talk? Have you time to come with me? There is so much I need to tell you...to ask you?'

'Georges, much as I would love to right now, I can't, I have to....' Georges face fell; David couldn't finish the words that would put him off and relented.

'Yes...soon...I'd love to"

'How about next week?' Georges' eager expression and wide-open eyes laid bare his feelings.

'Of course...I'll have more time then'

'Will you…will you really? I've been looking for you for so long…you have no idea…'

'Yes Georges, I promise.'

The earnest face looked up to him waiting for confirmation of a time and day,

'When…where?'

They agreed to meet up the following week at a place they both knew well and Georges held on to his arms in relief and gratitude, reluctant to let him go.

'I'll be there Georges…I won't forget.' David was bemused by the urgency. They hadn't seen each other for years, but here he was expecting, even demanding to see him again and so soon. The look of happiness on Georges' face made David smile, leaving him just a little sorry that they hadn't been in touch earlier.

Chapter 11

As the dinner party approached, before the arrival of the first of the guests, two caterers were busy in the kitchen with last minute preparations, and the young help Monique was finishing the place settings at the table. Simone arrived home a little earlier than expected and David brought her a cocktail from the bar he had stocked up earlier in the week in preparation for the dinner. She took an appreciative sip before showering and changing into a black Dior gown that flattered her slim figure and long perfect legs. What Simone lacked in conventional beauty, she made up for in every other aspect of size and shape and elegance. David came into the bedroom away from the noise of the kitchen and from Monique fussing around the table. Simone took an appreciative sip as David finished his second glass. 'Mm…I think you have got that down to perfection.' David had indeed mastered the art of an excellent martini, as well as several other cocktails that had become his signature drinks.

'What else have you been up to today, apart from practising this little delight?'

'I paid the bills… as promised…and what else…oh, yes, I nearly forgot. I bumped into Georges on the way back.'

'Georges? Georges? Georges Gaudet? Goodness… how is he?'

'Old.'

'What is he up to now? Must be retired surely.'

Simone sprayed perfume about her neck and wrists then stood to inspect her choice of outfit in the mirror. Straightening her dress at the shoulders and smoothing the lines across her stomach, she was satisfied she would do.

'He wants to meet next week at that café where we all used to go as students. Said he has something important for me.'

'Oh dear, I hope the place is better than I remember it. Do you know what he wants?'

David remembered the cafe with the greatest of pleasure and nothing but the happiest of memories.

'I've no idea…but I'll soon find out I guess'

The guests arrived on cue and pre-dinner cocktails were served with David's usual flourish; each glass contributing to the easy flow of conversation. As the temperature of the room rose, windows were opened slightly to welcome the cool evening air and eventually they were all led to a freshly prepared table. Crisp white linen, silver cutlery and an array of perfectly placed glasses greeted the guests as they found their allotted seats. As planned, David was placed next to Rene, much to her delight. He made sure that her glass was readily filled with wines especially selected for each course, and her husband was grateful not to suffer her demands for attention when talk of business threatened to take over. David provided something far more amusing, and much more to her interest.

The evening went well; Rene's expectations were met and plans made; and Claude was more than satisfied at securing Simone to the company for at least another three years.

Everyone left tired but happy and Simone was glad to retreat to the bedroom to change. It had been a long day, 'Thank you,' she called out whilst hanging up her dress.

David, contenting himself with a last nightcap was looking at the note Rene had slipped into his hand as she'd warmly kissed him on both cheeks before leaving with her husband. Her telephone number had been scribbled in pencil, along with several dates on which Claude would be absent on business. Rene was not a woman to leave anything to chance.

'What for?'

'Letting me talk business when I needed to…you kept things going…especially with Rene…she loved it. Claude was relieved anyway…I get the impression all is not well between them right now'

'Did you get your business sorted?'

'Pretty much'

'Good…good.'

David drained his glass and after another scotch, went through to his wife who was already asleep in bed.

Chapter 12

David arrived at the Rue Bel Homme earlier than planned and it amused him to think of the times Simone had berated him for being late. On a whim, he asked the taxi driver to drop him off at the end of the street rather than outside L'Etoile Vert. He stood a while as visions of a past life crept upon him, unbidden but not entirely unwelcome. He checked his watch and took the first steps into the street in possibly eighteen or nineteen years. A pale sun had already emerged from the thin clouds, warming his face and making the prospect of a stroll down memory lane a welcome one. At first he couldn't tell whether it had changed a great deal or if he just couldn't remember the detail but as he made progress, it all fell into place and he smiled at the recollections that warmed him as much as the sun.

Uneven stretches of pavement glistened underfoot, some still wet from the early morning wash where puddles gathered in potholes along the way. Small, gnarled trees lined his route with their tracery of branches casting skeletal shade on the ground. An abundance of buds were already bursting into new life with a hint of greenery and a promise of more to come.

There were few cars left parked along the way; those that were still there looked as though they had been sitting there all night as condensation streamed down their night-chilled windows. His pace slowed as the sleepy street returned to life after a quiet night. Most of the cafes along the route were still serving morning coffee and freshly baked croissants with tempting aromas greeting David as he passed each one by. He glanced inside Café Colombes where a clutch of customers sat, keenly engrossed in conversation. Familiarity embraced the scene as regulars took up their usual tables and chatted with ease to the man behind the bar. Several small tables outside were squeezed into tight spaces under windows and fluttering check table-cloths lay anchored against the breeze with a heavy ashtray. A young girl emerged, attractive, slim and dark-haired, to set out a collection of mis-matched chairs from a pile behind the door. It wouldn't be too long before the lunchtime customers appeared from offices and shops close by.

'M'sieur', she smiled, and nodded to David as he paused to check the menu. He would have stayed but for the fact that Georges would soon be waiting for him. He had grown used to pleasing himself, taking up opportunities as the fancy took him, but not today. He smiled at the girl, 'Bonjour,' he nodded back in her direction, reluctantly moving on when he saw how pretty she was. He lit a cigarette as he walked.

There were no familiar faces any more. Nights of working his way down the street with friends, building up their number as they went along, were long past. A couple of drinks would be downed in each bar, where David in particular proved adept at attracting the girls. Such evenings rarely failed to live up to their expectation and promise, and invariably finished at L'Etoile Vert where a newly installed jukebox played the Beatles and jazz, loud and long into the night.

He looked down at his expanding waistline and sucking it in promised himself he would do something about it soon. But despite the paunch, he was more than confident of his ability to still attract women when he set his mind to it. It had become automatic, a default reaction, but the excitement of the chase had recently diminished along with the allure of an expensive lifestyle. I must be getting old he mused enjoying the cigarette.

David brushed his fingers through his hair, greying at the temples but still thick and curling at the neck. He felt an ache for those early years when the world was opening up and the thrill of the chase was the best part, but only half disappointed that today the street was full of strangers. No one had spoken to him that morning, apart from the brief acknowledgement of the waitress, and he wasn't sorry. The mostly lone coffee drinkers at the outside tables barely looked up from their newspapers and morning cigarette, unless it was to check the time.

Those first days in Paris were a far cry from the grey university life endured back in Manchester. When the opportunity arose, he'd embraced it with enthusiasm; and where better to study seventeenth century French history than in France itself. It was an opportunity not granted to many and no sooner had it gone from suggestion to reality than his bags had been packed and a one-way ticket booked. He worked hard, it was true, but the times in between were embraced with equal enthusiasm.

A noisy delivery van brought him brusquely back from ruminations of the past when it thundered by. Its wide wheels hit a puddle as it passed David and splattered his new suede boots. The street and road narrowed at this point, allowing little room for manoeuvre. 'Thanks for that' he called to the disappearing truck and looked down at the dark splodges. The faces he'd sought from the past left as abruptly as they'd arrived.

He was only metres away from L'Etoile Vert without realising it and looking up from the spoiled boots, inadvertently walked straight into a solid, large figure coming in the opposite direction.

'Je suis vraiment désolé. Pardonnez-moi, je ne regardais pas'. The figure was no stranger, but certainly not one he expected to see here. 'Mme. Rubin!'

'Ça va, David. Tu étais ailleurs je pense'. David's confusion seemed to amuse her and wherever his thoughts had been, as she suggested, he was firmly back in the present now. Mme. Rubin, outside the confines of the foyer and her little office, came as a shock. He couldn't remember ever having seen her beyond the walls of the apartments let alone on the street. 'Que faites-vous ici? She looked different here where the harsh light of day revealed the full bloom of colours in her clothes and headwear, standing out against the drab stone and brickwork of the buildings. She remained immutable and let David back out of her path but showed little surprise at the encounter.

'David…,' she said, a growing smile curling around her mouth, 'I been to visit a frien'.' David tilted his head, eyebrows closing. 'Don' look so shocked. I do have friens, you know.' Her smile grew.

'Yes, of course… you…I…I just don't think I've ever seen you outside the apartment that's all…It's nice to see you on this fine day.' David recovered quickly enough to revert to his customary courteous response to her. Mme. Rubin nodded in reply.

'That all right. You are visiting someone too?'

'Yes, yes – like you an old friend, one from my student days. An archivist I used to work with in fact. We unexpectedly came across each other in the city the other day and arranged to meet up. Catch up on the past…you know what it's like'

'Ah, oui,' she replied, 'I like to catch up on the past too, if it don' catch up on me first. But I not keep you from your frien.' She brought her face closer to his, offering an embrace and kiss on both cheeks, and the overwhelming scent of patchouli caught his throat. Tapping her nose, she whispered in a lowered tone 'Prenez soin, David…prenez soin…Au revoir.'

The woman never failed to puzzle and unsettle him and his thoughts went back to the first time she had told him to take care, at their meeting in the foyer at the Belle Vue Apartments. 'I will…merci…you too, Madame.'

Mme. Rubin left a bemused David standing outside L'Etoile Vert and continued on her way. After a just moment's speculation, he turned to say 'au revoir', but the words faltered from his lips. She had disappeared as suddenly as she came. There was no sign of her, no open doorway, no alleyway into which she could have turned. The street ahead was almost empty, apart from a young woman in a long brown dress scurrying away in the distance.

Pushing the encounter with Mme. Rubin aside with no more than a shrug and quizzical brow, David shaded his eyes from the sun and peered into a side window of the café. The traffic of lunchtime diners at L'Etoile Vert was slowly gathering pace, and it didn't look too busy, but for a reason he couldn't fathom, felt reluctant to go inside straight away.

David stepped back to reflect on a place that had been such a big part of his early life in Paris, wanting to bask in the sight of the old familiar green shutters and flaking wooden sign above the front window. He lit another cigarette and sat at one of the small tables outside, tucked away and designed for sole occupancy. He tilted his head back and closed his eyes in pleasure of half-remembered nights amidst the rising smoke of the Gauloise, reliving hazy recollections of the people, the noise and the smell; evenings when cigarette smoke hung thick above their heads and the bar was always full. As the nights lengthened and turned winter cold, they would huddle inside for warmth, yelling out when an icy blast blew in from an open door. This had been his second home in those early student days, next to the cramped rooms in an apartment shared with four others. L'Etoile Vert was tucked away at the end of the street, beyond the main drag of tourists, and suited them perfectly. They claimed it as their own and the owner was more than happy considering the revenue it generated and the joyous, if raucous, life packed inside.

A young couple walked in from the street laughing at some private joke between them and David followed them inside with his eyes. From where he sat, the customers might not be the same, but the only other difference appeared to be a menu board propped up near to the door. They'd never served food when he'd been there otherwise he may never have gone home.

David had met Georges here only once before, and that was again at the old man's insistence. He'd tried to involve him in the precious Henrietta Papers even then, 'Don't you see? You have to do it, David! Take it on – the work was made for you…this is your era.' The eagerness in his face had been in stark contrast to David's when all he wanted to do was get back to the rowdy group of friends calling him over to the bar. He knew the history, what more could Georges offer? And were these 'Papers' really genuine? David had neither the time nor inclination to take on anything beyond his final dissertation, that and the tall, dark haired girl he'd set his mind on the previous week. 'You'll get the work done, Georges. Just take your time. Sybil will get well soon and you'll be fine.'

If David had felt any guilt that night it was subsumed into the immediate and pressing activities of the hours ahead. He wanted to get closer to the lovely economics student who, as well as being the brightest in her year, proved to be more challenging than most. Simone and her friends hung around on the edge of the main group of students; sometimes she turned up at the bar, but more often, not. That night she was there and the attraction far outweighed those of an evening in the company of an increasingly rambling archivist.

Georges' conversation was soon forgotten and once he'd retired David saw him less and less. The old man had no choice but to spend more time at home with his sick wife who understood, more than her husband, the pull of love. She had actively encouraged David to put thoughts of the Henrietta Papers out of his head – in fact she almost demanded it the last time he paid them a visit at their home with Simone. 'You have no idea what you would be letting yourself in for,' she told him, rather sharply he thought, 'it has taken over our lives.' Then when Georges was out of the room hunting for another bottle of red, and Simone was helping set the table, she'd gripped his arm and told him, 'It was the end for us as it has been for so many others, as I have found out to my cost,' until a fit of coughing shook her failing body.

That was the last time he'd seen either of them; there had been little communication beyond an occasional Christmas card once David and Simone left for England. When Sybil went into hospital, Georges had written a final plea; it was his last letter and had arrived the same day David handed in his resignation at school, the same time he and Simone had finalised their preparations to return to France.

David stubbed out his cigarette; ready to revisit his old friend who would look at the past from a different perspective. He went inside, suppressing any guilt he might have felt at not replying to that last letter, convincing himself instead that it had been unavoidable. Life goes on, he reasoned and he couldn't be expected to take on Georges' burden too. He tried to remember what he'd done with the letter and assumed it had been thrown out with rubbish that had been boxed and discarded from their little house by the sea. It was doubtful that he'd even read it all and was meeting Georges on the assumption that the Project was almost done and finished with. He was only mildly curious to find out if anything had been published. The visit today was out of respect to an old man who had shown only support, kindness and generosity in his early days in France.

Chapter 13

David paused for a second or two inside the café door and from his vantage point saw Georges sitting at a small table next to a window that looked out on to the street, eyes searching through the glass. Seeing David walk towards him, he gave a broad smile of relief. Georges had been waiting for at least half an hour and his eyes ached from squinting against the sun. He stood on unsteady legs to greet him as a father would a long lost son. 'Bonjour David. Bonjour mon ami!' They hugged and David perhaps regretted just a little that he hadn't been in touch earlier. It wasn't that he didn't want to, but Georges was yet another part of his life that had gone.

The intervening years had not been kind. His eyes were hooded and cloudy with cataracts and the collar of his shirt gaped, revealing a wrinkled neck and a suggestion that it was meant for someone much bigger. Years ago, he would have patted his expanding waistline and boast of Sybil's excellent cooking, but there was little left of that body now.

'Il est bon de te revoir, Georges.' David returned the

hug, conscious of the skeletal frame beneath the clothing and pulled out a vacant chair beside the old archivist. Conversations in the café were discreet and low as the waitress wove between the tables to take orders. She'd noted David's entrance and made a mental note to return to them as soon as she could. The table was covered in a red checked cloth upon which sat an empty espresso cup and a glass of half drunk cognac. The waitress came over within a few minutes.

'What can I get you, gentlemen?

'Er, same again for my friend and a large red for me'

He looked for confirmation from Georges who appeared not to have heard a word he said but was lost in his own thoughts.

'The house red will be fine, thank you…nothing to eat just yet…maybe in a while'

The house wine had always been a fine quality and as a nod to the past David determined to believe that it would be just as good, even though he could afford better. The waitress, Marcia, took the order back to the bar; glancing back over her shoulder to David as the two men sat close and began to fill the gaps of the intervening years. There was no recognition on David's part at all and she couldn't decide whether that was a good thing or not. It was hard enough to concentrate when she at least remembered every minute of the past. Wine and cognac were poured and whilst Marcia made the coffee she took the time to breathe deeply and collect her straying, disturbing thoughts.

Marcia had been a first year art student, working behind the bar to make ends meet; David, older and moving in different circles, was one of a crowd gathered at the other side. She was pretty then and they caught each other's eye more than once throughout the night. He was on his own as far as female company was concerned, and the tall, striking brunette so often with him, wasn't around that night. Although the mirror reflected a different Marcia today, the emotions of ten years ago overwhelmed her as if it had been yesterday. In her mind she reverted back to the young girl she was when he reappeared one night at closing time and under the pretext of a forgotten scarf, persuaded her to pour them both a goodnight cognac. She wouldn't normally be drawn in by such a suggestion but it had been a long night; her feet hurt; the attraction was too powerful to resist and she was on her own to lock up. He showed a great interest in what her plans were for the future and why she was working behind the bar, sympathising at the necessity to supplement a meagre income whilst studying. They finished the half-full bottle with ease and his seduction was complete when they staggered back drunk to her rooms close by. She shuddered in remembrance of how easily she had let it get that far.

Marcia smoothed her coarse bleached hair into place and came over with the drinks. David and Georges barely looked up from their conversation as they took the order with a polite 'Merci'. She did not linger, apart from taking a quick, closer look at the man who had coerced her into having sex with him all those years ago.

'How long have you been in Paris, David?' Georges quizzed.

'Oh, not that long,' he lied, taking a large mouthful of wine. He winced, holding the glass at arms length to study its contents. Perhaps not quite as good as he remembered, but then what was?

'And you never let me know you were coming.' Georges' cloudy eyes flinched.

'I'm sorry Georges…you know how it is. There was so much to do when we arrived…when one thing led to another, I put things off…couldn't even find your new address....I should have tried harder I know. But we're here now and I really am pleased that we came across each other when we did.'

'I'm sorry too. I know I am just an old man who pushes for too much. Sybil warned me not to force anything on to you back then, but she read too much into it.'

Georges drifted off at the thought of Sybil, lightly touching the gold cross hanging around his neck. David waited for him to go on, wondering whether or not to order a different wine. His own thoughts vacillated from the wine to making his excuse to leave as soon as he could, but he let the moment pass and ordered a more respectable glass from the drinks menu. He was impressed by the waitress's swift attention. Not wanting to interrupt Georges' ruminations, he sat back to survey the room and enjoy his fresh glass before Georges came back into the present.

'How is Simone? Have you got children yet?'

'No not yet...just the two of us still.'

David straightened slightly in his seat, dismissing that part of life where a child was nothing more than a shadow now, one too painful to share. Simone's latest miscarriage had barely been discussed between them and he would not get into that conversation here.

Georges became agitated and shuffled around in his chair.

'Is it late, Georges? Have you got to be somewhere?' David asked more in hope than expectation.

'No...not at all...time *is* pressing, but not in that way. I...I...never mind. Ignore me, I ramble too much nowadays. Tell me what you are doing. Such a promising student you were. Tell me, what have you done with it all?'

David selectively filled him in on the intervening years, knowing that they culminated in not a great deal. What had he done really? Beyond a couple of half-hearted attempts at tutoring and enquiring into work at the university, it amounted to very little. In fact, he struggled to think of what to say on how he filled his days since coming back to France. They passed well enough, but that too he would not be willing to share with Georges, or anyone else for that matter.

Georges eyes widened when he heard the words that David had no job to distract him from what he was about to propose and shuffled a little more animatedly in his seat. He leaned forward to take a sip of the fresh coffee before continuing, his hand shaking as he lifted the small cup to his lips. Drops of the thick brown liquid spilled down an ageing woollen coat, joining several other stains that looked as though they'd been there for some time. Now David had the chance to study the old archivist at close quarters, he was shocked by Georges' appearance, and not just the weight loss. Sybil would have been horrified and never have let him go out looking like that.

'I've not been too well, David,' he said, draining the last of the coffee, 'I found it hard without Sybil. I'm not very good on my own.'

'I'm so sorry Georges, I didn't know that Sybil had gone.'

'I did write, but…you know…well… never mind that now.'

He was embarrassed by any admission of helplessness, but let it go when he warmed up to his original subject; the real reason he was glad to see David again.

'You do remember my project, don't you – the Henrietta Papers?' A nod of David's head was enough for him to carry on.

'Of course I do. Have you finished your research, got a paper out of it yet?'

More fidgeting preceded the answer

'It had to be put aside, David, put on hold... far too long.'

He paused and looked in anticipation for some comment, some sign of interest at least. David waited and listened. Straightening out invisible creases in the table-cloth and steeling himself to broach the subject, Georges continued, 'Sybil died, as you know... she had been ill for such a long time.'

David wondered where all this was going and his eyes focussed on Georges' face. He was amazed that Sybil had lived as long as she had after he had last seen her. Georges stared into the distance as he spoke; in his mind's eye Sybil was standing right in front of him. His face relaxed a little and he began to smile, letting his voice trail into nothing-ness. David merely sat back in his chair and looked around the room. The waitress was back behind the bar having served the last of the lunches and he caught her looking in their direction as she dried the glasses on the counter. She quickly turned away and blushed in embarrassment. David gave a half smile and drained his glass; it was infinitely more palatable than the first. Georges had come back from wherever his mind had taken him and continued where he'd left off.

'I had to stop everything to look after her, you know... and eventually I had to stop working at the Archives too. I knew they had to let me go...taking too much time off you see.'

Georges had been waiting for this moment for such a long time, the pent up words struggled for a voice, but suddenly they found their way out, breaking free into an unstoppable flood and imploring David to listen. The Henrietta Papers needed fresh blood to keep them alive and he had to pass them on. It was only when he cracked under the strain that David encouraged him to slow down. What did it matter really?

'Georges, maybe it's time to let go…pass them on to the archives…why did you keep them for so long anyway?' Georges pulled out a frayed grey handkerchief to blow his nose. The thread of his argument lost for a moment. 'I seem to have a permanent cold in this weather,' he offered, wiping his eyes with the back of his hand.

'I'm so sorry, Georges. I never realised that things were so bad…Sybil was a beautiful lady in every way.' He reached across the table and put his hand over Georges' trembling fingers, trying to get back to something they had in common. 'I remember how kind she was to me when I was a student and my money had run out. I was virtually living off dry bread at one time and her cassoulet was always a treat.' Georges appreciated the kind words and vigorously blew his nose once again. 'I'm sorry…I'm an old fool.'

'It's time to let go, Georges, let me get you another cognac before we leave.'

'No, don't say that…please…we can't leave it there.' With a look of panic, he raised his hand to decline the offer of another drink and continued his story.

'It's my own fault…I should have looked after her better than I did. I was too wrapped up in my work to see how ill she really was…and now I am on my own.'

'Is there anyone looking after you now?'

David would prefer to think that there was someone around to ease his conscience at leaving him there like that.

'We had a daughter you know…soon after we married, but she, she…' The pain of remembering the child who had died in early infancy, around the time of his acquiring the Papers, tightened his brow, but he would not stop.

'If we'd had another child things might have been

different, but she couldn't...no she wouldn't. She believed those stories. I told her it was all nonsense but...and we needed the money it would bring'

When the tears fell, David interrupted and reached out to his arm, 'Look, why don't we meet up again next week? I have to see someone this afternoon, but we can talk more then...how about that?' David surprised himself at the suggestion; but Simone would approve.

'Yes, you are right...you've listened to me long enough. I am a little tired, but you won't forget will you?' Georges grasped David's hand.

'No. I promise I won't forget...how about the same time next week? Same place? We'll have lunch too.' Georges relaxed his grip and agreed as David motioned for the bill. The afternoon's exertions had taken their toll and he was exhausted.

'Sybil believed all that nonsense you know...but I told her it was just superstition. We didn't even know the woman. She turned up one day and put such stuff into her head. She never spoke to me...just Sybil. I can see her now... sitting at our table...bright scarf wrapped around her. But she disappeared as soon as I came through the door. When I heard about the nonsense she said to Sybil I wanted to give her a piece of my mind, but we never saw her again. I don't know why she didn't talk to me.' The ramblings were lost on David who instead went to pay the bill when the waitress reappeared. The lunchtime diners had mostly gone and she'd taken the opportunity to slip through to the back. David noticed immediately the bright lipstick and freshly combed hair. Must be meeting some-one, he presumed.

'I'll pay now, if that's ok?' She looked directly at him, searching for recognition, but receiving nothing. 'You don't remember me, do you?' David's furrowed brow gave the answer, not sure that he wanted any more renewed acquaintances that afternoon. It was getting late for his next meeting. 'Sorry...have we met?' This wasn't the kind of place he and Simone came to since returning to France and he was certain that they hadn't come across each other anywhere else. Marcia shrugged with a wry smile. Of course he didn't, she thought; it had been one night only.

'Mm...it was a long time ago...'68'

'Bit of a blur, the sixties,' he joked.

Marcia, against better judgement, reminded him of when and where, but left out the salient points that had indelibly left their mark on the occasion, the part when he had taken advantage of her inexperience; the part where he'd been the last in the bar and they had drunk too much and she'd taken him to her room; and the part when she'd been persuaded to take him to her bed. Following a series of awkward fumblings, they had made love of sorts before he fell asleep, unconscious until the next morning when he left and the night was never referred to again.

She took the blame along with the shame and pain of its consequences. Regrets following an abortion were not so much due to her stupidity, but the fact that subsequent tests that had revealed an underlying condition that meant she would be unlikely to conceive again.

'Good grief...you worked here then? ...and you're still here? You must have a few stories to tell about those days.'

'I did go away for a while...even got married...but it didn't work out and somehow I ended up back where I started. Unlike you, I suspect...? You look as though you have done very well for yourself, no longer the penniless student, eh?' She gave a short nervous laugh and David mused over what she had told him. He remembered nothing, but then he'd come across others before her who claimed to have known him. He looked back across at Georges and paid the bill.

'Who's the old guy? I've not seen him in here before?'

'Georges? He was an archivist who helped me with an essay or two in the past...student days'

As Marcia and David chatted at the bar, Georges, oblivious to the fact that he was on his own, continued talking as if David was still sitting opposite.

'We should have tried again...another baby would have been perfectly healthy, but she wouldn't hear of it.' He'd slumped down into his chair in defeat when David returned to the table. It was obvious that the exertion of the last couple of hours had taken its toll. Quiet now and lost in thought, he looked helplessly out of the window.

'Time to go, Georges.' David touched him gently on the shoulder. Georges gave a start.

'We always worked well together, didn't we, David?'

'That we did, Georges. No one knew more about my subjects than you, even my lecturers. You saved many a piece of work from abject rejection.'

Although it was warm in the café, the old man shivered and pulled his scarf closer round his neck. His small body, lost in the voluminous woollen folds of the coat, was finally coaxed into standing and he was ready to leave. He staggered a little and held on to the back of the chair, catching his breath.

'Are you all right, Georges? You look pale.' His ashen face clouded with pain.

'Have you seen a doctor recently?'

'I don't need a doctor...they couldn't help Sybil and they can't help me...far too late for that.'

He drained the last mouthful of cognac; the smooth liquid warming his throat and giving him strength to move. He took a deep breath and, as if the lines had been carefully rehearsed, spoke slowly and clearly, 'All I want now is to be with Sybil but before I can do that I must pass on my work, and the Papers, to someone who will understand them as I did.'

David was too busy looking out for the taxi he'd booked earlier, to notice what he said. The street was empty once again. 'I have to go soon, Georges…the taxi's on its way…please let me give you a lift home?' He looked at his watch and considered walking back down to the main road to seek it out and get Georges home as soon as possible, but he declined. 'You will help won't you? A little research in England… that's all… in Yorkshire…where you lived. I don't have long. I don't think I could travel that far now. But you are young. You can do it can't you?'

David had no intention of going back to England but played along, 'I'll see what I can do, Georges.' That had not been part of the conversation before now but none of it would amount to anything anyway. He had gone to England with Simone on a couple of working trips but that was all. His home was in Paris and there was nothing back there to tempt him. Relieved when the taxi eventually pulled up outside, he offered a softener to Georges, 'All right, we'll talk again next week, I promise…but I really have to go now,' he said pulling away from Georges' restraining arms.

'Yes…I'm sorry I've kept you so long. I'll be all right. You go…but we will meet again *very* soon, won't we?'

'Yes of course we will…just get yourself home now and rest. You look exhausted. Next week at the same time? We'll have lunch.'

Georges was beyond exhausted. In truth, he was dying, but wanted to keep that from David for as long as possible. For now, his plan was to call into the small Church on his way home and ask God to give him strength for a little while longer, at least until he could put his affairs in order. His bony hands gripped the table to rise again, blue veins standing proud above a frail translucent skin. The cross hung loose at his neck on top of the scarf.

'Won't you please let me take you back home, Georges? Come with me in the taxi.'

'No, no, I'll be all right. I want to walk a while…I have somewhere to go first…you go on,' he insisted. Reluctantly, David left when Georges wouldn't be persuaded. Marcia at the bar acknowledged his brief wave and 'au revoir'; both she and the old man watched David get into the taxi and disappear down the road.

Georges made his way to the door, but staggered before he could reach it. Too much cognac this time, he thought when his head spun and he felt around for something to hold on to. The room faded from view as the floor rose up to meet him.

Chapter 14

David paid for the taxi and now stood before an imposing apartment block on Rue Delphine. It was with little enthusiasm however. He'd stopped for a bite to eat on the way, disturbed by how much the meeting with Georges, as well as the flashbacks to student days, had affected his equilibrium. He felt out of kilter, without understanding exactly why. Why would a meeting with the old archivist, who was obviously losing the plot, hold such a sway? He wasn't in the right frame of mind to go back home and neither did he want to stay on the Rue Delphine; arriving there was nothing but an automatic response to the day and time. A growing hollow deep inside would not be filled by a visit to Rene, no matter what she wanted. Georges and days gone by were too much on his mind to be overcome by an hour in Rene's bed.

Reminders of a past life continued to resurface, unbidden and inexplicable, and the present was not coming up with anything like a favourable comparison. In a fresh moment of introspection, he was tiring of the life he'd slipped into over the past few years, even to the point of regretting how little he had actually achieved.

David looked up to the window of Rene's bedroom, brightly lit behind thin net curtains. She would be waiting, just as she had done every other Thursday afternoon for the past six months, the light denoting she was there and alone. But he would not go in today. The excitement and the pleasure of her company had long faded, and merely slipped into a habit. He wasn't even sure that he really liked the woman; she was tiresome and demanding, giving rise to the thought that maybe Claude had a point in his avoidance of intimacy with his wife. She was available and enthusiastic, but didn't come close to what he had with Simone. Their affair was a distraction during what would be another dull day on his own and filled in the time between other equally pointless pursuits. He thought back to the start of the affair and how he had let it get this far. They first met at a party given by Simone's office; a corporate function at an expensive hotel in the city for clients whose business was highly valued. Rene had sought out David when talk of investments, shares and hedge funds had become too much for those who just wanted to drink expensive wine and have a little fun. David had made sure that her glass was never empty and Rene was happy to finally find a man who paid her some attention. Invitations for dinners at their respective apartments inevitably followed and for a while she amused him with a sharp eye and acerbic wit on the lives of fellow guests. She was six years older than David with an edge on the society in which they moved, kept him updated on who was who and the latest gossip. He'd fallen into the affair with little or no planning on his part, but Rene drew him into her web easily enough.

At that first encounter, they drank until some point in

the evening when they needed more privacy and left the building for the lush grounds outside. David knew that he wasn't her first venture beyond a stale marriage, and most likely he wouldn't be her last. It amused him when she said that she thought they were 'two of a kind'. Simone had been too engrossed in conversation with a group of suited elderly gentlemen to notice; they staked a claim on her time when they found out they'd known her father, and so David and Rene took the opportunity to slip away.

It had never been his intention that anything should continue after that night; it should have finished with the last bottle of red drunk on the grass and out of sight, but Rene would accept no rejection and after dinner at the Belle Vue Apartment, a copious number of cocktails, wine and scotch convinced him that one more time would make little difference. Nothing David ever did was particularly planned, which he was coming to regret; he was usually the one who made the moves, the decisions, but this was not his. It no longer felt right; tonight did not feel right.

The window at Rene's apartment darkened as a shadow passed across the light, and David turned away from the building for what he intended to be the last time. With hands thrust deep into his pockets and looking straight ahead, he walked along the cool, damp street. It was getting dark; how long he had been standing there he couldn't say and time slipped by unnoticed. Street lamps glistened and began to light up the winding path, and the ugliness of what had descended into a damp grey after-noon from the beautiful promise of the morning, trans-formed into a jewelled portrait of Paris nightlife. As if to concur, a flash of bright colour passed between two trees, a figure in a hurry, vanishing into the darkness.

David loved the dark corners of Paris, loved the unex-pected encounters that they threw up when least expected;

turning off into an unknown side street, a sly glance from a stranger, meeting your gaze for a brief second, all knowing, then disappearing just as quickly.

He found an empty bench along a deserted stretch of the riverbank and sat to light a cigarette, in no hurry to get back home yet, just wanting to enjoy the solitude. His mind roamed around the earlier meeting with Georges, triggering a chain of thought that aspired to make sense of the day. Rene's irrelevance ensured that she was soon forgotten and when he started to relax, he put together an altogether different plan.

With one arm draped across the back of the bench, the other mechanically drew the cigarette to his mouth and he inhaled deeply, savouring the taste and the moment, satisfied that he was making the right decision. Across the river, offices disgorged the last of the workforce, each small figure collectively forming spokes of a wheel going out in all directions. The ugly building was not a place to loiter, but rather get away from, perhaps stopping at a bar beforehand, perhaps meeting up with friends, perhaps meeting a lover. Perhaps finishing with a lover.

The leaves on the trees, almost fully open here at this usually sunny spot, signalled the summer to come. The air had a different smell to it and the welcome heat of June would soon enough be upon the city. Paris would fill with visitors again after the paucity during winter and David felt a lightness he had not experienced for some time, almost happy. A weight lifted and he saw with unaccustomed clarity what needed to be done. It was obvious. He could not remember when he had last felt so energised. Perhaps Georges' project was the answer. Why not? It had viability, but even if it came to nothing, there was nothing to lose.

Sitting on the park bench, lighting up another cigarette, he went over their earlier conversation and considered that the project might just rekindle some of the old passion for work. Student days had felt so good, as the woman at the bar had reminded him, and he wanted to experience some of the same again, although this time he wouldn't go hungry. Perhaps this was what he had been waiting for, something on which to focus his energy and take him out of the all-consuming lethargy that was slowly creeping its way around and into every waking moment. He owed it to Georges, to Simone and to himself. To Georges for past help given to a struggling student, and an unfailing trust that showed he was worth it; to Simone for never questioning all he did or did not do with his life; and to himself to rise above the present apathy and get back to doing something he might actually enjoy.

This pleasurable reverie was interrupted by a rustling noise, loud enough to startle him back to the present. It came from the trees behind. He turned but saw nothing. There was no wind to disturb the trees and nothing to suggest he wasn't alone. He shrugged and felt foolish after asking out loud if anyone was there. They were hardly likely to answer if he was about to be mugged. He laughed at the absurdity, deciding that it was time to go, to make it up with Simone and try to get back something of the enthusiasm he'd felt when they'd first arrived in Paris.

David flicked away his cigarette butt; he needed a drink to celebrate his decision. The bench had grown cold and with a growing chill in the air he pulled up the collar of his jacket. Lights were switching off in the windows of the buildings across the river and somewhere in the distance a church bell chimed the hour. It was later than he had realised. As he set off for home, a dark figure watched from the trees, looking after David's retreating figure.

Chapter 15

Mme Rubin was sitting in her customary chair in the office when David returned home. Her bulky frame, topped by a red turban, shook as she nodded at his entrance. 'Bonsoir, David,' she called out, but did not rise.

'Did you enjoy your day, Mme. Rubin?' he asked.

'I did, David…I been arranging things…been sorting old stuff for new.'

'Ah, good.'

She offered no more.

'I hope you bought something nice?'

'It do fine, David…just fine.'

Her smile lingered long enough to see him enter the lift and dropped just as quickly when the door closed on a final 'Bonsoir'.

She spat a cherry stone into the dish and took another fruit. It was a rare occasion when David came in or left the building that she was not present, certainly rare that he should see her outside. Neither of them spoke of it again, and it was never repeated.

David's mood had lifted considerably by the time he

unlocked the door to the apartment and he was eager to share his plans with Simone. The answer phone was flashing but his first thought was to ignore it in the disappointment that she was not home already. Instead, he poured himself a large scotch and ambled over to his usual chair by the window. It tasted good but the flashing red light on the telephone refused to be ignored so he grudgingly took the calls. There were five messages, four for Simone from those clients privileged to have her home number, and the last one spoken by a voice he did not recognise. Relieved that at least it wasn't Rene with recriminations for not turning up this afternoon, he relaxed. It was the hospital. Georges had been admitted that afternoon and a nurse was asking if could he could call back when they had no known relative, or any other number, to contact.

Replacing the glass on the table and a fresh cigarette hanging from his lips, he immediately rang back to find out that Georges had been taken in after suffering a serious heart attack. He was stable but unconscious as other complications were discovered. David knew that he should have insisted on taking Georges home but relieved that an ambulance had been called quickly enough. His number had been found on a scrap of paper in Georges' pocket, given by David at the café before he left. It seemed longer than the few hours between then and now. Sadness shadowed the euphoria of the plans he was making, but they would keep.

The nurse advised him to visit in the morning when Georges was likely to be awake and more would be known more about his condition. For now, he was stable, not in any pain but in intensive care, under heavy sedation.

After reassurances that there was nothing to be done that night, he asked the nurse to contact him at any time should Georges wake up, then hung up and returned to his chair and the remaining scotch.

David was disappointed at no message from Simone; he felt the need to hear her voice, to talk about the afternoon and his plans for the future. She worked long hours and neither had usually found it an issue in their lives, quite the opposite. He poured another scotch. From the window, he watched the throng of people at the cafés, bars and restaurants, going about their usual business, but tonight he would not be joining them. His mind travelled to Georges and a realisation of just how alone the old man was. Where were his friends, his family? Who else should have been told that he was so ill?

It was late when Simone's key announced her arrival home that night; David had slept where he sat and was startled awake by the door shutting behind her.

'Ah, there you are, I've been waiting for you'.

'Really, you don't usually'. Simone was puzzled over his presence; it was Thursday and he was more often than not out with friends when they had no planned engagements. 'I know, but I wanted you here with me.'

His move to pull her closer to him caused Simone to back away. The smell of the scotch, and he'd had four large ones by then, made her feel nauseous.

'I'm tired, David…and what are you drinking?' she frowned.

Simone's face was pale and newly formed bags under her eyes verified her words. Conversation, despite David's best efforts, was a non-starter and when he commented on her appearance, she snapped 'I'm all right. I just need to get to bed early. I'll be fine tomorrow'.

She looked older tonight, David noted. Her face was drawn with lines etched deep across her forehead and her eyes were dull. She went to change out of her constraining work suit and emerged from the bedroom in silk pyjamas and dressing gown.

'I've got an early appointment tomorrow so I'll be going to bed very soon.'

'Yes you should...I'll see to things down here.'

After a light supper, rescued from yesterday's leftovers, half of which remained uneaten on her plate, Simone left the table. Conversation between them had been stilted, and when she did ask about his day, barely listened to his response. David wanted to tell her about Georges; he wanted to tell her about his plans for the future, but that would wait until tomorrow. The time wasn't right.

After thirteen years of marriage, they'd slipped out of the habit of telling each other the small details of their day, as much as they had slipped out of many other things that had once been important. Their sex life had become sporadic over the past months and this evening came with a shock of realisation how much he missed their old life together. Whatever betrayals he'd made, his love for Simone was still there and he was worried about her appearance.

'You get to bed. I'll clear up.'

'Thank you. It's Monique's day off tomorrow.'

He watched her walk to the bedroom on slow tired legs. 'Night darling...I won't be long,' he called after her.

SIMONE SET off early the next day and left a note saying that she would not be back until after midnight; she had a dinner organised with clients and he should not wait up. He never had before, unlike last night, and more often than not he'd been home long after Simone had gone to bed. She left quietly and without breakfast.

David had a restless night and slept on, unaware of her

absence until he woke up around ten thirty, drenched in sweat from strange disturbing dreams. Disorientated, he threw back the bedcovers and made his way to the bathroom and then the kitchen. The aroma of freshly brewed coffee invigorated his senses. He took it with a splash of cognac, a habit he'd slipped into after some wag at a party convinced him that it would help loosen the tightness in his chest. He wasn't going to argue and before long it had developed into a morning habit. The coffee was invariably accompanied by the first cigarette of the day as he sat at the breakfast bar. David closed his eyes and slowly exhaled a cloud of smoke. Last night's dream was fleetingly summoned, but as with most dreams, the last vestiges floated out of reach. He felt drained and tired. Yesterday's euphoria proved as elusive as the dreams and he was disappointed he hadn't told Simone about the positive decisions made the day before. It was then he remembered Georges and after taking a shower and dressing, decided to call the hospital. Georges' predicament left him with an empty feeling that his plans might come to nothing after all.

Calling the hospital invoked the same response as the day before. He was welcome to go in but Georges still remained unconscious. They advised visiting in the afternoon when the doctor had completed his rounds for the day and they would know more. In truth, David was relieved not to have to go out just yet. The pain under his ribs, begun several months earlier, angrily clawed its way back. It was sharper than yesterday and he needed to rest. The upbeat emotion in the park beside the river deserted him, left him depressed and lethargic.

The morning passed pleasantly enough, however. With a couple of books and the remains of food from the fridge, lunch was supplemented by a bottle of Saint Chinian, a gift from a grateful client of Simone's. Lunch then slipped seamlessly into afternoon and by four he fell asleep again in the chair. It was dreamless this time, but deep enough for him to be startled awake by a persistent ringing of the doorbell. An empty glass, laid across his knee, fell to the floor as he staggered to his feet. The room was gloomy and he gave a shudder. The bell rang again. It couldn't be Simone; too early, and besides she never forgot anything, let alone her key. Once again, he hoped it wasn't Rene trying to get in touch, although it was highly unlikely that she would call unannounced. She was persistent but not stupid. Relieved to be at least free from pain, he rubbed his eyes and brushed the hair from his forehead. It was in desperate need of a cut.

A key turned in the lock, perhaps it was Simone after all, and the door slowly opened and light flooded into the salon. Monique appeared in the doorway, coming to collect her pay, as she did each week, from an envelope in the kitchen. She gave a scream when she saw a figure coming towards her out of the darkness. Quickly recovering from the shock when she realised who it was, she garbled an apology for the disturbance,

'Je m'excuse, M. Weston, je ne pensais pas quiconque etait ici.' Her words stumbled over each other, heart racing from initial thoughts that she had come across an intruder. David recovered equally quickly from his torpor and surprise: 'Monique... pardonnez-moi.' He stumbled towards her as she looked away in embarrassment; her face flushed when realising her mistake in letting herself in. It wasn't often she saw David; more often than not her hours coincided with his absence. The last time had been several months before, when they'd had their last dinner party. He'd commented on her new hairstyle and she'd blushed at being noticed.

'I fell asleep in the chair.... The bell woke me up.

Please, please come in.' She smiled, nervous but relieved, looking around for Simone, unsure what to say to him. Out of courtesy, she always rang the bell first, but the apartment was usually empty. Monique turned towards the kitchen. 'I won't be a moment. Mme. Weston…she leaves my money…over there,' she indicated with a slight nod of her head, 'just on the side.'

Monique was young, no more than eighteen or nineteen, and cleaned several apartments in the block to supplement the shortfall in tuition fees at a local college. She was also a great help when they had guests and soon gained a reputation for speed and efficiency that ensured there was no shortage of work. A crop of white blonde hair framed her small, doll-like face that topped a slender body. David had already noted from previous encounters that she wasn't his usual type, but as if by default, complimented her anyway. She was training to be a beautician, experimenting with makeup that didn't always achieve the desired effect, but tonight she looked pretty; her makeup was light and for once showed her natural beauty beneath. She was in awe of Simone and the cut of her hair, if not the colour, was in acknowledgement of the woman she idealised as clever as well as beautiful.

'I will just collect my pay if that is all right?'

'Mais oui,' he nodded.

Monique put the envelope into her bag as David followed her to the kitchen and started to pull the cork from another bottle of red. He poured out two glasses and handed her one,

'Here, take this…it will steady your nerves. I'm sorry I gave you such a shock.'

'That's all right, I'm sorry if I gave you a shock too. I'm on my way out to meet some friends,' she garbled, trying to navigate her way around David to the door. He filled the frame, blocking her way.

'Please, just one then I won't feel so bad about giving *you* such a scare.'

Nervously looking around and not wanting to offend, the glass was reluctantly accepted and she followed him back into the salon.

'C'est bon...le vin...n'est ce pas?'

Of course it was, more than good in fact, and better than the cheap offerings she and her friends usually drank on a night out. After the second large refill, she convinced herself that they wouldn't mind if she was just a little bit late. The wine relaxed her nerves sufficiently to appreciate David's company and witty remarks, and although Monique smoothed and pulled the skirt of her new blue dress as close to knee length as could be managed. The dress was short, but her legs were shapely and slim. Ordinarily she liked the attention the dress drew, but here with David she wished it was longer.

After the third refill, each measure more generous than the last, David made her laugh with amusing anecdotes of people he'd met at parties attended over the past month or two. With each mouthful of wine, she let go of any inhibition she may have started out with and began to enjoy the moment; his world was as far from hers as was possible but for a while she revelled in the belief that gulf was not so very wide.

Monique did not leave the apartment until almost ten o'clock that night, light headed from a lack of food and barely walking straight. Her face was flushed as she hurried down to the ground floor and rushed outside into the cool air. Mme. Rubin looked up from the darkness of her little office when she heard the elevator door open and took note of the crumpled blue dress and the absence of makeup that had been so evident when Monique had first arrived. She did not go on to meet her friends, and when the shock of the night air sobered her sufficiently to think about what had just happened, she already knew that she could not return to the apartment block again. Filled with shame and embarrassment, Monique went home, made herself a coffee and lit a cigarette, despite having given up the week before. With a trembling hand, she sat to write a note to Simone to say she would not be able to continue with the cleaning job, as she needed more time to prepare for her course assignments.

Chapter 16

David sat smoking by the window once again. The brief distraction of Monique had been a pleasant interlude, but she'd all but gone from his thoughts when he remembered Simone. Undecided whether he should wait up or go to bed, the decision was taken away when the phone rang. Thinking it might be Simone, he quickly answered, but it was the nurse at the hospital letting him know that Georges' condition had seriously deteriorated in the last hour and become critical. He should go now before it was too late if he wished to see him one last time and they apologised for not being able to do more. The doctor had confirmed that all they could do now was administer pain relief. With little hope that his condition might improve, he was drifting in and out of consciousness, but in occasional lucid moments, he was asking to see David.

David stubbed out his cigarette and called for a taxi. Grabbing coat and keys, he headed for the door as Simone appeared from her night out.

'Hello, have you just got back?' she asked, puzzled why she hadn't seen him in the lobby.

'No, on my way out. I've just had a call from the hospital. It's Georges; he collapsed just after I met him yesterday...heart attack...complications...I told you I didn't think he looked well...and it's serious. He's unconscious most of the time, but when he came round, he was asking for me. They said I should go in if I want to see him.'

'No...oh I'm so sorry...poor Georges. Let me come with you.'

Simone made to put her coat back on, but David stopped her. 'No, absolutely not...you look done in. Get yourself to bed...get some sleep. I'll let Georges know you were asking after him.'

She looked no better than she had in the morning and David was in two minds whether or not to go himself, but there was no one else the hospital could call. He couldn't leave Georges on his own now, he owed him that much.

'I know how close you two were at one time,' she said, 'and you've only just got back in touch...that is so sad' She was sincere in her offer to go with him, but allowed herself to be persuaded to stay. She was tired, and in the stark light of the hallway, her loss of weight was even more noticeable. As David took the coat from her to hang up, he saw how loosely the blue, fitted dress fell from her shoulders. There was little flesh around her arms too. He leaned across to stroke her cheek, but she turned away and walked to the bedroom hoping he wouldn't follow. 'Stay as long as you need.'

'Get some rest, darling. I've no idea how long I'll be and wouldn't want you hanging around too. He might not even be awake when I get there. Go to bed and I'll see you in the morning. But don't leave before I come home though, will you? I need to talk to you.'

'All right, I'll see you later,' she replied from the

bedroom door, too tired to argue. 'I need to talk to you too.'

David's concern confused her. It had been a while since there had been anything like tenderness between them, at least not since that one night when she'd thought there might be something left to salvage. She placed a hand over her still flat stomach. The baby would start to show soon and she'd been told that the weight loss was only temporary due to the sickness, but her news would keep until the morning. It should have been a time for celebration but previous disappointments made her cautious. The magic and euphoria of that first time would always be clouded by anxiety and the strain of 'will it be all right this time'. They'd been trying for so long with no result, but now, when she had given up all hope of a child, when she felt that there really was nothing left between them, she was pregnant once again. This was the first time she had gone beyond three months and the doctor had said that all was well, so far.

IF SIMONE LOOKED THIN, Georges was skeletal. His frail body barely made an impression on the hospital bed. A thin sheet was tightly tucked in and he hardly moved as each laboured breath showed in the slow, almost imperceptible, rise and fall of his chest. His arms lay on top of the bed, the right one hooked up to a machine that blipped and blinked at regular intervals. David was shocked at the wasted body and sunken face; Georges was disappearing before his eyes.

The room was sparse apart from life-preserving equipment beside the bed and a nurse was adjusting a drip when he arrived. David introduced himself when she looked up, evidently pleased that someone had come to see her patient.

'Georges – your friend is here. David has come to see you,' she spoke gently, bending over Georges and placing her mouth close to his ear. Georges didn't respond even as she adjusted the oxygen mask over his face. She sounded like the nurse who had spoken to him over the phone,

'I'll leave you with him. If you need anything please press this red button and someone will come straight away. But don't be surprised if he doesn't come round yet. He sleeps for much of the time; it's due to the morphine we've given.' She checked her watch, and with a rustle of starched white uniform, made for the door when she was urgently wanted elsewhere. David turned towards Georges as he spoke.

'Has there been no improvement at all?'

'I'm afraid there's no more we can do for him except keep him comfortable. It's palliative care he needs. I'm so sorry. I'm just pleased that he has someone with him. Do you know if he has any relatives that we can contact as well?'

'No, none as far as I know. His wife died a while ago… they had no children…well none that survived…and I never heard him speak of any other relatives. If he had any, I never knew.'

'Ok thank you for that. I'll update his records with your name if that's all right? Would you mind leaving your details at the enquiry desk before you go?'

'Yes…yes of course.'

She left, relieved that Georges wasn't alone, and David pulled a chair closer to the bed. He picked up Georges' free hand studying what he could see of his face as he slept. If it wasn't for the confirmation of the machine, he would suspect that he had already gone. 'I'm so sorry

Georges. I had no idea things were this bad. You should have told me.' He kept hold of the lifeless hand, stroking it gently.

It was another half hour before the inert body stirred and Georges half opened his eyes. He managed something of a smile as he recognised the face before him, grateful it was not just another doctor or nurse.

'Oh...thank you, David,' he whispered in a hoarse voice, 'I've not...not...' Breathing was difficult and he gulped in the oxygen from the mask over his face. Pulling it away in frustration and wanting to talk, he summoned up enough energy to go on, 'I know I've not got long...' he paused a little to smile, 'Sybil is waiting...' He turned his head up towards the corner of the room as though he could see her. It gave him comfort through the pain.

'She'll have to wait a bit longer yet, Georges,' David's voice cracked under the strain of seeing him like this. 'You'll be fine. In a few days when...' But Georges cut him off and gripped David's hand with surprising strength. 'No...no time...I want you to do something for me.' But the effort was too much and he closed his eyes again. David sat back in the chair having replaced the mask back over Georges' mouth. He considered leaving to get back to Simone, there was little he could do here, but no sooner had the thought crossed his mind than Georges had pulled the mask off again and with great effort managed to tell David what he wanted.

'Go to my rooms...now...tonight. You must get the Papers.' He coughed, choking with the effort, but would not go back to sleep as David suggested. 'I want you to go while I am still breathing...while I can give you permission.' It took Georges several attempts to get across exactly where they were and how he should get there. Drifting in and out of consciousness, the intention was certain even if the directions were unclear. 'They are yours now...the Papers...my notes...findings. I told her I would pass them on...she won't let me go until...' With supreme effort, he motioned to the locker beside the bed. The key was in there, where he'd asked the nurse to put it from his jacket pocket, and he'd already managed to tell her that David would be taking it tonight.

'I should really get back to Simone, but I will get them...very soon' he began, but it was obvious he was talking to himself as Georges drifted back into oblivion. The pull of Simone was strong, but considering the time of night and the fact that he didn't want to disturb her sleep, he decided that surely this was one last thing he could do for Georges. He looked down at the sleeping figure for what would be the last time.

'All right, I'll go tonight. I promise.'

It was by no means certain that the old archivist had heard him but the lines on his forehead relaxed and his breathing became so quiet that David wondered whether he really was still alive until a slight twitch at the corner of his mouth told him otherwise. 'I hope that you find Sybil soon, Georges. Good night, my old friend.'

David straightened the mask over his mouth as the nurse popped her head around the door, on her way past.

'Everything all right, Mr Weston?' she enquired.

'Yes, thank you. He's sleeping, so I'll get off. I've taken the key from his locker if that's all right and I'll bring it back tomorrow.'

'No, it's quite fine. He told me that you needed to collect something that belonged to you. We'll see you tomorrow, then. And don't worry; he's not in any pain. I'll be here to top him up again soon and he should sleep through the rest of the night.'

But Georges needed no further medication; he did not

wake up again, and slipped quietly away in the early hours of the morning, free at last from pain and struggle.

IT WASN'T EASY FINDING GEORGES' apartment. Even the taxi driver struggled to make his way through the labyrinth of back streets and the half-occupied buildings that looked as though they were awaiting demolition, but eventually David approached an approximation of the right place. The driver was pleased to get away; it was not an area he often came to and was only there now because work was slack.

Georges had moved a couple of times since David's early days of visiting him and Sybil, but each time had seen them slip further and further down into poverty. There was little sign of life but as David wondered which way to go next in the oppressive darkness, the silence was disturbed by a piercing shriek followed by raised, angry voices. Moments later came the sound of breaking glass, making him twitchy and nervous. Pressing himself against a wall, he turned towards the sound of footsteps close by, at the same time looking for an escape route should he need one. A flash of red appeared and disappeared giving him little beyond the briefest glimpse. A trickle of sweat ran down his back. Metal grilles covered most of the windows; no pretty shutters with windowsills decorated by blooming geraniums here. Rust and decay and the detritus of a hidden underground world lay all around. Footsteps disappeared into the night and silence resumed along with David's suspended breathing. No one else appeared, although he couldn't shake off the feeling of being followed and invisible eyes caught his every move.

Searching the doors and windows for a sign of Georges' address, a stray cat jumped down from a wall ahead, the shock of which caused him to drop the key he had been clutching since leaving the taxi. The cat contemptuously flicked its tail and stalked off leaving David scrabbling around in the dark, wondering if he should just go home and come back in the morning. It was only the thought of not finding the place again that kept him going. 'This is madness,' he muttered to himself before at last the touch of cold metal rubbed against his fingers. He lit a cigarette to calm his nerves and decide what to do next. On consideration, returning in daylight was the better option, no matter what the outcome, but no sooner had he decided to leave, he saw that he had arrived at the right address without realising.

The door unlocked easily enough, but several bags of rubbish sitting tight behind it left a narrow gap to pass through. Regretting the extra inches in girth, David squeezed past and headed straight for the stairs that would lead to Georges' apartment. The intention was to grab what he'd come for and get out as soon as he could, hoping all the while he could remember the way back.

The apartment was three floors up and first on the left, just as he'd been told. Georges' home, if that's what it could be called, was little more than a single room; and the thin light given out by a single bulb in the middle of the ceiling revealed a stove and sink in one corner and a bed in the other. The window above the sink was thick with grime, impenetrable, not that there would have been much to see even if the glass was clean. The room itself was reasonably tidy, but that was more due to the few posses-sions it contained rather than their arrangement. A layer of dust suggested that it hadn't been lived in for some time. It was a sad testament to the man who had once held a post of such great esteem in the Archives where he'd worked, and to someone who had enjoyed the comfort and luxury of a fine home with Sybil. Shocked beyond measure at the depths to which Georges had fallen David wondered what could have had happened to him that he had to be living like this.

It did not take long to find what he had come for. The small brown satchel containing the Henrietta Papers sat inside a cardboard box under the bed. David brushed off the cobwebs and dust with his bare hand before removing the crumbling leather bag; at least the age of the satchel could not be in much doubt. He quickly scanned the contents to make sure he had the Papers he'd come for and then left in relief. The room was inexplicably freezing and his breath had started to form white clouds.

Chapter 17

1992

Manchester

THE ELEVEN O'CLOCK flight from Paris emerged from a bank of wispy clouds and came in to land at Manchester, England. On board the tightly packed plane with its knee-crunching seats, David shivered as he prised open his eyes to the captain's announcement of their arrival. Struggling to find sleep, he had finally slipped into welcome oblivion only ten minutes before landing. He yawned and pulled his coat tightly around, but an expanding waistline proved it a tricky prospect when trying to get buttons to meet buttonholes. Bloodshot eyes and a crumpled shirt were testimony to having slept little more than eight hours over the past three days, and he could have done with a few more on the flight. As the plane bumped along the runway, he rubbed condensation from the window and peered outside, squinting against a late autumn sun. It belied the captain's second announcement that rain was forecast soon.

It had been more than twenty years since David had left England for new beginnings in France and as they all waited to rush towards the exit, he recalled that, in all those years, he had never been tempted to return beyond those two working trips. With no family ties to drag him back, and friends who had been more than happy to visit him and Simone in their home in Paris, there was no point. He hadn't missed it at all, and even now the journey was made with reluctance amidst necessity. Not a man to burden himself with regrets, however, he still believed that all would be well and that the opportunity that he had chosen to take up would give him and Simone breathing space to sort out their life together. The visit was just a temporary foray to finish a piece of work started long ago.

When most of the other passengers had left, he prised himself out of his seat and hauled the remaining bag down from an otherwise empty overhead locker. Outside, fresh chilly air refreshed his lungs like a diver starved of oxygen. 'Welcome to Manchester,' he muttered under his breath, remembering why he couldn't wait to leave in the first in the first place as a student. The dampness was all pervading, mixing with the smell of the fumes of a dozen planes. David shivered again, but not just from the cold. He would definitely need a bigger coat now winter had seemed to have already arrived in England. He fished around inside the voluminous pockets for a cigarette before remembering with dismay that there was nothing to light up with. In the haste of leaving home, the gold lighter, the one with his initials, the one that Simone had bought him for his fortieth, was still sitting on the bedside table. He pictured it alongside the thick cut glass ashtray and whiskey glass and groaned.

At the bottom of the steps, he recognised the young boy who had been kicking his seat from behind for most of the journey, another reason he hadn't slept much. Quieter than he'd been throughout the flight, the boy stood strangely apart from the disappearing crowd. As David got closer he saw tears ballooned in his eyes as they frantically looked around. The receding forest of legs and bags had left him behind and he was calling out for someone in a small, strangled voice – was it Cecille? No one else had noticed in the rush to get away, assuming that a small boy wouldn't be left on his own. David at first made to join the rest of the passengers; another plane had just landed and the queue through immigration would be long enough already.

David calculated that the boy must be no more than four or five years old and started to walk away too, but something made him stop and look back. It was none of his business and he had too many other things on his mind, but he turned around anyway. The boy was still there. He looked over to see if he could work out who the missing Cecille might be. The air-crew were talking amongst themselves, as yet unaware of the small drama being played out, so against his original intention he went back to the boy and crouched down low to speak face to face, 'Vais-je vous aider a trouver Cecille?' The child looked up and solemnly nodded, grateful that someone might help him to find Cecille. David instinctively offered his hand and the little boy's fingers trustingly accepted and reached up.

'Comment tu l'appelles?' There was no reply.

'Je m'appelle David'. After a short pause came a barely audible reply 'Leon.'

'Leon, that's a nice name.'

The hand was small and soft, the poignancy of which tugged at something deep inside David and a moment of completely unexpected tenderness overwhelmed him. With eyes cast down at the blond, shiny head of curls, his free hand poised mid air, barely resisting the urge to stroke it.

'Allez Léon, trouvons Cecille'

Slowly walking back towards the plane, the need for a cigarette was momentarily forgotten in the concentration of helping the boy.

It wasn't long before a flushed young woman, struggling with a baby and a bulging flight bag, emerged from the plane, straining to look in all directions at once. The zip on an overstuffed flight bag had broken and the head of a small battered teddy bear poked out of the top. The crew had not noticed that she had still been on the plane, hidden between the seats, on the floor, searching for the creams and wipes that had spilled out of the bag when it had been dragged out of the locker. The baby, all the while had slept quietly beside her on the next seat. Leon, after two hours of containment had taken his chance in the rush to get off and disappeared in the crowd. A member of the crew followed behind this last passenger, smiling, but clearly annoyed at the prospect of being held up to search for a missing child; all she wanted to do was put her feet up until the return flight out in three hours time.

Cecille focussed on the disappearing backs of the other passengers that had now thinned down to a straggling few, until she saw the little boy with David, walking in her direction. 'Leon!' she cried out above the shouts of the workers waiting to unload luggage from the hold of the plane. The stewardess, obviously relieved that Cecille was now fine, went to join the other members of the crew and told them of the drama.

'Restez la, mon cher; je viens pour tu,' Cecille called out. She dropped the broken bag and rushed towards him, holding the baby tightly to her chest. Leon abruptly pulled his hand away from David's and ran to her, holding out his arms.

David thought her too young to have two children. In fact, she looked not much older than a child herself. She was very pretty though, flushed and completely dishevelled after the trauma of losing the little boy. Leon crashed into her legs and threw his arms around them so tightly that she couldn't move.

'Tu m'as laisse!' he sobbed, angry with her for leaving him, as the tears finally breached the dam and poured down his face. David went over to explain what had happened.

'Il était à la recherche pour vous.'

He spoke excellent French, sounding almost like a native.

'Merci, monsieur, vous etes tres, tres gentil.'

She prised Leon's reluctant arms from her legs, still smiling with relief, and all the while promising herself that she would definitely be more strict with him in future.

'Let me get that bag for you.'

David retrieved the broken flight bag and walked with them into the crowded airport, surprised at its weight. How could a small child and baby need so much stuff? Once inside, the boy and bag were safely ensconced in a trolley and all was calm amidst the surrounding noise and crowds. But as Cecille turned to thank David once again, the baby awoke and his mouth opened wide to let out a ferocious scream of complaint.

'S'il te plait pas maintenant.' It wasn't entirely unexpected since his last feed had been more than four hours earlier. A dummy was retrieved from underneath the blue baby blanket, hopeful that he would be pacified for a few moments longer. She wanted David to stay; he was really pleasant and maybe he would also help find their suitcases.

The company of small truculent children was not what she had planned as a career, but when the opportunity cropped up it had suited her purpose for the summer at least. Unprepared for their constant demands that were draining every ounce of her energy, any help would be welcome. Even if David did look old enough to be her father, he was attractive in his own way, and kind, and he might also help her to find a taxi when they had collected their luggage. It was wishful thinking. The baby spat the dummy out, took in gasps of air and let Cecille know that it was not enough.

'Votre bebe est…'

Non! – pas mon bebe. Au pair.'

Cecille's arms flapped in front of her face horrified that he thought the children were hers. Did she look that old? This was a huge drawback with the job of being a nanny, assumptions were made and opportunities missed when you were out with the little brats.

'Ah, oui', David raised an eyebrow in response and looked from Cecille to the children. The baby was laid across her shoulder being patted on the back as David focussed on Leon. He leant across the trolley, produced a franc coin from behind the boy's head and waved it in front of his face before rubbing it between two hands and making it disappear. Leon liked this game very much, especially when it reappeared again from his other ear. Cecille jiggled the baby in her arms and was happy to see that Leon was now sitting contentedly with his teddy bear, sucking his thumb and clutching the newly acquired coin. With a face still wet with snot and tears he was sorted at least. David stared at the child, lost in thought, barely listening to the nanny.

'Le bebe a faim…' she repeated, hoping he might offer to help with Leon, but David was already planning his escape. Cecille was surprised at the sudden need to get away, giving her no opportunity to put forward a plea for more help. A crowd had built up around the carousel and David told her that he had to go.

'Je vais vous laisser maintenant, Cecille. Bon vacance avec les enfants!'

'Au revoir – et merci encore monsieur….?

'David.'

'Ah, au revoir, David,' she replied as he turned to leave them, holding out her hand. For a fleeting moment only, he considered asking for her number as they shook hands, but the baby's loud wailing soon put a stop to any such thought. Instead, he mouthed 'Bon chance,' above the din and raised his arms in a gesture of 'what can you do?' and walked away, turning just once to see the noisy little group heading for the baby room before he went over to the carousel to wait for the rest of his luggage.

Much to his dismay, the carousel still showed no sign of life and the need for a cigarette returned with a vengeance.

Away from the growing crowd, he found a seat over by the toilets. He sat in resignation following an announcement that there was an unexpected technical fault. Unbidden memories had surfaced, triggered by the baby's wailing and a lost little boy, memories buried deep, but not so deep that they could not be heard and seen.

SIMONE LAY in the hospital bed with their baby in her arms, alabaster-perfect with just a slight smear of birth blood across his cheek. David rubbed it very lightly with his thumb but it was dry by then and stubbornly stayed. The oppression of silence closed in on them when there were no words to convey all that they felt. There was no cry, no baby wail of complaint when he emerged into a world that should have greeted him with laughter and tears of happiness.

A simple wooden cross on a stark white wall offered little comfort that day when, along with the baby, a part of himself had died too. After three miscarriages, this baby had almost gone full term and at forty-two was Simone's last hope that she might bring a healthy child into the world. Was it really twelve years ago? It could have been yesterday as the memory resurfaced with a pain that had never dissipated since their final loss. The need for a cigarette grew more intense as the gaping wound of that awful time would not be held back. Why now after all these years did it have to come back here?

Too numb to shed tears, too helpless to console his wife, he relived the sight of Simone slipping in and out of consciousness, along with the memory of holding her hand as if letting go would mean that she too would never return. How could anyone lose so much blood and still live? Against all odds, she did survive, but they were told that it was unlikely there would be any more babies. When the nurse took their son away, and when he thought he would lose Simone too, he stood looking out of the window and cried for the first and last time over this final baby who had never emerged from the shadows.

The pain had lost none of its grip over the years, it had just been relieved by an ocean of alcohol and cigarettes, and any other distraction that happened to come his way; exactly what he needed right now. Simone had emerged from her trauma by burying the memory under a mountain of work. She went on to create her own business and nurtured it with the energy that would no longer be required for raising a family. There would be no more babies.

. . .

DAVID CHECKED HIS WATCH. Phil knew when his plane was landing but they agreed that David would make his own way over to the flat. Phil had been the last visitor they'd had from England to their home in France. They'd known each other since early student days at Manchester, but to call him a 'friend' was pressing the point after the debacle of that last visit. Phil had periodically turned up over the years in an attempt to rekindle the 'great times' that had only ever really existed in his own imagination. God knows how he had got hold of his address in Paris. By the time David had received his note asking if it was all right to stay for a few days, Phil turned up at their door. It was too late to say they would be away. His visit was in part an attempt to get over his split from Jen, his wife, but David was the last person to give out a sympathetic ear. The reception was not the one Phil thought was his due and his request for financial help was not as much as he'd hoped for either.

David sat with arms folded and legs crossed, desperate more than ever to get out of the confining airport and escape from his oppressive thoughts. The noise inside grew with the swelling angry crowd and a sharp pain pierced his chest with renewed vigour. He rubbed at it with the flat of his hand, reasoning that he'd not eaten for a long time and needed food. Back at the apartment, the fridge and wine store were never empty, courtesy of Clare, Monique's replacement and her thrice-weekly visits. Simone would be in Milan by now, having packed the night before, leaving her briefcase ready on the hall table for a quick getaway. She would have caught the taxi at eight o'clock and stopped to buy the day's newspapers on the way. When she'd arrive in Milan, a car would be waiting to take her to clients, two or three before lunch, and the same in the afternoon. They would discuss the markets, their investments and their options, and make decisions on what to sell and what to buy. They trusted her judgement – and why wouldn't they? More often than not, she'd predicted the fluctuations in the markets long before they'd happened and they had all nicely profited from their investments. Then on top of the handsome fees that they paid for her services, gratitude was manifest in other ways – party invitations and extravagant functions, yachting trips, tickets to the opera and ballet. The perks were endless; the business was her baby and she nurtured it well. It thrived and grew and provided them with a more than generous income. He couldn't complain, but where did that leave him now? Along the way, David had forged relationships of his own in this privileged circle, as well as a taste for expensive wine and fine rich food; back to food again. His stomach growled even more loudly; it was almost lunchtime, and the airport continued to fill as later planes disgorged their passengers. He desperately needed a cigarette now, but perhaps more than that, he wanted to break open the duty free that nestled in the other bag at his feet.

At long last, the mechanical grind of the carousel came to life and a loud roar of approval belted out from an impatient crowd. Luggage began to spew out on to the snaking belt and before long his own large, battered, brown leather bag appeared. It had been a gift from his mother when he was a student, bought from Heal's when she'd visited London. The assistant had told her it would last a lifetime and she gave it to him as a parting gift the year before she died. He'd rescued it from the back of the wardrobe in the spare bedroom and took it in preference to the matching sets that Simone had always used when they went away together. There was no arguing that this, at least, was his.

He grabbed it with his free hand and made his way

out. At the other side of the airport, he glimpsed Cecille standing patiently with her trolley. The boy and baby were both quiet now and they made a pretty group waiting for their cases. He stopped and watched them unnoticed, just for a second, then walked towards the exit.

Chapter 18

Yorkshire

JULIA DUMPED FOUR HEAVY, fat volumes of Kelly's Directory on top of her desk. An orange cloud rose, atomic-like, and floated down over her.

'Bugger, I knew that would happen.'

She looked down at her front where powdered leather from the crumbling spines had settled like orange dandruff on her cardigan. Instinctively brushing at it with a hanky caused the small flakes to join together to produce something worse. She slumped down into her chair and threw the stained tissue into the bin wondering if Woolies would have a cheap enough replacement for the cardi. I could go in my lunch hour, she thought, and then remembered that money was tight this month. Money, or rather the lack of it, turned her thoughts to Michael, the recipient of all their spare cash at present. From the day he was born, or rather six months into the pregnancy, when she made it quite clear she was going to keep the baby despite the absence of a husband or father, money had been hoovered up before it could be earned.

The life that should have gone hand in hand with college, leaving home and then working and having money in her pocket, had never materialised for Julia. Leaving school as soon as the bump began to show went only a short way to appeasing her mother's shame that her daughter had not even reached sixteen. Working was out of the question, and to make matters worse, she'd refused to say who the father was despite the pleas and threats from her own father. She was equally adamant that she would not give the baby up either, and in the end, when Audrey and Tommy saw their first, and what would be their only, grandchild, they fell in love with the tiny bundle that had caused so much anguish.

Every time Julia saw Michael's face, as a baby, a toddler, a schoolboy running towards her at the school gate calling out 'Mummy!' the pang of loss haunted the love she still felt inside for his father. Even more now, whenever she saw Michael, she saw David. The pain had lessened over the years but at the same time was indelibly stamped into her being, like lettering through a stick of rock.

THE MIDWIFE at the hospital had gone out of her way to smooth the rough path that was being laid for the mother and child under her care. Possibly Caribbean, she kept a watchful eye over Julia and the baby; even visiting on one of her days off although Julia barely recognised her out of the blue and white uniform. She was instead mesmerised by the colourful hat and bright red lipstick. She'd sat on the bed, conspiratorially close, causing Julia to roll in towards her as she weighed it down, and spoke quietly into her ear,

'You stay clear of that man my girl, he not for you. You have beautiful baby, now let it all be.'

Julia wanted ask what she meant and to thank her before she left, but no-one on duty that day recognised a nurse who remotely bore the description she gave them. Julia never saw her again and was discharged with Michael in her arms. Audrey and Tommy collected them and drove back home full of apprehension, each ill prepared for their new life ahead.

At home, the questions and the probing eventually stopped. The demands that whoever was the father should pay for his upkeep, or heaven forbid, marry their daughter and bring respectability back to the family, faded along with the hope that Julia might relent and tell them who he was. Life wasn't totally unbearable however, and Audrey and Tommy showed little kindnesses in their own way, brought in gifts for the baby that they grew to love and cherish, and it was in this atmosphere of guarded love that Julia and Michael stayed until the day that Will came into her life ten years later.

THE OFFICE EQUILIBRIUM, having been temporarily disturbed, saw two bowed heads briefly pop up over piles of paperwork, but on finding that nothing too serious had happened, bent back down and continued their work. The noise in the office returned to no more than a scratching of pencil on paper.

Julia suited life at the Archives in more ways than one. Standing close to the shelves in the stacks, the muted colours of her clothes blended perfectly with the boxes, books and files behind her. She moved quietly through the symmetrical lines of moveable shelving, selecting and choosing papers and volumes, maps and charts, needed in her research. She worked with the efficiency and speed that came with over ten years experience.

It was generally known that she had a son who had reached his twenty-first birthday, and like her fellow students during college days, most assumed that she was older than her years, especially when her appearance bore out that assumption. Although not unattractive, few, apart from Maggie, got past the buttoned up blouses and over-sized cardigans that betrayed the slim figure beneath. Her hair had long outgrown its stylish cut of a year ago and would fight out of the band that had secured it at seven thirty each morning. Nowadays, she took less and less of an interest in her looks beyond a daily shower and clean clothing.

The years between Michael's birth and the day he left for university, the years during which it took him to look more and more like his father, something began to die inside her, day by day.

She pushed Will further and further away in their marriage, and found only relief in the fact that they no longer shared the same bed, assuming that he did too. Last winter, when he'd picked up a bad cold and his snoring became intolerable, she moved herself into the spare bedroom, made it her own and never moved back. There were plenty of excuses when he asked why she didn't return but thankfully he didn't press the point and it was accepted. She loved having the space to herself; being able to turn on the light and read when sleep evaded her was a luxury, as were two pillows in the middle of the bed and not having to manoeuvre her body as far away from Will's as she could when he wanted more than sleep. Turning from his attempts at intimacy was one thing she did not have to encounter any longer. If she had felt any guilt, it was subsumed by her own growing anxiety and helplessness to do anything about it.

In rare moments of introspection, it once crossed her mind that things might have been different if she and Will had had a child of their own, but the thought was dismissed as soon as it arrived. Will had made it clear that he would have loved them to have a baby together, but it was too late now and a decision she'd never regretted.

Coping with the turmoil in her mind was so consuming that there was little room left for Will. He showed only kindness when she was down, and patience when he understood what it meant to her when Michael moved out, but the closer he came, the further she pushed him away.

It had been over three years since they'd taken him to the cramped room at the halls of residence. She was miserable leaving him there, but Michael had been happy to get away and start his new life. He quickly found his feet and relished the newfound freedom from the start.

During those years, a vacuum had formed in Julia's heart, one that Will discovered he could not fill as the weeks turned into months and the months into years. It was the first time that they'd had the opportunity of experiencing married life with just the two of them, something Will relished, but Julia did not and the harmony of old never recovered its rhythm.

Julia lost her footing and floundered in a home that no longer gave purpose to her life. The part that had been so integral to the whole had gone and she could not function with what was left. Once the reminders of Michael's presence had been cleared, collected and tidied away, it felt as though Michael himself had been tidied away too.

When Will had taken up darts, Julia relished the regular Monday nights alone. It suited her needs, and for a while, so did the alternating Tuesdays of the reading and knitting groups. By Wednesday, she and Will would sit on either side of the sofa like bookends. He might try to move away the wools, patterns and books rooted in the middle, but she always found some urgent job that couldn't wait, or was so engrossed in a television programme, that he might as well have not been there at all.

A new routine settled into place, which saw Julia leaving for work earlier than usual, and Will invariably arriving home later than planned. He no longer found the time to engage his wife in conversation beyond perfunctory matters of domestic arrangements. It left him saddened beyond measure and frustrated with his inability to do anything about it. He loved his wife but increasingly found himself pushing at a closed door.

WHEN JULIA HAD LEFT for work, Will remained sitting at the kitchen table with a mug of half drunk, cold coffee. The impossibility of their situation burned inside. Try as he might, he found it harder than ever to find a solution. After ten years of marriage, was this the end of the road? He didn't want to give up but the options were running low. Whatever he said, Julia remained as cold as the coffee in front of him. A deep sigh of regret came from the depths of all he could not do to change things.

The tension at the back of Will's neck spread across to his eyes and the threatened headache hammered with a vengeance. Rummaging for an aspirin in a drawer, he slammed it shut when the packet he found was empty. Life had become a permanent state of confusion and incomprehension. The distance and coldness he experienced on a daily basis, the dismissal of any suggestions of what they might do together, set the pattern of his days.

Will put the kettle on to make a fresh coffee. He had a

free morning in which to ruminate on what to do next. More and more, he was asking himself if Julia had ever really loved him at all. Had that just been wishful thinking, a refusal to see what was in front of him when his love for her overrode anything else? His mind went back to happier days, as it had done so many times before; trying to work out at what stage the marriage had fallen apart.

Chapter 19

On a bright autumn day in October 1980, the only thing that had been on the mind of the chartered accountant sitting in Paragon Station's waiting room was next year's test match between England and the West Indies. That, and what he wouldn't give to be there in person. Then a shy young woman seeking a spare seat came along and changed his life forever.

Will recognised her as soon as she set foot through the door, despite the changes the years had brought. He didn't quite know what it was that made him hold back at first; perhaps it had been the remembered log-ago rejection, or perhaps it was the thought that she might give him a blank look before getting back to the book she now balanced on her knee.

Gone was the long blonde hair that used to cascade down her back, and gone the skinny girl from the same history class who was always the first to put up her hand in response to a question. The Julia before him fronted a neat bob that framed her pretty face, the blondeness having given way to a colour two or three shades darker. She was pleasingly dressed, but not in a way to attract attention.

On her part, Julia did not recognise the man sitting next to her in the waiting room, not that she had looked beyond the empty seat, and thereafter focused solely on the book she was reading. Having moved on from the classics and horrors of old, she preferred something more contemporary and was half way through 'Sophie's Choice'.

They were both waiting for the Leeds train, Will to meet up with a new client, and Julia on her way to a training course for her job at the Archives. The announcement that the train was delayed for at least an hour due to 'technical problems' came as no surprise to Will. It was not infrequent on that line and after a second's consideration; he left for the coffee bar opposite. It took Julia another few minutes to arrive at the same decision, following which Will watched her from his vantage point opposite the door.

Julia had joined the queue and bought a tea. Balancing cup and bag, she searched again for an empty seat. Will removed his coat from the seat next to him knowing it was one of the very few left.

"Is this seat taken?' she asked hopefully before recognising him as the man from the waiting room. She rarely travelled anywhere by train and felt awkward coping with the vagaries of commuter travel. Was a seat to be avoided if it had a coat or bag occupying it? At what stage do you ask if it's free? Fortunately this one was completely unoccupied.

'No...please help yourself.'

Julia sat in relief, moving the chair slightly away from his to maintain a greater distance between them.

'Are you waiting for the Leeds train too? Must be the third delay this month.'

Julia nodded, not wanting to get into a conversation with a man she didn't know. She

stirred her tea, unnecessary since she didn't take sugar, but it gave her something to

occupy her hands.

'Me too…it's Will by the way.'

Julia felt obliged to look up at him, but had no inclination to give her name in return.

'I'm sorry…I should explain. I know who you are…at least I'm pretty certain I do and I hope I've got it right… it's Julia isn't it?

'I don't think I …'

'Don't you recognise me? I knew you as soon as you walked through the door in the waiting room. I am right aren't I?'

Julia took a longer look at his face this time. The name rang no bells but there was something familiar about his features; something that resonated from the past.

'Goodness me…is it Billy? Billy Sanderson?'

Years fell away when realisation kicked in.

'It's Will actually… I've not been Billy since leaving school.'

'Oh'

Was this the boy she'd once had a date with? Julia blushed when the memory of his attempted, clumsy kiss came into focus, but at the same time she was relieved he wasn't a stranger desperately seeking attention. She drank her tea.

Will, enthralled by the beautiful woman Julia had become, felt the feelings of old overwhelm him as much as they had done years ago, even though she was nothing like the fresh-faced schoolgirl he'd had his first crush on. However, he did not let past experience put him off. They were adults now, and by the look of the third finger on her left had, hopefully both single. It was a promising start.

He recalled the café door opening to a fresh influx of customers that brought in with them a cloud of dust. Julia screwed up her face when a speck of grit caught her eye, but before he could offer to help she produced a hanky and managed to remove it without too much bother. He leaned in a little closer,

'Isn't this where I should tell you that I'm a doctor and produce a freshly laundered handkerchief from my pocket?'

Julia pulled back but smiled nonetheless, 'I've got it thanks…the speck and the movie.' 'Brief Encounter' was one of her mother's favourites that they'd watched many times on the video player at home.

Will took the opportunity to fill in the gaps of his inter-vening years, hoping she might reciprocate, but it wasn't to be, not that day at least. Encouraging others to do the talk-ing, and deflecting the need to talk about herself was something at which Julia was very adept. It was well prac-ticed since college days when Michael was a resolutely private matter.

Julia listened and looked at Will with interest as he described a life far removed from her own. She noted his hands: smooth with neatly clipped nails; office worker hands, unlike her father's short stumpy fingers that were cracked and calloused from years of hard manual labour. Then, unbidden, she thought of David's hands, blushed again and checked her watch.

However, there was time enough to discover that the office where Will worked wasn't too far from the Archives and for them to exchange numbers. He had managed to persuade Julia to meet him the following week for lunch.

He'd made her laugh today and lifted her spirits with amusing tales of trainees' excuses for turning up late; of clients who offered their own 'services' and goods in lieu of payment; and how he liked to be known as Will at interviews and work, thinking it sounded more professional than Billy.

School days were kept perfunctory and it remained unspoken that he had gone off with Julia's best friend Maggie after the rebuff at the school dance. Although he'd seen Julia with Mr Weston when they'd come running out of the school hall, he'd been more concerned that she should not see him with Maggie. He saw their kiss, however, and realised that he'd been dumped over a schoolgirl crush.

'I can't believe that we've not bumped into each other before now,' Will enthused, but all too soon came the announcement the train was ready and due to leave. From then on, the journey to Leeds was noisy and conversation kept to a minimum.

Julia had pulled her woollen green coat around her, tugging at the frayed cuff she had meant to repair the night before, but forgot when Michael needed help with his homework. However, they did meet for lunch soon after and other dates followed close behind. This time Julia did not repel his advances. She looked forward to his company. Pleased with the interest Will took in her life and work, his kisses were welcomed and enjoyed. His eyes never left her face when he wanted to know *her* opinions, *her* ambitions, what *she* wanted to do next. Will joked that he'd loved her since school, but that was closer to the truth than he let her believe.

. . .

WILL HAD ALWAYS ACCEPTED that there were parts of Julia's life where she broached no intrusion, but that was all right; there had been time enough, and now it seemed hardly relevant. He'd thought of her like Sleeping Beauty, waiting for that one kiss to bring her back to life and he would the Prince who would do it, but today, he finally accepted he would never be that man. Their marriage was dangerously faltering on the edge of a precipice.

Of course, he wasn't the first man she'd known but that didn't matter when he never materialised in their lives. She'd found Michael a difficult subject to talk about at first. Juila never mentioned it at their first meeting, nor during their three following dates, but when it became obvious they would be more than just friends, the subject of had to be raised.

Following a romantic dinner one night, at an Italian restaurant that was a particular favourite of Will's, Julia told her story when they'd finished eating, and several glasses of wine had given her the courage. She allowed no interruption until she'd finished what came across as a carefully prepared speech. He learned of a drunken teenage party, a one-night stand, and a man who disappeared shortly afterwards. She told Will he'd gone abroad and was never seen or heard of again.

Will had taken her hands in his and, overwhelmed by love, thanked her for telling him. 'The past isn't worth talking about now, and none of it matters anyway as we can do nothing to change it,' he'd said and that was the end of the matter. Will had accepted it all with good grace, understanding her need to be left in control over that part of her life at least. There was even a part of him that loved her for that too. Everyone had secrets and sometimes they were better left that way. He hoped that one day she might tell him more, but wouldn't push for it.

At the time of meeting Julia again, Will had been smarting over his last girlfriend, the exact opposite of Julia. She had frustrated him with her needs and demands, and the main reason he had ended their relationship was her jealousy and insistence on knowing every last detail of the women who had come before her. Looking at Julia, whose eyes were cast down and cheeks still flushed from the revelation, he could not love her more.

They were happy then and all Will could see was what an amazing future they had ahead of them, including Michael who adapted well to the introduction of Will into his life, showing little resentment, and bonding them close as a family. Will had come at a time when Michael was due to go to high school and he liked being the same as everyone else with a Mum *and* a Dad. Will made few demands on his stepson and was happy to let Julia provide the discipline. He took great delight in watching him grow and develop. Julia bloomed and flourished, basking in the family life she never thought would come her way. So, as well as taking Michael to watch Hull City, and play ball games in the park, Will took the boy to his heart. He remained curious about Michael's father but knew early in his relationship with Julia never to push for answers she did not want to give.

Will put aside the schoolgirl who had rejected him after only one date, but recalled it now as he finished his coffee. On their walk home from the bus, after the cinema, she'd let him hold her hand and he'd almost managed a kiss, but the next week at the school dance, inexplicably, she made it clear she wasn't interested in him at all and her rejection was absolute.

Neither of them went back to school after that summer break and neither saw or heard anything of the other until that memorable day at the station. Billy Sanderson, known now as Will, started at college, then went on to university to complete his studies in accountancy. Julia was consigned to a school day memory. Life moved on and girlfriends came and went. There had been no one he wanted to settle down with, and it might have stayed that way, but for their chance meeting. Will might be older, but deep inside there was a consistency of feeling that ran through from the boy to the man.

Over a fresh coffee, he still searched for the woman he loved, but found himself lost in the maze. The wedge between them was growing ever bigger, imperceptible at first, but had culminated into something irrefutable. Will could no longer hide from the fact that it was Michael who'd kept them together, and during the years since he'd gone, found little but the shredded remains of a marriage that was falling apart.

In recent months, there had been flashes of the Julia of old, but they were becoming increasingly rare. On his birthday, she had made a big effort, cooked his favourite meal of Spaghetti Puttanesca and bought an expensive bottle of Italian red, but as the evening drew to a close the anticipation of re-kindling their love died along with the snuffing of the candles on the cake. Julia retreated back into the spare bedroom using her usual complaint that she was tired and needed an early night. Will sat alone with the rest of the wine, in confusion, wondering what he had done wrong.

Shortly after, loneliness had driven him out on his own. Every Monday saw him at the British Legion Club, the first welcoming sight on a solitary walk into the night. At first it was just for a pint or two, then for the chance to enjoy a little banter and laughter with the regulars he was starting to get to know. One Monday, the captain of the darts team put a word around that they were short of a player that night and having played a little during university days, Will offered to give it a go. Apologising that he was probably too rusty, they gladly took him on in desperation, but when he proved to be more than competent, 'Darts Night' became a regular fixture at the end of every month.

Chapter 20

On that morning, before leaving for work, Julia had been oblivious to the fact that Will watched her a little more closely than usual. He did not get up to give her a kiss on the cheek as she left for the bus, nor did he mention how late he would be home that night.

Her cup and plate were washed and put away and supper sat ready in the fridge. She saw nothing unusual in his behaviour as she pulled her hat over her ears against the winter cold, and just wondered if it was going to rain before saying 'Bye'.

Her walk to work from the bus took longer than usual. A bitter headlong wind had picked up, slowing her pace as she pulled up her collar and the first tentative rain fell from the sky. She called into a bakery on the way to save going out later for lunch. Julia hated the winter, hated the incessant cold that numbed her fingers white and the wind that made her hair look as though it had never seen a comb, let alone used one. Will commented that she was too pale and didn't eat enough, but his words fell short of their mark. They were meant kindly, but only irritated her.

Julia enjoyed arriving at work before anyone else. She took pleasure in taking a coffee back to her desk, despite the office rules clearly stating it was strictly forbidden, and relished the time alone to plan her day and rid herself of the niggles in her head. Malcolm, the Manager, put in an appearance precisely thirty minutes later by which time she was ready for the day ahead.

It had been three weeks since Michael had phoned home and despite her trying to make contact with him, he was always out. Will shrugged it off as normal; he could remember university life well, the places to go, things to do, and none involved calling parents.

This morning over her coffee, Julia had tried to weigh up the myriad reasons to be grateful, listing the positives in her life, but it didn't come easy. Will was everything she could want in a husband: he was kind and thoughtful, cared deeply about her welfare; and he'd always loved Michael as his own right from the start, but – and there was always a but – there was a gnawing deep inside for something else, an empty space to be filled, a sadness and longing for something that did not exist.

Julia took a deep breath, closed the desk drawer on her empty coffee mug and set to work the pile of enquiries at her desk. They were much easier to navigate than the clutter in her head.

Rubbing at the red mark on her wrist, its dull ache always presaged the onset of rain. It had faded to a pale pink, a legacy from so long ago that the memory of its cause had faded too. Julia glanced outside to see if the heavens had seriously opened, but the greying sky had yet to release its burden.

The office began to fill, as it always did following a family history class the night before. Every inch of desk space was occupied and towers of registers were heaped on the floor, waiting to be returned to the stacks. Her arms hurt from the weight of the books that dug in, and her legs ached from walking up and down the steep metal stairs. It was on days like this that the job she had been so desperate to get didn't always live up to its earlier promise, and today, even the thought of no longer sweeping the floor of Marjorie's hairdressing salon did not cheer her up. The stain on her cardigan did not help either.

'I love my job, I love my job,' she repeated to herself as the promised rain started to fall and the room grew darker.

'Mm…taken to talking to yourself now?'

Julia was startled back into the room to find Maggie leaning over her.

'It's coffee time.'

'Great…but I think I need more than coffee, today.'

'Well, the day they put a bar in here will not arrive any time soon…what's the problem?'

As they walked to the staff room together, Julia pulled at her cardigan and made another attempt to rub away the marks. Maggie smirked.

'I know, I should have worn my overall…you've told me before.'

Maggie held open the office door, 'I've got biscuits,' she proffered as consolation and produced a couple of Kit Kats from her pocket.

Maggie and Julia covered the first shift of morning breaks and Maggie filled the kettle as Julia rinsed two mugs taken from yesterday's murky water in the sink. There were never any clean ones in the cupboard, apart from the remaining few with chips and cracks. On the wall was a note from the cleaner, 'The washing up fairy has retired. Do your own!!!!' The number of exclamation marks had been added to on a daily basis since it was put up, but the washing up still remained in the sink.

They sat at their usual table in the corner once Julia had cleared away a neat pile of pristine 'Archivist' journals and a tumbling stack of well-thumbed 'Woman's Own'. Maggie set down the coffee and biscuits.

'How's Michael doing?' she asked as Julia ripped off the paper of her biscuit.

'Really well,' Julia's face lit up at the mention of Michael, 'at least I think so,' she replied, momentarily distracted from the cardigan by coffee, Kit Kat and the thought of her son. 'The last time I managed to talk to him he was…and judging by the noise in the background, his nightlife's going well too. I miss him, Maggie. It's too quiet at home. I never thought I would feel like this. I know it's what he wanted and he's happy, he has lots of friends there, but….' Her voice trailed off and Maggie wondered if she was about to cry again.

'But nothing…that's the whole point of uni! Drink, smoke and get laid in the first two years. Study in the final. Job done. Isn't that what we all did?'

'I wish…'

'Sorry…sorry…I forgot…yours was a bit different, I know'

Maggie picked up her coffee and remembered too late that Julia had had Michael while she studied and lived all the while with her parents at home.

'Sorry'

'No, don't worry, it's all in the past, I'll probably have my adolescence in my sixties. You know…discover alcohol and pot and get banished to a lonely bedsit when Will throws me out.'

'I don't think he'll ever do that'

'Who knows what will happen?'

'Well, you're a bundle of laughs this morning.'

Maggie drank her coffee before steering the conversation back to Will.

'What do you mean, anyway?' she asked, 'Isn't it nice for you both to have the freedom to do just what you want? This is your chance to find some excitement together...to get closer...have a bit of fun while you're still capable.' Maggie raised her eyebrows.

'I think it might be a bit late for that...' Julia laughed, but her words trailed away before committing anything further. 'Just ignore me...it's one of those days.'

Maggie sat back in her chair, watching Julia closely. Their lives rarely coincided since Julia's marriage, and Maggie's love life was erratic, but she liked to keep up the connection with Julia and Will when she could.

'Let's have another outing. Just the two of us... Wuthering Heights is out this week... Ralph Fiennes as Heathcliff...we can drool over him with a bag of popcorn...while Will cries over England losing at cricket.'

Julia laughed for the second time that day, 'How did you know that?'

'Intuition, my dear; he doesn't strike me as a rugby man...footy perhaps...cricket definitely.'

'Really?'

'Yes...absolutely...Billy Sanderson was top bowler. Don't you remember? He used to get me to do the scoring but after two goes I was bored rigid.'

Julia remembered nothing of Will at sport, just saw him playing football with Michael and taking him to watch City on a Saturday afternoon. She then smiled at the thought of Wuthering Heights and wondered if she still had the book that must have been read at least twenty times.

Maggie sat back, her fresh white lab coat falling open to

reveal slim legs encased in a tailored, navy skirt. She pushed her hair back behind her ears. It was cut square, shoulder length, slightly curling under at the bottom. She visited Sassoon's in Leeds at least once a month for a trim and highlights, and at the same time would shop and replenish her wardrobe. Being in charge of restoration and binding did not require such meticulous attention to hair and wardrobe, but Maggie had never looked like the rest of the Archives team. Plain and drab were not in her vocabulary, or her wardrobe. She had often remarked that she could tell what day it was by the colour of the supervisor's socks, a different pair for each day of the week. Neither Maggie nor Julia were part of the several cliques in the Archives, formed over the years like calcified rock. As a constant outsider, Julia was grateful for Maggie's continued friendship.

Maggie was paid more for her specialist work, but apart from that had the luxury of only having to answer to herself. She was her own boss and Julia was more than a little envious. It was strange how their roles had reversed. At school, it had always been Julia on top. Julia the beauty, Julia whose grades were always impeccable and higher than Maggie's, and Julia the one most likely to reach the upper echelons in whatever she chose to do. Maggie was the one who always played catch up.

They sat in momentary silence, each absorbed in their own thoughts until the noise of raised voices preceded the arrival of Carole, the new trainee, and Colin, a lowly assistant, but arrogant enough to believe he always knew better. Carole, young and pretty, had Colin, pug-faced and flabby-jowled, trailing behind like a lapdog.

'Could his tongue hang out any further?' Maggie whispered and they both sniggered like children. Carole held court, looking across to see who was in the room, but they took her arrival as their cue to leave after arranging a date for 'Wuthering Heights'.

'It'll be a bit of escapism,' offered Maggie as she got up to put the mugs back in the sink, 'but for now, I have Pevsner downstairs, waiting for me to restore him to his former glory. Oh joy. I'll see you later.'

Maggie glided out of the room with the scent of Mitsouko in her wake. She never failed to capture at least one person's notice on entering or leaving a room and would have been disappointed if she had not. Carole, at pains to ignore her, re-filled the kettle while Colin followed her with eyes and mouth open, momentarily distracted.

Julia left soon after, with less enthusiasm and more than a little envy as the scent of Maggie's perfume lingered behind. The last time Julia had worn expensive perfume was walking through Boots where she took a spray of Chanel No.5 from one of the testers. She again looked down at her cardigan, a reminder of everything she would never be or ever own.

The conversation in her head now revolved around whether or not she had said too much about Will, hinted too much about their problems. Maggie knew more than anyone what she had been through since school, but her marriage to Will was a different matter, one that was kept in check.

Chapter 21

Manchester

PHIL'S spare room was just that – spare – and empty beyond a cheap single bed that creaked on tottering legs. Apart from the bed, there was an old kitchen chair and a tea chest upon which sat a lamp with no bulb. A small rug covered the floorboards, not quite big enough to hide a large stain hiding underneath.

On waking up from his first night back on English soil, David, still in yesterday's shirt, almost fell out of the bed. It was lower and narrower than he'd expected, and in the process he kicked over an empty whisky bottle lying on the floor. He swore as he banged his toe, and remembering where he was, stumbled to the window to open the curtains. He shut them again when the bright light was too much. Stepping out into the hall, he looked for any sign of life.

'Phil,' he croaked, 'Are you up?'

All was quiet and still, enough to tell him the flat was

empty. He found the bathroom and had a pee in a toilet that boasted no lid and a broken white plastic seat, after which he stared at his reflection in the mirror above the sink. Two red orbs stared back. The remnants of a pink soap, ingrained with grime, and sitting in a pool of mush, were ignored; there was no hot water either. David splashed his face before rinsing his mouth to get rid of the taste of last night's whisky. Too late to realise that there was no towel, he used his sleeve. The bathroom was as bare as the bedroom, but with more stains and a worse smell. He opened the cabinet on the wall to find a pack of razors, shaving foam and a half-empty blister pack of diazepam. He shut the door and stroked his chin; three days growth scratched back.

'What the fuck am I doing here? You are such a loser Phil.'

The kitchen was next to be explored, but he went with little hope of finding anything comforting there. On a tiny Formica table, a hastily scribbled note was propped up beside a dripping ketchup bottle. 'Dave - Help yourself. Free after 1pm. See you at the refec. Phil.' Help himself to precisely what he wondered as he picked up the sauce bottle and inspected the dried dark crust around the lid. A key lay next to the note attached to a length of blue string and an empty cotton reel. They could have been back in student digs. And it had been a long time since anyone had called him Dave. Once Simone had called him 'Daveed', he'd stayed with David.

He filled the kettle and opened several cupboards before finding a jar of coffee and bag of solidified brown lumps purporting to be sugar. There was no milk in the fridge and after two mouthfuls of the bitter brew he threw it down the sink. Instead, David recovered the last cigarette from the pack in his jacket found hanging behind the door.

With little conscious effort, he thought of Simone back home. She was never far away from his mind, but this was not a good time for reflection; the need to focus on the day ahead was all consuming. The window in the kitchen stubbornly refused to open, sealed tight by years of grease and paint so the room soon filled with smoke. Outside below, in a tiny yard, sat a collection of overflowing bins and sodden cardboard boxes. A washing line swung to and fro, from which a lone forgotten sock swayed in the breeze. The gardens on the Rue Bel Homme would be littered with nothing more than russet and red autumn leaves – and even then, they would be raked up by the gardener, the one whose daughter Monique used to come twice a week to clean the apartment. David sighed at the memory of petite, pretty Monique. As well as keeping the place clean, she'd sometimes leave fresh croissants or brioche for them to come back to. He wondered what had happened to her since that night they'd shared a bottle of wine and got to know each other just a little better. He had barely given her a second thought until now.

David rinsed the remains of the brown sludge from the sink and swirled his cup under the tap, before searching out some aspirin in his wash bag and refilling the cup with water.

At least one part of his life was making progress. A meeting with Ryan, an agent, had been booked for the following week in London, with indications pointing to a discussion on publishing and terms of payment. Against all odds, the work covering all previous research on the Henrietta Papers was in a position to complete, spurred on at last by the urgency of his situation. All that was left before the final write-up was searching out references alluded to by Georges, and completing the links with George Monckton and East Yorkshire. After that, the first draft would be finished. The second wouldn't take too long; he could almost write it in his sleep, it had lived with him for so long. The work Georges had put in was first class and had not been wasted. He was almost excited at the thought, but then felt his chest tighten and threaten with the recurring stabbing pain that usually followed. He rubbed at it; that usually did the trick, along with a rest and his feet up. 'I must be getting old,' he thought swallowing a couple of tablets and heading again for the bathroom where he took a quick cool shower and no choice but to use the slimy, pink soap. He dried himself with a towel found in Phil's room and shaved using water from the kettle. Dressed in chinos and a clean shirt, he checked the contents of his wallet, collected the key from the kitchen table and left.

The bus station wasn't far, but it was still too early to meet Phil, so he decided to kill time at the pub they had been to last night. It was preferable to staying in Phil's flat any longer than necessary. The Falcon Arms was handy, just at the end of the street, and as soon as he walked in, the landlord greeted him from behind the bar.

'Thought you would have been out for the count today.' He was wiping hot steaming glasses fresh from the washer.

'Takes more than that, landlord,' David countered as he sat opposite.

'Ted,' he replied and held out his hand.

'David. Pleased to meet you.' Ted shook David's hand. 'And what can I get you, David?'

'I'll have a pint, please, landlord. For old times' sake.'

Ted laughed; David had only been in once before, but he liked him and knew that he could do with a few more punters like him to keep the business going. The bar was otherwise empty and the lunchtime regulars were yet to arrive, not that there were many nowadays. The older ones were dying off and the younger ones had drifted away to the new cafés and bars that were springing up like mushrooms in town, choosing tapas and mojitos over pies and pints. The pub, like Ted, hadn't changed much over the years and couldn't even be considered retro enough to entice the new breed of real ale punters back into the fold. The pub and its landlord were both getting old, an intractable pair that would very likely expire together one day. Ted had not been interested in anything new since the brewery suggested karaoke nights. He ignored that one, along with the rest of the ideas that had been put forward, and they had left him alone – for the time being. There was talk of a smoking ban, but as David lit up, Ted said that if that ever happened, he might as well close down on the same day. The yellowing paintwork was testament to the number of smokers who gathered in the bar and you could almost chew the thick smoke-laden air when you came in from the street.

But Ted knew how to serve an excellent pint: hand pulled, just the right temperature, not warm, but not so cold that you couldn't catch the taste at the back of your throat, and crowned with a thick, creamy head. He took great pride in his beer, it was a work of art that he had been perfecting since 1971, and this alone made certain that he carried with him a core of regulars that just about kept the pub open, and the brewery one step away from calling 'time' for good.

David hadn't realised how much he'd missed a decent pint and sat at the end of the bar with his glass as Ted restocked the mixers on the shelves behind. He liked the pub and after his second pint, decided that he wouldn't even mind being called Dave again. He'd tried introducing Simone to an English pint of bitter when they moved to England back in the sixties, but never managed to persuade her of its merits. After one sip, she screwed up her face and told him 'no thank you.'

As Ted held a one-sided conversation, David's thoughts made a gravitational pull back to Simone, back again to L'Etoile Verte. No other woman had come close in his estimation, even now, and he was certain that she would take him back when he'd finished here. He'd never lost sight of the girl who first stepped into his life: the energy and style of her, and those long legs encased in black. She had him on the first night he saw her, but she soon proved to be far more than a tight skirt with a seductive French accent. Intellectually, Simone was more than his equal.

David closed his eyes and saw Simone's face. Forgetting the anger and pain of their parting, he preferred to think about when they met and she'd shown him how to have fun on the cheap, taking him to cafés and clubs away from the tourist traps. It was Simone who opened up a world of jazz and blues bars where singers bared their souls and sang with a cigarette in one hand and a glass in the other. It was a world he readily embraced and didn't want to leave.

Ted returned to the bar and looked down at David's glass. It was empty apart from four white, foam rings, left from four deep draughts.

'Another?'

David looked at his watch.

'Why not, time for just one more.'

He keenly felt the delight of a pub at lunchtime; the ease of a relaxed pint when not having to rush back to work and the slow pace of a comforting afternoon nap after closing time. It slipped into his stream of consciousness as he remembered how it had once been part of life at university. But after the third pint, and a pleasurably heated conversation with Ted on the preferences of

Manchester City against United, he remembered Phil. He was sorry to leave, the banter had just begun to warm up as a couple of regulars, retired men with nothing better to do with their day, had found it hard to resist the urge to join in, slipping into the conversation with ease. David liked nothing more than holding court at a bar over football, creating a little controversy where he could, and stepping back when the arguments were in full flow. He almost stayed, but the obligation he felt towards meeting up with Phil eventually, but only just, won out. As he headed for the door, Ted called out, 'Hold on, I almost forgot! There was some woman asking after you when you'd left last night. Can't remember the name. Foreign sounding...big lady...colourful. Certainly not from round here.'

David shrugged – even he didn't even know he was coming to the pub himself until Phil led the way, so how could anyone else?

'Did she say what she wanted? Are you sure it was me she was after?'

'Described you pretty well. And now I come to think of it, she did mention the name David. But I never knew it then.' Ted finished wiping the last glass and draped the cloth over the end of the bar.

'Did she leave a number?'

'No – said she'd catch up with you up later.'

'Ok...thanks...see you.'

Chapter 22

By one in the afternoon, Phil had completed his morning's lectures and headed off for the refectory. He sat at a corner table with a Cornish pasty, an apple and a glass of milk. He resisted the jam-filled doughnut as the button on his trousers was already straining with the expansion of his waistline. Still, however crap the food, he reasoned that it was cheap and saved on cooking and washing up back at the flat. It was always 'the flat'; he could never refer to it as home. Home was where Jen lived with the girls, the three-bedroomed semi he'd been thrown out of once the arguments took on a menacing turn; the home where he'd picked up one too many wrong-number calls. One year on, he still seethed over what little he was left with after the divorce. Apart from his clothes and a few CDs, there wasn't much to show for thirteen years of marriage, and he still had to pay maintenance every month. She'd sworn blind there was no-one else, but when the girls had let it slip that Uncle Malcolm had taken them all out for a burger at Wimpy's on Jen's birthday, no more proof was needed. Bitterness didn't begin to describe the gut-wrenching jealousy he felt whenever he thought of them together in the bed that had once been his.

Unfortunately, the visit to David and Simone in Paris had not achieved the outcome he'd hoped for either. In fact, just the opposite and the decision he'd taken in the aftermath of rejection was something he was still living with. The loan he'd asked David for wasn't a big deal. Looking at their lifestyle, it was nothing. He hadn't intended to go as far as he did with his revelations to Simone and his own thoughts on the subject, but it was too late now to do anything about it. David had always come up smelling of roses no matter how many times the past caught up with him but it looked like this time even David wasn't going to get away without paying. This didn't stop the strain of the visit and the gnawing question of whether or not Simone had told David what was said between them.

Phil licked his finger and picked at the crumbs left on his plate. He was still hungry. He pushed away the image of Simone that stubbornly lodged in his head; she didn't deserve any of it. She was the innocent one and Phil had made her suffer with words that should have remained unsaid. It was between him and David, no one else. The look on her face told him all he needed to know about his error of judgement and he regretted it. He loved Simone. But what did it matter now; she wouldn't give him a second thought. Phil's visit was cut short and he didn't get the chance to retract anything.

David turned up at the refec just as Phil was wiping sugar from a compensatory doughnut around his mouth.

'You look wrecked,' David said as he pulled up a chair and set down a mug of black coffee and a ham sandwich. He opened it to look at the pallid slices inside and pulled a face at the meagre filling, before facing Phil, 'You weren't that bad yesterday.'

'Not until you got me wrecked, I wasn't,' Phil scowled.

David had always despised Phil's self-pitying whine; it was nothing new, but he wouldn't be drawn in and took a bite of the sandwich. As he recalled, Phil hadn't objected to drinking with him at the time. As far as he could remember, Phil hadn't paid for that many rounds either. But for now, David kept quiet. He needed the room in the flat, even if it belonged to someone he despised. Once he had what he'd come for, he was out and back to France.

'Have you finished for the day?' he asked, changing the subject before Phil could continue.

Phil nodded with a mouthful of milk.

'Till ten tomorrow,' he replied.

'Good, good.' David took another bite. The sandwich was tasteless, but there was no food at Phil's flat. He was ravenous by now and money was too tight to be choosy.

'We haven't really talked yet about what your plans are,' Phil said, again mopping the plate with his finger, but this time more enthusiastically when it was sugar. Putting it down on the table, he asked as casually as possible, 'Heard from Simone?'

Without looking up, David replied, 'No, not yet. She wants to work something out and see if it suits us both without resorting to the courts. I'm waiting for her to get back to me. I've got enough to keep me going for a couple of months. But after that…'

'You really don't think you'll get back together then? Once it's all blown over…'

'The marriage is over, Phil. I've been stupid.' Although he didn't believe this for one minute, there was no way he wanted to get back into that discussion after last night. Phil looked away, not sure what to say. If it hadn't been for the pain that Simone was going through, he might have felt that some form of divine justice had happened.

'How could you let someone like Simone go? You had everything, mate. If you…' David cut him short.

'Water under the bridge, Phil. I know what a bastard I've been. And besides, I think Simone might be seeing someone else.'

'Did she tell you that?' Phil was relieved to think that their split might have reasons other than his revelation. He still had no idea how much David knew and he wasn't about to ask.

'No. But I'm pretty sure something's been going on. Let's face it; I've had enough experience… I can pick up the signs.' David half smiled as he said it. 'Can we drop the subject now, please? I think we pretty well covered it yesterday.'

Phil's head remained bent towards the table but lifted just enough to look at him through hooded eyes. He thought better of saying anything else and David wasn't about to give him the opportunity. David pushed away the half-drunk coffee that tasted only fractionally better than the cheap stuff at Phil's flat.

'Come on,' he urged Phil, standing up, 'should be quiet in the bar now. What do you say?' He couldn't resist watching him squirm; it was too easy when he had no idea how much David knew.

There was nothing Phil wanted less, but his need to find out more about David's plans overrode the disinclination that told him it would not be a good idea. He could smell the beer on David's breath when he leant towards him and said, 'you owe me that much don't you think?' Phil was in no position to argue and allowed himself to be steered in the direction of the union bar, despite the pile of work sitting in the bag at his feet. He knew that it wouldn't be looked at now until tomorrow.

David was right; the bar was quiet. He'd poked his head through the door on his way to the refectory to see if it looked the same as it had in their day as students. It didn't, of course, the ancient wooden tables and benches had all been replaced with padded chairs, drop lighting and modern art on the walls. It didn't seem right somehow, but it would have to do and it suited his purpose to ply Phil with alcohol to keep him on side while he needed a place to stay. They found two seats at the far end of the room, where David sat with a pint of bitter. Phil nursed a Coke and scowled when he realised it had been laced with Bacardi.

At the bar, a student in dreadlocks was talking to two first year girls. The buzz of freshers' week had fired them with a new-found confidence as they realised there was no one around any more to tell them 'no, you can't.' They giggled and flirted, soaking up promises of the night ahead. Other students drifted in and out, but no one was buying much. It wouldn't fill up until much later. A metallic clatter came from the kitchens at the far end of the corridor as lunches were finished, but apart from that, the place was dead. David remembered how it had been when they were students, many years ago. 'Ever wish you could go back, Phil? Relive some of the good times?'

Phil turned to David, 'That's just it; you can't turn the clock back, can you?'

'You're a miserable bastard today. You can't have had that much last night, so spit it out, what's your problem? Is it Jen? Is she trying to squeeze you for a bit more? You've got a great life here. The job's not that hard; you're on your own; and you can come and go as you please.'

'I need to go…'

'No you don't. Sit down. Relax and stop stressing...always your problem.'

'Look if this is about what I said in Paris, just get it out of the way. I'm sorry for what happened, but I can't take it back now.' Phil rubbed his face with both hands, desperate to get away. Even the flat beckoned to him as refuge from David's company, momentarily forgetting that David was staying there with him. Was there no escape?

'What are you talking about? If it's because I wouldn't lend you the money, I'm sorry, but you have to work these things out for yourself, and right now I'm skint too you know'

'I need to talk to you about something else.'

'Then fire away. Get it off your chest for God's sake. I'm supposed to be the one with the problems here, not you...for once.'

A girl with braided hair walked past in tight jeans and a scarf tied Fulham-style around her neck. David raised an eyebrow, 'Plenty of young ladies around here. What more do you want?' He looked towards the bar where the other group of giggling girls had already gone.

'It's Simone, she ...she...' He struggled to find the right words.

'...What about Simone?' he interrupted, impatient to be finished with the subject of his life. 'She knows. I know. You know. I'm an idiot. What more is there to be said?'

Phil decided that there was no more to be said, today at least, preferring to leave the facts of the situation for another day.

David really wasn't in the mood for a heart to heart. He'd had enough of that with Simone before he'd left. Her vitriolic condemnation of their relationship was the last conversation they had had together and it still rang in his ears. That one would take some moving on from. He certainly didn't want to go over it with Phil. He was the last person on his list of sympathetic ears.

Although David and Phil had known each other since the early days of starting university, they were no closer now than when they'd first met. Even so, Phil had always managed to appear at regular intervals in his life. They'd met at freshers, initially bonding over a shared support of City over United. In the beginning they would even go to the occasional game together. Afterwards, over a couple of pints, they would bask in the glory of a win, or drown in the sorrows of a loss, but beyond that there had been little else to cement any real friendship. As time went by, David's circle had broadened and he moved on leaving Phil trailing in the wake of reflected popularity. And David had let him, if only for the occasions when he had relied on the loans, the lifts and the alibis.

Phil had few friends and those that tolerated his presence did so under sufferance for the same reasons. It was a standing joke that he was still a virgin, even by the end of the second year, and it was often claimed that he couldn't even pull a pint. Even Jen was originally David's date, one of his rejects that Phil managed to summon up the courage to ask out. He found her in tears and alone at their table in the union bar, face streaked with black mascara, and he'd offered her a hanky. Phil couldn't understand how David could dump her so easily in the middle of a date. As it turned out, she was grateful for the attention and said yes to his advances after drinking far too much and watching David fondle another girl on the dance floor. Jen wanted to make him jealous, but when David saw her with Phil he was relieved more than anything else. The plot further backfired when she found herself in Phil's bed the next morning and realised that her place too, in David's life, was lower than she had led herself to believe. Jen stayed with

Phil in the belief that even he was better than no boyfriend at all and when she became pregnant, they married.

THE BLONDE FRESHER, who David thought had looked vaguely familiar, came back into the bar, giving him the opportunity to inspect her more closely. 'I'm going back to the bar', he told Phil, just as the blonde girl was joined by a boy with fair, curly hair. She smiled at something he said and they stood conspiratorially close, comfortable in each other's presence. She nodded in agreement and gave him a lingering kiss on the mouth before the boy walked past David and towards a morose Phil, still sitting on his own. He had been about to make his escape when David reached the bar, but stayed put at the request of the boy who was from one of his tutorial groups. That was nicely timed, thought David and continued to get refills.

'David! Hallo.'

The French accent caught him off guard. There was a fleeting moment of incomprehension and he looked behind in expectation of another David standing there. But it didn't take him long to place the young girl who, not so long ago, had been struggling at the airport with a young boy and a baby. He smiled broadly at the recollection, amazed that they should come across each other again. She really was so very young and he was glad that he had not embarrassed himself by asking for her number. Instead, he looked around in mock amazement,

'What no children? Don't tell me you left them at the airport when you'd had enough of them?' She laughed openly.

'No!'

'Well, it's good to see you. Amazing coincidence…what happened to them? The little boy,…what was his name?'

'Leon? I hand him back! Horrid little boy…far too demanding…and his sweet brother…mmm. At the end of summer, I get my money and come here as I always intend. I finish work for their parents and am back at my studies now. Final year!'

'You seem to have picked up English pretty quickly too.'

'Of course, my mother is English and that is mostly as we speak at home.' She paused and David raised an eyebrow.

'Sorry. I just wanted you to speak to me in French… which, as I remember, was just as good as my English.'

'Fair enough…what are you studying…apart from hapless middle-aged men who offer help to a maiden in distress?'

She gave David a quizzical look, hoping it wasn't a chat-up line. He was way too old and definitely overweight, although there was something about the eyes that drew her in. Not that she was in the least tempted; Michael was more than enough to handle right now.

'English lit.'

'Excellent…join me?'

She pointed out the tall curly haired student speaking to Phil.

'I'm with someone, but thanks anyway. That's my boyfriend over there.'

'Another time maybe,' and David looked more closely at the boyfriend

'He looks familiar.'

'You know him?' she asked.

'No, but I'm staying with the man he's talking to, his tutor. We've known each other since we were both students here.'

'Amazing…he's not moved far then.'

Phil had turned in their direction, talking all the while to Cecille's boyfriend, but turning in his seat so as not to lose sight of them. Michael was animated and spoke with his hands as much as his mouth and David studied the profile, sure that perhaps they had met before.

Cecille drew him back to the conversation. 'Maybe we could all go for a drink some time, yes? Then you'll know if you've met'

'Yes, perhaps we could. I'd like that,' David countered.

On impulse, she wrote down her number on the back of a flyer left on the bar.

'For now, I have a lecture to get to'

'I'll see you later, then. Bye for now.'

'A bientot, David.'

It wasn't so long ago, he would have arranged a day and time and he mused on the vagaries of life. At one time, where possibilities presented themselves, he felt almost obliged to take them up. Now, he wasn't so sure. 'Christ I must be getting old,' he mused, and the tightness in his chest confirmed the fact.

Phil and the student had now finished talking; the boy was stuffing a sheaf of papers back into his bag. David took the opportunity and walked over.

'Please, don't let me interrupt.' David motioned to the boy to continue who was making a move to leave.

'No, we've finished,' said Phil, 'There's nothing else is there, Michael?'

'No, that's fine, thank you.' He looked at David, 'History timetabling. Nightmare.'

'Ah, I remember it well. I came here too…with Phil as a matter of fact…back in the day. It's changed a bit since then…uni that is. Subject pretty much stays the same though, just different views…unless of course something fascinating and mind blowing happens to be unearthed.'

'Right…'Michael paused, 'I don't think there's much more to add to my field at the moment though, apart from interpretation maybe.'

'What's that, then?'

'Seventeenth century. Politics; French involvement in Britain at the mo.'

David pursed his lips in response, then held out his hand, 'David, by the way. Pleased to meet you.'

'Michael.'

Michael nodded and held out his hand.

If it wasn't exactly a mirror moment for either of the men, there was a flash of inexplicable recognition, enough almost to tempt Michael into accepting David's invitation to join him and Phil for a drink. David had already placed two pints of lager on the table.

'Join us?'

'No…thanks all the same but better not…saving myself for later.'

'The bitter's crap here, so I thought we should stick to lager,' David proffered, warming to his subject until Phil encouraged Michael to leave.

'Michael's one of my final year students. Plenty to do… don't want to hold him up'. His face was flushed as he turned to Michael, 'I'll see you later, then…OK?'

But when David broached the subject of what he had come to do, it piqued Michael's interest and he was no longer in quite such in a hurry to leave. His course was getting stale, his interest waning, and this sounded far more compelling. Ignoring Phil, who shifted uncomfortably in his seat and morosely looked on, Michael sat back down and they struck up a brief conversation.

David, feeling a little more generous with his time after a fourth pint, continued the conversation and asked a couple of pertinent questions. He took even more of an interest when he discovered that part of Michael's studies were along similar lines to his own research. He pulled his chair in closer, grateful for a conversation that actually drew him in. Phil kept looking at his watch, but he might as well not have been there. These two had much in common. David was more than happy to bask in a newfound enthusiasm for his subject and warmed to Michael. There was something about him that reminded him of himself at the same age. After half an hour, Phil was dispatched to the bar for more drinks.

'Not for me…I've really got to get off now, but it's been great talking to you. Maybe we could meet up again soon?'

When Phil left them, Michael gave his number to David. He also extracted a promise that they would talk again later in the week. David looked down at the scrap of paper; two invitations, one number, within one hour. Life was getting interesting.

'Great kid,' David commented on Phil's return. Phil's agitation had largely gone unnoticed. He downed the Coke and handed over the lager, insisting that he too had to leave.

'What, off already?' David sat back in his seat, thinking that perhaps the lager wasn't too bad after all.

'I have to…there's a few things I need to do in the office before I catch Michael later.

'Ok, I'll see you up at the flat when you've finished.' He then recalled the start of their earlier conversation.

'By the way, what did you want to tell me before?' David felt a little more generous towards Phil, enough to actually listen.

'Nah…nothing much…it'll keep. I'll see you later.'

'Ok…fine'

David took his drink back to the bar and looked for more congenial company but all was quiet, even the barman had nothing to say; not like Ted at the Falcon. He perched on a bar stool and thought about the Henrietta Papers, about Simone, and what he needed to do to get his life back on track.

A niggle of uncertainty was dismissed; there could be no doubts in his mind that everything had a solution, including his marriage. The alternative was unthinkable. He left another two empty glasses on the bar and headed back to the flat. He was due in London soon and more than happy to be leaving Phil again.

Chapter 23

The week after meeting David, Michael looked up at
Cecille sitting at the other end of the bed and wondered
how long she was going to stay. He was torn between
wanting his own space where the obstacles of Cecille and
her numerous belongings were not in the way, and the
pleasure of sharing a bed when he had time on his hands
at night, and no money with which to go out. Taking a
room in the house next to hers brought a cheaper option
than the one he'd left. It felt right at the time but soon after
he began to regret it. At times it was like being locked in a
cage where the bars keep closing in. She was too demanding. It had taken only a week for her to virtually move in.
How did he let that happen? Then he remembered.

Constantly short of money, precariously living from
one grant to the next, it was his saving grace when Cecille
received emergency funding from her parents. They
wanted her to live within her means but were not averse to
helping out when she pleaded poverty. And it would have
been good apart from the fact that she took up too much
room with her shoes (just in case we go out), clothes (I need

to change first), toothbrush and make up (shall I stay the night?) They spread around like spores blown from a dandelion. They were taking root, laying territorial rights, staking a claim.

'What is it?' she asked, looking up from her book and seeing him staring at her.

'I need to get on with some work.'

She stretched out her arms, yawning, 'I'm hungry.'

'There's a sausage roll in the fridge.'

'I bought that last week with three others…it's mouldy. Come round to mine, I've got bread left. We can make toast…you love toast,'

'Love to, but I've got to meet Phil in an hour and then David again, this afternoon, before he goes to London.'

'Please yourself,' she shrugged. You've seen more of them than me recently. I feel usurped.'

'And I have a dissertation that won't keep. Some of us do more than simper over Jane Austen.'

She threw a cushion at him, annoyed when he dismissed her course over his own, especially when she was in line for a first and he still struggled at a 2:1. Nevertheless he took it as an invitation to play, grabbed her and pulled off her top. She didn't resist but barely half an hour later, when his mind was already elsewhere, he jumped out of bed.

'I'm going for a shower.'

Michael's mood swings exasperated Cecille and she never quite knew where she stood in the relationship. He wanted her when it suited, made her feel like she really was the most important thing in his life, then at other times, she felt used. There were days when they were absolutely right for each other but they were getting few and far between. Listening to Michael in the shower, she thought of the good times: coming back from a night out, amazing evenings spent inside listening to music and smoking a little weed, it was perfect then, and once he'd even told her that he loved her. Then the next day he would make it obvious he wanted to be on his own, saying there was something he had to do, by himself, in peace and quiet, or some place he had to be that didn't include her, like now.

Cecille was still in the rumpled bed when he came out of the bathroom and he made no attempt to hide the fact that he wasn't too happy to see she hadn't moved. Cecille feigned indifference, unwilling to go anywhere at that moment. She crawled out to him and threw her arms around his still damp neck, 'I can

always go back to being a nanny if we are so desperate for money,

'Good God Cecille, we're not that desperate…anyway your Dad always bails you out.'

'Mmm…' she frowned but knew he was right.

'Tell me what you know about this David someone-or-other? He's not a lecturer is he?'

'No…not exactly. I met him through Phil.'

She did not tell him that they had already met and was secretly hoping that they might bump into each other again one day. He had a presence that intrigued her, something Michael had yet to master. Michael pushed her away from him, back to the bed

'I really do have to go.'

She knew defeat when faced with it. Underneath the flamboyant personality, he had a temper that simmered on the back burner before boiling over and although it didn't happen often, she knew when to back off. She was not impressed by the abrupt dismissal, but wouldn't risk him getting angry again. Recently he was always angry about something, more than usual. He hadn't always been like this and she wasn't sure how to handle it – or even if she wanted to.

'Ok, I get the message. I suppose I should go and get something done myself. Will I see you tonight?'

'Can we leave it until the weekend? I've got a lot to get through.'

'Sure…maybe you will be in a better mood by then.'

Cecille bounced off the bed to get dressed, trying to keep her feelings light. Before she left, she planted a kiss on the top of his head,

'See you later, Monsieur Grumpy.'

Michael looked across with a half smile as she went out, wondering why she wanted to stay with him. There was no space for anyone in his life right now he decided; she would have to go.

A more pressing problem than Cecille was the bank statement that arrived this morning. He checked the figures again, but they hadn't miraculously changed. The account was way overdrawn and with no time to take up a part-time job, the bank wouldn't extend his already outstanding overdraft. Julia's monthly letter, which usually remained unread, was gratefully received if only for the two tenners she slipped inside. If the money didn't go far, it gave him a reasonable night out in between uni work and a few basics. Cecille fared better but he resented having to ask for a sub. She made a fortune from the nanny summer job but that and the regular allowance from her parents rapidly disap-peared on shopping trips into town.

Michael collected together the mass of papers spread around on the table and meticulously put them back into order. Forgetting about Cecille and money worries, he moved on to thinking about the issues he wanted to discuss with David. It went through his mind that it was a pity

David wasn't his tutor instead of Phil as he fastened his bag and searched around for the door key.

MICHAEL HAD AGREED to meet David at the uni bar after two. Recently, this had become their regular meeting place. It was as good as any and fairly quiet in the afternoon. No real thought was given to David's choice of location at first, and the fact that he managed to down two or three pints every time wasn't questioned, but Michael was beginning to wonder if a drinking problem lay at the root of the fact that David's hand always shook when he reached for his glass. If there was a problem, it was well hidden otherwise.

This morning, David had sounded vague on the phone, as though his mind was elsewhere, but Michael was just pleased that their meeting hadn't been cancelled. They were getting on really well and the connection between them both was amazing, evident in mannerisms and attitude, as well as work, and an appreciation of the young women who happened to pass by.

David wasn't there when Michael arrived. He scanned the almost empty room and went to their usual table at the far end, a spot where they were guaranteed to be free from interruption, but after over half an hour, Michael was still sitting on his own. He was on the point of leaving when David walked in looking strained and even more crumpled than usual. He went straight to the bar, looked round for Michael and gestured across to ask if he wanted a drink. Michael held up his glass and mouthed 'No, thanks, I'm fine.'

Shortly after, David came across with a pint of lager, less a large mouthful taken at the bar, and sat down to join Michael.

'So, how's the dissertation going?' There was no mention of the fact that he was late, so Michael let it pass.

'Slow. One or two gaps I need to fill, but it's coming along ok. There's a few things I'd like to ask your opinion on though, if you don't mind?'

'Not at all, you fire away. I don't know how much of a help I'm being to you, but while I'm still around I'll do what I can.' He took another large swig of his drink and started to relax,

'Don't you see Phil much? He really should be the one to talk to.'

'No…not really. I mean…he's great with me when I see him. But…and don't get me wrong here, I just think a different perspective can be a good thing sometimes… and you've been really helpful on that.'

Michael knew that David was leaving soon to continue his own research up in Yorkshire and was fascinated by the mysterious Henrietta Papers. He was intrigued as to why the work had not been completed long ago. The talk of sudden illnesses and untimely deaths meant nothing to Michael and sounded like vague excuses. How hard could it be? He would give anything to be in that position, to work on something so original. He'd work for free if he didn't have the dissertation to finish. As time passed, he accepted that realistically any job prospect would centre on teaching, but the thought didn't thrill him. David's experiences confirmed what he knew already; teaching was not his vocation in life either. After enrolment, he hadn't considered much beyond student life and what he enjoyed, but now he was at the stage of finishing the dissertation, he had no idea where to head next. As his final year was coming to a close, work was still a distant and unattainable prospect. One thing he was sure of though was that he did not want to end up like Phil.

There was a big world out there and he wanted to explore it.

Over the next hour, they worked well together; probing, questioning; expanding ideas that Michael had not considered before. It was as though it had been common practice for much longer than the short while they had known each other; heads close together in a shared interest. Even David had found himself looking forward to their sessions and in a short space of time they developed a mutual respect and friendship. David also considered that Michael might also be useful to him on his own research. He couldn't explain why he was so drawn to him, beyond their interest in seventeenth century France, but it felt good.

The working part of their meeting came to a close and Michael relented enough to join David for a drink back at the bar. Relaxed in each other's company the conversation took a more personal turn.

'I won't be able to join you next week I'm afraid…off up to Yorkshire for a few days…following up a few leads and references at the Regional Archives.'

'You might get to meet my Mum, then.'

David raised an eyebrow.

'Oh yes?'

'Yeah, she works in the archives up there…has done for years.'

'What's her name; I'll be there anyway and can look her up…tell your Mum how much you're missing her.'

Michael laughed, 'It's Julia…Julia Sanderson.'

David took another mouthful before replying.

'So…is that where you're from originally'

'Yeah, lived there all my life…couldn't wait to leave though…I prefer it here'

'Your Mum must miss you'

'Suppose…but she's got Dad'

'And what does Dad do?'

'Stepdad actually…Will's an accountant. Married Mum when I was nine.'

David studied Michael's face, curiously drawn by a compulsion to get to know more. He didn't want to appear too curious, but Michael was more than happy to furnish a few more details of where he'd grown up and life with his Mum, and before long, David kept him in conversation when he bought another round.

'So that's where you're from originally?' He wanted to confirm.

'Mmm, a small village just outside Hull, you won't have heard of it.'

David badly wanted a cigarette, he had run out but with each revelation of Michael's life, he stayed, transfixed.

'Mum's a senior archivist. You should ask for her, she's good. She's the one that got me interested in history in the first place. There's no way I was going into accountancy… I'd die of boredom after the first week.'

'Yes. Yes, I'm sure she is…good that is.'

'Tell her I sent you. Tell her I'm working hard. She thinks I'm out too much having a good time… probably because I usually make the duty calls from the bar.' They both smiled at the mutual understanding that university life involved more than just work and that the bar was an essential part of life.

David studied Michael's strangely familiar profile, working out that he must be what, no more than, twenty, twenty-one perhaps? Straight from school to university probably. But then they all looked young and fresh-faced. There was so much more that he wanted to know but wouldn't push it. The world opening up before him was something he hardly dared contemplate when the enormity of it threatened to overwhelm him. The lager sat full and forgotten on the table as his mind came sharply into focus.

'Was your mother a brilliant scholar…like you?'

'I'm sure she could have been…and better than me from what Gran says. Apparently, she was the first one in the family with brains. First to go to uni and all that…but it took some time to get there. She had a few problems to get over first.'

'I guess we all have our problems somewhere along the line.'

'Having me just after her sixteenth birthday was hers. It took me some time to work that one out, but then again, it's not something you think about as a child. Your parents are old, full stop. But mine isn't, at least not *my* mother.'

'Your stepdad is older then?'

'No, not really, they're roughly the same age. Knew each other at school, even had a date once he told me, but she dumped him and then he left school early, before doing 'A' levels. Told no one. They only met up again when he came back…although god knows why anyone would want to go back there.'

David tried to recall a Will from school but most of those days had long gone. There was nothing there that he'd cared to keep hold of. Until now. This was different and he struggled.

'I never met my real Dad…never really knew what happened to him…just he moved away, that's all. Mum never liked to talk about it, drove Gran mad but she wouldn't. Anyway…water under the bridge…couldn't care less to be honest with you. I think it was a big deal at the time, but really…now?'

David remained silent, taking it all in, absorbing, computing each fact he was given.

'Sorry I must be boring you with all this…never spoken to anyone before about it. Taboo subject at home soo…'

Nothing was lost on David, his eyes searching Michael's face as if trying to grasp an elusive thread of memory that would not be caught.

Michael brushed his fingers through his hair, mirroring David's action moments earlier, then stood up. He'd never even told Cecille about his childhood yet, or taken her home to meet his Mum. He'd said too much. Why would anyone else be remotely interested, let alone David who he had only just met?

'Sorry, but I'm going to have to go now. I've got to take these books back before I get another hefty fine.'

'Sure, that's ok. As I said, I'm away for a few days from Wednesday, but I'll be in touch when I get back.'

Michael hoped that David wasn't too put off by the family revelations, but surprisingly, he seemed almost interested.

'Hope so, you've been a big help and I'm grateful. And good luck with your book. I can't wait to read it.'

Michael held out his hand and David shook it firmly, holding it a little longer than he had intended, while his left hand rubbed at the shooting pain under his ribs.

'You ok?'

'Yes…it's nothing…touch of indigestion…I'll see you soon…when I get back, Michael. And the family thing… we all have a story to tell somewhere down the line… makes us who we are.'

Michael smiled and left. David sat back in his seat and finished the pint. He wiped his mouth with the back of his hand and went back over their conversation, trying to get the year right. Was it sixty-eight or sixty-nine, when he and Simone had moved back to France? All he could remember was the energy of leaving, the endless packing and clearing the house; and the excitement of Paris.

Of course he remembered Julia, the young girl he'd taught history in year five, the one so eager to please; the one who'd turned up on his doorstep on the first day of the summer holiday, so pretty and oh so keen. The kiss on the night of the school dance; of course, that's where it all started. That's all it was, but then she'd come back for more. He tried to remember the day she came to his house, but the more he chased down that road, the more it tantalised with a glimpse, then turned the corner and disappeared. It was just one day; over before it started; a pleasant distraction at the beginning of a long summer that continued and ended in Paris.

David couldn't breathe in the stuffy warm air of the refectory and headed outside for a cigarette. There were too many questions he couldn't answer, so he made for the only place he could relax since coming back, the bar at the Falcon where he could openly talk football and enjoy Ted's company for an hour or two.

London, and the agent Georges had put him in contact with, loomed large and the business of the book had to be sorted out before anything else. The rest would have to wait until he got back.

The temperature outside had plummeted as it approached teatime and it was getting dark. Lights at the windows of the red brick building cast long shadows outside. It felt cold and damp. David shivered and pulled on his overcoat, heading back from the bus, towards the Falcon, a better prospect than Phil's flat at that moment.

Chapter 24

London

THE CRICHTON AGENCY was on the third floor of a narrow building in Holborn. The dark blue paintwork on the door was peeling, but past experiences of London taught David that nothing was ever as it seemed on the outside. The traffic was thick and impenetrable, but had it always been *this* bad? It took longer than expected to reach the office and in reality, his knowledge of London had lapsed since the occasional visit in the eighties to music gigs with a few mates he kept in touch with. The last one in particular worked well with Simone's business trip. Watching Dylan at the Hammersmith Odeon was a night to remember. It blew them away so much they went back for a second night and were lucky enough to get tickets. Simone had dinner with clients leaving him free to enjoy the music. He looked back fondly on those days. Life was easy then.

The plaque on the wall was weathered and grained

and he couldn't hear whether or not the bell underneath was working, but after a lengthy wait, the small grille beside it buzzed and a woman's voice, cracked and muffled, asked who was calling.

'David Weston for Ryan Pierce.'

A short click released the lock.

'Come up.'

The stairs were steep and led to another door equally in need of paint.

The tiny office was occupied by a middle-aged woman with a flushed face and greying hair fighting its way out from a few clips at the top of her head. She wore little make up beyond a smear of lipstick, and with a slight nod of her head, gave him a brief unsmiling glance of acknowledgement. David was clearly an intrusion she could do without. Her desk, pushed into a corner, was overflowing with an untidy pile of papers and files. She continued tapping at a keyboard with remarkable speed, and again motioned with a nod of her head, 'You can sit over there; Mr Ryan will be with you soon,' and continued with her work. It was obvious that she would broker no further interruption.

David looked behind to see a single chair pressed against the wall and hoped he'd made the right choice of agent. Ryan had come out top over three others he investigated and was very interested when they had first spoken on the phone. In fact, the reason he had approached him originally, was that Georges had his name on file. It was too late in the day to go scouting around the others anyway. Money was getting tight and the thought of staying a day longer than necessary with Phil was not an option up for consideration.

He needed a strong coffee but soon realised that one would not be on offer any time soon. The woman opposite was still typing furiously; she hadn't looked up since he sat down and hardly paused for a break, so it was unlikely that water, let alone coffee would come his way.

David checked his watch, refusing to consider that the work might not be accepted; he knew it was exceptional. He rubbed his neck and circulated his head in an attempt to dislodge the nagging pain he had felt since leaving Phil's, but his main concern was only whether Georges had given the name of the right person to do the Papers justice. With no plan B, and an abhorrence to ask Simone for any more money, he would pull out all the stops and hope for the best. He had long since been convinced of the authenticity of the documents and was confident that the world beyond, starting with Ryan, would be ready to respond with a great deal of interest.

Ryan was at that moment looking over the paperwork that had previously been set up to broker a deal with Georges. On top lay David's letter informing him of Georges' death and asking to see him. He finished the last mouthful of coffee, straightened the pile of papers in front of several other ongoing concerns and decided that it would still be worth his time.

'Sorry to keep you waiting but I had an urgent call to take.' A tall, lean man looking somewhere in his late forties, but perhaps older, came out of the room behind the typist and squeezed past. He held out his hand to David. 'Come on through to my office. Sorry it's so cramped...we're waiting for something bigger on the next floor when they get round to finishing the re-furb.'

'That's ok. I'm getting used to cramped premises.'

'You're staying in London, then?'

'No, I've got a friend in Manchester...handy for my needs at the moment, but I'll be going up to Yorkshire pretty soon to follow up the final leads for the book.'

'Good…good…well it's nice to meet you David. I was really shocked to hear about Georges. You were a friend of his?'

'Yes…known him since I was a student in Paris.'

'Come on through.'

The clacking of the keyboard abruptly stopped and a printer sprang into life as they both made their way to the office.

David Weston and Ryan Pierce were probably roughly the same age, but the difference in appearance couldn't have been more pronounced. Lean, fit and freshly shaven, Ryan exuded a scent of expensive cologne, subtle and woody, David bore the scent of the remains of the pink soap. Casually dressed in white tee-shirt, dark blue trousers and grey, unbuttoned jacket, his hair was cropped short and neat. 'Let me get you a coffee.' He looked back at the woman. 'Would you mind Lynette?' Lynette scowled and looked at the pile of work in front of her, before asking David how he liked it. 'Black…no sugar.' Lynette replied without looking up, 'Just give me a sec and I'll bring it in'.

Ryan led David through to the inner sanctum where he was offered the only spare chair available in the room, each weighing the other up before either spoke again.

'So…' Ryan was the first to speak as he sat back in his chair looking David square in the face, and trying to judge what to make of him. David had been in too much of a hurry to shave that morning and his shirt, though clean, had not met an iron.

'I was really sorry to hear about Georges. I wondered why he hadn't been in touch recently…not like him at all.'

'I know. I didn't realise how ill he was…only saw him a couple of days before he died too.'

'He was an amazing man…so enthusiastic, and enigmatic. I'm really sorry I won't see him again.'

Before David could reply, he was overtaken by a bout of coughing.

'Would you like a glass of water?'

David nodded, unable to speak the words that he would prefer the coffee brought in by Lynette, laced with cognac. He took the glass fetched by Ryan from down the hall and gratefully drank until restored enough to continue.

'I'll be straight with you, David, I'm only seeing you because Georges did mention your name once or twice in the past as someone he wanted to work with. But you weren't too keen back then, I think? Why was that? And why now?'

'No...I wasn't in a position to take it up then...too much going on...but when we met later, curiosity got the better of me. I hadn't been certain of their authenticity...'

'But you are now I hope?'

David paused, uncertain where the conversation was leading, before replying with a question of his own.

'How did *you* meet Georges...you're a long way from Paris.'

'Publishers and writers conference a few years back in France...I specialise in Anglo-French histories. I was also intrigued by the back-story given to me by Sybil as to why they hadn't seen the light of day before now. Well I say intrigued....I really don't know what to make of what she told me...strange visitors in the night...the warnings...all very odd. I wondered about her mental heath at the time.'

'Poor Sybil. You know she never recovered after the death of their daughter?'

'Yes, I heard. Georges told me something of what she'd been through.'

Ryan relaxed a little more; there was something about David's manner and expression when talking about

Georges and Sybil that resonated with care and affection. He obviously thought well of the old man.

'I do know that Georges was well respected at the Archives and no doubt would have published earlier if circumstances had been different. Life just got in the way and held him up. What do you know about how he got hold of them?' Ryan was keen to fill in any gaps of what he already knew.

'He told me long ago that he'd found them in an old chest left behind at the apartment they'd lived in some time before…bundled together in old newspapers with notes tucked inside dating back to the 1850s. When Georges realised what he had in his possession, they started to take up more time and energy than he could spare but eventually it was Sybil's illness that put paid to his plans. They were going to establish his reputation and make a decent profit, but sadly he never made it that far.'

'Right.' Ryan nodded, hiding disappointment that there was still work to be done on the initial draft. 'I have to say that the book has been a long time coming. One or two publishers I have in mind are keen to see more…I was hoping to show them something quite soon. How far on are you with it?'

'It's almost finished…won't be long,' David lied, but confident that given a deadline, he would focus better.

The downturned mouth told David all he needed to know of Ryan's scepticism.

'Georges and I met only briefly…I was visiting another client at the time, but he insisted I look at the Papers… wanted me to know exactly what he had. I'm not a complete novice…but he convinced me.'

David had already scanned the shelves of published works behind the desk, concluding that they were sufficient

reference to Ryan's credentials, if indeed he was the insti-
gator of their publication.

'You mentioned that it was almost done when we spoke
on the phone last week. Has there been a problem since
then?' He watched David's shaking hand as he reached
over for the coffee that Lynette brought into the office, and
took note of his bloodshot eyes. He was convinced that
Georges had been going the same way too in the time he'd
known him. As David sipped the hot drink, black and
strong — how did she know? — conversation danced around
logistics and a timetable of the project until Ryan finally
spoke the words that David was waiting to hear. 'I've got
the name of one particular publisher I think we can get
you signed up with pretty soon if all goes well. He wants to
take a look at a completed draft as soon as it's ready — if
that's all right with you?'

It was more than all right and gave David the incentive
he had been hoping for. He too relaxed a little more and
sat back in his chair as they discussed a proposed date for
completion. It was agreed that within weeks rather than
months it would be ready. In the meantime, David
broached the subject of an advance. Ryan did not exactly
dismiss it out of hand, but told him straight that the
publisher would need something more substantial to go by
before they would discuss finance.

By lunchtime, business was concluded. David agreed to
complete the first draft by the end of the month and they
would take it from there. Ryan looked at his watch; he had
an hour free before his next appointment. 'What time's
your train? Time for a bite to eat before you go?' He
wanted to get to know him a little better, away from the
office. He wanted to know that he had made the right decision in taking him on, for reasons other than David's
knowledge of the subject and his intellectual ability to do

the work. When Simone had picked up Ryan's last call it was obvious that something was wrong at home. 'No, David is not here any more. He is in England now,' had been her curt reply before hanging up. She did not give an alternative number, or offer to take a message and Ryan had no choice but to leave it to David to get in touch with him.

They set off for the nearest pub for lunch, which suited both their purposes. David needed a drink and Ryan wanted to observe. He recognised his former self, five years earlier, when drink had almost destroyed him too. He hadn't always worked on his own and, luckily, had managed to cling on to one or two indebted clients who owed him enough to start again when he finally dried out – of course, at a considerably lower percentage than the one he'd been used to.

By the second round, close on the heels of the first, a pint of beer for David and a lime and soda for himself, he knew that David would need careful monitoring over the next few weeks.

'So, tell me, I'm curious, how come Georges gave the papers to you? You weren't working with him and you said yourself, you hadn't seen him for years. How come you want to take it on now? No one else interested?'

'It's a long story', he began, but it wasn't one that David was keen to go into with someone he had just met, not the personal side anyway. He gave Ryan an abridged version of the history between Georges and himself.

'Basically, I knew him from his days at the Archives in Paris when I was still a student. I learned about Henrietta Papers shortly after he'd helped me with some documentation I needed. Since living there with Simone, my girlfriend at the time...'

'Simone…your wife? I think I spoke to her when I called you.'

David ignored the comment and carried on, 'I got to know Georges better over the years, and he and I often discussed what could be done with the Papers. Unfortunately, after his wife's illness, he became a bit of a recluse and struggled with his own health. Just before he died in hospital, we'd met again and he insisted that I take them. I couldn't really refuse. I had hoped he would recover but… well the rest is history.'

'But why wait to give them to you? Why didn't he just sell them? I know he was short of money'

'I don't know… some superstition in his head. He didn't say much, but when he became ill too, he talked about being cursed ever since he'd had them. I think his mind was failing at that point as much as his body and at the end he turned back to the Catholic faith, spending more time in the Church than anywhere else.'

'And what about you? Do you think there's a curse? Will it pass on to you?' It was said more as a joke and David laughed out loud.

'Really?'

He looked across at Ryan and smiled at the thought of Georges. 'We were very close. I'd known him for years. I respected him enormously and we liked each other's company, but…his mind was starting to play tricks. Still, in memory of Georges, if nothing else, I'd like to see the project through; with your help, of course.'

The two men shook hands and David left for the train back to Manchester. 'Call me as soon as you're close to finishing,' Ryan said and passed David his card to remind him of the office number.

'And don't get sidetracked.'

Chapter 25

Manchester

WITH DAVID IN LONDON, Phil was relieved to be back on his own. The day started well; there was enough milk for cereal and coffee for once, and he mulled over the events since David's arrival. So far, he'd successfully put off talking to him about Simone and as time went on, felt less inclined to say anything at all. Life was bad enough as it was without piling on more trouble for himself. David hadn't mentioned anything, so maybe Simone hadn't told him what he'd said to her about the student in his tutor group. Best to let sleeping dogs lie was the best line of reasoning he decided.

Cheered by the thought that he hadn't been found out, he even considered a spot of cleaning on his day off. It was getting late, but even in the gloom, the flat looked disgusting, even more of a mess than usual was now there were two of them living there. Neither of had any notion of cleaning and emptying bins. Makeshift ashtrays of two tin cans and an old saucer sat on the floor poking out from under the sofa; the room stank of stale cigarettes. Phil threw them in the bin in the kitchen and managed to open the one window in the living room that could easily be freed. He was starting to relax, happy in the thought that David might never find out what was said to Simone after all. David had too much to drink most of the time they spent together anyway. How could you have a reasonable conversation with someone in that state? Phil discovered an empty whisky bottle and dumped it with the ashtrays.

Life was full of maybes, he reasoned with himself. Maybe Jen would stop pressing him for more money now she'd found someone else. Maybe the kids would realise that he wasn't such a bad Dad after all. On the other hand, they'd not been round for more than three weeks; last month's bills were still unpaid; and Jen still wanted more.

David hadn't offered any contribution for his stay either, merely a promise of something when he was paid for his book, if it ever materialised. Maybe this was what rock bottom looked like. Looking round convinced him that he couldn't get much lower. Cleaning the flat didn't get past dumping the makeshift ashtrays and whisky bottle; he lost interest when he thought of thought of Jen and another man in the house he still considered his.

The flat was quiet, apart from the distant drone of a television upstairs and he realised with an ache of resentment that the last time he'd felt a woman's body even remotely close to his own, had been during the fateful time he'd spent with David and Simone at their apartment in France. He cringed at the thought of what he'd done. How could he have got it so wrong? Making that clumsy pass was only the start. Maybe if he called Simone he could explain himself better and they could go back to where they were. He wanted her out of his head but all he could see was the look of incredulity on her face when she thought that David might be the father of a child in England. Why did he have to say that? It hadn't been planned that way at all. It had started off as a joke, but completely backfired when it all went too far and she took it seriously. How could David be the father anyway? Or could he? The more the thought swam about in his head, the more he realised that perhaps it wasn't beyond the realms of possibility. There was an uncanny likeness between the two after all. The years were right.

Phil scraped the crusts of a cold pizza from a plate on top of the ashtrays, beer cans and whisky bottle and decided to call it a day. It was gone eleven and he had to deliver a double lecture first thing. He was tired and his head hurt with thinking too much.

Leaving the kitchen in darkness, and halfway to the bedroom, the doorbell rang. He decided to ignore it when drunks and druggies regularly came out at night; it was that kind of area, hooded yobs in the dark, threatening and demanding, looking out for easy pickings when no one was home. He made a noise to let them know the place wasn't empty but when the ringing didn't stop, went to the window and pushed the curtain aside to look out, but it was too dark to see down below. He shrugged it off and turned to go back, but after the third urgent repeated ringing, reluctantly went to the door.

He opened it slowly, suspiciously. 'Who is it? What do you want?' he shouted through the narrowest of cracks. He didn't want any trouble, and picked up an old cricket bat he kept handily close to the door, just in case. They'd made their point and he would make his.

'Ah, good, you are in Phil, I was beginning to think I had the wrong address.'

He fumbled with the security chain until it was free and opened the door in amazement.

'Good God, what are you doing here?' The nearest streetlight had given up long ago and had not yet been fixed but there was no mistaking the sound of that voice and the owner of the dimly lit face before him. Simone. She stood waiting for Phil to register her unexpected presence.

'Aren't you going to invite me in? I'm sorry it's so late, but I won't keep you long. I know that David is not here right now and I want to speak to you if it is all right.' Struggling for what to say in reply, he opened the door and let her in.

'Simone…yes…come in. What… why…why didn't you call me first?'

'Because I didn't have your number for one and for another I didn't want David to answer, of course.'

Phil stood aside to let her pass and leaned towards her to kiss her cheek, which she successfully evaded. The day's earlier optimism melted like icecream in the sun. He too was grateful that David wasn't around.

'Have you spoken to David?'

Simone had called Ryan in the belief that David would be seeing him at some point and when she found out the date of their meeting, made her own plans and booked her flight to England.

'I do hope that I am safe in here with you.' She smiled with a look that was anything but amused. The last time he had seen her stung with renewed vigour at its repercussions. He cringed at the thought.

'I'm so, so sorry about that…you were…I mean…I only…'

'Stop it, Phil. It's done and we won't mention it again.'

'No…really I am sorry. It wasn't a good time for me. With Jen gone…and taken the girls and…'

'And you thought I would be willing to take you on?'

'No! It was just the heat of the moment. I've regretted it ever since.'

In hindsight, the visit to David and Simone's had not been a good idea so soon after his wife had left him, but it was too late to backtrack now. His anger at David, triggered by envy of his wife, his life and his seeming ability to get everything he wanted from life, was too much; it was unbearable. Simone's crumb of sympathy had been all the encouragement he needed. They were on their own; she smiled at him as they shared a glass of wine over lunch together. How could it have gone so spectacularly wrong? Then the suggestion about Michael; said more in anger than anything else, it wasn't meant to be taken seriously, just something that David could easily have let happen, that's all. But now this; Simone was the last person he expected to see at his flat.

'I've not come to make you feel bad about what happened, but about what you told me of one of your students. I can't get it out of my head.'

Even as he'd told her, he knew he would regret it, but years of jealousy had surfaced when he saw the life they were leading in Paris and he could no more help himself than he could stop breathing. David had everything that Phil could only dream about. When Jen had left, he thought a visit to Paris would be good for him but two days into the trip, he realised just what a mistake it had been. On arrival, David's first comment was to ask when was his flight back. It was obvious that he had only agreed with reluctance. Phil felt snubbed but determined to get something out of it; he'd never been to Paris before and anyway, he'd done David plenty of favours in the past.

Over the first two days, Simone had been absent for much of the time, working, and then a client dinner. David showed him how to get to the usual tourist spots but always had the excuse of a prior arranged meeting to leave him to go on his own. But on the third day, when David made out he had to see an old friend, and for one morning only, Simone and Phil were alone together. The memory stayed with him long after. The sting of the sharp slap across his face that followed his clumsy advance was swift and hard. Words that came out of his mouth betrayed not just a heat of the moment retort, but years of bitterness, jealousy and unbridled resentment. The clumsy uninvited kiss sealed his fate and Simone demanded that he leave immediately unless he wanted her to tell David, but the words could never be unsaid.

'You know, I teach someone who is the very image of David when he was the same age? The amount he's shagged around I'm surprised there's not a whole brood of them out there. How do you live with him?'

Simone's face had flushed as though she had been the one slapped; stung by words she had more than once considered herself; not that there were any children of his out there, at least as far as she knew, but the fact that their lack of children was solely on her account. David could have had a child with someone else. They'd not had the tests, David wouldn't hear of it, and she had been too distraught to argue.

She did not rise to Phil's suggested accusation, but the seed was sown and it quickly grew in fertile ground as she watched him leave the next day. Neither had she allowed herself to ask the thousand questions that demonically flew around her head but instead let the thoughts take root and grow out of all proportion. Over the years David had been forgiven many times over his affairs. Knowing that they'd never meant anything, she watched silently, wondering what he wanted from a life that increasingly looked like a vessel drained of vitality. To the outside world he was content, full of life, good to be with, but there were times she caught him unaware, looking into the distance as if seeking an unattainable goal. Quite simply, she loved him and forgave him; their life together had been good in so many ways, but recently she'd felt it unravel and couldn't quite suppress the nagging doubts and their inability to talk. Cracks appeared in the marriage, running too far and too deep to repair. And now, should there be a child some-where, a boy who had reached manhood, a son who was not hers but his, that would be too much to bear. David had always made her feel loved as no one else could; she forgave the evenings spent apart, and what man did not have the occasional mistress? But this, if true, cut so much deeper and she needed answers.

Phil showed Simone through to the living room, glad that he'd at least cleared away some of the mess, although the stale odour of cigarettes still hung in the air. At first she refused his offer to sit on the sofa and did not want a drink. He noted how pale she looked and at forty-eight, how at that moment she looked nearer fifty than forty in her face, if not in her perfect body.

'Come on…please…sit down. I'm sorry about last time…'

'Forget it; I don't want to talk about your clumsy pass. I haven't come all this way to...' But the room began to spin before she could finish and she held out her arm for the proffered seat.

'I will sit for a moment, thank you'

'You don't look well…is everything ok?'

'I'm fine, thank you, but a glass of water would be good. It's been a long day.'

She had not slept well since David left. Dreams of the child that had not survived re-emerged. How could someone like Phil even begin to understand the devastation of losing a child, of knowing that you will never give birth to a healthy...She choked on the words before they were even spoken. When Phil mentioned his daughters it was always tinged with cost and the drain on his dwindling finances, not with love.

Phil returned from the kitchen, his eyes inevitably drawn to Simone's legs elegantly encased in silk. She perched on the edge of the sofa; loathe to sit back amongst the numerous stains it held there. Her perfume rose above the stale cigarettes, reaching Phil with a reminder of the luxury of the apartment in France.

'It's good to see you, Simone, I did want to apologise. I respect you more than anyone I know...it was crass...I...'

'Stop' she interrupted, 'I've already said that's over and done with. It's not why I'm here.'

'I guess this isn't a social call, either'

'No. It's not you I've come to see, and not David either...not yet, anyway.'

She looked him straight in the face as she spoke, her usual composure only slightly disturbed by the quickening of her pulse.

'Before I serve David with the divorce papers there is one thing I have to do first.'

Phil knew exactly what she was angling for but wasn't about to help her out. He squirmed at the thought. 'What do you want from me?' He would love nothing more than have someone like Simone beholden to him, but the feelings of inadequacy she never failed to elicit stood in the way. The mere sound of her mentioning his name was enough for him to burn inside, but as he cogitated over his feelings towards her, she finally brought up the subject he had instigated in France:

'I want to meet the boy you told me about at the apartment. I want to see him for myself.' Phil looked away, searching for the right words to put her off and get her to go back to France. He laughed at the absurdity of it.

'That's really not a good idea…he would…he wouldn't…it was just something I said in the heat of the moment, not a statement of fact. I can't just…'

'You seemed quite certain when you came over and told me about him; his looks, his manner, his hair. You knew David at that age too and now I just want to see if *I* think it is true. It's important to me, Phil. You have no idea what you have started…it changes everything.'

Her face betrayed little emotion. Phil couldn't tell if she was upset, or angry, or had just resigned herself to the fact that David might have had a child with someone else and kept it from her. He'd never considered why they'd not had children together, always assumed that they liked the life they already had and didn't want to spoil it. It was a lifestyle he would gladly have swapped for his own. His own children, having both reached the surly teenager stage, barely acknowledged his existence.

'I don't know…look, what good would it do anyone after all this time even if it is true…which I'm sure it's not? He has two perfectly good parents. I met them…lovely people'

'I don't doubt that. I will not cause any trouble, but I will see him for myself. If you won't introduce me, I will just have to turn up where you work and look for him.'

'No… no, don't do that. Okay…I…I'll arrange something tomorrow if I can.'

'You will?'

Phil shifted uncomfortably in his seat, wondering how to get out of it.

'I'll think of something. I've got him for a lecture in the afternoon. But *please* don't say anything about what I told you. Just say…'

'Say what exactly?' Her cheeks flamed, betraying the icy coolness of her response,

'Do you have a father, because my friend here thinks that you could be the long lost son of my husband?'

'I'm sorry, Simone. I shouldn't have said anything. You deserve better. You know, I probably got it all wrong… It's…'

'It's a little bit late for that now. I am not going to put anyone in a compromising situation. I just want to meet him, that's all. I need to do this.'

She stood up and gave him a card from her hotel, 'I'm in Room 416; you can call me there' she said and left as abruptly as she had arrived.

The threadbare carpet and the cracks in the wall stood out in all their shabby glory as he followed her to the door.

'Goodbye Phil…I will hear from you tomorrow, yes?'

Phil nodded, but said nothing. He locked the door again and went back into the sitting room. The smell of her perfume lingered as he sat alone with his thoughts on why she had come. He didn't want to be any part of it, had enough problems of his own. It would be another restless night. Everything had gone too far and David was due back in the morning. He'd achieved nothing and only heaped even more misery into his life.

Phil went into the kitchen and made another coffee, black this time. He hated black coffee but the milk hadn't stretched to another cup. A hazy memory of Simone's kitchen in France with its well-stocked fridge, and gleaming white cupboards, flittered through his head and the bitter bile of envy rose once again.

How had David managed it, he snarled. They'd started out together at university, both getting a 2:1, although if the truth be told, David had sailed through his on what seemed to Phil to be very little work. Phil struggled, and when he got the opportunity, copied, borrowed and plagiarised for his result; but got it all the same. Everything came so easily to David; the pretty girls who'd hung around; the invites to parties; it was as if it was his right. Even Jen, his own wife, had been one of David's early cast-offs. Phil had been more than grateful to get her attention when David had made a move on someone else at the bar. Jen saw everything, he made his move and she seemed grateful that night. He thought they were right for each other, but Jen had different ides when she casually informed him before she left him for good that he could just as easily have been any other man that night.

Chapter 26

The lectures Phil delivered that morning were uninspiring, perfunctory at best, and given to a group of students who responded with equal boredom and disdain. Thursdays were never good, but the job was beginning to depress him even more than it usually did. It would be different if he had a life to go back to at the flat, but he couldn't even find a woman through a dating agency. Four dates in and not one of them had wanted a second; and two had left early on the first. The Phil he saw in the mirror and the Phil he heard in his head were some way off the Phil who came across to the dates. Each rejection brought a fresh reproach of a life unfairly dealt and depression came in its wake.

The day was spent in abject misery when around every corner he expected to see Simone. The card she'd given him burned in his pocket and he wondered how long the agony would last until her flight back to France. By three thirty, he started to relax; maybe he'd pulled it off after all. His afternoon lectures were mercifully short and Phil determined to make his escape as soon as they were over.

However, the hope was short lived by the arrival of Michael at his door.

'Hi Phil d'you think we can re-arrange my next tutor-ial…I'm a bit behind with the work…just a couple of days'll do it.'

It was getting to be a habit but he wasn't about to argue today.

'Fine…fine…look Michael, I'm in a rush right now. Got another appointment… see me tomorrow ok?'

'Won't take a minute, I promise'. Michael stood his ground and even though Phil did not want to give way, when he caught sight of Simone walking towards them, knew all was lost. As she got closer, her eyes revealed what he needed to know. She saw Michael and in his face saw David at the same age. She blanched. This was not what she expected at all.

The shock of seeing Michael, this young man in the flesh, this image of David made incarnate, was electrifying. Simone had been prepared for the possibility of a likeness, but this was on another level. With supreme effort, the emotion that threatened to engulf her whole being was suppressed. Outwardly composed, she spoke without taking her eyes from Michael.

'I am sorry to interrupt…'

'No, please go ahead.' Even the voice was David; at least as it was before years of cigarettes took their toll. Constricted as it was, Simone cleared her throat.

'You are one of Phil's students?'

'Yes.' Ordinarily he would have left but there was something very seductive about this attractive French woman standing before them and he couldn't resist. 'I'm Michael'

'Ah…Michael. I do believe that Phil has mentioned you…a most promising student.'

He was flattered, if a little confused as to why he would have merited a mention, but Simone's smile captivated him and he was shocked to realise that he was blushing. For the first time since primary school when Amanda Hewitt had kissed him in the playground, and told him she liked him, he stumbled over his words. She was looking right through him. Did he know her? Had they met before? Surely not; he would definitely have remembered.

'Well…I don't know…I'm not…I mean…well…'

'Never underestimate yourself, Michael.'

He couldn't believe that Phil knew anyone of such class and she didn't look old enough to be a parent.

'I understand too that my husband has been helping you with one of your assignments.'

Michael's face lit up at the realisation of who she was,

'David…Mr Weston…he's your husband?'

He smiled and held out his hand, 'So nice to meet you, Mrs Weston…David…Mr Weston…he's been really helpful…probably forgotten more than I will ever know.'

She took the proffered hand and held it for a moment longer than intended as she continued to study his face.

'I wouldn't put yourself down too much. David doesn't know everything…just likes to make out he does.'

She laughed, making light of the comment, then told him what a pleasure it was to meet him.'

'Au revoir Michel. I hope that we meet again.'

'Cool, Mrs…er…Mrs Weston.'

'Please…call me Simone.'

'Simone,' he said with a slight nod of the head. With pleasure at the thought of meeting her again, however unlikely, he failed to notice Phil's face had turned grey. What was it with the French? Cecille was pretty enough, but this woman was in a different league altogether.

'It'd be great to see you again some time,' Michael replied more in hope than expectation.

'If you don't mind Michael?'

'Yeah…yeah…I'll see you tomorrow.'

Neither Simone nor Michael had paid him any heed during the encounter, but were abruptly brought back into the moment.

Simone watched him walk down the corridor, taking in the familiar gait and the soft brown hair curling at his neck. They had spoken for no more than two minutes, three at the most, but it was enough; Simone was satisfied. Ignoring Phil, she turned to leave.

'I'll see you out.' Phil struggled to keep up with her as she rushed towards the door, her face still fighting to contain the tide of emotion ready to breach the dam. She briefly turned,

'Thank you for making me aware of your student…I'm sure that you must have thought about it a great deal before telling me…but I am glad that you did…even though your reason is a far distant one to mine'

With that, she disappeared amongst the crowd of students disgorging from the lecture rooms. A taxi, already booked, was waiting for her at the front of the building. Phil had to run to keep up. Flushed and anxious, he pushed his way through the crowd, desperate to know her next move. 'What are you going to do now? Where are you going? Please…Simone…talk to me.'

'I am going back to my hotel. I've done what I wanted to do and I have seen the boy. Thank you again for that at least.' At the roadside, she bent to the driver to confirm that the cab was hers, climbed inside and firmly shut the door on Phil.

'Simone wait…'

'Dorchester, please.'

Simone's breath came in short gasps. Released from the constraints of the last half hour, she could finally face the truth. There was no doubt in her mind that Michael was David's son. Another woman had given him the one thing that she couldn't. Tears scorched her eyes; when she closed them, she saw nothing but Michael's fresh young face and the curling brown hair. Looking out of the cab window, she saw nothing but his lovely face and familiar voice of old. The driver asked if she'd had a pleasant day, but held off any further conversation on seeing the look of distress in the face of his passenger. Simone heard nothing but Michael's voice. 'It'd be great to see you again some time.' He was everywhere: crossing the road; in every passing car; in every café they passed; on the busy streets. She heard nothing but the fine clear voice of this young man who was not *her* son, but *was* David's.

Simone sat in silence; lost and hollow inside, unable to comprehend why in God's name could she not have produced anything so perfect or so beautiful? Why did her son have to die? There was nothing she would not have given up: the apartment, the cars or the job, for just one more hour of her own baby's life. The desolation of that day rang a death knell for her own fertility and felt like a mockery of all she had strived to be, or become.

Chapter 27

The day after the meeting with Ryan, David caught the ten fifteen train back to Manchester. The hotel had been cheap, the bed uncomfortable and he was left nursing a sore back. A constant stream of traffic below his window and the irritating thump of music down the street left him tired and irritable despite all hopes from the day before. The fact remained that the book had to be finished before he had a chance of seeing anything approaching a decent return on the work. Sitting in a pub near the hotel, he worked out that with two or three weeks finalising the research, and a short spell in Yorkshire, it should be complete by the New Year. It would mean paying for accommodation, but sharing with Phil any longer than necessary was out of the question. Commuting to York-shire would be impractical anyway. Money was dwindling rapidly but he'd manage it somehow.

Time ran away in the reverie of the moment and finishing his pint he checked his watch. Somewhere in the distance a clock chimed and confirmed the hour. It was getting late for the train. David attempted to run to the station but hadn't allowed enough time to get across London. However busy Manchester got, it was nothing like this. He flicked away the cigarette butt, but within less than a minute, a sharp pain gripped his chest and pulled him up short. His head began to spin and everything was going out of focus. He bent over to regain his balance, hands on his knees and head sunk low, desperate not to pass out. He was jostled and dodged by the passing crowd, but of course, no one stopped. He wasn't laid out on the floor or unconscious, just another drunk or junkie. It was no one's business but his own. When the pain eased enough to stand up straight again, he hailed a passing cab and managed to catch his train with seconds to spare. It was full of course, apart from one seat next to an old lady sitting by a window.

'Is this free?' he asked hopefully, his face flushed and his voice breathless as he clung on to the headrest.

'I think it is now, dear. There was a lovely woman sitting next to me earlier but she seems to have gone when I nodded off. Very colourful she was, such lovely bright clothes...I can't see her now and her things have gone.'

She wanted to chat, and even though the last thing David wanted was a conversation with an old woman, he was in no position to ignore the last empty seat on the train. He duly sat and the pain in his chest began to subside in the relief of leaving London.

'Are you all right, dear...you look a bit flushed?'

'Ha...not as fit as I used to be.'

He put his head back and closed his eyes until the pain had eased sufficiently for him go and find the buffet car. The old woman went back to her book on realising that the man next to her would not be as talkative as the woman in the bright clothes.

In the twenty minutes it took to buy a cheese sandwich and two small bottles of rioja, the first being drunk at the counter, David was relieved to see that the old woman was no longer there when he came back and he had room to spread out.

Leaning down to pick up a fallen napkin, something bright on the floor caught his eye under the seat in front. A red scarf. He looked around for any sign of the woman but she had definitely gone; her book, bag and coat were nowhere to be seen. He laid the scarf over the empty seat and thinking no more about it, ate the sandwich, drank the wine and slept soundly for the rest of the journey.

IT WAS dark by the time David arrived back at the flat. Reaching for the bobbin and key in his pocket, he let himself in, hoping all the while that Phil would be out or at least in bed, but instead he found him in the kitchen eating a Chinese takeaway. An assortment of foil trays spread across the table, the unpleasant smell of which pervaded the kitchen. After years of the finer fare in Paris, he pulled a face in contempt.

'You're back...all go well? Phil asked stuffing a forkful of gelatinous chicken and noodles into his mouth.

'Pretty much as I expected.' David sniffed, 'That stuff stinks. What on earth are you eating?'

'What are you talking about? You used to love noodles...go on...help yourself, there's plenty left,' Phil offered. David was hungry, but far from certain that this Chinese was the answer.

'You OK? You look crap.'

'Long day...anyway why are you in such a good mood? It's not like you.'

'Sticky problem at work sorted. Thought I'd treat myself to this.'

What he did not say was that a few hours earlier he'd called Simone and extracted the promise he wanted. She wouldn't say anything about seeing Michael to David. He chose to ignore the nagging doubts that she'd only said it to get rid of him, and returned with a celebratory takeaway and a four-pack of lager.

David put aside all repugnance of the food in answer to the growl in his stomach and fetched a plate from the cupboard.

'Thanks' He helped himself to rice and a gloopy spoonful from a tray that purported to be lemon chicken judging by the colour and wedges stuck on top.

'So what's up with you?' Phil persisted.

'I'm all right, just tired. You know what London's like.'

He filled the plate, but his appetite waned after the first few mouthfuls. An uncomfortable sensation in his chest threatened to erupt again into the pain of earlier in the day, but he chose to put it down to a mix of hunger and stress and continued eating anyway.

'There's a beer in the fridge if you want one…What did the agent say?'

'Still keen, but I need to finish soon,' David replied between forcing down chicken that tasted even worse than it looked.

'Ryan confirmed what I already knew…that I need to go up to Yorkshire for a few days. Check out the Archives and follow up a fair number of references.'

He drank his beer straight from the bottle and remembered the half bottle of whisky that was still in his room; it just might help him sleep better tonight.

Phil nodded, smiling; the evening just got better and better. David was definitely still leaving.

'Pity, I was getting used to having you around,' he lied.

'Yeah.'

With nothing more to say, David scraped what was left on his plate into the bin.

'I'll leave you to it. I need an early night and have to pack.' He'd already found out the time of the mid-morning train and planned to be gone well before Phil returned from work. There would surely be somewhere cheap enough to stay; it couldn't be anywhere near as bad as London and he'd worked out that there was enough money left to keep him going for another two months at most, if he was careful. He would either have to appeal to Simone after that, which he was reluctant to do, or quickly find a job, which was equally unlikely.

David kicked off his shoes and lay on the bed; the take-away lay heavy in his stomach. Without undressing, and a whisky glass in his hand, his eyes closed on Simone back in France, at their apartment. Oblivion soon arrived and the empty glass dropped to the floor next to another empty bottle.

PHIL SAT in front of the TV; David's leaving had been a subject uppermost in his mind since the day he'd arrived, but now all was resolved and he could relax. Things were looking up. With David gone, he could focus his mind on other matters. When Simone had left after meeting Michael, on impulse he'd taken David's advice when one of the post grads sought him out. She was a mature student, around thirty-five or so, and in need of a lot of reassurance that she was good enough for the course. Divorced with no children, she looked up to Phil as someone who could help to get her through. Perhaps she was a little overweight and no real beauty, but she made up for that with a pretty smile each time they met. But more than that, Phil was attracted by her dependence on him and how she hung on to his every word. Perhaps he should ask her out one night.

The last thing he wanted was David in the next room, or worse still, laid out drunk on the sofa. This little boost to his ego was just what he needed. He settled down to watch the Sweeney, turning the volume up to drown out the rain that sounded more like gravel being thrown against the window. It was a bitterly cold November night and the gas fire spluttered in defiance at being turned up so high.

PHIL WAS the first to leave the next morning. David, half awake had listened for the door to close before struggling out of bed. He sat in the kitchen with coffee and a cigarette, ready to finish packing his bag, when the phone rang. He didn't want to answer it, but thought better of it on the chance that it might be Ryan who he knew had Phil's number on file.

'Hello.' There was a moment of silence at the other end.

'Hello? Who is this?'

He was about to hang up when a woman finally spoke,

'David?' The softly spoken voice was unmistakable.

'Simone! Is that you? Are you ok?... is everything all right?'

He perked up and his face became alive at the welcome sound of her.

'I need to see you, David' There was another long pause. 'I am in Manchester…are you free to come over to my hotel?'

'Manchester?…You're here?'

Of the myriad reasons she may have had to come over,

the one he hoped for was that she wanted to see him, to put their problem behind them. He missed her and raised his hopes that she wanted a reconciliation as much as he did. He'd tried hard to ignore his feelings, to not miss her, but there was a vast emptiness inside that wouldn't be ignored.

'Yes…of course I'll come…you know I will. Why didn't you let me know you were coming to England?... I've missed you, Simone.'

Confident that she must have had a change of heart about the divorce, he wouldn't push his luck, but Simone offered little in the way of hope. She merely told him where she was but David, going on past experience, was still left with the expectation of Simone taking him back. Ignoring the packing, and ignoring the train he was due to catch, he sat on the bed with an uplifted heart at the thought of seeing Simone.

A huge weight lifted from his shoulders and the headache he'd woken up with began to ease. Surely she felt the same way. Simone was the only woman he had ever loved and she'd always taken him back before.

He made another coffee, lit another cigarette, and took them both to the bathroom. A decent shower gel had replaced the sludge of pink soap and he'd bought himself a large white towel to replace the thin green postage stamp left out by Phil. He felt happier than he had at any other time since arriving back in England.

SIMONE WAS SITTING in the lobby, back straight and looking down at her hands neatly clasped on her lap. Behind the green plush chair sat a suitcase, waiting and ready to go.

David saw her immediately he entered and watched for

a moment, unseen, taking in the loveliness that could still take him by surprise. She looked at the watch that hung loosely from her wrist, turning it to see the face, and then lifted her head towards the door. She didn't smile when she saw him, just gave a look of recognition.

David's longing to go back to their life together manifest in a desire to hold her and not let go until she relented; but something told him it might be different this time. The old familiar, forgiving, welcome in her face was nowhere to be seen. It was hard to gauge what was going on behind those eyes and when he bent down to her she made no move to welcome the proffered kiss on her cheek.

Simone had been sitting in the same spot for an hour. The coffee on the table in front remained untouched, cold. The hour was spent looking back over the twenty-five years they had been together. That was all she had done since yesterday's meeting with Michael. Arriving back in Paris after her father's death, the years had slipped by so quickly. She had come to terms with the fact that there were no children, there would never be a child in their lives; she had even accepted the demands made on her over David's behaviour and the strain it had put on their marriage. But it came at a price. She long ago accepted that there would always be a part of him that would not be hers and that forgiveness was the only answer when the alternative was too painful to consider.

Of course his judgement came into play; the women who hadn't taken no for an answer and the indiscretions that too easily followed. Somehow, he'd always managed to convince her of his love, and she finally understood how her mother must have felt when her father strayed and betrayed. 'They need their mistresses, but not nearly as much as they need us, darling,' she would say. Or perhaps it was because David had never truly been hers that she had held on to the marriage for so long. For much of the time, they led separate lives and even during their first year together, he'd challenged her and tested her loyalty to its limits. Her father had been right, of course, when he disapproved of her choice of husband, but she would never have admitted it, and perhaps that was another reason why she'd stayed with him for so long; that and the Catholic faith that she kept alive. He'd never interfered, never questioned, and her attendance at Mass was sporadic, but none the less her faith remained intact and divorce had been out of the question; until now, and despite how much she missed him. She felt his absence from her bed since he left and until yesterday would have taken him back yet again. The night before he left, they had made love, still love, not just sex, and the poignancy of those final hours was the most painful of all. The act of sex was also for the procreation of children, the one thing they would never have together.

'Not going back already?' David had seen the suitcases, 'I was hoping we might have dinner together.'

'No David. I've finished my business here and I have to get back soon,' she coolly replied, 'I just wanted to say goodbye and let you know that I will have the divorce papers for you to sign as soon as my lawyer has completed the formalities. I can't say how long it will take, but you must understand that there is a lot to take into account. There will be some money due to you, of course, but it is out of my hands now.'

His body stiffened at her unexpected coldness and the early morning optimism disappeared like the sun behind a dark cloud.

'You could have told me that on the phone this morning.'

She nodded, 'Yes, I could have done that but I wanted to tell you personally.'

He waited for her to go on, scrutinising her face for any sign of regret, but it remained immobile. Things had never gone this far before; he wanted her back, wanted some small sign that she might relent, but there was nothing.

'I'm not going to be here more than a couple of weeks. We can talk when I get back can't we?'

'No more talking David…it's over. I will give you space to clear your things but you need to move out. Perhaps you want to move back here? I'm sure your friend Phil will put you up until you get sorted.'

'Simone come on…why are you doing this? Why now? Rene was nothing to me you know that.'

Simone gave him a scornful look and shook her head.

'You have no idea do you?'

'What do you mean? Why have you come all this way to tell me now?'

The hotel doorman came up to Simone, 'Your taxi is here Mrs Weston. Shall I take your case?'

'Yes. Thank you. I'll be right there.' There was a moment's silence before Simone said goodbye.

'I have a flight to catch.'

'Does it have to be so final?' David reached across, wanting to hold her close once more, make her realise that it didn't have to end. She evaded his attempt.

'I love you Simone…always have…always will. You know that.'

'It's gone on long enough, David. I don't want a life with you any more.'

She paused a while, considering her words carefully before saying 'Perhaps it would have been different if *we* had had children?'

'What?'

A puzzled look passed across David's eyes. Did she know something? Is that what this visit was about? She posed the last statement as a question and he wanted to ask what she meant by it, but let it rest there. There was no certainty about anything. Not yet. There were never going to be any children between them, not ever. Simone was forty-eight and besides they'd known years ago it would not happen, not after the last time. She could not conceive and could never go full term; and with equal certainty, they would not consider adoption. They'd equally accepted both premises.

There were many questions he wanted to ask her, but no time to give them voice right now. He made up his mind to go back to France once the work was completed, once he knew for certain all he suspected about Michael. She would understand then surely that he had been as much in the dark as she had been, if indeed she knew anything, but the question remained; how? Was Phil behind it? Was that the reason for his sudden departure from the apartment? It had to be.

'I'm sorry Simone but I won't let it stop there. We will talk when I get back I promise.'

Simone followed the doorman and left him standing alone amidst the throng of newly arriving guests. She did not look back.

ON RETURNING to Phil's flat, it didn't take David long to finish the packing started earlier. Grateful to be focussing on something other than the immense weight of sadness at seeing Simone, he scribbled a hasty note of thanks to leave on the kitchen table along with his bobbin key. More than anything, he was glad to be leaving Phil's flat for good. Talking to Simone and the unfinished business with

Michael left him disturbed, but he wouldn't dwell on it right now, it would keep; so would the meeting with Michael that had been planned later that day. There was no question of letting him go now and the more he thought about the boy, the more the bitterness of the years he'd missed churned inside.

Chapter 28

As usual, Julia siphoned off some of the easier enquiries to take over to Carole's desk. If she gave her anything too complex, it would only bounce back later in the week, or sit untouched until a customer complained. Carole's desk was its usual mess; since starting at the Archives, she had demonstrated little or no enthusiasm for getting through the work, no matter how many times Julia broached the subject. Carole was twenty-two, the age at which Julia had had a six year old son and was working her way through college.

Placing the work in a prominent spot on Carole's desk, where it could not be missed, she caught sight of herself in a mirror that had been recently hung on the wall. Shocked at the image that looked back, tears stung behind her eyes at what she had become. Not so long ago, her response to an unexpected glimpse of herself would be to turn away unconcerned, but today, in the silent and empty office, she let her eyes wander over the reflection; on the face she no longer bothered to cover with makeup and the hair that had not been to a salon in so long. Wisps had already worked their way loose, blown free in the strong winds on her walk from the bus and she brushed them back behind her ears. Julia stood transfixed by the image and tried to remember when she had last worn makeup. Not that Will ever minded; he even said that he preferred her without any. Julia turned her head to different angles, trying to imagine how she might look with a little more effort. The face looking back was still unlined; set with deep blue eyes that hid another world behind them. She was not unattractive, still two years away from forty, but inside, and the face Julia chose to see, was so much older than that.

On Carole's desk, alongside the tub of blunt and broken pencils, was mascara and lip-gloss. She picked up the mascara and unscrewed the lid. The brush was curved and matted with a thick, coal-black, substance. The office was still quiet as Julia applied the mascara to her own pale lashes and then stepped back to survey the result. She noticed memo notes stuck around the computer monitor, telephone numbers with reminders of who to call, numbers that Julia was sure had nothing to do with work: Mickey, Darren, Jess, but no surnames. Julia turned back to the mirror and surveyed the effect of newly blackened lashes as voices echoed from the corridor outside. The mascara was hastily returned to the spot it came from and Julia went back to her own workstation.

It was Thursday morning and they would be busy. On days like these, Julia felt that she knew and understood the lives of the dead better than her own by the time she had finished with the family history enquiries. More than once it came as a shock to realise that the dead had lived more of a life than she ever would.

The door opened behind her and Colin propped it back with a wedge as he always did on arrival. It was all the better to hear what was going on from his vantage point on the other side in the reading room and he didn't like to miss anything.

'Morning, Julia,' he boomed across the room. Colin was a man of indeterminate age, easy to dislike, but hard to ignore.

'Hello, Colin,' she replied without turning. She had no desire to look at the figure that always made her think of a character from a Dickens novel. The tight black trousers and lank black hair framed a face that had more than once elicited the comment it was one 'only a mother could love'.

'You look different today,' he continued, walking in front of her desk despite Julia's reluctance to get into a conversation. She remembered the mascara and put her head down to continue.

'No Colin, the same old me.'

It was generally known that Colin was lazy, but his powers of observation were not lacking; he was good at picking up on detail. Not the detail required in the job of work, but detail in the people who worked around him. He was the first to know when a new haircut appeared, or notice a change in dress. He knew what went on inside and outside the office and was willing to impart that knowledge to anyone who cared to listen.

The office started to fill and Colin left for his province in Collections and Returns. The rest of the staff arrived on cue, the usual pleasantries were exchanged, bags were stuffed into drawers and computers booted up.

Julia started work on a few donations that had arrived for her attention and headed past the enquiry desk to the photocopying room to copy a delicate pamphlet donated by a member of the public.

At the main desk, she noticed that a queue had already built up, fronted by a man in a long blue mac. His collar was turned up so she couldn't see his face, but as she got closer she heard a voice that stirred a distant, vague memory. She dismissed it as probably someone she had helped out before and went about her duties. Repeat visits were the norm and the Archives had plenty of regulars who came in at least once a week when they got hooked on treading the ancestral trail. More and more of them were the newly retired, keen to follow up a promising start, all hoping for that elusive link to someone important or famous, but more likely finding the poor and mundane. If anything more interesting was unearthed it was more likely to be on the criminal side. Judging by the demographic, the closer they got to death themselves, the more they wanted to make links with the ancestors who had gone before.

The man in the mac was talking to Carole and had obviously been holding up the line for some time. As it so often happened, she was out of her depth. Martha Baines, from the comfort of her seat further down the counter, did not like working with the public and wasn't happy at having to leave her desk to help out. She may have been a fount of knowledge and experience but her talents were marred by the ungracious manner with which she dealt with the public. On more than one occasion, Martha had made Julia go out at peak times when she could easily have done it herself. Julia passed close to the desk, ready to step in, but stopped short and blanched when it hit her who the man was.

She quickly walked past the desk, head down until reaching a post wide enough to be hidden from view. The man in the blue mac was far too engrossed in conversation with Carole, however, to notice anyone else, let alone a silent member of staff blending into the background.

Julia knew that there was no mistaking him. Older, yes; greyer, certainly; more lined, obviously, but it was him. The voice was loudly audible, above the usual hushed tones in the building, and even from this distance, came across as rich, deep and authoritative. It wasn't easy to make out what it was he wanted, but she caught the words 'Civil War' and the name 'Monckton'. Of course, Carole wouldn't know where to start. She'd been there three months now but hardly took in the training she'd been given. Julia would have no problem, but backed away even further when Carole started to look helplessly around for someone else to take over. The other assistants had gone for their break and Martha was already tied up with someone else.

'If you'll just give me a minute, I'll try to find someone to help you.'

'Please do.'

Julia backed away to the photocopying room, leaving Carole to search out the other staff coming back down.

This was not how she'd imagined it would be if she ever saw him again. She wasn't prepared. She sat on the lone chair next to the photocopier, putting her head down in her hands as the room spun.

Colin appeared at the door with an armful of directories and looked at her with undisguised curiosity, 'Hello, is this where you're hiding?' He'd suspected that something was going on with Julia since first thing that morning; the day just got more interesting by the minute.

'Will you be long?' he asked brightly.

Julia didn't notice his presence, let alone heard him.

He repeated his question and moved closer, immediately noticing Julia's ashen face when she looked up from her hands.

'What's the matter with you? You look like death.'

'Nothing, Colin' she snapped, 'I just felt dizzy for a minute. Do you want to use the copier?' She stood up, slightly unsteady on her feet, but determined that Colin would not get the chance to probe further.

'Oops, not pregnant are we?'

'Don't be stupid. I'm going up to the tearoom for five minutes to get a glass of water. I won't be long if anyone asks for me.'

'Do you want me to come with you?' Colin also loved an excuse to escape work and wanted to know more.

'Good God, Colin, I think I can manage.'

Colin held up his hands in disappointed resignation 'Ok, ok.'

Julia left to go up by the back staircase, holding on to her chest as her heart thudded painfully inside. The others had just left, break time was over, and the room was thankfully empty. She took a glass from the cupboard and let the tap run cold before filling it, then walked over to the window, breathing deeply and willing herself to be calm. The clumpy mascara felt heavy on her eyelids; she would not cry and make it run. Perhaps he might be gone when she went back down.

THE WINDOW AFFORDED one of the finest views from the building. The church on the hill in the distance shone in an early winter sun that had broken through the black clouds. It would be its last appearance before the first deluge of the day. Julia looked out, seeing nothing but the image of the blue coat and the back of David's head. Anxiety and uncertainty clouded all rational judgement of what to do next but the decision was taken from her when a tap at the door made her jump. Malcolm poked his head around, unsure of the state in which he would find Julia. Malcolm didn't like illness, or indeed anything of a personal nature, especially when it concerned female staff.

He found it a constant strain working with staff that consisted mostly of women.

'Ah...Colin said you were up here...not feeling well... are you all right?'

'Yes I'm ok. Just felt a bit dizzy, that's all. I'm fine now, really.'

'Good...good'

Malcolm walked in, relieved there was nothing for him to worry about. He stood for a moment in his badly fitting suit, with its shiny knees and fraying cuffs. There was no longer a wife at home to encourage replacements when the trousers of both work suits never seemed quite long enough, each finishing some way short of his shoes. He was the butt of a lot of jokes in the office, but whether or not he noticed, he chose not to let on. He was good at what he did and never felt the necessity to get close to anyone he worked with or listen to their prattle. His preference for Julia came with the understanding that she came from the same mould.

The crease between his eyes deepened as he considered whether he had enquired sufficiently about her health or whether he could get on to the real business of why he had come up to see her. Julia had never been part of the gossiping set, but all Malcolm cared about was that her work ethos was similar to his own and he liked that. She managed her time well, and apart from a couple of recent slips, never reneged on her workload or tested him outside his comfort zone with that mysterious complaint of 'women's problems'.

He kept hold of the door handle, relieved at being able to take her at her word. Following a moment's silence, Malcolm cleared his throat, remembering the reason he had come up to see her.

'Right...well, if you're sure you're all right, there's a

gentleman downstairs with an enquiry that I think that you're best to deal with. He's looking into North Newbald at the time of the Civil War. I remember that you once gave a talk at that same village last year and took some material with you.'

He paused, waiting for a response, eyes raised in expectation. 'Are you up to taking this one? If not, I can always ask Martha later.'

Julia had little time to consider what to do and took on the default reaction of agreeing to take the enquiry. 'No, don't do that. I'll be down in two minutes... just give me a minute first.'

Malcolm nodded, happy with that. 'I'll let him know then. Apparently, he used to teach around here years ago but spent the past twenty years in France, according to Carole. Pleasant chap…you'll like him.'

'Yes…I'm sure I will.'

Malcolm left, content in the thought that he would not be losing a member of staff due to illness when they were already short on numbers, and also that Julia was well enough to handle the enquiry.

What Malcolm did not see was the look of panic on her face as he left. She went to the toilets where she splashed cold water on her face. The shock momentarily at least put a little colour back into her cheeks. She tried to smooth back her hair, but her hands shook so much that she could not manage even that. Her hair looked flat and lifeless, and now it was damp too. She tucked it behind her ears in an attempt to give it some semblance of a style and headed slowly to the reading room.

Chapter 29

The reading room was getting busy, but David's presence was unmistakable; he sat large at a small table, the only one as yet uncovered by yellowing documentation and ancient volumes. A briefcase was by his side and he was waiting, staring straight ahead and deep in thought. Julia stopped for a moment at the other side of the glass partition where the last vestige of doubt that it might not be David disappeared. She went into the room.

'Mr Weston?'

He turned quickly, startled from his reverie and stood to face Julia.

On his part, their last encounter of 1969 started to resurface; on her part it had never left.

'Yes, that's me.' He smiled the old smile she remembered so well and recalling the last words of Michael, knew that she must be his mother.

'Julia…hello…how are you? It's been a long time.'

David smiled but beyond that betrayed little emotion as he registered the plain unmade up face and drab clothing.

A very different Julia, standing before him now, had replaced the pretty young girl from the summer of '69, the eager girl with the tight blouse and short skirt. He registered the change with shock and surprise.

The buzz of conversation in the room quietened down as yet more papers and files were deposited on the waiting tables. Chatter was replaced by the sound of pencils scribbling on notepads and pages turning. To keep their conversation low, he moved to close the gap between them, in keeping with the sign above the door requesting silence. Julia instinctively stepped back, her face had become a burning a beacon in the coolness of the room. At this vantage point, Julia too registered the changes in this man from the teacher at school.

Luxurious curls, once a rich brown, were now grey and in need of a cut, hanging limply over his collar. The once bright eyes were hooded with a network of lines mapped out beneath, and the whites had a yellow tinge, even more noticeable when he'd moved up close. But despite the ageing, she still saw the attraction he commanded, and the compulsion he found easy to extract from those around him.

'What are you doing here?' Julia tried to keep her voice level and calm despite the turmoil inside.

'Work…I need to complete some research and I'm reliably informed it should be here.'

'Right…do you want to tell me what it is you're looking for?' The hammering heart did not ease for a moment and it was all she could do not to run out of the room.

'Do you mind if we sit first?' The events of the past week had left their mark on his health both physically and mentally and the pressure was taking its toll. They sat on opposite sides of the small table oblivious to the flurry of activity in the rest of the room and Julia produced her pad and pencil.

'Yes…yes of course…I'll make notes and see what we have…if we have…'

Neither chose to raise the questions that demanded answers. Not yet.

Pertinent questions only were asked, and the business side was concluded with relative ease. There wouldn't be much, not all that he had hoped for, or led to believe was here, but it would be enough to go on with.

'I'll see what I can find for you.'

She stood up, keen to get out of the suffocating room but David indicated for her to sit back down.

'Don't go just yet…please?'

Julia reluctantly sat back down.

'Tell me… how long have you worked here? It looks as though you've done well'

She answered after a moment's pause 'I've been here a few years now.'

'I'm pleased to see that all my hard work with you paid off…did you come straight from uni?' He sensed the discomfort but would not be put off the subject of her past and determined to penetrate the wall of silence. She would give nothing away.

'Are you married…family…?'

This was too much, too soon; too personal. This wasn't the time or the place to divulge her private life and it was none of his business. The topic was deflected.

'I've been told you're writing a book. How far on are you with it?'

She spoke quickly, her throat tight with the strain of maintaining a conversation at such close proximity, worried that the nervous tremor in her voice would betray her. He ignored the question and continued with his own.

'You've not moved far from home. I always thought you were keen to travel...or did you?' He was relentless, staring into her face.

'No...that never happened.' He raised an eyebrow in the hope that she would go on but Julia sat implacable.

'I'm sorry about that.'

Her heart thumped even harder, telling her to leave. Now. They were two strangers on a stage enacting roles where they had neither the capacity nor the wherewithal to make sense of two very different scripts.

Julia was desperate to get away. Confirming what might be available from the archives, she stood to make her escape. David, reluctant to let go of his former line of question, had to concede he had little choice for now.

'I'll see what we have. The information is scattered around and might take me a while. You can wait here if you like or come back later.'

As Julia walked away he called over 'It is good to see you again...and Julia?' She froze as she heard him speak her name and gave a slight upward incline of her head. 'Yes?'

'Shall I wait in here?'

She coughed nervously, but felt on safe ground again. 'You'll have to leave your coat and bag in one of the lockers over there first. Just bring paper and a pencil. No pens. And you'll need to show some ID before I can give you anything to work from. Carole will help you.' David recognised the young woman bent over a pile of old catalogue cards waiting to be inserted into a wooden drawer taken from a cabinet beneath. Her short dress was in obvious contrast to the outfits of the others in that day.

'Yes...I've met Carole.'

He smiled, having already appraised the dress that

emphasised every curve of her body and also revealed the slim legs encased in black tights.

'There may not be as much information as you think, you know. Don't expect too much, will you?'

'That's ok. Just let me see what you've got.'

He paused as if waiting for more, but Julia turned away.

'Perhaps you'll come for a coffee with me later?' he called as an afterthought.

She ignored the request and pointed to the lockers before going to get the documents.

THE STACKS on the first floor provided a momentary, and much needed, refuge as Julia tried to regain control over her body and thoughts. A thunderous headache had taken hold and she could taste the bile rising in her mouth. 'I will get through this,' she said to herself over and over like a mantra, as she sought out the files. Locating what David needed was laborious but occupied the time before going back down. Unbidden memories tinged with rejection and pain confronted her at every turn despite every effort otherwise.

Within the hour, Julia found David where she had left him, this time deep in concentration over a thick and half full notepad. He looked up at her arrival, his face more relaxed and less lined than it seemed when he came in. The pain in his chest had subsided.

'I was going to send a search party.'

'Sorry…I've brought all I can find, but going back well over three hundred years…I did say there's wouldn't be that much…'

She put down a thin pile of papers trying to avoid looking at him.

'No problem…thank you…but before you rush off again, what about that coffee later?'

'I don't know. I'm really busy today…I doubt I can get away.'

What she wanted to say was an emphatic no but David would not be put off.

'Come and get me later…when you have your lunch break. Or shall I come and find you?'

JULIA WAS FLUSHED AND ANXIOUS; her eyes darted towards the door. The blackness was closing in; chasing faster and faster. She had to leave quickly. Find safety. Usual place. Now. She reached the storeroom at the back of the office, unseen, closing the door behind. Heart thumping wildly; blood searing through her ears; gasping for air, sinking low, low down. The heat was unbearable. Shaking uncontrollably as the darkness closed in. Am I dying? She fell to the floor.

TIME DID NOT EXIST. Julia had no idea how long the darkness stayed until she managed to come round again; when the shaking stopped, and she could see again.

She found the familiar office chair with the broken back and sat, slumped forward with head in hands. Damp hair prickled her scalp. Her name had been called several times but the office was silent now.

It wasn't the first time this quiet, secluded room had provided a refuge. When the noises in her head would not be shut out and the darkness threatened, she knew what to do. When the pressures at home became too much; when emotions got in the way and the panic set its trap, this was her retreat.

It wasn't the first time and wouldn't be the last, but it was still her secret at work. The panic attacks began when her fifteenth year had drawn to a close, when the carefree childhood had been replaced with a dread reality from which she could not hide for long.

Michael had become her world and life revolving around a series of lies that kept her just the right side of sanity, took its toll. The lies she told her parents, the lies she told Michael and the lies she told herself had become so inextricably linked to her existence, they almost became true. Almost.

The episodes increased during the early years of Michael's life and it had been a strain for her mother to watch when nothing and no one could pierce through the impenetrable wall of the dark and cavernous place that Julia retreated to. The first concluded with a violent outcome on the bathroom floor with a razor at her wrist. Counselling had helped but the process was slow and painful and shortly after, her father had taken the heartache of losing the innocent daughter he loved to the grave following a heart attack. They had all loved and cherished the baby but the after effects were difficult to deal with.

THE HEAT of the tiny room became unbearable and it was close to lunchtime. Back in the office, Julia saw Carole staring vacantly out of the window. She'd been more than happy to be on her own and not have Martha complaining about her work, making the most of the time with a few personal calls to arrange a night out. Just two months into the job, she was overwhelmed by the repetitious nature of the work; lugging registers around that not only listed death but, in her mind, smelled like it too. The only part she really liked was payday, that and the fact that her parents stopped nagging her for lying in bed half the day. But it was not the job of her dreams.

As Carole looked out of the window, she drifted back to Kuta Beach in Bali, where she had spent the previous summer, filling her head with sun, sea, and parties; and, of course, Rafa, her short-lived lover. She was startled into the present when the storeroom door opened and quickly picked up her pencil in pretence of working. When she saw that it was only Julia, and not Martha, she relaxed.

'Did you have to do that? You frightened me to death!'

Julia turned her back on Carole and made her excuses.

The message she'd had been given for Julia by David was long forgotten, and by the time she thought about it, Julia had disappeared anyway. Carole, on her own again, closed her eyes, lay on Kuta Beach and slipped back into the arms of Rafa.

Julia went up to the toilets where she again splashed cold water on her face and rearranged her hair away from her neck with a band. The hope of getting away unseen was short-lived when she met Maggie coming up the stairs in the opposite direction.

'I've been looking all over for you, where have you been hiding? Are we still on for tonight?' she asked, until realising the state Julia was in. She had seen that look more than once before and knew well enough that it wasn't a good sign.

'Shall I call round your place first? You look as though you need cheering up.'

Julia had completely forgotten that they were going to the cinema that night.

'Sorry...yes...I've been busy all morning...er...yes... yes. I mentioned it to Will...it's fine. I'll see you later

Maggie, I've got to go right now. Can't stop. I'll be ready for seven.'

Maggie looked at Julia's disappearing figure, rushing down the stairs.

'Are you sure you're all right?' she called out.

'I'm fine, really…don't worry…it's nothing. There's just something I've got to do this lunchtime. I'll see you later.' Maggie wasn't convinced but let her go, without another word.

Julia prised her coat out from the overstuffed rack downstairs, and tied the belt tight around her middle. Almost as an afterthought, she went to the public toilets nearest the door. They were empty and Julia took the opportunity to look for the old Rimmel lipstick she was sure was still in her bag. Frantically searching amongst tissues, purse and a comb, she eventually found it tucked away at the bottom. It was still unused; an impulse buy from Boots when she'd been out with Maggie one lunchtime and she'd been told it was definitely her colour. It was carefully applied to two pale lips, but as soon as she put it on it was obvious that it was a mistake and much too dark against her porcelain-white face. Rubbing it off with one of the tissues left a red stain that wouldn't budge but it would have to do.

What am I doing, she wondered as she leaned against the basin, still trembling and looking at her reflection. Beneath the open coat, a pair of shapeless trousers, worn from yesterday, stood out in accusation that she really should care more, and at that moment she wished that she'd put on a skirt instead. 'It's all too late, anyway. What does it matter?' she confided to the face that looked back from the mirror, grateful that at least most of her outfit would be covered up by the coat.

David was still at work in the Reading Room, holding

open a large volume with one hand, trying to keep it from closing up in its new binding, and writing with the other. Julia was automatically drawn to the hair curling around his neck and the hands that had once touched her so tenderly. She didn't notice Carole at first, walking up to him with another book. He turned to her and they spoke, close up and laughing about something she said.

The table was full of documents and books, more than the items she'd brought down earlier. Carole must have been dispatched as a last resort when Julia had left for the office. They made a charming picture: David looking up and smiling, and Carole chatting freely and touching his arm. Julia froze as she watched Carole turn to leave, flashing him a wide smile before she went.

'Thank you Carole…much appreciated.'

'You're welcome, Mr Weston.'

Restored in the warm comforting confines of the Archives, David looked relaxed and the pain in his chest had subsided enough for the old charm to return with very little effort. He sat back in his chair watching Carole's disappearing figure before seeing Julia walk through the door.

'There you are. I've been waiting ages for you. Didn't you get my message?'

'No…no message. Who did you give it to?'

'Carole…a while ago, I should have checked with her just now…too busy helping me out I suppose'

Julia stood transfixed by the voice before replying.

'I've only got forty-five minutes,' she told him stiffly, 'then I've got to be back to relieve the counter staff.'

'Then let's not waste time.' He looked straight at her, intent on something, but she couldn't fathom the meaning behind his eyes. David gathered up his notes and pencils and left them in a neat pile on the table. He took her arm as they walked to the locker to get his coat. He was too familiar; it was too urgent.

'I was told that I could leave my things there until I get back. Is that right?' He paused, 'Will they be safe there?'

Julia took back her arm, 'They'll be fine, don't worry.'

Chapter 30

Julia led the way out of the Archives building, on to the street, keeping a distance between them, but occasionally glancing in his direction. David had turned up the collar of the long, faded blue mac and, despite the age of the mac and its owner, presented an attractive enough man nonetheless. He'd always dressed well, although twenty years ago the clothes might have been a couple of sizes smaller. Tension rose with each step until Julia broke the silence between them.

'How long are you here for?'

'I'm not sure just yet…it all depends.' He didn't elaborate, but instead asked if there was a decent café close by. 'I've been away too long. Nothing's familiar in town any more.'

'It's not changed that much.'

'Then I've just forgotten what's here.'

She took him to the far side of Westgate Lane, away from the parade of shops, and towards a small café where it was unlikely they would be seen by anyone she knew. As they got closer, she hoped that it would not be busy. She'd only been once before, a long time ago, on an unsuccessful date, just before she'd met up with Will, when she was on a work placement at the Archives. His name was Gareth, a family historian who had been very persistent in asking her out until she relented to a coffee on her morning off. It had been a disaster. They had nothing in common. What she mostly remembered was the dandruff on his collar and afterwards she made it clear that the coffee had been a once only.

The sky had turned a darker grey, heavy with the promised rain, and despite the best efforts of the shops with their early Christmas displays, no one looked happy to be out on this late November day. She caught sight of her reflection in a shop window they'd passed. It paled into insignificance against the mannequins behind the glass, each dressed in Christmas-party finery. Then she remembered the stain on her cardigan.

The Corner House Café was not busy and David took her arm again to go in; and again she shrugged him off. 'It's all right, I just want to make sure that you don't run away,' he said, smiling. 'You didn't seem too happy about coming out with me but I really want to talk to you.' He made light of her indifference when the only reply she gave was, 'don't worry…I'm here aren't I?'

The café was over warm and the steamy air mingled with an aroma of fried bacon from morning breakfasts. A waitress indicated that she would be with them as soon as she finished taking another order, so they found a table in the corner, away from the door and from the cold air that had followed them in.

'I really can't stay long?' she repeated once they were seated.

'I know…I know, I won't keep you out too late.' He picked up the menu propped between the salt and pepper cruets and ketchup bottle. 'Let's order shall we? I haven't eaten all day.'

The harsh strip lighting in the café was flattering to neither of them. His face looked gaunt, but the paunch around his middle told of a comfortable life. He'd shaved that morning, but not close enough, and it gave the impression of neglect. She wanted so much to know what had happened since they last met, but was reluctant to start that conversation.

'I'll just have a coffee, thank you...I'm not hungry.'

The waitress returned to take their order.

'We'll have two coffees and two cheese sandwiches please'

'Ready in two minutes,' she said without smiling. She was working on her own due to sickness and grimaced as another influx of customers arrived through the door. Julia shuffled in her seat, straightened her back and looked around at the unfamiliar faces, grateful at least that there was no one here she knew. The café was filling up and the buzz of conversation grew louder.

'You should eat something...or have you already?' David drew her back into his intense gaze. She flinched and fixed instead on the ketchup bottle with its congealed neck, an obsession she'd always loathed at home.

Again he assessed the changes in the face of the woman sitting opposite; a woman who bore little resemblance to the young girl he'd taught. Here sat a middle aged woman and not the thirty-six year old he knew her to be beneath the sallow cheeks and tired eyes. Pulling off the blue woollen hat, her dark blonde hair had flattened to her head and did not respond well to fingers that tried to coax it back into shape.

Drinks and sandwiches arrived to break the silence. Julia stirred a coffee she did not want whilst David eagerly made a start on his cheese sandwich. He pushed the other towards her and the memory of the last time they had eaten together was not lost on either of them. Julia took a small sip of the hot drink and it loosened her throat sufficiently to speak as David ate with enthusiasm.

'How long are you staying around here?'

He paused with the sandwich halfway to his mouth, then put it back on his plate and took a drink of the thin tasteless brew.

'You asked me that earlier.'

'But you never gave me an answer. Are you living around here…or just visiting?'

He ignored the question and after a short pause, asked one of his own.

'I think it's time we talked about the other reason I'm here. You know what it is so please don't pretend otherwise, Julia. Don't make it difficult for me…it's hard enough as it is.'

'I don't know what you mean.'

'Ok…have it your own way… I'll ask you straight…'

He searched her face for a glimmer of reaction, but none came and her eyes were still fixated on the sauce bottle.

'Why didn't you tell me about Michael?' He'd stopped eating now, losing his appetite for the sandwich that was as tasteless as the coffee. Julia crossed her arms tight across her chest, swaying slightly backwards and forwards, trapped like a hunted animal. Her eyes darted around the room.

'What about Michael? What do you know about my son?'

'*Your* son? We've become quite good friends Michael and I over the past few weeks…we met in Manchester…at the university in fact…I've been helping him with his dissertation.'

'Really? You lecture there now?'

'Good god no…I've been staying with a friend who happens to be his tutor.'

'And how did you know he was my son?' Her face burned at the thought of what they might have talked about.

'It was Michael who told me that his Mum worked at the Archives when I said that I needed to come up here. We got talking…he told me your name, what you did… where he was from…he's a really nice kid. Spoke well of this clever mother of his who'd had a difficult start in her career…the mother who'd had a baby at a very young age.'

Now that David had started, he warmed to the subject. He wanted more than anything to talk about Michael and dispel any last doubts that may have lingered. If he felt some small sympathy for Julia, it was put aside in the desire to open up and embrace this new opportunity that was just within reach. He leaned over and put his hand on Julia's, but she quickly snatched it away.

'I have to go,' she replied in a voice barely audible.

'No!…Not yet…I want to know about my son.'

'And what about me?'

This wasn't the conversation that she had been expecting after convincing herself that there was no way David could know about Michael, but he wouldn't stop now.

'Have you any idea what it was like when I finally realised who I was talking to?'

'You didn't say anything did you?' The panic in Julia's voice was rising but David continued.

'He reminds me so much of myself at his age.'

'Does he?' The reply was given more with sarcasm than denial and the gulf between them widened further. On his side, twenty-four years of a childless marriage had slipped by. No knowledge of a son for all but a few weeks. On the other, a woman grown bitter from early rejection and a love frozen in time.

'Why didn't you tell me that you had a child?'

'What about me?' she asked again, her voice now reduced to little more than a whisper.

'You should have told me Julia.'

'How could I? You let me go and didn't tell me where you'd gone. I went back to your house and it was empty…sold.'

David put his face in his hands. 'The school had my address. You could have found a way.'

'What for? Would you have come back for me? I never moved away and you never got in touch with *me*! Not once. Not to say hello, or sorry, or how are you? Not even to say a proper goodbye.'

Hot tears flowed freely down her flaming cheeks.

'I know… and I am so sorry.'

'Of course you are… now… but not for me. You're not sorry for what you did to me!'

'I don't know what else to say to you. You came to me…I didn't ask you to…'

He knew as he said it that this was not the time for that conversation and stopped himself going further. The words, once spoken, killed the last vestige of hope that Julia had so carefully preserved, along with a faded black and white photograph hidden at the back of her wardrobe.

'Julia, I've missed out on more than twenty years in the life of a son I never knew I had.' There were tears in his eyes too, but they failed to stir any sympathy and something inside Julia finally snapped.

'My life has nothing to do with you! Why do you need to know about my son now?' She spat the words out. There was nothing left for her to say. David tried to be conciliatory, 'Michael is a lovely boy. You've brought him up well. And now I want to get to know him. I've a right to that at least, haven't I? And Michael has a right too.'

'What? What do you know of Michael? You met him…when? And now you tell me that he's a 'lovely boy'. You don't know anything,' she hissed.

David wiped his face with a thin paper napkin from the table and Julia's coffee spilt as she scraped her chair back to stand.

'I have to go back,' she told him, her voice empty and quiet now, drained of emotion. 'We have nothing more to talk about.'

Before she could leave, he tried to reach over for her hand. She let it stay just for a moment, before taking it back; it wasn't her he was pleading for.

'Why didn't you tell me, Julia? For God's sake, didn't you think that I had a right to know? Or that Michael had a right to know about me?' he repeated, 'Didn't you tell anyone?' His pain turned to anger when he saw that she wasn't about to welcome him into Michael's life. Through the tears and years of pent-up denial Julia was confused and frightened when she saw the determined look in his eyes. One or two faces in the café turned in their direction, but neither noticed.

'Have you no children of your own…in France?'

David regretted not suggesting a pub. He desperately needed a drink. The memory of Simone in agony at the Hospital de St. Petrie rose to add to the pain of knowing that there had been a child somewhere all those childless years. Simone had almost died after giving birth to a baby who would not live. He had sat with her, still dressed in his dinner jacket and tie, holding her hand after the operation. He couldn't remember the journey there, or when he left, but vivid in his mind was the cross on the wall above her bed. He'd fixed his eyes on it as a talisman to bring her through. He prayed to it, making a promise that if she survived he would show Simone that it wasn't a problem to be childless, that they were fine as they were. They had each other, what more could they need? The memory was fleeting only and David came back into the present.

'I've business to sort out for the rest of the week…but I will come to see you again,' he called out to Julia's retreating figure. 'I won't leave it like this.'

The waitress had quickly put their bill on the table when she heard raised voices. They wouldn't be the first arguing couple to leave without paying and she wasn't paid enough to kick up a fuss and go running after them. The bill was the last thing on Julia's mind and the café door slammed in a gust of wind as she left.

David held his head in his hands, thoughts raging, why couldn't the boy have been his and Simone's? Why did fatherhood have to come at such a high price? To not see the baby turn into a boy and the boy turn into the lovely man he'd met was hard to bear and he would not, could not, let it rest there. Michael would know of his real father. They both had that right.

The conversation with Julia had not gone well, that much was no surprise, but David was glad it was at least out in the open now and the knowledge of it could not be ignored. Julia was no longer a naïve fifteen year old girl but a grown woman who had had a life with the son he had yet to know.

Out on the street, another pair of eyes watched Julia leaving. Mme. Rubin had viewed the scene inside the café with interest before disappearing back into the shadows.

Chapter 31

A heavy rain whipped up, lashing Julia's face. Christmas lights from the shops shone on wet pavements, reflections distorting in the puddles as she rushed past to get back to work.

Soaked and cold, with hair dripping down her neck, Julia met Malcolm on the way in, looking equally bedraggled.

'Got caught as well?' He laughed, stating the obvious.

'I'm glad I've seen you…can you spare a few minutes before you get back to work?'

Julia was about to protest other pressing matters but he pre-emptied her objection,

'Don't worry, there's enough staff on the counter this afternoon and I need to talk to you…come to my office when you can…when we've both dried off…I'm in all afternoon.'

'All right…just give me a few minutes to get myself sorted.'

It was the second time she'd been late back that week; he might have been preparing a warning but that was the last thing on her mind. Whatever she did this afternoon, she would make sure that it did not involve seeing David again and keep clear of the public rooms.

Drying off her face and hair, Julia made the best she could of her appearance, and composed once more, tapped on Malcolm's door. He was on the phone and gestured to her to come in and take the one clear seat in front of his desk. The other three were covered in a variety of fusty donations needing to be checked for validity and duplication. Almost the entire office floor was in chaos: piles of books, boxes and other ephemera lay in disorder, all at varying stages of decomposition. She recognised the collection as the rescued remains from an old, local engineering firm, closed and ruined after the recent floods, and assumed that the work was about to be passed on to her.

The office window looked down on to the side street below and Julia's eyes drifted from the mass of boxes to the water-puddled pavement. It was still raining. The mesmeric sound of the occasional wash of tyres from passing cars sailing across overflowing drains was the only sound other than Malcolm on the phone.

The revelations at the café could wait to be dealt with later and the internal doors of her mind closed one by one until Malcolm's voice brought her back into the room. The phone call had ended and her attention was needed.

'Well Julia...Julia?...what do you think?'

'Sorry...to what?...to this?' She gestured towards the debris in the room.

'No...not this...not yet anyway...I just said I've been talking again to the gentleman you were helping this morning.'

He leant forward, obviously pleased with himself on recent developments.

'He told me he's willing to pay the department for our

services…to help with the research. He's close to finishing his book on the Civil War and Henrietta Maria's involvement, but has a tight deadline from his agent. He asked for you specifically…wanted to know if you could work with him as you seem so familiar with the subject.'

Malcolm looked for a response before continuing, 'You know, we could get some good publicity from this when the book comes out. We could do with higher visitor numbers if we don't want to see further budget cuts.'

Julia attempted a smile at such enthusiasm, but it waned as the internal doors of her mind threatened to open again.

'It's good to find someone who actually believes our services are worth paying for.'

'Yes…it is,' she said, flatly, 'I'd love to do it. But don't see how I can fit it in with the pile of enquiries already on my desk. I don't think Carole can cope with them…and I presume you'll want my help with this lot here.'

'Don't worry about all that, I'll have a word with Martha this afternoon and she can take your urgent enquiries. Mr Weston's not coming back until next week so we have a couple of days to get something sorted. Talk to Carole…she's got all the details.'

'I bet she has…'

'Sorry?'

'Yes…I'll go and see Carole.'

Julia got up to leave as he added, 'Oh, I almost forgot…your son rang while you were out. Did you get the message?' She shook her head, puzzled as to why Michael would call her at work. 'He's tried a couple of times this morning apparently. You might want to give him a quick ring first to see if it's important.'

'Ok…thanks, I'll do that.'

Two messages she'd not received that day, but on the

way back to the office, she didn't get the chance to ring him. Carole called after her when passing the enquiry desk.

'Julia...Julia...you got a minute?'

Carole had rarely looked so animated when working at the counter; it was a transformation nothing short of miraculous.

'What is it?'

'Come over here'

She took Julia over to the public shelves where it was quiet.

'What's the matter?' Julia asked, surprised at the secrecy. 'Has Martha had another go at you? You know I can't...'

'No, nothing like that... no...I was talking to that man David Weston this morning. You know, the one you were working with earlier. He was telling me about the book he's almost finished.'

'The book...and?

'You know, the one about the Civil War?' Julia nodded, 'What about it?'

'You'll never guess what...at last we have something interesting. He told me that you'll be helping him, but after we talked a bit more he asked if I could help too... typing up...you know, that kind of thing. Then before he went, he wanted to know if I would like to go for a drink with him after work. Said we could work out the details over a glass of wine. That is, if I was interested. Do you think I should go? I'd really like to but...'

'No, I don't think you should go! You don't know anything about him.'

'No, but you do. He told me that you've known each other for years. And for an older man, he is rather attractive don't you think...that voice...very sexy.'

'I can't believe what I'm hearing. He's old enough to be your father!'

Carole was disappointed at the response but refused to be put off.

'Come on, he's not that old.'

'Are you so desperate, Carole? Anyway, it was a long time ago and even then I didn't know him that well. I don't know anything about his life now; if he's married or has a family, or anything.'

Carole shrugged 'I'll think about it, then. He said he'd wait for me at the Rose and Crown if I wanted to meet up and we could…'

Before she could say anything else, Colin had wandered over with a pile of books warning her that her absence from the counter was not going down well with Martha. A queue was already building up. Carole looked over and saw the scathing look aimed in her direction.

'I'd better go,' she said, 'thanks, Colin. I'll see you later, Julia? Yes?'

Julia didn't answer, but watched Carole sashay back behind the counter, her dress looking shorter than ever. She'd forgotten that there was a time when she would have worn hers just the same.

It was gone three by the time she had the opportunity to call Michael. As usual, there was no answer to the student house phone and she had to be content with leaving a message instead. He'd probably be desperate for another loan, although 'loan' had a variety of meanings in his vocabulary. It wasn't the end of term yet and not even the weekend, so he was unlikely to say he would be coming home. It was his final year and he rarely came back as much as he used to.

For the rest of the afternoon, Julia successfully managed to avoid the public areas and sorted out the workload on her desk. She later found out, through Colin, that David had collected his things and left the building an hour ago, in a hurry. She managed to fend off Carole, who was desperate to talk to her again on why Julia thought that she should not see David after work. Thankfully, Maggie was too tied up to ask where she had been at lunchtime.

Julia's head pounded; she recognised the signs of a migraine only too well when there was much to cope with. She rubbed at her wrist and looked at the clock, relieved to see that there was only another fifteen minutes to go before finishing for the day. There had been no other call from Michael so it couldn't be that urgent.

IT WAS six o'clock by the time Julia climbed aboard the bus for home, facing the ever-present battle for a seat. The rain had still not let up, swelling the usual number of passengers with those who might otherwise have walked. Julia was shored up on both sides by damp coats and plastic bags. Her stomach reminded her that she hadn't eaten since breakfast and the strain of the day left her feeling so tired she could have slept on her feet. Pitch-dark outside, a grey fug of light strained to illuminate the inside of the bus. She remembered the cinema, but the last thing she wanted tonight was to see a film with Maggie and decided to cancel as soon as she got home. Apart from which, Michael might call back and she didn't want to miss him.

At her home stop, Julia squeezed past the line of unhappy commuters. It was a relief to get out but after the warm cocoon of the bus, the chill wind was a sharp reminder of the long haul of winter ahead. Julia also remembered her hat that she'd left in the café.

Chapter 32

Battling to reach home, the light shining from the living room window went unnoticed until Julia unlocked the front door. Positive that Will would not have left it on this morning, and knowing that he wasn't due home until late that night, she went inside hoping to be wrong on one of those counts.

It wasn't Will; it was Michael. Overwhelmed with happiness at Michael being home, the joy of seeing him was just what she needed right now and her spirits lifted.

'Michael...why didn't you tell me you were coming... it's so good to see you'. She went over for their customary hug, but Michael barely responded and remained sitting on the sofa. He didn't look happy and looked up at his mother without smiling.

'I did! Left messages all over the place this morning before I left, but you never got back.'

'Oh...I'm sorry...I didn't get the message straight away and then I was tied up with Carole...but I did try to call back...honestly. You never answered.'

'No I'd gone by then.'

'This is such a nice surprise…I thought you were busy with the dissertation…is everything ok?'

'It's fine…fine…I just need to talk to you about something else and it couldn't wait…I can't get it off my mind'

'Oh…what about? Is it money? Are you short?'

Michael sat with hands clasped together, searching down in the carpet for the right words. Julia backed away to take off her coat and hang it in the hall.

'Have you eaten? Shall I do you something…are you hungry?' she called out while Michael sighed in frustration.

'Mum I've come to ask you something. Please…come back in and sit down. I'm not hungry…I don't want anything to eat.'

Julia reluctantly returned, her eyes opening a little wider as she held her breath and waited for him to continue. Something wasn't right. Was this it? Had David already said something to him? Was this the time Michael demanded more than she wanted to give? She sat on the sofa next to her son, and put her hand across his as she studied his profile. He could so easily have been David twenty years ago.

The house was cold, but her face burned at the thought of David. The darkness threatened once again that day and the waters of anxiety crept higher and higher when there was little she could do to hold them back.

Michael turned and took her cold hands in his, 'I want you to tell me Mum…truthfully this time…who is my father?'

'What…?' she pulled back her hand, 'what's brought this on?'

'Please Mum…talk to me…I'm asking you for once to tell me more than you have.'

'I've told you, he…' she stopped short at the old lie,

'Why now...why today this minute? Has something happened?'

'You could say that...'

'What? What's happened?'

'Someone I've got to know at uni...friend of my tutor's.' Julia did not need to ask who but played along,

'What? Who was that?'

'Someone over from France...doing research... someone who's going to visit the Archives very soon and will be asking for you...I told him about you.'

Of course he did. The lies and cover-ups, denials and ignorance, were they to be wiped out now by the boy in front of her? She still couldn't think of him as a man; he was *her* boy, *her* son, and it was enough that he had had a happy life with her, and with Will. He hadn't needed to know any more than that. What would have been the point? But he wasn't a child any longer and demanded answers she still did not want to give.

'I've told you, Michael. It was someone I met at a party. A friend of a friend who'd been visiting and a man I never saw again. We had too much to drink. I'm sorry. He went away....I...I don't know where. There was no secret...'

'Stop it, Mum. I know there's more to it than that. Just tell me the truth...please...tell me!' he shouted.

'What do you want me to say? I never saw him again and that *is* the truth,' she said, confident that that part at least was true, 'please Michael there's no point in bringing it all up again. It can't do either of us any good.'

They were both angry although Julia wavered at this point. She knew that he'd made friends with David, but didn't know what they had spoken about, or how much had been revealed by their meeting.

'Who have you been talking to, Michael?'

'I already said, someone at uni, a friend of Phil's. You know Phil, my tutor.'

She nodded, hoping against hope that this wasn't going where it might.

'This friend of his is a guy who's been helping me with my dissertation. There's something about him I can't work out. We have a subject in common and he was very interested in what I'm doing…interested in me. We've met a few times to talk it through, but it's more than that…more than my dissertation. His name's David Weston. He spoke as if he knew you. Do you know him, because he was *very* interested in you? Did you know him? Before he left, he'd been probing more into my personal life than the dissertation…and there's something else…'

'What else Michael?'

'I met his wife…she came to the university and took more interest in me than was normal…I didn't think much of it at first. A beautiful French woman who seemed to know about me. I didn't think anything of it at the time but really? She seemed upset about something. I couldn't get anything out of Phil. He doesn't get back to my calls either. So what's going on Mum?'

Julia's head sank down to her chest as Michael waited for an answer. He knew something he'd said had struck a chord. She took a deep breath, and spoke slowly, searching for the right script.

'It was such a long time ago, Michael. I'm sorry. It *was* just one night, and then he did disappear from my life. Abroad, yes…France. There really is nothing more I can tell you.'

'Yes there is! Did you sleep with him when he was married? Did you have an affair?'

Julia blanched at his words as Michael sat waiting for an answer. Michael wondering why she hadn't made any attempt to get in touch with David, or if not that, why David didn't want to know his son. Why did it have to be so hard to get at the truth? The look on his mother's face told him all he needed to know.

Neither of them heard the front door open, but when Will appeared in the room, Michael rushed past, ignoring the surprise on his stepfather's face,

'Michael? What on earth's going on? Why's Michael home?'

Julia pulled herself together just enough to think of a plausible answer.

'Uni problems. He's a bit stressed out about the dissertation, that's all.'

'Anything I can help with?'

'No, it'll get sorted...he needed to get away...'

Julia rubbed her hand across her forehead to ease the pain that refused to budge. Will went over to her and put his arms around her shoulders.

'Want me to get you something for that?' He stroked her head, but instead of relaxing into the gesture, her body stiffened and she moved away.

'It's ok I'll go get some aspirin.'

Snubbed, but no longer surprised by the reaction, Will went upstairs to look for Michael and leave her with her own thoughts. It was always the same when she got together with Michael since uni; his exclusion could not be more pronounced.

JULIA WENT UP to bed early that night. Michael had already gone and she was left to piece together what they had each said.

Will stayed downstairs and pulled out his diary, checking the pages for the following week. Monday nights at the Legion were still inked in, but they had been taken over in recent weeks by other commitments. Quietly closing the living room door, he picked up the phone and dialled the long-familiar number. His talk with Michael had been enough to fit together the missing pieces of the puzzle.

'Hello, it's me.'

He kept his voice low, glancing at the photos on the sideboard as he listened to the voice on the other end.

'I'll be over in about fifteen minutes, then…if that's ok?'

Despite an early night, and the tiredness that ravaged her body, Julia hardly slept. She watched the hours crawl by on the bedside clock and when she could no longer bear the repetitious loop of thoughts in her head, pulled back the covers to go and make some tea. The floor was cold; too early yet for the heating to have switched on. The fleecy dressing gown and slippers were little help against her shivering, but tea and another aspirin would help alleviate the cold and the pain that still throbbed in her head.

The house was quiet, too early for Will to be up, but after a couple of hours, when the clock shifted towards seven, there was still no sign of him. He was usually around by that time, making breakfast and listening to the news on the radio, but not today. She went back upstairs and stopped at his room. The door was slightly open and responded to a gentle push. The curtains too were open and the bed still made. She went inside.

'Will?…Will, are you there?'

Silence was the only answer.

His bed showed a slight indent where he must have been sitting and on the floor lay an odd sock. She picked it up; curious, and pulling the bed covers back felt the sheet underneath. It was cold, still as fresh as when it was made.

It hadn't been slept in. A quick search around the room and a check inside the wardrobe and drawers revealed gaps and spaces; the opening and closing of each generated an increased feeling of dread. Some clothes were still there, but certainly not all. She searched through the house, every room, every corner, but it brought no answer, no note even, and no relief from the growing tension wrapping itself around her head like a vice.

It was getting late and she needed to get ready for work. The motion of showering and dressing were carried out on autopilot. Scenes of the night before still lingered, and the anger that came from Will, when he'd come back downstairs to confront her, had been vitriolic.

'I'm sick of being excluded Julia…there's not much more I can take. I've had enough.'

There were too many problems to solve without Will adding to them. She'd gone to bed where her own inner rage burned alongside the thumping pain at her temple that no amount of painkillers could shift.

THE ARCHIVES PROVED a useful escape as long as she was undisturbed. Thankfully, David did not turn up the next day; perhaps he had already gone back to Manchester? However, it didn't stop Julia checking the study room at every opportunity to see if he was back. Malcolm was persistent, 'How are you getting on with Mr Weston? I've not seen him recently.'

'I've no idea…not heard from him. Maybe he changed his mind. We didn't have that much anyway.'

Was it relief that he didn't come or disappointment? The two emotions grew, interchanging with each passing day as working life slipped back into normality and the usual routines continued. Not so the routine at home, but that was a relief too when she did not have to face Will's questioning either. It was strange having the house to herself but as the days went by, although angry she that he hadn't been in touch to let her know where he was, she was not curious enough to try to find out.

Maggie was taking leave for a couple of weeks but that was good too; she was happy not to have to answer more probing questions. Even Colin remained subdued on the subject of David and Carole, and was disappointed that that road of gossip had been a dead end.

It was after three nights that Will re-appeared, waiting for her when she got back from work.

'Hello Julia.'

'You're back...where have you been? No message...no call. I didn't know what to think.'

'No...I'm sorry...no forget that...I'm not sorry...but I had to get away. I'm only sorry I didn't let you know...I should have.'

'Are you going to tell me where you've been? Is it permanent?'

'Is that what you want?'

Julia didn't answer straight away but glanced over to the glass of whisky poured from a bottle of malt bought the Christmas before. It was half-drunk and sitting on the table beside him. From the sound of his voice it wasn't his first, even though Will rarely drank at home.

'Yes I'd like to know...if you want to tell me'

'I went to stay with a friend.'

Julia didn't ask who, and will didn't elaborate.

'I don't think I can live like this any more, Julia. Neither of us is happy...you don't let me come near you... you don't talk to me...we don't even share the same bed. I've had enough and I'm leaving. For both our sakes.'

The weight of silence hung in the air and neither

moved until the shrill ring of the telephone broke the spell. Will chose to ignore it and Julia could not move as she absorbed what she had just heard. Was this what she wanted?

'You have to agree don't you...surely... it is for the best?'

He reached out for her hand, silently crying out for her to say no, for her to tell him that she did love him after all, that she wanted him to stay; but there was nothing. No response, no look of regret.

'Don't you even care what happens to us?'

She stared at Will with a blank expression.

'I'm sorry... I don't know what to say.'

The phone finally stopped ringing and Will went to pick up the suitcase with more of his clothes from behind the sofa.

The door closed with barely a sound, all anger spent, all emotion drained; and Julia sat alone until darkness enveloped the room.

It took some time for the enormity of what had happened to sink in. Again she probed the question: was that really what she wanted? After the emotion of the past couple of days, there was nothing left inside; no tears, no regrets and no longing for what she could not have.

WILL ARRIVED at Maggie's apartment, uncertain, but with no other plan in mind than he'd had to leave home. It still felt like a betrayal, but he had tried everything in his power to make it not so. Part of him also felt happy to be with someone who actually wanted him, made him welcome and loved. But the other part paced restlessly as Maggie flitted to and from the kitchen. The aroma of a chicken casserole filled the air, and a bottle of expensive wine lay waiting in the fridge.

'Let's go out', Will suddenly announced when she came back into the room. She was flushed from her exertions in the kitchen, and basked in the thought of their night ahead, together. Maggie's face fell in confusion.

'But you've just got here…dinner's almost ready...'

'Please…please Maggie I need…I need to just…'

Maggie did not want to do or say anything that might make him change his mind. The past three nights had been all that she'd wanted. It had taken long enough to get this far and time was running out.

'Of course we can, darling…whatever you need to do, I understand.'

Maggie stroked his cheek; there was nothing she wouldn't do to keep him here. She thrilled at the sight of his suitcase by the door and grabbed her coat from the hook.

They headed for the same rendezvous always used due to its quiet location and the fact that no one they knew was likely to be there. 'Café Rendezvous' was where they had met every Monday night for several weeks now: eight pm, when darts at the Club would be in full swing. They had slipped comfortably into the routine, alleviating the pressure of an oppressive home life from Will, and giving Maggie the opportunity she had waited for years to come to fruition.

It hadn't stopped Will wishing that it had been Julia waiting so eagerly for him each time he approached the table where Maggie sat, but he was grateful for her welcome and sympathetic ear. He ordered a beer and wine from the waitress hovering by.

'You look done in. Did you talk to Julia?'

The look of concern was tempered only by the rush of

pleasure at the thought again of another suitcase in the hall.

'She still won't talk…I don't understand any of it. It's as if there's nothing left inside her…'

The sorrow in Will's face did not deter the hope in Maggie's that he had at last come to accept the end of his marriage to Julia, and the start of a new life with her, with someone who had always loved him.

'You said yourself that once Michael had gone, nothing had been the same.'

'I know…it was always about Michael…but I loved… love…him too…as my own. I gave up wanting children because she only ever wanted Michael. And I only ever wanted the two of them. What did I do wrong Maggie? What happened?' Will appealed, searching for answers where there were none.

'That last night Michael came over…then suddenly going off again without saying a word to me…I don't even know what it was all about…I tried talking to him but got nowhere.'

'Maybe it's a mother and son thing. You know, Dads sometimes become an irrelevance? Don't understand. He's always loved you though…you know that.'

'No I don't know that…not any more. He was acting very strangely. Julia said he was having problems with his dissertation, but I think there's something else she's not telling me…I just don't know what.'

Maggie put her hand on his arm; Will looked up and gave a thin smile of gratitude.

'I don't even know if we should be doing this, Maggie. Not yet, anyway. Julia worries me…her behaviour…everything about her is shutting down. I can't get through but should I be walking away just now? I think she's ill.'

'Will, you've gone through this so many times. I'm here for you...always have been...always will be.'

'And you have to see her at work...how will you cope with that when she finds out?'

'I'll face that when the time comes...anyway it might not be for much longer.'

The comment went over Will's head, and the movement of Maggie's hand across the flat of her stomach was unnoticed. She was going to tell him over dinner, but sensed that it still wasn't the right time, not just yet.

He winced at the thought of them together at work, of Julia finding out what her best friend had been up to. Maggie persevered 'All I know is that I don't want to give you up...I love you, Will.'

Although they now shared a bed together, Will hadn't meant it to go that far. He'd just wanted someone to talk to, someone who knew what he was going through, but when they were alone at Maggie's apartment, it had been too compelling – the wine, the soft music; and Maggie wanting him in a way that Julia hadn't for so long. It was bittersweet. Will turned in his seat, looking for the waitress returning with the drinks.

'I know,' was all he said in reply and Maggie could only take comfort in the fact that he was with her now at least.

Convincing herself that the rest would follow, Maggie was beyond distraught when the suitcase, still packed, went back home with Will later that night. 'I have to find out what's wrong with her Maggie. Please understand? What if she really is ill? I'd never forgive myself' And Maggie could only console herself with the belief that he would be back again when nothing changed. He would be back when it all went wrong.

Chapter 33

Four weeks passed and David had not reappeared at the Archives. It was time enough for Julia to slot back into the normal working week and accept that Will had come back home; it was a time during which Maggie took extended leave on the pretext of visiting friends down south; and time for Will to regret decisions hastily made.

Of course Carole had gone out with David for that drink at the Rose and Crown, despite Julia's advice, and the next day she had told Julia every detail. 'He was amazing company, but nothing happened. He *is* a bit old really. But what a life he's had in France...I don't know why he gave it all up. He could have finished the book over there, surely, and we could have just sent over the information he needed. We get enquiries from all over the world, don't we?'

Julia had hidden her feelings under a mask of reproach that Carole had been so taken in by a man who obviously drank too much and would probably never finish a pamphlet, let alone a full book. She was relieved to hear that the one drink did not go further. Carole's last remark hit home, however.

'I thought he was going to invite me back to his place, but he said that he needed an early night. Not disappointing really. Most of the guys I know don't have much to say for themselves but want to get you into bed as soon as they can.'

'Will you see him again, though?'

'Oh no, I don't think so. Seb's back and he wants to take me to the new Italian in town…ve-ry expensive…'

And just like that David was dismissed from Carole's conversation and from her life. How easy it was for some. Go out with a man, find it's not quite right and move on. But if David had said yes to her all those years ago, how different would her life have been?

Michael paid one more visit home after the last confrontation, stung into apologising for his angry words, and saddened when he learned of Will threatening to leave. It hurt that he might have been responsible in any way and thought too much of Will to want that. It did not stop him wanting to talk about David, however. This genie was out of the bottle and would not go back no matter how hard Julia tried. He arrived on a Monday evening when he knew Will was out and she listened as he talked and asked the questions he demanded answers to.

In hope more than expectation, she initially stuck to the same line of defence, refusing to shift when he wanted to know more; but the relentless questioning wore her down and eventually she admitted that yes, David was his father. It could have been such a relief to say those words, 'David is your father,' but the repercussions left her in no doubt that it wouldn't end there. Would David's presence mean he would want be part of Michael's life in more ways than she was prepared to accept? After years of denial, of lies and a refusal to acknowledge the truth, where did that leave her now? The wall of self-preservation was crumbling, brick by brick. Her only hope was that David had gone back to France.

Michael left two days later in a state of shock. He needed to be on his own to absorb what he now knew for certain to be true. Julia was left broken. With no place to retreat with her own version of the truth, she would have to endure whatever Michael decided to do next. She begged him to not to say anything to Will just yet; she would do that in her own time, and Michael, too overcome to object, had more than enough to think about on his own terms.

AS THE DAYS and weeks passed by, with no word from David, Julia relaxed into a certainty that he must have gone back to France. It was little consolation to Michael who went back to Manchester in the hope that David might answer the remaining questions his mother evaded.

Amongst the relief of David's prolonged absence, Julia fought the same old demons inside of wanting to see him again. Despite the fact that it wasn't her he had come to see; despite the fact that he knew the truth; despite the fact that Michael knew, the urge was still there.

When David re-appeared by the public computers talking to Martha, it came as no great shock. Half feared, but half expected, the desire to know what was going on prevailed. Michael insisted he'd not seen him back at the university, but in light of what he knew, she wasn't sure what to believe.

David had his back to her, but by the look on Martha's face, something was not right when her hand took hold of his arm. A hacking cough bent him double and several heads spun around at the distressing sound. David turned away from Martha and put a large red-stained handkerchief to his mouth. When the episode finished he put up his hand in an apologetic wave and spoke to her again.

Gone was the arrogant stance and booming voice, and in their place a man who had aged considerably over the past few weeks. He had lost weight and the blue unfastened mac flapped around his legs. Julia watched from a safe distance, reluctant to move or say anything just then. Martha took him to find a seat in the public area and Julia was left to only imagine what had happened in the intervening weeks. Perhaps Michael was telling the truth. She went back to her office, unsure what to do but tried to imagine herself in his place. How would it feel to suddenly find out that you have a son in his twenties? Perhaps she should have been more gracious in letting him know, but amidst that thought, the old bitterness of her feelings of rejection reared up to vindicate her reaction.

It wasn't long before Martha came through to see her.

'Can you come out please, Julia? Mr Weston's back and wants to have a word with you. I've left him in the public area…not looking too well actually…he really should be home in bed I would have thought…don't get too close to him either, he has a dreadful cough,' she warned.

'He wants to see me? Can't you handle it, I've really got a lot on here?'

'You know you started this one…it's yours. I'm just as busy'

'Ok…tell him to give me ten minutes…I just need to do something first.'

Martha was more than glad to leave him on his own with a glass of water and went to wash her hands before scurrying back to her own desk.

Julia collected her bag out of the drawer and went up

to the toilets where she coaxed her hair into place and applied a thin coat of the new lipstick she'd bought to replace the old garish colour. Her usual pale face was flushed, but that was at least better than being washed out. She wished she had some perfume, but was out of practice using anything. On her way back down, she met Malcolm,

'I see our friend has returned...I wondered what had happened to him. Got a strange look about him though.'

'Yes, I know, Martha told me...I'm going down to see him now.'

Malcolm was startled at the unaccustomed lipstick and the flush in her cheeks, but thought how attractive she could when she made the effort. The effort was to no avail, however. David was in a much worse condition than she thought.

The lines around his face had deepened and his eyes more red than white, were sunk beneath the weight of the lids. His breathing was painful to hear and his words were spoken with a rasping noise from the back of his throat. Julia pulled up a chair besides his; it was a busy time, but at least the noise was low.

'Where have you been all this time?'

'Not well...think it was a touch of flu.'

'You don't look too well now...are you sure you should be out?'

'No...but no choice'

'Have you seen a doctor?'

He held his free hand to his chest, wincing, waiting for the pain to pass.

'He couldn't do much. Had me in hospital...tests...the usual. Don't drink... don't smoke...I left this morning.'

'What?'

'I'll be fine in a few days.'

Another fit of coughing told her otherwise and he could barely speak.

'You shouldn't be out…you really don't look well enough.'

'Another day in that place would kill me…too noisy. No bar… and no smoking' he attempted a smile despite the pain but his words trailed off in the effort.

'You're not seriously telling…'

'No,' he interrupted, 'I'll be all right…I have pills… if I keep taking them…'

'Where are you living? At least go home to bed for a few days.'

'I've rented a flat…above a takeaway…handy when the fridge is empty.'

Neither laughed at the comment when it was overtaken by another bout of coughing. Julia looked around, uncertain what to do for the best. She couldn't leave him like this.

'I need you to help me but I can't keep coming here.'

'No you shouldn't be here now. Look…stay put…I won't be long I promise. Will you be ok for a few minutes?'

He nodded; the walk to the archives had been too much and he was in no position to argue. Julia disappeared for about twenty minutes before returning with her coat and bag.

'There's a taxi outside…I'm getting you home.'

Julia gripped David's arm as they left together under the watchful eye of Maggie. She'd recently returned to work and had been trying to catch Julia on her own all afternoon. During the intervening weeks, loose trousers and more accommodating tops had replaced the tight skirts and dresses. She turned to Carole at the desk.

'Who was that with Julia? He looks vaguely familiar.'

'Oh, that's Mr Weston. He's writing a book… we've

been helping him with some research. Haven't seen him for a few weeks though. Looks to me as though he'd better hurry up with it, the state he's in.' Maggie raised an eyebrow.

'Do you know where they're going?'

'No idea. Julia just said that she was leaving early and to tell Malcolm that she'd make the time up next week.'

At the far end of the counter, Colin, noting every movement and every word, was smirking over what snippets he could piece together with this one.

IT WAS GETTING dark by the time the taxi pulled up outside David's flat. Julia couldn't see clearly enough what kind of takeaway it was but from the pervading smell of curry hanging in the air, it was easy to guess. The place had either closed down or wasn't yet open for the evening. Julia paid the driver and managed to get David upstairs via a side entrance, stopping every few steps to let him catch his breath. She closed the door behind them and managed to get him to the nearest chair.

'Is this really where you've been staying?'

'Home sweet home...but not for much longer.'

Julia did not have to look far for what purported to be the kitchen. If nothing else there were tea bags, milk and sugar on hand and by the time she returned with two hot mugs of tea David's face had taken on a slightly healthier pallor.

'Thank you...your colleague was all for calling an ambulance until I asked her to fetch you instead'

He sipped the tea, warming his hands around the mug. How many years had it been since they'd last shared a tea together? Julia thought again of the small house by the sea, where the promise of a different life was held in the balance; a life that belonged to a different world than this.

'I don't really understand why you're here'

'Long story…but you must know I didn't come back to England with the intention of upsetting you…I had no idea what I would be coming to…no idea at all…it was just work.'

'No…none of it was ever intentional…never was…'

'Tell me…tell me now…I need you to say it…I am right aren't I? He is mine?'

With nothing to gain by not telling him what he desperately wanted to hear, she spoke the words

'Yes…he's yours…but Will is his Dad in every other way…and always will be…but yes, he is your son'

David slumped back, as he immersed himself in the knowledge and pictured Michael when he'd last seen him. He was Michael's father. He had a son. Emotions vacillated from anger to exhilaration; the barren years of not knowing swiftly moved on to a future with him in his life. David closed his eyes, content at least that all trace of doubt had gone; Michael was his. Almost forgetting Julia's presence, he started at the sound of her voice, not quite understanding what she was saying to him

'It doesn't change anything I said…you do know that?'

'What? What are you talking about? It changes everything…for me anyway…and for Michael.'

'Michael thinks you've gone back to France and I want it to stay that way…please…it's for the best.'

'Best for who? Me? Michael? You!'

David wouldn't push for anything more right now. Rubbing at his chest, he did not have the energy, and the euphoria of knowing that he had a son gave him comfort enough for now.

'All right…we won't talk about it just yet.'

'I'll get off if you're all right.'

'No…please…stay a bit longer…there's something else I want to ask.'

Money was tight, hence the run down accommodation; Simone had not reneged on her earlier promises, but funds were getting low and he was sure that her legal adviser was prolonging matters. More than ever, he needed to complete the book and get through the next few weeks before tackling the state of their marriage; of salvaging whatever he could.

Julia put down her mug, 'What do you want?'

'I need your help.'

'I told you, I've gone as far as I can…there is no more information…you've got it all.'

'I know that…most of it was wishful thinking anyway…no there's something else. As you can see I'm not at my best right now…not well. I'm struggling writing up this lot.'

He gestured to the piles of notebooks and papers on a table in the middle of the room.

'And you want me to do it for you? No…definitely not. There's no way I could…'

'Hear me out please.'

'You come back here…force your way into my life… make me tell you things I never should…and you want favours from me? Have you any idea the trouble you've caused me and my family…and not just now?'

David repressed the bile rising and the words he wanted to fling back.

'I don't know who else to ask…please think about it Julia. When it's done I'll be able to pay you…acknowledge your part in it…I know you can type, I asked Carole.'

'Of course you did.' Julia spat out the words.

'Don't be like that…she looks up to you…spoke really highly…'

David was stopped by another spasm of coughing so bad Julia wasn't sure how safe it was to leave him. She looked at the pathetic figure hunched in the chair, failing to connect this man with the one she'd know years before and brought him a glass of water. The episode eventually passed.

'Please Julia,' his voice no more than a whisper, 'There's a word processor…'

The machine had been bought second-hand from a stall in the market the day before he'd been taken to hospital.

'Bit battered but workable'

'I don't know…'

The eyes implored her to change her mind and an idea formed in Julia's mind.

'All right…I'll give you a couple of nights next week if that will help…but I want you to promise me something in return'

'What? I can't pay you in advance…'

'No…not that…I don't want your money.'

Looking around at the appalling state of the room, it told her he was in far more need than she.

'Stay away from Michael.'

'What…why? Has he said something?'

'No not to me…but he doesn't need you in his life. Will's been a great Dad and always will be. He's been there for both of us when you were long gone.'

David knew defeat when faced with it but believed that once the work was finished he would convince Simone to take him back and then contact his son again. He would have them both in his life and show them he was worth it. There would be time enough afterwards to repair his marriage; time to show Simone what life could be like with Michael in it. Beads of perspiration stood out on David's forehead and the room spun when he stood up.

'Agreed.'

He staggered to the door 'I think I need to lie down for a bit.'

'Let me help you.'

'No…I'm fine. Will I see you tomorrow?'

'I'll see what I can do.'

'Please…I am grateful…'

Julia left by the same door, thankfully not too close to the entrance to the takeaway. Light radiated from its window in an otherwise dark street; it was open now and two people waited inside. She quickly made her way down to the main road and found a taxi to take her home, wondering what she had agreed to in return for keeping David away from Michael and Will.

Chapter 34

Will arrived home at his usual time and hung up his coat and scarf on their usual peg in the hall, surprised that Julia's coat was missing. The house was unusually quiet, no clatter of plates in the kitchen as Julia prepared supper; no hum of the radio in the background; nothing. He tried to remember if it was tonight that Julia was at the cinema with Maggie; not a comfortable thought but preferable to any alternative. He'd not seen Maggie since returning home; she'd been in touch only once to say that she would wait, but not for much longer.

He checked the phone and saw the message light flashing.

'Hi it's me…I might be a bit late home…something's come up at work…I won't be too late…I don't think… 'bye.'

Her voice was hesitant, but obviously she wasn't at the cinema with Maggie. That was a relief at least. The message was typical Julia now, perfunctory, no detail; nothing about what time she might be home.

Despite his best efforts, coming back from Maggie's had not been much of a success, but then nothing about Julia gave encouragement that it would be. Trying to win her back to how things used to be was proving to be a longer battle than he'd hoped and he was tiring of the enormous reserves of effort it demanded. Running back to Maggie wasn't the answer, but then neither was staying, waiting for Julia to make a move in his direction or at least meet him half way.

Will went to the kitchen with a heavy heart and opened the fridge to find a plate of cold meat and salad looking as appetising and welcome as his cold and empty bed. He went back to the telephone and called the familiar number.

'Hello, Maggie Ryedale.' Will didn't speak and after a few seconds hung up, still unsure. Was Maggie the answer to his problems? After all that had happened between him and Julia, would she just add to it?

He went back to the kitchen to heat up a can of soup; even that would be better than a plate of salad. The phone rang as he stirred a pan over the stove. Maybe it was Julia.

'Hello'

'Hello it's me.'

'Maggie?...hi'

'Did you just call me?' He paused before answering.

'Yes...sorry, I shouldn't...'

'I've been waiting so long for you to get in touch. Has something happened?'

'I don't know...Julia...she left a message saying she was going to be late home but never said why...or where... what time. I don't know what to think any more Maggie... it's all been just a waste of time.'

'Come to my place, Will...come now...I need to talk to you about something...have you eaten yet?'

He looked at the unappetising soup in the pan and shifted it to the back of the stove.

'No not yet...but is that a good idea? You know what happened last time.'

'Yes to the first and I never regretted the second.'

Although Will couldn't see the look on her face as she spoke, excitement and hope for the future registered again in her voice. When he'd left her last time, she was determined that was it, no more waiting, but still couldn't resist the need in his voice.

MAGGIE'S smart terrace house lay in the fashionable part of town, looking nothing like the home he shared with Julia. From its stylish sofas to the sophisticated modern artwork on the walls, it looked and smelled expensive.

After speaking to Will, she'd quickly changed, added a little more makeup and opened a bottle of cabernet sauvignon. It sat upon the low table in front of a rich brown leather chesterfield, along with two glasses.

As Will drove over, he knew how easy it would be to succumb to a life here with Maggie. She demanded so little of him but gave so much, wanting him in a way that Julia never had. Maybe the time had come to embrace someone in his life who saw him as a person to love and need and desire; the compulsion grew as he drew closer, leaving behind years of rejection.

Maggie kissed him lightly on the cheek and led him in by the hand to the sitting room. She'd changed into a pale green silk shirt, open at the neck, and loose black trousers. Her hair, recently cut into its usual bob was freshly brushed away from her face and her skin glowed. She smelt of Chanel. Each move, each piece of clothing had been carefully selected before his arrival.

'So…what's happened this time?' she asked as she poured out the wine, a large for him and a much smaller one for herself, which would barely be touched.

'I don't know what's going on. I half thought that you might be able to tell me…if she'd said anything to you at work. I did think it was your film night…she said something had been planned a while ago.'

Maggie raised a quizzical eyebrow.

'I've hardly spoken to Julia since I got back. She's been distant, but…well…you know how she's been and don't need me to tell you. We were due to go to the cinema but nothing came of it in the end.'

'Nothing's happened at work then…recently? Something that might make her go off and not tell me? She's been acting odd…like she's a different person…talking to me even less than before…and I've no idea why. To be honest, I've given up. I can't say anything…do anything. It's like living with a stranger.'

Maggie passed him a glass. She felt ashamed to feel a thrill at what he was saying, but not enough to send him back home.

'I shouldn't drink really…not if I'm driving.'

'All right, let me make you a coffee,'

'So you've no idea what's going on a work?'

'I'm not sure exactly, but Colin…'

'Colin! What's he got to do with it?'

Will knew of his reputation, Julia had told him many times of the embellished stories he liked to put about.

'Let me finish my darling…there's a man Julia has been working with, a Mr Weston…David Weston. You might even remember him…our old history teacher? I hardly recognised him at first. He's aged…over from France doing some research for a book he's trying to finish. It covers an area Julia knows better than anyone so it was natural she should be the one to help him out.'

Will sat forward, searching back over the years to picture David Weston but only came up with a hazy recollection.

'Well...he didn't turn up for a few weeks...we thought he'd got what he wanted and left...but then he suddenly came back again...this afternoon. According to Colin, he had a funny turn and Julia went off with him in a taxi.'

'What?...Why? Why Julia? What did...?'

'Look that's all I know.'

Will stood up, 'I should get back, Maggie...I want to know what's going on. I'll be in touch later...I promise... just bear with me a bit longer. I know I ask too much of you but...'

'Yes you do, you got that right...call me.'

'I will. I promise.'

'Then I suppose I'd better be satisfied with that...for now'

'What was it you wanted to tell me...completely forgot in all my woes. I'm so sorry.'

'It'll keep.'

'You sure?'

'Yes I'm sure,' although Maggie knew it couldn't keep for that much longer.

IT WAS GONE ten o'clock when Will heard Julia's key in the door. She came through to the living room, where he sat in the gloom of a single lamp. Julia's ashen face betrayed the smile she forced from her lips.

'Sorry I'm late.'

'How was the film?'

'The film?...oh, yes...the film...great thanks...we enjoyed it'.

'You and Maggie?'

'Yes...it was longer than we thought.'

'Really...and what was it about?'

'Look I'm tired...I'll tell you in the morning, but now...'

'No. Tell me now.'

'What is this? I'm tired and...'

'Stop it Julia! I know you've not been to the cinema.'

Julia, long past caring to ask how he could know, or express anything other than resignation that he knew, merely replied, 'Then why did you ask?'

She went to the kitchen and filled the kettle. Will followed close behind, irritated that he'd left Maggie to come back to this shambles.

'Are you seeing someone else? Just tell me now...'

'What?...no of course not. If you must know I took someone home who wasn't well at the Archives that's all.'

'And it took until now did it? Why not call an ambulance or call for a relative if he was that bad? Why lie to me Julia?'

'Who said it was a 'he'?'

'I rang Maggie. She said you've been helping someone. And Colin saw you both leaving in a taxi suggesting something more than work. I recognised the name...not at first...Maggie told me then it rang a bell...it's that history teacher I saw you with...that night at the school dance?'

'What are you talking about?'

Julia flushed crimson.

'You've really no idea? Don't treat me like an idiot. I've never mentioned it before but I saw you both and it was more than just a friendly kiss...wasn't it?...I saw where his hands were going. No wonder you dumped me.'

More than twenty years of supressed jealousy and resentment exploded into the room that night. Never straying into that forbidden territory, the past stayed with him, unspoken.

'I never said anything to the others and I don't know if Maggie realised what was going on but she was nice to me that night.'

'All right…yes it's him but this is not what you think.'

'How long has it been going on? How long have you been seeing him? Is he the reason you won't talk to me… won't let me near you? Where do I fit into any of this Julia?'

'I've promised to help him type up some notes, that's all. He's ill…seriously…ill. I felt sorry for him'

'You felt sorry for him! Typing his notes…is that what it's called now? For fuck's sake!'

Will's normal calm demeanour shattered into a thousand pieces; he frightened Julia and shocked her with his language, Will who had never shown such anger towards her before or even raised his voice.

'What has his work got to do with you? Is this a new 'personal service' the Archives are offering now? Was there really no one else? No wife…friends? Why *you* Julia?'

Julia began to shake and the tears welled ready to fall.

'He's on his own and when it's done he'll be gone.' Her voice grew softer in contrast to Will's but she stood firm in her resolve no matter what he thought.

'I will go back to help…there's nothing more to it than that but it won't be for much longer.'

Will, faced her, a figure of defeat and loss, and watched her leave the room. His voice, cracked with emotion called after her,

'Fine…do what you like…it's obvious my opinion doesn't matter in the least…'

She didn't reply.

THE NEXT DAY brought an uneasy truce; Julia made every effort to be her old self but the subject of David was not mentioned again. She called Michael in the forlorn hope that they might have a normal family meal once again but he was too busy with his dissertation. Two days later, she was back at David's rooms as Will found out from the note she'd left for him to come home to.

He made a show of accepting the arrangement, even told her that it was fine if it was something she needed to do, but what he did not tell her was that he was already preparing for the day when he would leave for good.

Julia showed her gratitude; she was solicitous to his needs and made sure a hot meal was prepared before she left in the morning. They still slept apart though and on that she would not, could not, shift. For Will, it was just another nail in the coffin of their marriage. Michael eventually came the following weekend, but the conversations between him and his mother were mostly out of Will's earshot and, not being privy to what they were saying, he kept his distance. The torment was relentless, leaving him with less doubt over the plans he was making with Maggie.

On the nights Julia was out, when they met, her sympathy grew in line with his growing dependency on her support, but the conversation she needed to have with Will still never materialised, and it wouldn't, not until he made the decision to leave Julia, and come to her, for good. At their last meeting, her patience finally snapped

'For God's sake Will, what are you waiting for? I can't keep this up for much longer. You know I love you…I always have…but you have to decide soon…please.' Her patience and forbearance grew as thin as her waistline expanded, and with it came the stress of worrying that Will's reaction might not be what she'd hoped for. Her last check up showed an unhealthy rise in blood pressure, not helped by the overwhelming desire to look at baby clothes and plan for a future that was far from certain.

Chapter 35

Julia collected the key to David's flat from beneath the mat outside his door. It was strange how quickly they'd all adapted to the routine. Will no longer pressured her into stopping the visits and she felt relief at how quickly David had stopped pressuring her over Michael. She would not renege on her promise as long as David kept his side of the bargain, and Michael would be no part of his life.

The flat provided a far from pleasant working environment. In the narrow confines, there was no escape from the all-pervading odour of curry; it inhabited every hollow in the walls and every fibre of the chairs and curtains. An almost empty can of air freshener sat mockingly on an old sideboard, it needed replacing soon but as the time flew by, she noticed the smell less and less. Deciphering the notes he gave her took up an inordinate amount of time before typing.

There were moments when her hands refused to co-operate and demanded a break from the unaccustomed overuse. Occasionally she would have to stop, flex her fingers, and make a coffee for them both in the tiny

curtained-off portion of the room that beggared the defini-
tion of 'kitchen'. It held a sink, a two-ring Belling cooker
and a unit that had peaked popularity thirty years before.
The sticky circles on the surfaces had been cleaned, the
unit sanitised and mugs scrubbed free of the stubborn
brown stains. At least that part of the flat now smelt fresh.

'I need a break.' she would announce decisively to his
querying glance when she stopped. Her confidence and
authority increased with each visit, in contrast with David's
evaporating energy and his reliance on her presence.
Coffee was made from a jar brought with other essential
supplies Julia arrived with, although by the time the kettle
had boiled he'd usually fallen asleep from the pills he now
took at regular intervals throughout the day. He slept much
of the time now, with Julia ever mindful of his delicate
state of health. She carefully placed the steaming mug on
the table beside his chair and watched the rise and fall of
his chest as she drank her coffee. Spread around his mug
was a half-smoked pack of Gauloise, a cheap lighter, an
almost empty bottle of whisky, tablets and water, all that he
demanded for the duration of his day. The dishes of food
she carefully prepared the night before to tempt him and
give him strength sat mostly untouched until replaced with
a fresh offering. The lack of food belied his swollen
abdomen and legs, but the shirt enveloping his otherwise
shrinking frame, gaped at the neck.

Their first conversation of each visit invariably went
along the same lines,

'You should eat something,' to which the response was
always the same 'I'll have it later.'

'Please let me get a doctor to look at you' was her
appeal when the pain and discomfort became unbearable
to watch.

'No…I've already said…no doctor…no hospital…not yet. The tablets just need to kick in.'

Julia took the burning cigarette from his relaxed fingers and ground it out in an overfull ashtray. He barely stirred and for once looked peaceful, almost comfortable. The ever-present blood-flecked handkerchief lay across his lap, and one arm draped in languid fashion over the arm of the chair. She listened to his short, laboured breaths. Her stomach lurched at memories of the past that still arose, unbidden, of her visit to his house when they were both so much younger. It was a far different world to the one they inhabited now.

'You should be in hospital,' she said gently to his sleeping body.

By the time David awoke, the coffee was cold and Julia had retreated back to the notes and typing.

'Thank you, Julia.'

She stopped and turned to him, a slow smile growing on her lips, basking in the need and gratitude he now showed her.

'I have to finish now…I'm tired and my fingers are getting stiff.'

Before he could reply, another fit of coughing shook his body leaving him too exhausted to speak. Julia tidied up the notes and put on her coat, scarf and hat after ministering painkillers and water. On the way out, she stopped at the shortening pile of work by the computer, and laid a hand on top of them.

'How *did* you get hold of these? You never really said how they've managed to survive and end up with you.' She gestured to the satchel, still sitting central to the mound of paperwork. David merely repeated the old mantra; 'Left to me by an old friend…he thought…thought I would…

would be the best person to…' He clutched at his chest, waiting for the knifepoint of pain to go.

'I need the money…it will sell I promise…you will get…'

'I don't want your money…I told you…all you have to do is leave Michael alone. We made a bargain remember?'

The yellow fragile papers lay untouched in their crumbling leather satchel and the gold cross sat dormant inside.

JULIA MADE her way home with an uneasy heart that evening. After working out the nearest bus route to get her home, she struggled on the walk towards the stop against a biting north wind. Despite a thick winter coat, scarf and gloves, they offered too little protection. Intense cold numbed her fingers as usual and the icy blasts chilled her face. She ran into a woman walking the other way when keeping her head down. It was dark but her colourful attire still stood out, incongruous to the grey and dark night air.

'I'm so sorry!'

'Don' worry…you go in the right direction.'

Julia smiled but thought it strange thing to say. The woman looked vaguely familiar, but she'd quickly disappeared down the street leaving Julia wondering where she'd gone. By the time Julia arrived home she'd forgotten her entirely.

It was increasingly hard to leave David alone in that place. A single storage heater and spluttering gas fire proved no match against the cold and damp that penetrated the flat's windows, walls and doors. She'd left him wrapped in an old woollen blanket, rescued from the back of the airing cupboard at home, and wondered if he would stay in the chair all night.

Slowly thawing on the overheated bus, Julia's thoughts

again drifted, as they so often did, to that other bedroom, the one with the small bedside lamp, the unpacked clothes and the unmade bed where Michael had been conceived. She rubbed at the steamy window; it was pitch black outside and in the slatted glow of headlights, the rain continued to whip up in the wind.

The urge to take care of David grew with each visit but the impulse of old was fading. She took stock of the toxic feelings of love and obsession and found that they fell short of what she felt now. Loving David had long been a habit, the force of which had been so compelling that even when Will made love to her, when they had still shared a bed together, when she closed her eyes, it was always David's face that she saw, always David's voice she craved to hear.

Will was in the kitchen sitting over the remains of a makeshift tea of beans on toast when she got back. He did not look up when she came in.

'I'm so sorry Will. I didn't get a chance to make anything before I left today.'

'It doesn't matter, I'm fine with this.'

She did not tell him about the time spent searching out the blanket and the trip to the shops for food for David.

'Shall I make us a tea?' Her words hung in the air and fell redundant.

'No? Ok…well I'll get off to bed if you don't mind….it's been a long day.' But before she could go, Will's body switched to life, and the threatening scrape of his chair as it fell back when he stood, shocked Julia into staying put.

'You're tired? Nowhere near as tired as I am, Julia! This will be the last time I am going to ask you; what is going on? And please don't insult me by saying that it's just work. Do not tell me that it's normal to go to someone's house to do what you are doing, night after bloody night!'

'Please…please…it is different…it's…'

'Stop it…just listen to yourself!'

Will moved close to where Julia stood, so close she could feel his breath against her face and again the eruption of long pent-up anger. This wasn't the Will of old, it was a creation forged from months, even years, of rejection and isolation.

Julia stepped back.

'Please sit back down…I…I'll tell you. I'll tell you why I have to go…it is work…'

'It's not fucking work!'

Julia was again shocked by the language and the force with which the words were spoken.

'I'm trying to tell you. Please don't shout. Let me explain. Just sit down…please…give me a chance.'

Will rubbed his forehead with one hand and straightened the upturned chair with the other. The flash of anger spent, he sat back at the table, hands resting in front of him with eyes locked on to Julia's face.

'Well?'

Julia, sitting opposite, looked away from his hard gaze.

'When Michael came that first weekend, and stormed out before speaking to you, he'd come to tell me about a man he'd met and got to know at university…a friend of his tutor's…someone helping with his dissertation… someone who knew a lot more about his subject and…'

'Julia, what are you on about? What man? Surely not David Weston? Does he know about him?'

'Yes he knows.'

'So all those cosy chats between the two of you…the ones you kept me out of were all about the man who is his father. I don't believe this. All that time you thought it a good idea to keep me out of it.'

'It wasn't like that.'

'No? Well what was it like?'

'I never wanted David to get involved in our life. I still don't. I go to help him now on the promise that he keeps Michael out of his. When we're done he will go back to France and that will be it.'

'Then you are even more gullible than I took you for Julia. Do you really think that he will leave and not make any further attempt to get to know Michael?'

'He promised me…in return for me helping finish the book and I believe him…and you have to believe me'

'I don't have to believe anything anymore…I'm done.'

'What? No…you can't…'

'Julia I set you free to do whatever you want…go to him. He obviously needs you far more than I do.'

Chapter 36

On the night that Julia decided would be her last visit to David, whether the book was finished or not, she found him in an advanced state of agitation. Slumped in the chair, the only sound beyond his heavy breathing was the pick, pick, pick of loosened threads of the fabric of the chair arm beneath his fingers. He barely noticed her arrival until she began to clear the night's debris from the floor. A cloud of ash floated in the air like the aftermath of a volcanic eruption when she dusted the table with a dry cloth. His vacant eyes registered nothing and the odour of his unwashed body was overpowering. Julia knelt at the foot of the chair to get his attention.

'David?...David...you need a bath.' He looked up, relief spreading across his face on realising she was there.

'You're back, I thought you...'

'Of course I'm back. I said I would...David I'm going to run you a bath.'

Julia resigned to the fact that there would be very little work done that night and slowly got up from the floor, but

David grabbed her arm with surprising strength before she could walk away.

'Tell me…how's Michael? Is he well? Have you heard from him?'

'He's fine…why do you ask?'

'She came again you know…last night. Again… Simone…Sybil…warned me about her.'

'Who came? Simone?'

'No…no…not Simone…her!'

The ramblings weren't new; he'd been doing it for some time but usually she ignored them.

'Well there's no one here now David…I'm going to run that bath for you and just hope there's enough hot water.'

Thankfully there was and David did little to resist her help when Julia came back for him. He'd obviously not moved for some time and the stiffness in his joints made progress slow. There was no embarrassment during the act of helping him undress although a recollection of another time was not lost on Julia; a time when he'd helped her undress.

David slowly eased himself into the steaming, hot water that rose up high. There were no scented oils, no bottle of bath foam to hide his nakedness. A bar of soap was found in the sink and a small bottle of shampoo on the window ledge. David's body visibly relaxed into the warm water's enveloping embrace.

In a moment of tenderness, Julia knelt beside the bath, and lathered up the soap to wash his back. His hair was next and rinsing was done with a plastic jug that sat on the side of the bath. No words spoken; none were needed until she'd finished.

'I'll go find some clean clothes for you.'

The bedroom had the stale smell of neglect. A suitcase

lay open on top of the roughly made bed, but its contents were barely touched. She found the warmest items and returned with clean underwear, shirt, corduroy trousers, a thick jumper and woollen socks.

Dressing was slow and painful, but once achieved he returned back to the chair and began to look something like his old self once the stress of the exertion had passed. He even drank the tea she'd made and ate most of the buttered toast. Julia, satisfied that he looked and smelled better, continue with her work, pleased he hadn't bothered to light a cigarette. The notes weren't too far off completion; two, maybe three more nights might do it.

During a break, when David was not sleeping, she offered small details of Michael's life when he was a child. He took whatever crumbs she cared to give, and worked out where his own life was at the time, how the boy could have fitted in so easily.

'He's working hard now...the dissertation stresses him but that's only natural. Still seeing Cecille...off and on... I'm not sure how long it will last'

'Cecille...yes...I remember her...the little boy...Leon'

'Who's Leon?'

The anger and resentment so recently shown on both sides left like a bad dream, in a fresh desire to listen and talk about Michael. Julia was confident enough that was all that would be wanted of her, and it sustained David as no food ever could.

That night saw the beginnings of forgiveness and Julia's realisation that in the end, the past, the anger, the longing and waiting, none of it really mattered now. She saw glimpses of the man she had loved, but came to accept that the idealised image nurtured since childhood, had gone for good.

She encouraged him to talk about the Henrietta

Papers, although his words became a strange abstraction of thought and reality and it took a while to grasp what was said. The toxic cocktail of tablets, alcohol and cigarettes were having a strange effect on his mind as well as his body.

'You have to understand what you are taking on,' he repeated time and time again.

'I'm not taking anything on,' she replied, 'I'm only here to type up your notes… remember?'

'But you know what happened to Sybil…and to Simone…and the others before them…so many…I told you…Georges told hinted at it…'

'No, I don't know. You're mistaking me for someone else.'

She went back to her final batch of typing, but stopped when she saw his sunken red eyes fill with tears.

'Enough now…shall we call it a day? You look done in.'

He looked around the room as if in need of affirmation of what he'd said and rubbed his fingers roughly through the grey curling hair that comically stood on end.

'The Henrietta Papers…they need to…they must… must be completed…put away…done with.'

Picking up the refilled whisky glass with trembling hands, he drank, ignoring the remnants of the toast. The Henrietta Papers, still on the table in the satchel, sat between them like unclaimed baggage at the train station, and Julia sighed with relief at the almost completed pile of notes.

'No…no… you can't finish yet… please just a few minutes more?' he pleaded, draining the glass, and sitting back in the chair as the lines across his forehead deepened with each painful breath.

'All right,' she consoled, 'a few minutes more… then I have to go.'

Julia's chair had one leg slightly shorter than the other three; it rocked unsteadily, but helped keep her mind focussed on the job in hand when it gave her an unexpected jolt. She worked quickly in the belief that she might yet get David to the hospital once the work was finished. His rambling, more frequent and more confused as time went on, became a mix of fairytale and self-pity in between more lucid historical facts about the book.

The apocryphal tale of a dying queen and a murdered girl fell on deaf ears as Julia tried to focus on the job in hand. What bearing did this three hundred year old story have on David's life in Paris, let alone hers in Yorkshire? In other moments of clarity, she would try to get answers from the same unanswered questions.

'Why do you have the Papers? Shouldn't they be in a museum or the Paris Archives? It's doesn't seem right that they're here and I am the one to type this…this lot up.'

'You're not listening to me. I'm trying to tell you why you need to take care…'

He took a long drag of the Gauloise, disregarding the hacking cough that closely followed each intake of breath.

'Take care of them…then they go back…but now… just help me finish… let me leave...' but the cough again took over.

'It really is time for me to go home now.'

He didn't argue, but a loud crash outside cut in. Julia went to the window and pulled aside the curtain. A pale, wan moon cast a little light in the yard below where over-flowing bins took up one corner, but all was silent.

'Must have been be a cat.'

The more gentle thump of David's glass falling to the

floor signalled his drift into unconsciousness, but his last words prayed on her mind.

'She put a curse on anyone who had the Papers…they have to go back.'

It was almost nine; Will would be home soon from the Cricket Club meeting and she wanted to be there first for once.

David's eyes opened slightly as she passed by. 'I have to go now. Do you want me to bring anything in for you next time?' He gestured towards the almost empty bottle of whisky that sat beside the restored glass, then looked across to the satchel.

'Another bottle…please.'

'You really would be better in hospital, David,' she said but knew that he wasn't listening. A dish of homemade soup sat in the kitchen, still untouched. Undeterred, she brought him a final hot sweet tea and David placed his hand on hers as she set it down beside him.

'You will come back, won't you?'

'Yes…I *will* come back.'

'You will help me finish this?'

He looked remarkably alert and even made an effort to stand when she went to the door. The bath had done some good at least.

'It might be in a couple of days but don't worry…I am coming back. I've left you food…bread…milk…please eat something.'

He didn't object and Julia, satisfied with the state she'd left him in, went as she'd arrived, unseen and in the dark. Heading down the back stairs and out into the biting air, she thought of Will and what this was doing to him. The light from the takeaway shone out on to the street and she could see three customers waiting inside. Pulling up her collar, she walked her usual route for the bus and felt a stab of conscience. Perhaps it would be good for them both if she stayed at home for a couple of nights; show him that their marriage really did mean something; that she did care. David had enough supplies to get him through two nights at least and she convinced herself that he did look a little better tonight.

Julia felt unique pleasure in the new experience of letting go: shedding the baggage that had no more meaning to her life than carrying a concrete block. The heart can recover and the mind can be freed, and for a couple of hours, she felt that recovery and freedom. She felt it on her way home; it nourished her when she bought the wine; and it stayed with her as she uncorked the bottle and waited for Will to walk through the door.

It was gone midnight before she went into his room, a last resort after searching through the house for a sign of where he'd gone or what he might be doing. She found it in his bedroom where a note lay waiting for her on the neatly made, unused bed; it was lit by a shaft of light when she opened the door.

JULIA

I'm sorry to have missed you and tell you face to face before I left, but perhaps it's better this way. I rarely see you now and we never talk do we? I think it's time for me to move out – this time it is for good. I am so unhappy and obviously you are too. I have tried to make things right between us but I know I have failed. There's nothing left for me here. I'll leave it to you to tell Michael but please let him know that I will be in touch very soon. I'm sure you have all you want now with David

Will

. . .

UNDERNEATH, as an afterthought, he had scrawled

I'LL LET *you know when I can come to pick up the rest of my stuff.*
   I hope things work out for you
   W

WILL'S room was drained of his presence. Drawers and hangers had been cleared leaving only a smattering of summer shirts and trousers. The bedside cupboard door hung open, swaying in the breeze from an open window, giving the impression he had only just left.

Julia's fingers lightly touched the fabric of one of the shirts in the wardrobe. Pulling it to her wet face, she fell to the floor on her knees, dragging the shirt and the hanger down with her. It went with her to his bed where she lay on top of it and closed her eyes. Sleep did not come easy but when it did, bizarre dreams jolted her into waking.

For two days Julia did little but roam the house, lost, as though she did not know her way around, touching, moving things, staring at the door waiting for Will to walk back in as he had done so many times before.

All hunger gone, she neither ate nor slept in the desolation of the rooms devoid of life. On the third day, the local paper dropped through the letterbox and in an absent minded scan through its pages she saw the notification of a man found dead in a flat above a takeaway on Brierley Road. There were no suspicious circumstances.

The paper lay open over the next day, read and re-read as Julia remained in denial that it could be David. He was well enough when she'd left. He couldn't die just like that, she would have known. No, he was waiting for her to go back. She would go today, maybe bring him back home where she could look after him properly.

Forced by hunger, she sought out the meagre contents of the fridge and managed a breakfast of boiled egg and toast. Spurred on by the thought of what to do next, she showered, washed her hair and dressed. She threw the paper in the bin and left for the flat above the takeaway, ignoring recorded messages from work and from Will.

Chapter 37

The street looked longer in daylight, hardly the same place at all. The night-time youths lingering in doorways were nowhere to be seen. Doors were shut tight and there was a different silence, like the aftermath of a great disaster. Families had moved out long ago, and houses had been left to an underworld of dealers, users and pimps. At night, the grafitti'd walls indicated how far she had to go, but the scrawls didn't look quite so menacing in full daylight.

She arrived at the faded blue sign above the takeaway door that read: 'Taj Mahal – Purveyor of Authentic Indian Cuisine'. Julia had always used the entrance down the alleyway, the one David showed her on the first day she'd come with him from the Archives. It had been dark even then, on that cold winter afternoon. Each night she came he would be waiting in the chair by the window, waiting just for her. She had a spare key to get in without disturbing him.

There was no entry today. The door had been bolted from inside and no amount of hammering on the door could wake him up. How could this be after so little time?

She went back down to the takeaway and looked inside. It was empty and in darkness. A handwritten notice had been stuck to the inside of the window, and an untidy scrawl read: Flat for rent. Good rates. Apply within. A phone number was given underneath. She wrote it down and found a telephone box down the road. Surprisingly, it still worked even though two of the windows were smashed and shards of glass lay all around the pavement. After a short interval, a man with a strong Indian accent answered and within a few minutes he'd agreed to a viewing within the hour.

Julia walked along nearby streets to fill the time, papers blowing in the rising wind, until anchored on a street lamp or wall. A nagging pain in her head grew with each step as thoughts of Will and David fought inside her mind.

Julia passed shops and other takeaways with frontages stuck like parasites to buildings that had once been beautiful houses. Ornate brickwork and carvings remained above one or two, but most had been lost over the years and doors rotted in frames where they were not boarded up.

At the far end of the street the Catholic Church of the Sacred Heart sat stoically resistant to change and abuse, although its windows were protected with iron bars. The door, slightly open, was inviting enough to escape the cold outside. A paint-flaked Jesus, nailed to a cross, looked down on Julia as she went inside. It was cold but at least provided shelter from the wind, and a thin ray of sun shone down on to a row of pews. Julia pulled her coat around tightly and sat in the comfort of the sun.

A black-frocked figure at the front turned at the sound of her footsteps and nodded in acknowledgement of her presence

'Good morning…beautiful day is it not?'

Julia smiled in return, but said nothing, relieved when he continued his job of removing dead flowers from the altar. He was used to the occasional visitor seeking the peace and solace of his Church and would not intrude on her solitude unless asked.

She closed her eyes, but the only image that passed behind them was David in his chair, haunting her every thought.

Mr Syed had sounded very keen to show her round when she told him she was interested in renting the flat but needed a little time to prepare. It was ten fifty two, still early, but unable to wait any longer, Julia got up to leave.

'May your day go well,' the priest said as she left.

Inexplicably crossing herself, she realised it was the first time she'd set foot inside a church since Michael's christening. Her father had wanted Michael to be Catholic, same as he had been christened, but he wasn't practising and her mother thought the 'nice little church' in the village would be more suitable. Julia hadn't cared one way or the other.

Back at the takeaway, Julia stooped to look through the glass door, shielding her eyes to block the sun's reflection. It was dark and lifeless.

She knocked, and a few seconds later could make out an old man shuffling towards her. Bolts were slid along the top and bottom and the Yale released. An old man greeted her, giving a warm gap-toothed smile.

'Hello, welcome.'

'Hello, Mr Syed?'

'Yes that is me. And you are Miss Harris?'

He took her hand and shook it in both of his. An oversized brown cardigan covered a pale blue tunic, both of which looked old but freshly laundered. His face was clean-shaven, from which his eyes and mouth wrinkled more from smiles than misery.

The local paper had made a great issue of police finding a body in a 'shabby little flat', down a 'grimy backstreet', but there were no tell tale signs now to indicate that anything untoward had happened.

Familiar smells assaulted Julia's senses as the door opened. It was surprisingly small inside the takeaway and newspapers spread across a waiting bench lining one of the walls. Decorations on the wall comprised faded posters of the Taj Mahal and other exotic locations. Mr Syed urged her in; 'too cold to keep the door open long.'

He liked to use his hands when he spoke and made encouraging gestures as the door was locked behind them.

'You are lucky it is still free. I have had other enquiries…very colourful foreign lady was the first.' His accent was strong, but Mr Syed's command of the language was excellent. Julia spoke little as he beckoned her to follow him behind the narrow counter.

'There is another entrance round the side, more private, if you should want it.'

'Yes,' she answered, but already knew that.

Her legs weakened as he led the way up a narrow staircase through a second door. Darkness fell all around when the tightly sprung door slammed shut behind them. The dark was unexpected, causing Julia to gasp and Mr Syed apologised for the broken light.

'It will soon be fixed, no worries there. You will be all right, just hold on to the rail.'

The stairs were bare, steep and narrow, creaking with every step. It was intensely claustrophobic. Mr Syed apologised again, this time for the arthritic knees that painfully slowed his progress.

At the top of the stairs where it was a little brighter, she recognised another door as the same one she used at night, the one that led to the fire-stairs outside. A small skylight, obscured by dirt, let in a faint shaft of sunlight, revealing a row of black plastic bags piled up outside David's door.

'These will be cleared very, very soon, miss. It won't take long.'

Mr Syed shuffled over to the wall, breathing heavily after struggling with the climb. The wall switch operated a single bulb that starkly lit the lino-floored landing. There was nothing here but the bags and a screwed up ball of police tape.

Mr Syed produced a key from his cardigan pocket and held it up to Julia, 'This is it,' he said, 'my flat for rental.'

He took Julia's silence as a sign that she was impressed by the new door, the old one having been broken in the attempt to gain entry, and smiled in encouragement, but the key was a poor fit and it took a while to release the lock. Julia's heart lurched when it eventually swung open and she looked in. Her feet became leaden, weighted to the floor. The walls swayed and Mr Syed turned, puzzled when he saw her holding on to the wall.

'Are you all right? Come in…come in.'

'I'm fine…yes.'

'Much brighter in here, a nice big room for you.'

The dizziness subsided and equilibrium returned. The room was empty but for the chair with the threadbare arms; no belongings and no clutter; the paperwork and satchel were all gone. Julia shivered and rubbed her arms; it was as cold as the Church and a smell of disinfectant joined the odour of curry. It was not the flat as she remembered and a wave of confusion spread to find that there really was no-one else here but Mr Syed.

She walked to the window and pushed it open to get some air, standing with arms on the sill until Mr Syed's voice brought her back into the room.

'Are you ready to see the rest of the flat now?'

He spoke as though there were several rooms to inspect; causing Julia to smile at the thought of how little there was left to see. She closed the window and half listened as he talked about other prospective tenants he'd already shown around: two teenagers with a baby.

'They are from down the road, living with his mother, hardly a penny between them, no right to be having children so young, don't you think?' Julia nodded and smiled at the irony. He told her that he would prefer a single person, 'someone just like yourself, who will give me no bother. Or the other lady who came this morning.' The raised eyebrows and nodding head were given to encourage a response, but none came.

'They are not even married I tell you,' he continued nevertheless. My Syed shuffled closer until she could see every detail of his face, the deep lines with whiskers sprouting where he'd missed with his shaver. His smile revealed brown stained teeth with a gap at the front. He was too close but poor eyesight kept him moving closer. Julia stepped back, 'Please Mr Syed, show me the kitchen if you would.'

The tiny space, partitioned by the same old curtain, had been scrubbed bare. Cupboards left open to dry, gaped empty and the floor was damp where it had recently been mopped. Gone were the tins and packets, the soups, ham and butter she'd left on her last visit. There was no sign of life anywhere; notes, word processor and the ancient satchel, were all gone.

Mr Syed went on talking. 'My daughter-in-law was most scrupulous in cleaning and clearing the flat...too many empty bottles,' he remonstrated with a wagging finger. Julia recalled the cheap whisky she would bring with the cigarettes and food. Mr Syed spotted his nephew from the window and opened it to call down in Hindi as Julia went back into the living room.

She stopped dead in her tracks when she saw David sitting in the chair with the threadbare arms, red eyes accusing and following her every move. He spoke 'Why didn't you come back?'

'David!…how…' Her heart pounded in shock and disbelief as the accusing image began to fade. Mr Syed came back and saw Julia's grey face staring at the empty chair.

'That chair will be replaced…I know…not good…not good…threadbare arms…' He paused. 'Are you all right? You don't look at all well, miss…please sit for a minute'.

Julia whispered hoarsely, 'I have to go…I'm sorry…I can't be here.' The old man reached out, puzzled at such strange behaviour, but she pushed him aside in the desperation to leave. Julia pulled at the door but when it wouldn't shift, panic rose further. A bewildered Mr Syed came over and turned the handle firmly when he saw her distress and the door opened quite easily.

'I'm sorry,' she repeated and rushed out.

The sudden darkness of the hall was disorientating. The light, on a timer, had gone out and fumbling around, she missed the first step, falling headlong down the stairs. The floor met her head with a sickening thud and her right foot caught at an unnatural angle behind. Before slipping into oblivion, David's accusing words returned 'Why didn't you come back?'

A SHARP PAIN shot through Julia's foot as she slowly came round. How long had it been? Seconds? Minutes? Hours? A muffled voice, urgent, spoke close to her ear, 'Miss Harris…Miss Harris, are you all right?'

She tried to open her eyes. Who was Miss Harris? The room was spinning and a powerful smell of curry made her feel sick. She could taste bile at the back of her throat and the wrinkled face of an old man hovered over her.

'Please dear God, not another in my house.' he said, clearly distressed.

'It is Mr Syed here…Miss Harris are you all right… please say something.'

He shook her arm, unsure of what to do for the best. Julia tried to sit up and put her hands flat on the floor to push, but couldn't manage more than lift her head.

'My foot…' she winced in pain.

'Lie still for a bit longer…I will go and get help.'

'No…I'll be all right…just…just help me get up…please.'

For an old man with arthritis, his arms were surprisingly strong and with help she struggled up on to her right foot. The room continued to spin and the pain made her cry out. Mr Syed supported Julia through to his own kitchen, where she fell gratefully onto an old, but comfortable chair. It was the same as the one that had been in David's flat, but with arms still intact.

'I will call an ambulance now.'

'Please no! I don't want an ambulance. I just need to get home…no ambulance.'

Mr Syed was in many ways relieved to do as she asked. He had had enough of doctors, ambulances and police when Mr Weston had been found upstairs. But how would she get home otherwise?

'You rest here for a minute,' he insisted. 'I will make you some tea, yes? Then you might feel a bit better and we will see what is to be done.' He asked if there was someone he might call. Julia struggled to remember. Names, places, her mind was a blank. Where was she exactly and why?

She told him that her mother would be at work until six and that her dad was away before realising that they were both dead.

'Please just get me a taxi.'

'I will see to that,' he promised.

She then remembered Will, of course Will. What was she thinking?

Mr Syed went to make the tea and whilst waiting for the kettle to boil, shuffled back with an ice pack to put on the sizeable lump that had appeared on her head. She felt something sticky across her eye and saw from her finger that it was blood. She tried to wipe it away as the old man nervously fussed around. She then pulled down her sock and discovered that her ankle had grown to at least twice its normal size.

Mr Syed eventually brought over some tea brewed in a pot by the stove, and poured it into a delicately flowered china cup, carefully adding milk with two heaped spoons of sugar. Julia gratefully accepted the hot drink, as she did the footstool gently placed under her foot. It was warm in the kitchen, very different from the shop and the flat. Julia winced and bit her lip as she attempted to get comfortable. Her hands shook when she raised the cup to her mouth and Mr Syed tried to distract her as they waited for the taxi. The flat and its availability were never mentioned again.

Mr Syed spoke of his life at the takeaway and she found the cadence of his voice comforting, slow and soothing. It was difficult to keep her eyes open and very few words were taken in until another jolt of pain brought her round. She paid more attention to Mr Syed when she heard him mention David's name.

'Maybe if I had known how ill Mr Weston had been I could have helped him too.'

'Mr Weston?'

'My last tenant,' Mr Syed replied in a quiet voice, slowly shaking his head. 'No-one knew him well. He was keeping much to himself. He was a very private man, I think. Lady came to see him a couple of times…same colourful lady came to look at my flat before you, maybe French with her accent but dark skinned like myself. Bright scarf around her head, I think she must have been the last person to see him alive. I ask her about Mr Weston, if she had seen the police but she seemed to know everything that happened. I tell the police about her but she cannot be found now. They find a wife though…'

'Tell me what happened.'

'No wrong doings' he emphasised, 'he was just very, very ill. I didn't know.'

Julia tried to make sense of what he was telling her, searching in the dark for the last time she'd seen him. Who were these other women?

'Why did you run out so suddenly? Had you heard what had happened? You should have given yourself time…the whole place is now quite as good as new.'

'Yes…I'm sorry.'

'I was very upset by the death of Mr Weston. I don't think he could have set foot outside or spoken to anyone for a long time, apart from colourful lady. Maybe she brought him the food. I used to try to make conversation with him when he first came, but he didn't want this, so I left him alone. I don't interfere in other people's business. He paid me my rent every week, on time, and I let him be. I understand the need for privacy.'

The old man was still visibly shaken by the death of his tenant.

'It was only when he didn't pay, when I thought he had left…I had to see what was wrong…something very wrong.

We had to break down the door, you know. I was helpful to the police. I told them that no-one ever came to visit him before, no-one at all, apart from lady they could not find.'

Mr Syed looked at his watch, 'Taxi here soon.'

If Julia kept perfectly still, the pain eased slightly, but the haunting vision of David sitting in the empty room with its overpowering smell of disinfectant and curry, would not go away. All she could see was David in the armchair, by the wall, head slumped to one side. 'Why didn't you come back?'

That wasn't how she'd left him; he was fine then; he wasn't ready to die. The book, the papers, were all waiting for her, it couldn't end like this.

Mr Syed looked at Julia with fresh concern when she didn't respond. Drained of colour, her battered body sat inert.

'Are you sure I can't call for an ambulance? You are not at all well.' Julia turned towards him, 'No...don't do that. Nothing is broken. Look, I can move my toes.'

The taxi arrived, relieving Mr Syed of the worrying burden of Julia. Mr Syed's nephew, Shamil, a muscular, sullen man, drove it, unhappy at being taken away from his usual shift. With little effort, he carried Julia into the back seat of his car as Mr Syed hovered by the door,

'I hope you make a quick recovery, Miss Harris. Please come and see me when you are better.'

The journey home was painful but did not take long with Shamil behind the wheel. He took her key to open the house and helped Julia into the living room, before getting back to his usual shift as soon as he could. Paying customers were already waiting. When Julia looked for her purse he shook his head.

'Not necessary...my uncle has taken care of that, thank you...you fine now?'

Shamil was glad to get away; he'd covered an obligation to his uncle and did not want to get involved after the goings on with the last tenant. The last thing he needed was the police coming round again.

The house was cold and empty but Julia couldn't even make it to the bedroom. Her head raged with pain and her foot could not withstand even the slightest pressure. The house, the room and the sofa encompassed her world. Thoughts vacillated from year to year until she no longer recognised who or where she was. The phone flashed to show there were several messages waiting; it was the last thing she saw before drifting into unconsciousness.

IT WAS two days before Will's key turned in the lock and he let himself in, and another thirty minutes before an ambulance arrived. Will knelt beside Julia's motionless body, still laid on the sofa where Shamil had carried her. He was relieved to find her still breathing, but each breath was erratic and shallow. The blood on her cheek had dried where it had run down from the top of her head. If his first instinct was to try to rouse the still, inert body, his second was to call an ambulance. The sight of her condition was disturbing in the extreme. He held her hand and stroked her white, swollen face where the left eye had now turned yellow and purple.

'What on earth happened Julia? Who did this to you?'

Agitated and helpless, a surge of guilt overwhelmed him to think that he might have caused it in some way, that he hadn't been there to protect her. Searching the room for some clue to the mystery produced nothing; it was the same as always, everything was in order: furniture, chairs, sideboard, ornaments; nothing damaged, nothing missing. Framed photographs adorning the wall reflected and mocked happier days when they were all together; Michael on Will's shoulders at the Fair, chocolate around his mouth and a big grin for the photographer; a faded black and white photo of Julia's mother in the garden of their old home, sitting on the grass with Michael as a baby, dribbling as his first tooth was about to poke through; and one of Julia on her own, captured by Will when she thought no-one was around, looking wistful under the cherry tree they'd planted together, sitting on the ground hugging her knees and looking up, sad but beautiful. He'd loved her more at that moment than any time before and knew he wanted to be with her always, with or without another child. All taken long so ago, and where they once made him happy, he was now overwhelmed with sadness at the memories they stirred when he looked back down at his wife.

Julia stirred a little when Will put water to her parched lips, gratefully taking in the cool liquid that ran down her chin. He wiped it solicitously when she turned her head away.

'What's happened Julia? Have you been in an accident? Were you attacked?' Julia half opened her eyes, confused and incapable of speaking to the strange man looking down at her. He was close, too close. She could barely move, too weak. 'Who…who are…?' But the words wouldn't come and she drifted back into oblivion. Will covered her cold body with a blanket from the bedroom and resigned himself to waiting for the ambulance. He called Michael, giving him the barest of details, not wanting to frighten him, and trying to hide his own fear, asked him to come home when he could. He then rang Maggie but before she could answer, the doorbell rang, it was the ambulance at last, and he hung up.

Chapter 38

The Catholic Church sat equidistant to the Archives and takeaway flat where David had lived and died; it was small but appeared bigger when so few pews were occupied. David's coffin rested on a stand at the front, and on top of it droplets of holy water caught the light as they trailed along its lid. There was no requiem mass, and no bread and wine taken for Holy Communion. Apart from Simone, the only others attending were Mr Syed and his nephew; Michael and Will; and Phil, none of whom embraced the Catholic faith. An uneasy silence hung in the air when they were unsure of what to do, or what was expected of them. The church was cold, and white plumes of breath rose from the mouths of those present.

It was prettily decorated however; the flowers at the altar were fresh and plentiful, and it must have been well used over the years judging by the worn patina of the wooden pews that lent a comforting smooth touch beneath the hand.

A passage was read from the Gospels and two prayers incanted for David to rest in peace. The eulogy given by the priest was heartfelt even though circumstances decreed that he knew neither the deceased, nor the widow who had arranged the service from France. Simone had arrived the night before having grieved at her own church, in her own way, beforehand. David had converted to Catholicism to please Simone, and in an unsuccessful attempt to placate her father, before they married, but took no further steps to confirm the newly proclaimed faith. Simone never wavered in hers; she sat at the front, immutable, looking into the marble face of the Virgin Mary holding the marble-cold infant Jesus. She thought of the few precious moments she had had with her own baby son when he lay lifeless in her arms. That deep well of tears had long since dried leaving in its place unimaginable sorrow and regret over the loss.

The news of David's death arrived via the police the day following their investigation into a man found dead and alone at the flat. A polite, apologetic call was made with relief that it was highly likely no further investigations would be needed. An autopsy confirmed death by natural causes and Simone's number was discovered amongst his meagre belongings. The body was no longer their problem.

On hearing the news, Simone sat alone in her apartment, in shock, but not entirely surprised. She allowed herself only brief moments of reflection on the last vestiges of their marriage, pushing anything further away when there was much to organise, not least informing his son, who now sat in the pew behind with Will.

Simone closed her eyes and prayed that David might now find the peace and contentment he had lost. There would never be any other man in her life and it was time to say goodbye.

Michael watched the still, dignified figure of Simone, his own thoughts going from the man he barely knew, to his mother who could not attend. He couldn't quite bring himself to think of David as his father, but neither could he understand why he had never been allowed to get to know him. What was the big deal? Schoolgirls get pregnant all the time; there had even been one in his final year. What did it matter? Suppressed anger at his mother finally breached the dam when he heard about David's death but fell apart when he knew she was in no position to respond. In the bitter fallout of his inability to know more, his resentment ensured that Cecille went back to her parents, leaving him alone when she couldn't handle the situation any longer.

Today all anger was gone for Michael, leaving in its place an interminable sadness for a father he would never know and a mother who, more often than not, barely recognised him as her own son. He desperately needed the comforting presence of Cecille in the claustrophobic confines of a cold church, and the desire to have her close once again, was overwhelming.

In the pews to their left, Phil was still coming to terms with what had happened and how he might deflect responsibility from himself. Any guilt at having been the cause of David and Simone's split was long erased by his own humiliation and rejection by them both. An attempt to talk to Simone outside the Church was cut short by a curt retort, 'I don't think we have anything to say to one another Phil...please leave me alone.' She left him standing like the fool he'd always been.

Fr. James Morrison concluded the service and quietly asked Simone to stay behind to conclude the formalities. She spoke to Michael first, thanking him for coming and hoping that they might keep in touch. He gave her his new address and phone number in the knowledge that they were highly unlikely to be used, but it was a good way to part and they wished each other well. Phil had left as quickly as he could without a backward glance and Mr Syed and his nephew quietly slipped away.

The only other person in the Church remained in a dark corner at the back, arriving alone and unseen. She watched in silence until the Church had emptied. 'I told you long time ago, David...I told you take care. You didn't listen...none of them listen'

David was buried in the churchyard and Simone made arrangements for a headstone to be placed in his memory.

Chapter 39

1998

Manchester

AFTER THREE DAYS of dull skies, a bright sun broke through to shine on the wedding of Michael and Cecille. The time spent apart ensured a reunion of two people perhaps a little more mature, but much chastened from what they had learned.

Michael took away something of his father from two conversations held with Simone before she went back to France. They were brief, but long enough for him to get a better understanding of the man he had only just begun to know. Simone was kind enough to emphasise the positives and forgive the indiscretion with Michael's mother. Simone's love for his David was obvious, however; she did not hold back on his shortcomings and did not want Michael left with an unrealistic view of who he was.

Michael concluded that although they had many similarities in looks and traits, they were far apart in other ways. He looked at Simone as she spoke with an understanding that went beyond his comprehension. How she could have allowed herself to be treated in such a way? He took it to heart when he looked at the relationship he had with Cecille. When she returned from her parents' house in France, and a reconciliation between them was not entirely out of the question, he made a vow that he would change for the better. He would not be his father incarnate.

Jean and Marie Garnier had welcomed their daughter home with relief following the revelations of Michael's family history and Julia's subsequent breakdown, but they couldn't make up for the devastation it brought to Cecille. Michael's regret over his behaviour, if not a Damascene moment, followed weeks of soul searching and coping with the gap she left in his life. Cecille had gone, his mother was all but a stranger and the father he had only just met was dead.

Cecille did not make it easy for him, but that only inflamed the desire to get her back. He fought hard to get over his sudden dark mood swings, but when he did struggle, allowed room for her proffered care and sympathy and the ever present contact with Will.

The register office held a small but close gathering of friends and family and Cecille looked as radiant as any glossy magazine bride on her special day. She wore a loose-fitting soft ivory dress that fell just below her knees, its billowing fullness successfully hiding a belly that was growing by the day. Her hair hung in flowing blonde curls at her shoulders, setting off shining blue eyes showing the happiness and excitement of a day she thought would never come.

As ever, throughout the weeks of grief and torment,

Will had stepped into the breach and made sure his stepson was not alone. Together they put his life back on track and Michael came to realise that not all was lost to him. Over time, he also accepted the changes in Will's life and took pleasure in being a big brother to the baby girl born to Will and Maggie. It had at first taken supreme effort for Michael to forgive him for abandoning his mother, and the arrival of Flora at first caused a seismic shift in their relationship, but slowly, over time, as the facts of the past became known, he had come to an understanding that not everything in life was as simple as he would wish it to be. It was obvious to all who knew Will, including Maggie, that he still cared for Julia despite everything. The blame that Michael harboured and placed firmly at the feet of Maggie was eventually left behind too.

Michael's life slowly came back into focus with complete acceptance that Will was much more of a father than David could have ever been, even if he had lived.

Three years into their reunion, Michael did his utmost to live up to the promises made to himself and to Cecille, and the wedding, although hastily put together, was a joyous occasion. Any sadness that could have transgressed the happy day did not materialise. Guests were deliberately few: a handful of close friends along with Will and Maggie and two-year-old Flora; and Cecille's parents over from Chatou, on the outskirts of Paris.

Julia came for a short while, but was in close attendance by her carer, Ruby, a large, colourful woman who took charge and looked happy to be out on such a beautiful day. Ruby took in the surroundings and the faces of everyone present; she missed nothing in her summation of the small crowd and the parts they played. She kept Julia close all the while.

The emotions of the afternoon exhibited only happiness for the young couple. The bride's mother kept back her tears at the placing of the rings; if it wasn't the wedding she had hoped for, for their only child, she felt that she had got the measure of the man who was finally proving a worthy partner for her daughter. Over the years since David's death, Michael had visited them several times in France and won them over, not just with the charm that he did inherit from his father, but also with the resolutions he soundly kept. Her husband, Jean, no longer grim and unsmiling, accepted the situation too, if not with good grace, then with the resignation he felt his dignity required. He had been in no doubt that it would not last and that before long she would be back home as she had been so many times before on breaking up with Michael, but was happy to have been proved wrong on this occasion. At least they'd both finished their degrees and one of them had a decent job. Sales and marketing might not have been Jean Garnier's idea of a solid career, but then he'd dealt in facts and figures since the age of eighteen, the solidity of which he could understand. He would concede, however, that Michael was earning a decent salary, for now at least, and he would certainly need that with a baby due in four months time.

Julia, with Ruby by her side, looked upon the proceedings with some confusion, unsure why she was there, but enjoyed the ceremony. Afterwards, she looked around for David, as she always did, and when her enquiries produced a blank look and she became anxious, would calm down only when Ruby whispered in her ear.

Jean chatted to Will, in his impeccable English, outside the Register Office.

'We are to be grandfathers then. What do you make of that?'

'I'm happy for them. It's been a bumpy ride. I know

Michael has not always been easy, but…'

'Non, it *was* difficult…'

'But he's been through a lot.' Will looked across to Julia who appeared lost at that moment, looking around as though she'd misplaced something but couldn't remember what. He watched as Ruby led her gently through the process of the wedding, from the registry to outside, staying close.

'Better line up for the photos,' suggested M. Garnier when their conversation had dried up.

Flora squealed and danced with happiness after the confines of the ceremony room. She was being chased by Maggie who was struggling in high heels and a tight silk dress. Will took the opportunity to go over to Julia and Ruby.

'Hello Julia…how are you?' She looked at him with little recognition despite the occasional visits he made to the home. He rarely spoke of them to Maggie, nor of the place he still held in his heart for the woman he had once loved. He would always care what became of her and had pieced together the history of the fragile girl whose life had been so blighted from such an early age. Will talked about it to Michael when they tried to understand how she had come to disassociate herself from reality.

'Hello, how are you?' she politely replied. Ruby stepped aside but listened carefully to every word.

' It's good to see you out.'

'Yes but I seem to have lost David…have you seen him?'

Ruby gently reminded her that David was not there, as she frequently had during the course of the day and Will was grateful that Julia was with a woman who showed much compassion, along with an ability to take command of the situation throughout the course of the afternoon. When Julia might have created a scene, Ruby stepped in and calmed her down.

Post traumatic amnesia the doctors had labelled Julia's condition and no matter what treatment she received, little changed as her time in the home drifted into years.

Julia posed in the photographs in a simple floral dress that had first been worn at Michael's graduation, a time when they all still hoped that she might yet recover; but the damage caused by the fall, and the pressures of the past, proved too much and she slowly disappeared into her own world, rarely to emerge with any acknowledgement of the present. Michael's wedding gave her some small pleasure, it was a fine day to be out and she smiled back at anyone who smiled at her first, but always asked the same question to anyone who would listen, 'Have you seen David?'

An old university friend of Cecille and Michael's who had studied photography, agreed to take the photos as a wedding gift, and the small group assembled on the steps of the Register Office. The final photo was ready to take; everyone was present, even Julia, escorted by Will in place of Ruby, with Maggie and Flora on the other side; all lined up and smiling. As they collected close enough to fit into the viewfinder, a sharp wind picked up disturbing the carefully arranged clothing and hair, causing a mix of mild panic and amusement. Ruby, watching from a safe distance, murmured under her breath, 'It not finish yet,' as the sky darkened and the expected rain began to fall. Within seconds there was a scramble for cars and taxis to escape the downpour.

'See you all back at the hotel,' called Michael to the assembled guests before seeing to his mother.

'I wish I could get you to change your mind and come with us...just for me?' he asked as Ruby bundled her into her coat. She reached up to push back a lock of Michael's curling hair that had blown across his eyes, a look of half recognition crossing her face.

'I have to go back now. David is coming for me and I don't want to miss him.'

'Ok, Mum...I'll come and see you soon...I'm glad you came.'

He gave his mother a hug and thanked Ruby before nodding to Will, who was standing close by, as if he too wanted to say something to Julia.

'See you in a few minutes, all right?' Michael said to his stepfather before heading back to his bride, impatiently waiting in the wedding car.

''Bye, Julia,' was all Will had come to say as he pulled up his collar against the rain. Julia merely looked beyond him to the rushing figure of Michael and said nothing.

'She tired now, Mr Sanderson. I need to take her back.'

'Of course...I just...'

Maggie and Flora were already in their car as the rain fell heavily and the steps outside the Register Office lay empty once more.

'You look beautiful,' Michael whispered to Cecille as he settled beside her on the back seat, 'I'm so happy,' and he gently placed his hand across her rounded stomach.

'Will your Mother come?' she asked, picking up his hand to kiss it.

'No...I'll see her some time at the home.'

He looked out of the window to see Will talking to his mother and wondered, 'if only things were different.'

'I'm glad she came to the wedding though.'

'Trouble is I never really know how much she takes in. One minute, I think she knows me...that she might be

322

improving...the next she's gone and I don't know where her head is. I know I shouldn't be hard on Will...we get on great now, but sometimes I can't help wondering if we both could have done more to help her. It was hard watching them both at the wedding...then going their separate ways.'

Chapter 40

Cecille and Michael's honeymoon was a long weekend in the Lake District at a small hotel alongside Lake Windermere. Funds would not stretch to Cecille's first choice of a beach in Barbados. The wedding had gone as planned; no one made a fuss and even Cecille's Father had been conciliatory, giving Michael a welcome gift of cash on top of the cost of the day.

Michael laid on their king-sized bed with his hands behind his back, watching Cecille taking off her makeup and marvelling how beautiful she looked with or without it, basking in the now permanent nature of their relationship.

'What? What are you looking at?'

'You...you, me and a baby on the way...it's unreal.'

Cecille patted her stomach.

'Oh it's real all right...want to feel him kick?'

'Tell me...when exactly did we decide all this? Is it too late to back out now?'

Cecille aimed a cushion at his head.

'Money will be tight you know.'

'I know but something will come along…it always does.'

'I'm not relying on your Dad.'

They took long walks by day and made love at night in the honeymoon suite, after which Cecille chatted happily in French, trying to teach Michael more than the basics. He tried to keep up then switched on the television.

It was hard to leave after breakfast on Sunday but travelling back by the scenic route was a pleasure and they took their time. A mountain of post on the doormat welcomed them back home; mostly cards with best wishes for their future happiness and the usual platitudes printed inside. Cecille read every one while Michael looked at the covers and the name at the end of the messages. The thin airmail letter sitting in the midst was almost lost, it was so small, but when spotted, took up Michael's interest more than the cards. He turned it over to look for a sender. It was Mme. Weston, Isle de Paris, France.

'It's from Simone.'

'Who?'

'Simone…you know…David's wife.'

'What does she want?'

'Let me read it and I'll tell you.'

The second and last time they had met had been at David's funeral, the first being a brief meeting at university with his tutor. He remembered how lovely she looked, and how sad, on both occasions. He recalled how gracious she'd been to him, even though they had never met before. It was only later he realised she must have known her husband was his father even then; that she had known it even before he had. The letter was addressed to him only, not both of them, but then there was no way she could have known he was married.

'She deserved better,' he murmured.

'Hmm?' Cecille was too busy ripping open letters and cards and the remaining wedding presents to take much interest in Michael's puzzled expression as he read the letter. The baby gave an extra kick making her laugh out loud, 'Whoa there young man, it's not your time just yet!' They knew it was a boy after the last scan, Cecille couldn't wait of course, and it was obvious how happy that made Michael.

Michael came over to her, 'You all right?' 'Oui…all is well in baby world…so…what's the letter about?

'Just Simone…she wants to send me something of my…Da…of David's.'

'I thought you have finished with all that business,' she pouted on remembering the upset they had all been through because of David. Her first meeting with him, at the airport when the Marechal brats were in tow, was a whole lifetime ago. Thinking of her own baby, she would never hand him over to a nanny as inexperienced as she had been, no matter how desperate. David had been nice then, but caused so much trouble for them all, not least Michael and his mother and Will. It was strange to think that she'd met Michael's father even before he had.

'She's written to tell me that she's only just got round to clearing the rest of David's belongings…the stuff she took back to France…says here that there are items that she thought I might like…stuff he was working on when I first met him. Should be here in a couple of days apparently. She just wanted to give me warning to look out for it all very soon.'

ON THE DAY the parcel arrived, Cecille was in the nursery, hanging a print of 'Where the Wild Things Are' on the wall above the cot; it had been lurking amongst a pile of junk yet to be sorted at the Oxfam shop in town but had cleaned up very nicely. The knock at the door was annoying; she'd not even dressed yet. Michael had taken a call from the care home manager that morning and left in a rush so she wanted to do something nice and cheery for his return. Julia wasn't well following a bad chest infection and after his last visit, the doctor emphasised she should go into hospital for tests considering the poor state of her health. She'd refused and become agitated with the staff when they tried to reason with her.

Cecille signed for the package and put it on the kitchen table, itching with curiosity, wanting to open it but her better judgement deciding against.

Chapter 41

Yorkshire

'I LOOK OUT WITH YOU, Julia. But you know, you don'
have to wait for that man any more…he made bad choices,
but they not your fault. He gone now.'

Ruby's voice quietly purred in her ear, but Julia had
stopped listening long ago, the words were repetitive and
meant nothing. Julia asked again if she knew where David
was, but Ruby just shrugged and told her to get on with her
life and not to worry, 'That man gone now Julia. Someone
else take his place. They don' learn, any of them.'

Julia sat by the window every day since her son's
wedding in the belief that he had been and she'd missed
him. She waited, looking out in full expectation that he
would come again. The only person she talked to was
Ruby. Ruby knew David and could help her find him if she
wanted to, but was being difficult.

'Course I know where that man is, but you better off
not and he not coming here.'

The night before, she hadn't slept; her dreams were filled with wild, impossible landscapes and tortured faces of people she didn't know. This morning she hadn't eaten and the doctor had been called in when she was doubled in pain from so much coughing. Her health was a cause for great concern.

'They want me to go into hospital but I'm not leaving yet, not until he comes,' she told Ruby, but Ruby had already gone.

Looking out of the window, the last of the summer roses in the borders were clinging to life after the high winds of the previous night. Most had lost their petals, leaving a carpet of red on the lawn, but soon even they would disappear; soon they would turn brown and rot. It was late morning before Ruby returned again.

'When did I come here, Ruby? I can't remember…you sat with me when all the others had gone…you stayed with me.'

Ruby's dark eyes missed nothing and she watched Julia's tired face and the body wracked with pain, shrinking day by day. Her shiny black skin, plump and soft, glowed in the light from the window; Julia wanted to touch it when she came close but Ruby was always just out of reach.

'Where do you go to Ruby?' Julia asked, 'when you're not here?'

'I got things to do. But you know I come back.'

Julia worried constantly that he might come late in the night and that he won't be able to find her, but Ruby told her that no visitors are allowed in after supper and put her mind at rest. On days when the weather was fine, Julia might sit outside in the garden, but mostly she felt better inside, near the window on her own, or with Ruby. She once confided to Michael that, 'when Ruby is in the mood for talking, she tells me stories about her childhood in

France; about a castle where her daughter used to work.' Michael smiled and was pleased they got on so well.

'Hello Julia...who are you are talking to now?' Julia didn't answer. 'Would you like a biscuit with your tea?'

It's not Ruby standing there but a young woman called Claire according to the badge pinned to her uniform. Julia wanted to say no to the biscuit, but Claire had already left two besides a cup of weak milky tea and moved on to the old man across the room.

'Where's Ruby?' Julia called out. No one listened or answered but moments later she could sense Ruby standing behind. She could feel her breath close to her ear and would smell her even before she saw her; a mix of exotic spices and perfume. For a fleeting second, an old takeaway came to mind, but she couldn't place where or when. 'What was his name?' she asked looking around but addressing no one in particular.

'That long ago Julia...forget that now' Ruby whispered, 'today you will have a visitor.' Julia turned to look up as Ruby tucked the gold cross around her neck back into a tunic straining across her chest.

'That's pretty.'

'This is no pretty decoration, Julia', she answered, 'it was my daughter's and one day she will have it back.'

Dark clouds loomed in the distance, putting paid to the promised fine morning, and the driveway and gardens were empty of life. Visitors would be few that day.

'Not long now, Julia...but don' be mistaken. He not the one you think, so don' build up your hopes.'

Her tea grew cold and the biscuits remained untouched until they were collected and taken away. Julia was in no mood for tea today and for once didn't want Ruby close either. The chair was uncomfortable and the cushions, hard and lumpy. She was restless.

'You don't know everything, Ruby.'

'I know too much,' she said, and Julia felt her piercing eyes staring deep into her own, 'I tell you, he made bad choices.'

A trolley of tablets and medication rattled on its round and reached Julia's chair. She took two small, pink pills handed to her in a plastic container, with a beaker of water. She had become adept at keeping them under her tongue until they could be spat into a tissue, having learned soon enough not to make a fuss about tablets she didn't want to take. It was easier that way; say nothing and get rid of them in her own way. Ruby gave a sly smile, but said nothing. As the trolley left for the next on the list, Julia turned back to her, but she'd already gone.

Visitors mostly came in the afternoons and at first Julia had quite a few. A man and two women, strangers in uniforms, disturbed the tranquillity of her days and caused a stir of excitement; too much excitement for the staff who did not like disruptions to their routines. They asked endless questions; mostly questions she couldn't answer. Other people came too, claiming that they knew her, or said that they were related, but they stopped visiting quite so much. She gave them blank looks and after a short while would ask them to leave, all but the one person she did like, someone who knew David, but had only paid the one visit. She'd been nice to her and kind. Julia told Ruby about the stranger, 'I liked her but I don't know why she came. She told me she was married to Michael's father, but she must have been confused. I told her she couldn't be and she cried. She held my hand for a while...then left. I don't think I will see her again.'

. . .

TIME DRIFTED SLOWLY by with little variation in the days and weeks, but Ruby's prediction was correct when an unexpected car arrived that day. Julia watched it pull up, black and shiny, and she thought she would like to go out in it. The man getting out looked familiar, slim, tall and confident-looking with curling hair flopping over his eyes. Julia shifted uneasily in her chair, straining to get a better view, sensing something, someone she was expecting. He looked over to the large windowed building and the door set in ivy-clad walls, before slowly walking over.

It was several minutes before he arrived in the lounge with Mrs Carey, the manager.

'Thank you for coming so quickly, Mr Sanderson… your Mother really isn't well at all. She needs to be in hospital but refuses point blank to leave. I was hoping that you might help persuade her.'

'I know…I heard her coughing last time'

'The doctor has been and done all he can but she needs more than that now…you do understand?'

'I know she's not in a good place'

'She's in a world of her own…talking to herself… waiting for someone to turn up to take her away. All she does is sit by the window looking out. We try to get her to mix with the others but…'

'Let me go and have a word. I'll see what I can do.'

'Thank you…you know where she is.'

Julia's face lit up in recognition as Michael walked towards her but it was replaced with a look of confusion as he came close. He was younger than she remembered, but the hair, the face and the soft brown eyes were unmistakeable.

'David?' she whispered.

'Hello, Mum…it's Michael…how are you doing?' He

bent down to kiss her cheek and they both looked at each other.

'What are you talking about...you're David,' she flushed pink with a gaze that blocked out everything and everyone else in the room. Mrs Carey came up to them.

'Michael has come to take you out for a ride in his new car Julia...he wants to talk to you...'

'Michael...oh...oh yes...I see.' Julia pulled Michael close to whisper in his ear

'Best not to use your real name or they might not let me go.'

'Would you like that, Julia?' asks Mrs Carey.

'Oh yes' and she beamed back at her.

Tears of joy fell down her cheeks and she searched for a hanky from her sleeve. Michael couldn't fail to notice the fleshless arms and tiny wrist and looked towards Mrs Carey.

'I know and we're keeping a close watch until we can get her into hospital.'

'You've come back for me...I told her you would...I told Ruby'

Mrs Carey left to get Julia's coat.

'They told me you were dead you know, but I knew better...I knew you'd come back for me.'

'I've come to take you for a ride out Mum...and have a little chat.'

It was Claire who came back to them, having taken great care in choosing the warmest coat and scarf for Julia against the cold. A fresh supply of handkerchiefs were produced and put into her pocket. Claire and Michael supported her ailing body on the walk to the car until Julia pulled up short.

'My suitcase...I can't go without my suitcase,' and a look of panic crossed her face.

'You don't need that now Mum…we won't be long. We're just having tea at that café you like.'

'I need it!' she persisted and refused to move any further until Claire went back for it and put it into the boot.

Nothing surprised Michael any more and he fired the ignition when Julia was safely strapped.

'Where are we going first, David? Have you got the tickets?'

Michael turned to face her before moving off.

'Mum…I'm   Michael…remember…Michael…your son?'

'You can stop it now…we're on our own…no one can hear us, David.'

'Mum please…David died …I told you before.'

'I don't know any Michael…if you're not David, who are you? Why did you pretend to be David if you're not him? I don't understand.'

Julia's agitation grew as her voice became louder. Anger and confusion mixed as Claire looked on with concern from the door.

'Where are you taking me?'

'Just a short drive Mum…I just want to talk to you… have that tea at the café…just like last time… remember…when we…'

'I've never been to a nice café with you before. David is taking me to France so we can be together. He'll be here soon. I'm not going anywhere with you!'

She struggled to get free of the seatbelt, panic rising in her chest and the hacking cough threatening to erupt.

'I want to get out!'

Michael had no option but to release the belt and open the door. There would be no outing today. Claire rushed over to help Julia, still shouting, back inside,

'I'm not a fool you know…leave me alone…you're a doctor aren't you? Trying to get me into that hospital again…well I won't go.'

Mrs Carey took the suitcase; the scenario wasn't new, and she resigned herself to leading Julia back to her usual chair. Michael followed their return to the lounge. Julia's anger and confusion, as expected, was replaced by a violent attack of coughing. The pain returned causing fresh alarm but Julia refused to be taken back up to bed.

'I'll sit with her Mrs Carey…wait until she's calmed down'

'I'm so sorry it's come to this, but I think it best if you leave us to settle her…she's very confused and it's not doing her condition any good. We'll try again to get her back to bed when you leave and get the doctor to come in.'

'Just give me a couple of minutes with her…please?'

Mrs Carey was unsure but relented when she saw Michael's dejection. She understood the cruelty of the situation having experienced it many times before in her twenty years at the home; the helplessness to do anything other than watch and listen and give whatever care they could.

Michael thanked her and pulled up a chair to be close to his mother. Her agitation had subsided sufficiently for her to have all but forgotten the episode outside, although the cough still lingered. He said nothing at first but took her hand and put it to his lips. She liked that. 'Who are you?' she asked. A deep crease formed between Michael's eyes. He wouldn't tell her that he's her son any more,

'A friend…just a friend visiting.'

'That's nice…I don't get many visitors. Have you been here before?'

The second tea trolley of the afternoon was doing the rounds. Michael wiped his eyes and blew his nose before accepting tea for them both. The hacking cough that had been plaguing her since her last visit to David's flat subsided and she was brought medication to ease the pain. It couldn't be hidden like the tablets and the liquid is taken.

'All right now, Mrs Sanderson?' Claire asked. She put two teas and a glass of water on the table, and Michael chose a biscuit he knew Julia liked from a selection in the tin. With calm restored and the cough easing, a little colour returned to Julia's face.

'This is nice,' she said, 'You can come and see me again if you like…what's your name?' and she smiled at the son she no longer knew. Momentarily free from pain and comfortably settled in the chair, she watched Michael sip his tea and took pleasure in watching how he brushed his hair away from his eyes and how it fell back down again a minute later when he moved his head. Julia liked the curls at the collar, it was familiar but she wasn't sure why.

Before Michael left he promised to come back again very soon. Julia was tired by now and let him go without a murmur. Her head sank back into the chair where sleep became a welcome release. She dreamt of a summer many years ago; of a home vaguely remembered; and of a time when everything made sense.

Michael had not persuaded her to go into hospital, but the time would come very soon when she would have no choice. He'd asked her why she wouldn't go and the answer was lucidly given, 'There's nothing they can do for me now…and besides, I have to be here when David comes for me.'

Michael had opened his mouth to argue but let it pass. It was a conversation that would go nowhere and she always had the last word. What Michael didn't know was that they would be the last words he would ever hear from her. Julia suffered a severe stroke that night and never regained consciousness sufficiently to speak again.

Chapter 42

Manchester

MICHAEL ARRIVED back home to find the kitchen table strewn with paper bags and boxes, and a guilty Cecille sitting looking at them.

'What's this?'

'They came today…just after you'd gone. The box was a bit damaged so I thought it would be best if I opened it…just make sure everything was ok.'

'Did you indeed.'

Michael bent down to kiss his wife's upturned smiling face; he was happy and relieved to be back home after the trauma of seeing his mother. He picked up the letter first and read it as Cecille made him a coffee.

'Whoa, don't put the mug there…leave it on the side' he announced on realising what was in front of them.

'What are you going to do with this fusty stuff? Do we have to keep it here?'

'Mm…don't know yet…I need to think…just give me a minute will you?'

There had been nothing amongst the papers to interest Cecille but the curiously beautiful gold cross she'd found separately wrapped amongst them was a different matter altogether. It was ornate, a beautiful design with a large diamond in the centre. She took it through to the sitting room to examine it in detail, going over to the window where the smaller diamonds caught the light. All it needed was a delicate chain and she might even consider wearing it. Or perhaps selling it; they could certainly do with the money and if it was that old, it might be valuable. With a bit of a clean, it would be as good as new. It really was quite exquisite, especially when it caught the sun. Now that she had time on her hands, she formed a plan to take it to the antique jewellers in town and see what they thought of it.

She went to the sofa and flopped down in a happy heap, surrounded by an array of baby magazines, books and knitting patterns, although she had decided soon enough that perhaps knitting was not something at which she would ever excel. Cecille placed the cross in the centre of the low table where she could look at it and tidied the magazines into a neat pile. Michael came through and found her deep in thought.

'I just don't know what do with those Papers and David's half-finished book…what do you think?'

'Honestly? I think you should get rid…they smell like someone's died. I don't like having them in the house… they give me a creepy feeling. He doesn't like them either…he told me,' she said as she patted her swollen belly.

Michael laughed.

'You have no idea.'

He showed her the letter from Simone. As an eminently practical, intelligent and sensible woman, she set out in black and white all she knew of the Papers and their past, but included the conjecture and hearsay of those who took possession. She encouraged Michael to read the notes inside.

'You know what? I think we should take them back to where they belong...Paris...the Archives there. I haven't got the time to finish all that David started. It's a mess I really don't need right now.'

'Ok then do it...get rid. But not the cross! Pleeease?'

'But that's part of the package. It should really go with them.'

'No it could be valuable...please, please...we still need so much stuff for the baby...please?'

'I don't know...' In her state of pregnant happiness he found it hard to refuse Cecille anything, but in this instance wanted the cross to go with the Papers.

'I tell you what, let's have a road trip...take all this by car and we can visit your parents at the same time.'

Cecille squealed in delight at the thought and clapped her hands with childlike pleasure.

As good as his word, Michael wrote a letter to Simone that same evening, to thank her for the Papers, but also to tell her what they planned to do with them. As he pictured the beautiful woman he'd met at the university, he was sorry that it was unlikely they would ever meet again and briefly wondered what kind of mother she would have been to him if things had been different.

THE JOURNEY to France began in a fervour of optimistic planning amidst the blaze of a late summer sun. Cecille eased her way into the passenger seat of their car with as much grace as she could muster considering the expanding belly in front. Two months to go and it couldn't come too soon but the thought of seeing her parents was too irresistible to miss, and besides, she felt so well.

The drive to the ferry, however, was tiring, needing frequent stops for Cecille to pee and eat, but the short crossing passed without hold-up or incident. From Calais, she slept most of the way following a couple of restful breaks. With a pillow stuffed between her head and the door, the rhythmic motion of the car proved too soporific to resist and Michael was relieved to get a break from her constant prattle. As the sun went down and the skies darkened, he turned up the heat in the car.

Light showers had been forecast for the evening, but on getting closer to Paris, the weather was more akin to a storm threatening in the distance. Soon a low roll of thunder preceded the first heavy downpour. The windscreen wipers were put on to full speed although they could hardly keep pace with the sudden deluge and forced Michael into looking out for a suitable place to stop. The driving rain was as unexpected as it was fierce and lightning forked across the sky. On the motorway, the last sign indicated that the services were just three kilometres ahead although it seemed much further when they were going so slow.

'Not far now,' Michael glanced across at the sleeping figure of his wife who was blissfully unaware of the unfolding drama outside. His glance towards Cecille could be measured in seconds only, but the consequences of that look would last a lifetime.

The dark figure in the middle of the road loomed large and quick as Michael turned his full attention back to the windscreen. Her body, clearly visible, stood in a long dress, flapping in the storm. Immutable. Too fast to stop. Michael swerved. Brakes screeched in the wash of the flooded road. Hands tightly gripped the wheel but to no avail as he lost control. Cecille jolted awake to see a car racing towards them from the other direction, headlights blinding her eyes.

The crash took on a balletic quality as the two cars glided and spun. The steering wheel locked and took no part in the dance macabre and Michael could only look on in helpless horror, at the face of the inevitable crash. They collided front against side forcing Michael's car into a roll, throwing open the boot and leaving its occupants unconscious.

Emergency services arrived to a floating maelstrom of clothing as the contents of carefully packed suitcases lay strewn in the floodwater. The angry wind worked through the last of its rage and the rain slowed as two ambulance crews carried out their assessments.

MICHAEL MIRACULOUSLY ESCAPED with injuries that were not life threatening but Cecille lay in a coma in intensive care. Distraught beyond rational thought, he managed to call Cecille's parents and garbled a brief explanation of what had happened. They arrived two hours later in a state of shock, immediately demanding answers that Michael could not give. Police found no trace of anyone else at the scene, other than the driver of the second car, despite Michael's repeated insistence that he'd tried to avoid a woman in the road. He'd suffered nothing more serious than whiplash, shock and a sore arm but concussion wasn't ruled out entirely. Intensive searches were undertaken and appeals made but to no avail and it was eventually concluded that the lack of vision, and distortion caused through the heavy rain, had affected his sight.

'No…no you've got it wrong…there was someone I swear…you've got to keep looking…I saw her!' If Cecille and the baby died, how could he live with the thought that it was all his fault, that he'd swerved for no other reason than he'd imagined a figure in the middle of the road? It made no sense.

Cecille lay motionless and hooked up to the life preserving equipment that gave them all hope of her survival, but it didn't stop the accusatory looks and the tightly reined in anger that simmered inside Jean Garnier. All three in turn tried in vain to coax and cajole a response but never gave up hope as Cecile and the baby clung on to the thin connection to precious life.

Michael did not want to leave Cecille's side but after twenty-four hours without sleep was persuaded to go to one of the hotel rooms that had been booked by Cecille's mother. Jean and his wife would stay with Cecille with promises given to report immediately if there was any change. Cecille and the baby were alive, just, but a more hopeful prognosis was too early to predict the future.

BAGS of wet clothing and a hastily stuffed suitcase sat on the floor of Michael's room. Too tired to cry, too drained of rational thought to register the raw pain that engulfed his whole being, he looked down on the mass of items so carefully packed just two days before. A pretty yellow summer dress, mud stained and ripped lay on top of a black plastic bag. Cecille had put it in at the last minute; a final item of clothing before forcing their case shut. He heard her voice clearly in his head, 'I need a nice dress in case we go out for dinner…I'll make it fit in!' He heard too his impatient reply; 'You'll bust the catch if you put anything else in!' But as usual, had capitulated and made it fit.

Michael pulled the voluminous maternity dress close to his face; she'd worn it when he took her out for dinner the week before and beneath the mud and the damp, it still smelled of Cecille.

He sat on the bed, too tired to sleep just yet, staring at the bags and case. Before long, something else caught his eye, a dark box almost hidden at the back. Sitting like an uninvited guest, sullen and incongruous amidst the damaged bags and clothing, it alone had remained totally intact.

He took off his shoes and lay down, still clutching the dress, still watching the box, but his eyes grew heavy, and despite the turmoil in his head, sleep came at last. Between each fitful doze, he tried to make sense of the past two days. Why hadn't he just posted the Papers? What was he thinking of? Cecille was seven months pregnant but it had seemed such a good idea at the time; she had been so excited, he didn't even consider changing her mind. The weather had been fine too, no storm had been forecast when they left. Cecille was to see her parents and the Papers would go to a place where they belonged. It had all been so simple.

When a deeper sleep arrived, it was not of the restful kind. Wild dreams ravaged through the hours left of the night and the woman in the long dress rose out of the shadows, accusing and pointing to a bloodstain on her chest. Her face was contorted with pain and she screamed at him before fading back into the mist and mire of her surroundings. Michael woke with a start, bathed in sweat. He looked at his phone to check for messages and the time. It was seven in the morning; he needed to call the hospital before anything else.

. . .

THERE WAS no change in Cecille's condition; both she and the baby were neither worse nor better; still critical, but stable at least. Michael took a shower, shaved and brushed his teeth before searching for the cleanest clothes he could find. His mind cleared and in the silence of the hotel room, he experienced clarity on what he had to do. It was obvious. He dressed, picked up the box and headed for the hotel reception.

IT TOOK another three days of slow and painful waiting before Cecille awoke and was able to sit up in bed. The worst was over and the baby was thankfully thriving inside the womb. Cecille's eyes went down to her protruding stomach and her eyes filled with tears when she heard the news that he was well and healthy as far as they could tell from the tests. Michael took her hand.

'The baby's fine. They're as certain as they can be that he should be all right but it looks like he will be born in France…they won't let you leave.'

'Mon bébé va bien? she whispered, relieved beyond words as she cried in his arms.

'Oui', he replied gently placing her hand with his over the bump. Tears of joy flowed for the life of the baby yet to be born.

'Bébé Louis.'

They had discussed names and Louis was the favourite of them both, but Cecille then added: 'Bébé Louis Jean William.'

'I like that', said Michael.

. . .

CECILLE AND MICHAEL arrived back home with far more luggage than they'd started out with, not least a tiny baby in tow. Born early, his small wrinkled arms, legs and face were yet to fill his skin but he came with a surprising amount of hair. It was brown and soft, and in later years would curl around his neck and flop unbidden into his eyes like his father's and grandfather before him.

Michael's workplace were understanding about his extended leave of absence, but his basic pay fell short when commission wasn't included in the salary. The euphoria following confirmation of the health of the baby and Cecille's recovery was gradually replaced by the practicalities of day-to-day life. Whilst baby Louis brought a great deal love and happiness into their lives, reality bit hard when their bank overdraft reached its limit and there was no imminent prospect of replenishing lost funds. By the time Louis was two years of age, their only salvation rested with the bailouts provided by Cecille's parents.

Chapter 43

2000
Manchester

EARLY ONE AUTUMN MORNING, Cecille sat on the floor with two-year old Louis; piles of baby clothes that no longer fitted were strewn around a cot that was becoming a tight fit for the toddler's growing frame. The last cheque from her father had given them breathing space to pay the bills, but it was rapidly dwindling and Cecille struggled to think how they could bring in more money. If she worked, her pay would be absorbed in childcare and Louis was nowhere near school age yet. She daydreamed of some unknown rich aunt dying alone and finding herself the recipient of a marvellous windfall, an inheritance that would save them from the money misery that overwhelmed their daily life. Thoughts drifted to the past, when they both worked, and all they had to worry about was which new restaurant to try next.

In the living room, with Louis toddling close behind

and clinging to her leg, she took their wedding album down from the bookshelf and looked through its well-thumbed pages. She showed an uncomprehending Louis the happy smiling faces in the photographs, naming them one by one; even Michael's mother Julia managed not to look too confused. Cecille's train of thought moved on to his father and the sad way in which he died, and then to the Henrietta Papers that Simone had posted after David's funeral. The day they'd set off on that fateful trip to Paris started with such hope and excitement. Perhaps they should have tried to sell the Henrietta Papers; who knows what they might have brought, but Michael had been intent on getting rid of them and Cecille had been in total agreement. When they first inspected the contents of the package, they'd scoffed at the notes stuffed inside by some old archivist who once owned them, fantastic tales of children who failed to survive, 'Shadow children' he called them, and issued warnings to any future owner who had taken them on. It had sent a shiver through Cecille but neither of them gave any real credence to the superstitious nonsense. Now they would be in the Paris Archives; it was their problem. Michael had posted them from the hotel after the accident.

Cecille looked at Louis' chubby face when, bored by the album, he plonked himself on the floor and concentrated on his building bricks and cars; he was a picture of health with no repercussions following their brush with death in the car crash just before he'd been born. Thoughts moved on from the Papers to the cross. The cross, of course, she still had it. It had been completely forgotten amidst the frenetic times between leaving home and returning with a baby who took up almost every waking moment.

The cross was exactly where she had put it two years

before, enveloped in a nest of crumpled tissue, tucked amongst a broken watch and several pieces of jewellery that were no longer worn; mostly paste of course and worth very little. She unwrapped the cross and held it in her hands, turning it this way and that to catch the light streaming into the room. It was a beautiful object. Louis had followed her into the bedroom and she kissed the top of his head when he wanted to drag her back to the toys. His hair smelled deliciously of the baby shampoo it had been washed in the night before. It shone and curled about his neck and a surge of love overwhelmed her. She stroked his hair, 'Mummy's just thinking…why don't we go for a walk into town?' He clapped his hands delightedly, 'Choc,' he said as a 'walk into town' usually meant a treat was in store from the sweetshop.

And thus, later that day, on a bright crisp morning late into October, when Michael had gone to work, Cecille retrieved the gold cross from the jewellery box and set off into town with Louis, soon fast asleep in his pushchair. She'd never told Michael she'd kept the cross and let him think that it was still sitting amongst the papers when they'd packed.

The jeweller, no stranger to the occasional piece arriving without due provenance, inspected the cross. Within a short space of time, and without speaking, he counted and assessed twenty three old table rose cut diamonds and inspected the embellishment of mille grain repeats, around a fully diamond encrusted centre. It was almost certainly eighteen carat gold, but bore no hallmark. He had never come a cross like it before and held his breath before looking up at Cecille, asking, 'How and where have you managed to acquire such a piece?' He gave little away as to potential value, but his gut reaction told him that he could be reasonably confident of its authenticity. For now, he accepted Cecille's answer that it was inherited from her husband's father and had been brought back from France some years before. The provenance could wait; all that concerned him at that moment was confirmation of the value and how much he would have to invest to buy it from this woman in his shop. He asked her if she would consider leaving it with him and come back in a week's time.

'But can't you at least give me some idea of what it's worth?'

'I need to check with an expert in the field and do a little research first.'

'I don't know...'

'Just let me see what I can come up with...you *will* make a tidy sum from it...'

Cecille was not in a position to go traipsing around anywhere else with Louis in tow but at the same time was wary of what the jeweller was asking of her.

'And to show good faith, I will advance you two hundred pounds as a deposit if you agree to leave it with me.'

'Two hundred?'

'Don't worry...I'm not going anywhere and I'll write an agreement to purchase from you only if a price is agreed between us...when I've a better idea of its value. If you don't agree, you can pay me back the two hundred and I'll return the cross immediately.'

Cecille still looked doubtful until he added,

'But...just so you know...someone else may demand more information about where it comes from...want to see the paperwork...proof of ownership, that sort of thing...it could take a very long time and involve a lot more people than one jeweller like myself.'

His meaning was clear and Cecille reluctantly agreed.

. . .

EVENTUALLY, the cross made a surprising amount of money for both the jeweller, who located his own purchaser with very little difficulty, and for Cecille who made plans of her own. There was enough to clear their overdraft, pay the bills and buy badly needed essentials for Louis. In some ways, she was sorry to see it go; the more she looked at it, the more she appreciated its beauty and would have liked to have known about its history, but that was for someone else to find out now.

On the day they agreed a price, and the exchange was finally made, Cecille held the cross for one last time. A shock of electricity ran through her fingers and along her arm, leaving a tingling sensation when she put it back down. Misreading her expression the jeweller asked,

'You are happy with the deal aren't you?' and held out a hand.

'Oh yes,' she replied, rubbing her arm as darkness started to envelop the shop. With the cheque safely in her purse, her only thoughts had been what to do with the money. She shook his proffered hand and left as Louis started to wake up. He yawned and asked when they would get his 'choc'.

On the way to the bank, a few doors down from the jeweller's, Louis, clutching his Milky Bar from the sweet-shop, giggled as a cloudburst caught them unawares. Cecille, drenched by the rain, laughed at the thought of what she had managed to achieve, and how thrilled Michael would be when she told him.

SHORTLY AFTER THEY'D left the shop, a woman who had been sitting in the café opposite, the one who had followed

Cecille's every move until she left the jewellers, stood up to pay her bill. The waitress had admired her colourful head-scarf when she'd served her, but the dark woman in the colourful outfit ignored the comment as well as the coffee that sat cold on the table.

Her large figure cast a shadow over the jeweller's shop window and she stood for some moments reflecting on the displays that had recently been rearranged. She scoured the items before briefly looking behind her, and then went inside. A door security alerted her entrance and the jeweller looked up, raising his eyebrows at the woman standing before him.

'Good morning, can I help you?'

'I come for the cross you purchas' from that woman who just left.'

The jeweller looked confused.

'How do you know what I bought from her...I haven't even...?

The woman cut him off short, raising her hand, palm out and giving him a cold and hard look.

'I know...I wait for this for a very long time... you don' know how long. It was once my daughter's and I would like to get it back...'

'I still need to do a definitive valuation...I'm not sure you know...'

'I know. But you bought it and I want it back.'

'Look...come back next week when I've done my final valuation and we can talk then.'

He was in the process of arranging a very lucrative deal with a buyer in Paris and almost certainly this woman would not be in a position to match it.

The bright headscarf trembled slightly as she stared at him with unflinching eyes.

'Do what you must then… but I come back for it. Tomorrow.'

The jeweller hadn't noticed anyone else come inside the shop, but was suddenly aware of a young girl standing by the door. She was wearing a stained, long brown dress and appeared to be cradling something in her arms. She looked vaguely familiar.

'I know you don't I?'

The door had not sounded its usual alert, which was strange considering that all the security systems had been checked the week before. The young girl said nothing but stared straight ahead. He half smiled from behind the counter, assuming they were gypsies on the make, and in readiness of trouble, held a finger over the siren button beneath the counter just in case there were others waiting outside. It wasn't necessary. The woman and girl left when he announced that he would see what he could do and the cross was quickly deposited in the safe at the back of the shop.

Chapter 44

The disappearance of the jeweller was never fully resolved. When the shop remained closed without notice for several weeks, and when no one could get hold of the owner, questions were asked and investigations made. The shop was sealed off from the public by a police presence and the local community made up their own stories on what had happened when their questions received unsatisfactory answers. It was headline news for a couple of days in the Press and on the radio; and a television crew appeared one day when the story caught the public imagination even further afield.

A notepad by the shop telephone revealed a French number, hastily scribbled in pencil, but when it was dialled, was found to be a disconnected line. All other leads came to an equally unsatisfying dead end. No known relatives were traced; no friends came forward to speak up for him; and although he lived close by, there was very little information to piece together much of a life for the missing jeweller. Thorough checks were made against an inventory of the shop contents but they revealed no theft or break in;

and as no one else knew of the cross he'd taken possession of, apart from Cecille, it was never a factor in the police investigation. Lines of enquiry slowly ground to a halt and the eventual conclusion by all concerned in the case was that the debts he had accrued, exacerbated by a recent very large withdrawal of cash, and the imminent bankruptcy he faced, lay at its root. He was placed on the Missing Persons file and remained there.

Six months elapsed after the end of the investigation before new ownership of the jewellers shop was announced on the window and in the Press. 'Fabrice Jewellers' had been obliterated.

About the Author

S.F. TAYLOR writes in a rambling three-storey Victorian house, a four-minute walk from the bracing North Sea in East Yorkshire. Having published two non-fiction books, this is her first foray into fiction

To find out more about her books contact:

facebook.com/sftaylorauthor

twitter.com/suefrasertaylo1

instagram.com/soofraser

Coming Soon in 2022

Paris, Picasso and Me

'Well I've made it this far'. Olivia stood at the front path of her new home, a half smile playing across her lips. It was an amazing achievement after all. A long and arduous journey, with pitfalls too dark and numerous to escape without some remnant of pain still trailing behind, but here she was. The words of Elton John, heard on the radio before leaving her parents' house that morning, still rang through her head:

'Don't you know I'm still standing better than I ever did

Looking like a true survivor, feeling like a little kid'

She laughed to herself. It had to be a good omen, didn't it? It had been a hard wrench for all of them this morning but they knew it was needed.

'GO SEE to your Mother Olivia…she's not stopped blubbing all morning,' her Dad had asked. Liv had found her in Bee's bedroom, gathering up the last of the clothes she'd washed and ironed for their new home.

'Look at this! Four odd socks. Your Dad's just the same. I can never do a load without ending up with odd socks.'

'Doesn't matter Mum, I'm not moving to the other end of the Earth…you and Dad can bring the waifs and strays when you come to visit us.'

'I know that love…it's just…'

'Just nothing…think about the positives, your washing machine won't be on half as much.'

'That doesn't matter…it's just such a big change…it'll be so quiet round here.'

'Mum! You've been asking for a bit of peace and quiet for as long as I can remember.'

'This is different Olivia…I'll miss that bairn'

'Please don't cry…you'll set me off and Bee won't understand if we're all sad. This is supposed to be a happy day remember.'

'You're right…get yourself off love…but I should be helping you with the move. Today of all days'

'Plenty of time for you to help out…you know Dad's not well enough right now and I'd rather you came when things have settled down…anyway I've got Dom and Patrick.'

'Dom's been a great help…lovely man…but let me know if you're short of anything'

'I will I promise…I love you Mum…you and Dad have been so good…getting me back on my feet…I wouldn't have got this far without you two'

'Oh get away with yer before the waterworks start up again'

'I am going to miss you…but I am looking forward to a new start…and cooking for you in my own kitchen.'

Barbara wasn't too sure about that but smiled after she'd given her nose a final blow.

'Where's your Dad got to now? I told him to stop fretting over those boxes'

Outside, the van's horn tooted, signaling they were loaded and ready to be off. Most of the furniture had either come from Barbara and Arthur's loft, or taken out of circulation on assurance that it was surplus to their needs. The budget was tight but Barbara thrived on frugality; she loved nothing more than making limited means stretch beyond their expected capacity. 'Barbs it's not war time y'know…we're not scraping burnt bits off toast any more.'

Liv was more than aware of the difficulties that lay ahead for her but there was enough of her mother in her that told her she could do it. Between them, they'd rescued several items from the charity shops in town. 'It's all good stuff in here,' her mother re-assured her when Liv sniffed the odour inside the shop. But they lived on the fringes of an affluent area and it showed in quite a few finds they'd picked up.

Robert wasn't convinced about the move of course, but then he always managed to make everything she planned sound like a bad idea. He'd been happy enough knowing Liv and Bee were living with her parents; satisfied with regular access he had once the divorce was finalised; but something changed when she told him she would be moving away to be on her own with Bee.

Having survived the worst of what life had thrown in her direction, Olivia Smithson now found herself at the door of 59 South Street, just about intact, and ready to face the future. Two plastic bags sat waiting at her feet while she took in the enormity of her achievement. The sold sign drooped almost parallel to the ground following the high winds of the night before. It pulled out easily enough and she laid it out on the lawn.

For the first time, Liv took note of the garden. It was a far cry from the well-tended plot at the neat little semi she'd left, or indeed ex-husband Robert's. Weeds here were well rooted and the only sign of cultivation was the occasional yellow daffodil that managed to rise above the couch grass, dandelions and briars. 'I know exactly how you feel,' she murmured to herself and hummed the Elton John tune as the taxi disappeared down the road. Olivia picked up the bags after dusting her hand free of mud from the sale post and smiled up at the impatient little girl who had already bounded up the steps to the front door. This was their house, hers and Bee's. Beatrice Rose, otherwise known as Bee was the saving grace of a life that had struggled, like the swaying daffodils, to rise up and be seen after six years of suppression.

Overcoming death and divorce, and the ignominy of moving back in with her parents, this small house with its overgrown garden and peeling paintwork was where a new life would finally begin. Here was the opportunity to get back the person she had once been and reclaim the life she would choose for herself. If there was any cause for anxiety, it would be over the future of the little girl waiting at the top of the steps, the one whose patience diminished by the second.

The old house might have peeling paintwork, dirt-smeared windows and weeds, unlike the immaculate house next door she noted, but it was hers. Relief and happiness arrived in waves as she embraced that moment. Clutching an old stuffed toy in one hand and a small bag in the other, Bee jumped up and down shouting, 'Come on, come on, come on…Mummee!' with her four-year old's exuberance.

From the window of the house next door, the one with the neat doorway and tidy garden, a net curtain twitched and pulled aside at the bottom corner and the elderly face of Frances Fenton looked out.

TO FIND out more about this and future publications, subscribe to S.F. Taylor's mailing list on her website: www.sftaylorauthor.co.uk